The Second Coming of Hell

By

Joshua Griffith

ISBN: 978-0-578-65091-3

Cover Art designed by BooksGoSocial

Contact Joshua Griffith on Facebook or

Follow him on Twitter @jdgriffith78

To Stacie: You're my greatest inspiration in every aspect of my life!

Table of Contents:

Chapter 1

Present Day

"Listen to my words, brothers and sisters. It's not too late to repent!" the old man—a preacher—cried out as he dramatically waved his tattered Bible around.

The patrons inside the bar kept drinking, and people outside didn't acknowledge the old man's presence as they hurried along, which only added to his passionate rant. The man was far from well kept, his clothes dingy and tattered. Pages from his Bible hung loosely and littered the area around his feet. With each passing car that flew by him at the busy intersection, the fallen bible pages swirled in the wind.

"The Lord is coming soon. If you haven't given your life to Him, you'll feel His wrath. Just give your life over to the Messiah, and you'll be spared eternal damnation. You shall be granted eternal life in Heaven!"

As the old man dropped to his knees to gather the loose pages, the bar owner walked up and stood behind him. He pitied this old, mad soul but, on the other hand, he didn't like the commotion he was causing outside his establishment.

The bar owner had to play it cool when he asked this religious zealot to move on, especially in this day and age of social media.

Everyone had a phone with a camera. He didn't want to be seen berating a poor, defenseless, old man. If something like that went viral on the internet, his livelihood might take a terrible hit. The bar owner cautiously looked around and spied several pedestrians holding their smart phones towards his direction. "Fuck!"

He took a deep breath to calm down, but as he inhaled the plethora of odors that emanated from the unwashed preacher, he nearly gagged. The bar owner couldn't hold back a coughing fit, causing the preacher to look over his shoulder.

The old man smiled, revealing a mouthful of decayed and missing teeth. "The end is coming sooner than anyone expected. You, my friend, must be made ready. Join me in my crusade!"

The bar owner tried to slowly back away, shaking his head, but the preacher reached out and hugged him tightly. "You're the first person to come join me in the Lord's cause. Please allow me to savor this monumental moment!"

Feeling uncomfortable, the bar owner had two things running through his mind: I hope his vest is actually green velvet, not mold growing under his crusty, stained jacket, and how can I keep my lunch down?

"What is your name, sir?" the preacher jubilantly asked.

"Todd," he wheezed, biting back the bile in his mouth and throat. "Todd Riggs. I—"

"TODD!" The preacher cried out as he waved his right arm around, still holding Todd next to him with his left. "Todd has seen the signs and has chosen to stand with me and profess his love for the Lord as we await His return!"

Embarrassed, Todd scanned the streets around him, noticing more on-lookers gawking, probably recording this whole scene. He wanted to bury his head so no one could see his burning, red face but that would mean tucking it into the preacher's coat. Hell, Todd thought, it might be worth it! I could pass out and hopefully get driven away to the hospital—

Suddenly, a loud boom was heard in the distance. Was that an explosion? Todd looked around but saw nothing.

"Sir, I'm only out here to ask you to move away from my business," Todd explained. "You're scaring away my patrons with all this end of days talk. Could you possibly do this across the street...in front of O'Bannon's Pub, maybe?"

"No, I can't do that!" the preacher insisted. "I must stay here in this spot until it is my time to go!"

"I can call the cops and have you moved," Todd replied as he broke away from the old preacher's grip. "Is that how you want this to go down? You getting dragged off in handcuffs for disturbing the peace?"

"I won't be here long enough for that to happen. I'll be taken away to the Promised Land for my heart is true, and I've devoted my very soul to the Word of God!"

Todd decided the old man was probably off his medication, if he had any. He was about to turn toward his bar to call the police, when he felt a small ground tremor. The sound of sirens wailed in the distance somewhere. Confused, Todd looked around. To his surprise, he saw black smoke climbing high into the air. "What's happening?"

The bar owner looked back at the preacher and saw the strangest thing. The man had a look of sheer jubilation on his grizzled, old face. Creases on his visage grew brighter as the dirt encrusted on his wrinkles fell away. He spread his arms wide, as if he waited to embrace someone and hollered, "I'm ready, Lord! Take me home!" And then…

He vanished!

Todd fell backwards against his bar's sun-warmed bricks, his head swimming, uncertain as to what had just happened. Several people who had been recording him and the old man ran across the street towards him, probably wanting to know where the old preacher had gone — how the trick was done.

Hell, Todd thought, I'd like to know the same thing! Sirens seemed to blare everywhere at once as the cacophony of metal crunches mixed into the symphony of chaos that surrounded him. Cars wildly flew by like missiles out of control, mowing down the gawkers in the street. Their bodies either flew into the air, slamming hard onto the pavement or were dragged along, caught on the cars' undercarriages.

To Todd's horror, none of the vehicles had drivers in them!

Everything was now a potential accident waiting to happen as more cars rammed their way down the streets. He ran back into the bar for his own safety and saw that the place was now empty. "Where the hell is everyone?" He looked around, hoping to find someone…anyone. "There's no other way out of here except the front door."

Well, there is a back entrance, Todd thought. But it was used exclusively for deliveries. Had everyone left out the back? Why leave at all? He glanced around the bar, his brain swimming in confusion. Purses sat on the counter, and jackets still draped the backs of chairs or lay on the floor. It was an eerie sight, and it made him think everyone was about to pop out from somewhere and scream "SURPRISE!"

He wanted that. He wanted everyone to scream at him—*anyone* to scream at him!

In the dim light of the room, he saw that behind the bar station, there were several bottles of alcohol broken on the ceramic tile. The bottles' contents pooled up and invaded the air with the odors of Jack Daniels, Jose Cuervo, Vodka, and Bacardi.

In one fluid movement, Todd pushed himself up and twisted, landing on top of the bar. He sat there, letting his right foot kick against the wooden side, as he took in the eerie scene.

Suddenly, a loud crash broke the silence. He instinctively rolled over backwards behind the bar, landing awkwardly on his side. Shifting his body, he struggled up and perched himself on his knees. When he did, he grimaced in pain.

Todd looked down and saw that there was now a new red liquid mixing with the alcohol on the flood.

Blood! His blood!

Using the fingers of both hands, he pressed along the left side of his body. He gasped each time he found a tender spot. He looked down at his hands. They were covered in blood, as was his left side. Glass shards had embedded into his skin. Todd gingerly rose to a standing position and cautiously inspected his bar to see what had actually happened.

"Can this day get any more fucked up?" he growled aloud. While surveying the wreckage, he managed to pluck pieces of glass from his side.

The room was no longer dim, and he realized the brightness was caused from the now gaping hole in the wall where his plate glass window had stood, just minutes ago. Through the hole, he could see that his decorative metal tables on the sidewalk were gone. He squinted against the brightness to see better and gasped in surprise. On the sidewalk, in place of his tables, was the tail of a small airplane.

Airplane?

Still holding his side, he worked his way through the chaotic destruction that was once his pride and joy to determine if he was really seeing this or going crazy. As he stepped outside, Todd saw the rest of the small aircraft. It had smashed into the building next to his bar, its tail ripping off as it hit his place.

People ran in a panic from something Todd couldn't see. "Maybe I should run too," he muttered. He decided he definitely needed to find a better shelter…away from all the chaos.

He began a trek down the sidewalk. Everywhere he looked vehicles were crashing or shooting erratically down the streets. No one was in any of them!

More earth tremors hit, but now they were accompanied with the sounds of ear-splitting explosions. As his walk shifted into a jog, he looked back, trying to see where the explosions were coming from. Not paying attention to where he was going, he ran into a woman, nearly toppling her.

"Sorry," he said and grabbed her upper arms, trying to help stabilize her. As he did, he stared into her deep brown…*vacant* eyes.

She had an eerie expression on her face — the kind one might see on the walking dead. He couldn't help himself. He stared, and as he did, a vicious shudder stabbed down his spine.

A single thought shot through his brain: *zombie woman!*

At that moment, with no warning from her, she vanished, leaving him holding—air! He gasped and shivered violently.

"What the hell is happening?" Todd screamed out. He clutched the sides of his head. Is this what madness is like? Am I hallucinating?

To Todd's left, a sudden flash of light lit up the sky. It was followed by an explosion and a shockwave of intense heat. It forced Todd to drop to the sidewalk, and he instinctively covered his head.

Peeking through the slits of his fingers, he couldn't believe what he was seeing.

Chapter 2

A half a block away, a fiery crater, about the size of a city bus, had punched through the street like it was made of glass. The flames emanating from the crater seemed to dance and move like they were alive!

Todd looked up to the clear skies and saw more fireballs reigning down like some sort of cosmic shit-storm. With his mouth gaping open, Todd could have sworn he saw the figure of a man flying in the sky.

That can't be right, can it?

He scrambled to his feet and ran as fast as he could, glancing up at the sky to keep an eye on the firestorm and the "man". Sheer terror caused people to trample over those who fell, and they knocked others down who were too slow.

More fireballs fell, slamming into buildings, causing them to explode like a macabre demolition show. Smoke and debris filled the air, blanketing everything around him. Todd ripped off his tie and wadded it up in his hands. Holding it over his mouth and nose, he tried to keep from breathing in all the glass-filled dust.

"I gotta get away from this," he mumbled and started to run. He tried to avoid the crowds and chaos by ducking down a deserted alleyway.

Was this the end of days that the old preacher talked about? Where did he go? Where did that zombie woman go? They just disappeared! Who started the cars?

Other than an alien invasion, what else could explain what was going on? People vanishing! A man flying around in the sky! And this firestorm—what is that about? Its projectiles seemed to come from out of nowhere! Was this mysterious man in the sky causing the destruction? Was this the return of the Messiah? "If so," Todd muttered worriedly, "I'm so screwed!"

Todd's mind raced as he ducked behind a large trash bin to avoid a fire that swept through the alley. He heard screams of pain and terror from somewhere around the corner. As the explosions continued, Todd mentally cried out, *"Fuck! I don't want to die!"*

He peered around the dumpster. Through the myriad of heat mirages, Todd spied an old cemetery off in the distance. Strange as it seemed, the fireballs struck everywhere, except in that graveyard. Was it because the land was hallowed?

Clutching his left side, Todd decided to make his way to the cemetery. If I'm going to die, I might as well be in a graveyard. Suddenly, a thought occurred to him. Will I be safe in there since I'm not the church-going type of guy, or will I get fried for even trying to enter?

Todd jogged to the end of the alleyway. The stench of burnt hair and flesh assailed his nostrils, and he gagged. Charred remains of people were scattered everywhere — their eyeballs fried in their sockets.

Again, the sickening odor of burnt bodies slammed into him, and he gripped the side of an old pick-up truck. He dry heaved a couple of times, and then he proceeded to empty the contents of his stomach. He squeezed his left side to keep his muscles from tensing up and going into a full on charlie horse.

Todd took a moment to wipe his mouth. He gazed up at the sky. The flying man looked like he was making bigger fireballs and was targeting the taller buildings and skyscrapers, seemingly with the intent on bringing them down. When the first one hit the rooftop of the nearest skyscraper, the building's exterior walls on each floor exploded outward as the fireball pushed through with so much force that when it reached the foundation, it blew it apart.

Only a flaming crater of concrete and twisted metal remained. No building it seemed could withstand this fiery onslaught, but that didn't deter terrorized people from using them as shelters, giving them a false sense of security. There was a sporting goods store up the road to Todd's right that people were running towards, but the people inside had already claimed it and were now defending it. The defenders had busted out the bar-covered windows, shooting anyone who tried to enter.

With fire and gore to his left, and a human target shoot to his right, Todd decided to make a break for the cemetery straight across the street. It seemed to be the one piece of tranquility amidst all the chaos. The cemetery was surrounded by a black, iron fence that had sharp spiked tips at the top of the bars, and the land was the size of two full city blocks.

The main gate into the cemetery had been knocked down by a runaway rental truck and was blocking the way inside. As he ran across the street, Todd thought back to what the old preacher had said. Feeling like a hypocrite and having nothing else to lose, Todd spoke aloud, "I don't want to die, so if You're listening up there…I repent ALL my sins and give myself over to You, Jesus…just spare my life!" He cringed, feeling foolish for even thinking such a thing, but he was desperate.

He ran across the street and yanked the door of the rental truck open, sliding inside. The motor was still running, but no one was in the cab. Unlike some of the other vehicles he had encountered today, the windshield had a massive hole in it and was covered in blood. Someone had been ejected from the cab at the time of impact.

Quickly, Todd scooted his way to the other end of the cab and opened the passenger door. He hopped out. Cautiously, he approached the prone woman's body and noted there was a lot of blood loss from going through the windshield. She had gone headfirst into a large monument stone. Her blonde hair was covered in blood, and her head was contorted underneath her chest, giving the erroneous impression that she had been decapitated.

Todd's nausea came back full force. He clutched his knees and started to throw up again, the bile burning his sore, parched throat. He turned to look away from the dead body but noticed that the cemetery was quiet — eerily quiet.

He could see more fireballs striking everywhere outside the cemetery. Inside the cemetery, though, there was no noise. The vibrations from each impact could be felt, but even those had been dampened somehow. How was that possible? Then again, today was a day where the impossible had become a reality.

Maybe I was right to assume this cemetery was hallowed ground and protected...but why?

From the safety of the cemetery, Todd could see things from a new perspective. The flying man was definitely the one causing the destruction. The man, if you could call him that, would dramatically wave around what appeared to be a staff in his hand. The tip would glow the same color as the fireballs and then out of thin air, a fireball would coalesce and hurtle towards the city.

Todd noticed movement out of the corner of his eye. He tried to ignore it, figuring it was someone wandering aimlessly through the destruction. He wasn't willing to run out into the open to aid whoever it was because he felt safe here in the cemetery. He certainly wasn't a hero. If they want to find sanctuary like I did, they can come in here on their own, Todd thought as he tried to justify his cowardice.

With guilt nagging at him, Todd gave up and sprinted in the direction of where he saw the movement. I don't need to leave the cemetery; I can get their attention. They can decide if they want to join me in here or not.

He frantically waved both his arms over his head. When the pain from his wounds seared through him, he clutched his left side and waved with his right arm only.

As he neared the fence, he noticed that the figure was a man walking calmly down the sidewalk on the other side of the street, as if he was out for an afternoon stroll. Todd also noted that the man was strangely dressed. He was wearing several layers of tattered robes made of shredded fabric while having a sickly green/brown cloak on his back. The man was completely bald. He had a dark complexion, like he was from the Middle East or some other desert region, and the boots he wore had the same sickly green/brown color as the cloak.

The man lifted his hands to his lips and blew on them, releasing some sort of sparkling dust. It got caught up in the wind and was carried away. As Todd watched, he kept thinking this can't be good either.

Turning his attention back to the dark, bald man, Todd saw that the guy was staring back at him with a creepy, skeletal grin. The man's teeth were rotten and broken. His face, as well as his arms, was gaunt. *Dachau-emaciated* were the words that settled in Todd's head. As he got a better view of the man, everything about the guy screamed starvation, but the man moved like he had the vitality of a healthy teenager.

Within a split second, and causing the space to warp between them, the bald man went from the sidewalk across the street to being mere inches from Todd's face, with only the iron fence separating the two men. Now that the man was directly in front of him, Todd cringed and felt a chill crawl down his spine. The guy's eyes glowed with a sickly green/brown color that perfectly matched his cloak!

"Boo!" the man shouted, cackling with laughter.

Todd stumbled backwards from surprise. Before he could regain his balance, he tripped over a gravestone and fell on his back. Sprawled out on the grass, his legs were left comically draped over the stone. He blinked his eyes several times, trying to make the black spots disappear. Rolling off the grave marker, Todd scrambled to his feet. He watched as the man moved on down the street, using his robes to fan the air, causing the sparkling dust to waft over the area.

Some of that dust landed on a small sapling and several potted plants. Each plant instantly shriveled up and died, like they had been hit by a drought on steroids. Todd gaped as the weird man turned again to look at him. Mentally, he heard a strange voice scream inside his head, *"I'm the bringer of famine! Enjoy my plague, you cowardly worm!"*

Todd's hands instinctively shot up and over his ears as he tried to block out the maniacal laughter that followed the words. As the guy left, so too did the voice inside his head. He sighed heavily and began to brush off the grass and dirt from his pants, relaxing a little.

At that moment, he had the strangest sensation that he wasn't alone. Looking around, he warily searched for anyone else that could be in the cemetery, but he didn't see anyone. He couldn't see all of the graveyard because of a rise in the middle of it, so he decided that maybe he should walk around, just to see if anyone else was in there with him. He wanted no more surprises.

As he rounded one of the many oak trees in the place, a soft hand touched his shoulder. Todd gasped and froze dead in his tracks. The hairs on the back of his neck stood on end as fear seized his stressed-out mind.

He whirled around and saw a pale, petite woman standing behind him. She wore a very old but clean, long-flowing, blue gown that matched her sapphire eyes. Her nose was red as if she had been crying recently, and her eyes were puffy with dark circles under them. She seemed sad, making him believe that she had lost someone she loved.

"Todd Raymond Riggs?" the woman asked coldly.

Todd blanched and warily backed away as fear covered him like a shroud covers the dead. "Who are you?" he demanded.

The woman blinked and said again, "Todd Raymond Riggs?"

"Who wants to know?" He narrowed his eyes suspiciously at the stranger.

"I do, of course."

"But who are *you*, and how do you know me?"

"I don't know who you are; that's why I asked."

"How can you say that when you just said my name?"

"I did?" The woman looked confused and distraught. "When did I say your name?"

Todd growled irritably, "My name was the first words out of your mouth, you idiot! So I demand — "

The strange woman's entire body started to shimmer and glow. Suddenly, she rose in the air and hovered there, staring at him. Terror filled Todd's eyes, and he stumbled, nearly falling, as he backed away from her.

"You have no right to speak to me like that, you insignificant worm!" the woman hissed angrily as her sapphire eyes blazed with her fury. "With the blink of my eye, I could kill you where you crawl!"

Todd hunkered down behind a large monument, cowering there, but he never took his eyes off her. He put his hands up in a submissive way, showing that he believed her. If she could fly and glow, she could probably follow through with her threat.

The woman descended, landing softly on the ground, her bare feet making no noise whatsoever. She continued to glare for a moment longer, but then all emotion seemed to melt from her pale face. She looked all around, like she wasn't sure where she was. Maybe she was looking for someone or something, he thought as he watched her.

When she had finished looking at the cemetery, the strange woman stared at Todd. "Todd Raymond Riggs?"

He gulped, stood up straight and rounded the monument. "I'm Todd Raymond Riggs."

The strange woman beamed him a toothy smile as she strolled up to Todd like nothing had happened. "My name is Purah, and I'm here to take you away from all this!"

He felt a cold shiver cover his body. "Where are we going?" he asked suspiciously.

"To the Promised Land, that's where. It's what you asked for."

"When did I ask to go there?"

Purah blinked several times at Todd and then asked, "Go where?"

"The Promised Land," Todd explained irritably, suspecting something was out of whack in Purah's brain.

"Yes, that's where you wanted to go," she replied. "You're on my list to be taken there!"

"How did my name get on your list, Purah?"

"Only those who have truly repented of all their sins get to go to the Promised Land," Purah declared with a sudden twinkle in her eyes.

Holy shit! Todd thought as his face paled. That prayer actually worked for me? He sat down on top of a gravestone, still feeling stunned that his pleas had been heard and that he was going to escape all this chaos. Another thought occurred to Todd. "So, is this the apocalypse?"

"Apocalypse?" Purah laughed lightly. "No, no. This is the end of days, silly."

Todd pinched the bridge of his nose and frowned. "And that's why you're here? It's the end of days for all Mankind?"

"No, I'm here because your name is on my list."

Todd thought this over and then realization hit him. "It was you, wasn't it? You're the one who's been making people disappear, aren't you?"

Confused, Purah responded, "I have no idea what you're talking about. I'm here for those who are on my list."

Todd inched towards Purah. Being this close to her made his chest tight. His anxiety filled his entire body to the point of overflowing. He noticed that her skin appeared flawless, like that of a porcelain doll. He also noticed that he found the woman, or whatever she was, very attractive. If it weren't for the whole end of days thing, Todd would have considered asking her out for drinks…maybe even more. He gazed at her for a moment longer and then asked, "Are you an angel?"

"A fallen angel, yes. Now we must go, Todd Raymond Riggs. You're the last one on my list, and I need to start on my next list."

"What will happen when I get to the Promised Land?"

"Have you never read your Bible?" She smiled sympathetically at him. "I'll bet you have memory problems like me."

Todd's cheeks heated slightly. "I never went to church much. I've read the Bible a little, but that was so long ago that I've forgotten most of it." He grinned sheepishly. "Please forgive me?"

"It's not my place to forgive," she explained cheerfully. "I've got no idea about what needs to be forgiven."

Todd felt bad for Purah, so he repeated his question. "What will happen to me when I get to the Promised Land?"

"Mortals will be cleansed of all impurities and will be granted ever-lasting life."

"I'm going to be...immortal?" Todd was both stunned and overjoyed by this new revelation.

"Of course you will be, silly. Which part of ever-lasting life did you not understand? Now, take my hands, and I will take you to your new home and then I can start on my next list."

As Todd took Purah's hands, he noted how soft and delicate they were, forcing his mind to wonder about other soft spots on her angelic body. Curiosity got the best of him. "What's on your next list to do?"

Purah smiled at him as if he were a small child who knew no better. "Why raise the dead, of course!"

They both vanished.

Chapter 3

In the Future

In the small farming village of Melona, the people lived their day-to-day lives in relative peace. The villagers were out in the early morning, setting up their carts and makeshift tables for any outsiders who wished to barter for their crops and wares. The village had a reputation for having plentiful fruits and vegetables to choose from, and traders quickly spread the word, mainly because not many in the area had the abundance of food year round. Fruits and vegetables were their main staple, but they also had several wells and small creeks that ran through the village, yielding a steady flow of fish, turtles, crawfish, and frogs, and travelers could barter for different meats.

Melona was founded by Rose Macready, an outspoken sorceress who had a strong connection to nature and was able to use her vast knowledge and powers to make the village thrive. Leading by example, Rose used both compassion and tough love to rule; however, if anyone tried to question her authority or replace her, Rose stood her ground with a pack of wolves backing her, ready to take out any threats. There were whispers that she could "see the future" because she could predict when bad weather or a freeze was coming within a three-day span. Her people saved their crops while others around them failed.

The landscape of the world had dramatically changed since the firestorms had rained down on the entire world. No one could give an explanation of how it had started or from where it had come, but those who survived it knew it hadn't been man-made. Cities and rural towns had been razed; the scorched land had turned to ash. Nothing had withstood the impact of those fireballs.

Twisted metal and concrete chunks were left as permanent skeletal remains of a destroyed civilization. Many people had fled to the subway systems for cover, but those proved to be deathtraps. The subways became tombs as the tunnels collapsed, killing outright or burying alive the people in them. There were rumors of a being who roamed Earth during the firestorm, bringing famine by releasing a powdery substance which caused the crops of whole regions to wither, making the landscape barren and uninhabitable. As time went on, many trees and vegetation grew back, but not everything in nature recovered.

The oceans had boiled to the point that there was more land than water; only the deep trenches and abysses contained the last remnants of ocean water. Ocean floors resembled a vast marshland, treacherous and deadly because most areas were like quicksand. One wrong step and a person would be swallowed whole.

Water everywhere had become scarce and was worth its weight in gold. Those who had their own personal wells or water sources, kept them secret from the water-raiders — people who would kill to possess the water.

Over the years, small villages popped up everywhere out of necessity. Barter was the new form of currency which allowed the purchase of basic staples: food, water, clothing, hand tools, and weapons. Skilled craftsmen were coveted by their villages, which tended to go out of their way to keep them happy.

Every village that survived had one thing in common: walls! The walls had quickly been built to keep out marauders and the ghouls that had arisen from their graves shortly after the firestorms ended.

Ghouls came in all shapes and sizes. They wanted nothing more than to kill and eat the flesh off anything living. In the early days of recovery, people had tended to be over-confident in their assessment of the ghoul threat, mainly due to all the zombie movies. "Kill the brain, kill the zombie" was the mantra in those early days, but that advice turned out to be a myth. When people realized that a bullet to the brain wouldn't faze the walking dead, they changed the name from zombie to ghoul.

The simple act of renaming the zombies allowed for a paradigm shift in the minds of the living. In other words, they thought of the walking dead differently. They weren't zombies; they were ghouls. After a lot of trial and error — and deaths — it was discovered that beheading was the only way to kill a ghoul. A new mantra was born: lose the head of the walking dead.

Of course, getting close enough to take a ghoul's head off was dangerous. They tended to travel in small packs of a dozen or more, and the worst part was that they could coordinate and speak to each other.

The walls surrounding Rose Macready's village were built using stones from a nearby quarry. Embedded in the mortar was razor wiring, making the walls treacherous for invaders to scale. The top of the walls was wide enough for a walkway. This allowed villagers, who volunteered to perform guard duty, to watch the perimeter and alert the others of any impending attack. And attacks came often because of the village's reputation for plentiful resources.

*

Rose looked to the sky and noticed storm clouds rolling in from the west. Already, the flashes of lightning colored the horizon. Storms from the west weren't as severe as those coming from the east. Those storms brought acid rains that burned on contact with the skin. Tornadoes came from the east too, but with climate changes caused by the firestorms, one needed to take a storm from any direction seriously and prepare for the worst.

The dawn of a new day was breaking as Rose walked by the merchants setting up their wares. Her voice boomed out as thunder rumbled in the distance, "Trade well, my friends, but be prepared to close up quickly. A storm's a coming, and I have no good or bad feelings from it. Be safe and be well!"

Everyone smiled but an uneasy feeling could be felt all around as the merchants kept looking over their respective shoulders. A couple of people murmured about pulling their carts over to the storage building and calling it a day, even though the day was just beginning. The building was only a dozen posts in the ground with a tin roof on top, but that was better than lugging home their carts.

Whether anything got traded this morning or not didn't bother Rose. She was more concerned with the possibly nasty storm that was on the horizon. She cringed at what the storm might bring to her village. There would be more people looking for shelter or bad guys looking to take over and enslave her people. And, of course, with more people coming out of the woodwork, more ghouls would follow.

Rose strolled over to a wooden ladder that leaned against the wall. She climbed up the rungs to the top of the wall where she could survey the land and get a better view of the dirt roads leading towards her village.

I've got to prepare for the possibility of housing more people because of the storm, she thought as she paused at the end of the ladder. If we run out of lodging, the storage building could provide shelter, albeit not the warmest or coziest place to be during a storm.

A loud crash of thunder snapped Rose back to reality, and a gloved hand appeared in front of her face. "I'm quite capable of getting up here on my own, Duncan," Rose insisted as she jutted her chin up at him.

"True, but I love it when you get your panties in a bunch by being all indignant," Duncan replied with a sly grin.

Rose smacked his hand away as she bulled her way up to the top of the wall. She stomped past Duncan who followed right behind her chuckling, with his hands clasped behind his back. She glared at him over her shoulder as she stalked to the north corner of the wall that gave the best view of the main road.

He watched her every move with interest, noting that she was as graceful as a cat and just as inscrutable. The sorceress was in her early thirties and stood just shy of six feet tall. She had the lithe body of an athlete, but her chest was well endowed, which Duncan very much appreciated. A petite nose sat above her pink, full lips, but it was her eyes, both alluring and unsettling, that always seemed to grab the man's attention.

"Is the lovely sorceress expecting trouble or a new shipment of fine, regal clothing?"

"No to both but with that storm coming, anything could happen." Rose narrowed her eyes and added, "Why do you assume that's all I want—more stuff, like I'm a rich woman?"

Duncan perused Rose's clothes. She was wearing a long turquoise dress that had puffy shoulder padding, and it clung to her upper body tightly, accentuating her breasts. She wore several gold necklaces, and one had the Earth Goddess pendant attached to it. Her gloves were made from silk, and they rode up to her elbows. And although it was hard to see them, he knew she was wearing calf high, leather boots.

"The shoe fits, Miss Macready. I've seen on more than one occasion where you've given much to have the finer things in this world. Though I must say, you could do better with more things that have a functional purpose, like work clothes or—"

"What I do with my barter goods is no concern of yours!" she snapped. "If I look presentable to those who come through these gates, maybe they'll come back…hopefully, bringing in more traders with them. I need to look professional and memorable."

"And the fact that we have plenty of goodies that everyone wants isn't memorable enough? Do you really have to dress like an aristocrat?" Duncan swished his hand at her dress.

"I'm a woman," she growled irritably. "I can wear whatever the hell I want! If I want to wear luxurious fabrics, I have every right to do so! And for your information, I have plenty of functional clothing. If it's one thing I know how to do, it's how to dress properly for the occasion. You have no right to tell me what I can or cannot wear—I'm not your wife!"

"Thank the gods for that!" Duncan snorted. "I'd be in the poorhouse if you were mine." He stood there laughing at her.

"Is this how you treated your wife before she vanished? If I were her, I'd be grateful to be gone and no longer under your suffocating, tight-wad ass control!" Rose whirled around and turned her gaze back to the road.

Duncan abruptly ceased laughing and moved next to her. He angrily grabbed her arm and spun her around to face him. With murder in his eyes and only inches away from her face, he growled, "Rose, you should know better than to poke fun at me like that!" All amusement had melted from his face. "My scars run deep for a reason, and you blatantly cut at them, splitting them open again. Trust me when I say I always remember those who hurt me; I always make them pay!"

"Unhand me or I will give you some new scars to whine about!" Rose moved her hands to show Duncan the deadly magic that was pulsating in them, ready to strike at him.

Duncan roughly pushed her away. "What you said has already scarred me, so no need for your crap magic! I'll remember your words and one day, they'll come back to haunt you!"

"This crap magic has kept you living comfortably while you've been here. It's put food in your belly too, so mind your tongue, warrior. You can be replaced by any thick-headed buffoon who can wield a sword."

Duncan stood, silently glaring at Rose, but she could see he was thinking, which could mean anything. He was a stubborn and strong-willed man, but he was also a good man. From the multiple scars that covered his strong, square jaw, Rose figured he'd seen his fair share of brawls. This morning his blond stubble covered the slight cleft in his chin, and Rose resisted the impulse to reach out and trace it. The rest of his face, though, was unmarred, with the exception of a thin scar that traced from the bottom of his left eye down to the top of his protruding cheek.

Why did she always end up fighting with him? She sighed. Rose had known better than to bring up the memory of his wife.

Duncan's wife had been one of the many people who had gotten "reaped", which was what everyone called it. When all hell broke loose throughout the world, some people were taken—they just vanished into thin air. A few had seen otherworldly beings taking them. "Must have been grim reapers taking them," people would say. "They were reaped."

Rose didn't like being badgered about her looks, and her pride dictated that she had to say something hurtful to save face. Now, though, she felt bad for hurting him. Instead of apologizing, which was out of the question for her, she changed the subject. "Any problems on your hunt last night?"

"Nothing I couldn't handle with one arm behind my back," Duncan replied, his anger ebbing slightly. "There were more Chouls out and about than usual."

"Chouls?" Rose blinked. "Don't you mean ghouls?"

"Same thing, Miss Macready. I've come to the conclusion that since this was the Christian's apocalypse, all the dead who were brought back to life were actually dead Christians."

"And you believe this...why?"

"Go to any graveyard around here, and you'll see that not all the dead came back. If the living ones were snatched by some unseen force, then who's to say that same force didn't raise the dead followers of Christ?"

"You have a point, Duncan, but I'm still going to call them ghouls. Any ideas on why there are more of them out there now?"

He shook his head. "None, but something's got them stirred up. I've got a bad feeling in my gut about this." He glanced over at her. "You feel worried about that storm that's coming in from the west?" When Rose nodded, he added, "Well I sense a different kind of storm coming." Duncan used his chin to point at the road. "I see the first of the traders coming; you better head on down and be all *memorable*."

Rose nodded as she walked past Duncan towards the ladder. She knew he was a smart man and had great fighting instincts, as well as spot-on intuition. She tried her best to nurture those qualities in him because they were good skills to have around.

She had difficulty divining what it was about Duncan Morgan that made him so special. His reasoning that the dead were Christians was spot on. Only the Christians had arisen; the dead who were pagan, atheist, or of non-Christian religions had been left undisturbed in their graves. Their living non-Christian counterparts had not been reaped either. Only Christians had been reaped. For some strange reason, she couldn't fathom, some Christians had been left behind in the world. Weren't they all supposed to be in Heaven?

Once she got to the ground, Rose tugged and adjusted her dress. She walked towards the main gate, which consisted of two massive wooden doors made from fallen trees bolted together. The door was locked in place using three thick planks of plywood. As Rose got closer to the gate, she called out, "If there are no ghouls around, open the gate so the trading caravans can enter."

One of the watch guards on the wall gave the "all's clear" thumbs up to the gate masters who then proceeded to remove the wooden planks from the gates. Huge, metal hinges creaked loudly as the massive doors were pushed open.

The first of the horse-drawn carriages crossed over the village threshold. Most of the caravans that came to the village consisted of people walking with large backpacks or people in old flatbed trailers, retro-fitted to be pulled by a horse, a mule, or even a cow. The savvier traders who had the time and resources tended to ride in style, usually having gypsy-like covered wagons. Many of these wooden gypsy wagons could be used as a store to trade from or used as a dwelling place to be lived in.

So far this morning, there were more walkers than wagons in the small caravan. Only four flatbed trailers and two green gypsy wagons rolled inside the village. But it was the one bringing up the rear that was really different from the rest.

"Oh crap!" Rose growled.

Chapter 4

The wagon, which was a wooden, covered vehicle—gypsy-style, had flashy gold trim on the borders and doors. Its artwork on the sides and back consisted of angels and crosses.

Rose's muscles tensed as she shook her head. "Great, just what we needed today," she growled sarcastically. "Christians!" She felt torn because she knew that not all the Christian followers had gotten taken away during the firestorms.

Those who stayed behind almost always preached about repenting and joining them. These left-behind people were far more aggressive than Christians were before the reaping. They felt they hadn't made the cut. They hadn't been worthy to be with Christ. Now they preached—forcibly, sometimes—at any kind of gathering, trying to get people to repent and follow Christ's teachings.

Rose had read the Christian's bible, as well as the Torah, the Quran, the Vedas and Bhagavad Gita and even the Tipitaka. She never understood how people who followed Christ—a benevolent being who preached peace—could be so violent. Maybe the left-behind people thought they would gain brownie points if they forcibly converted people. She'd never heard of a quota system in Christianity, but maybe they had one. They sure acted like it.

She sighed heavily as she watched the wagon of a left-behind guy enter the compound. In a few minutes, he'd probably be preaching about the "Promised Land". In the past, Rose would let them get on their soapboxes and speak to the villagers.

She shuddered now, remembering one group that had come out brandishing machetes and torches. The villagers either hid or stood their ground, trying to fend off the group. The leader of the zealots kept whipping the traders up into a frenzy, until finally that frenzy turned against the surprised Christians. After an entire day of sermons filled with religious bigotry and hate, one of the traders strolled up and beheaded the preacher in mid-rant.

That was the day Rose had met Duncan Morgan. He picked up the preacher's severed head and threw it at his stunned followers, coldly stating, "He wanted to cleanse this place of bad people; I'd say he got in way over his *head*. Anyone else want to join him? If you do, just step right up, and I'll send you to your Heaven…minus a head, of course."

The missionaries quickly dropped their weapons and torches and fled out of the village as Duncan charged at them with murder in his cobalt eyes. Ever since that day, he chose to live in Melona to help keep the peace. Rose knew there was something different about him, but she couldn't quite place it. She felt that if Duncan stayed here, then she could glean the truth one day.

"Duncan!" Rose pointed to the wagon as she called out, "Your presence is needed down here!"

Duncan looked towards the road and let out an oath in disgust, which made Rose wonder if his hatred for the "Bible-thumping hypocrites" left on Earth had anything to do with his wife. He was a private man that seldom talked about his past, and Rose suspected that was a form of defense to keep from getting hurt. "Can't add to the scars if you don't open yourself to another's blade," Duncan once told her. It was his go-to reasoning for not trusting anyone…not even Rose.

Not wanting to waste any time, Duncan straddled the sides of the ladder with his steel toe boots and slid down. He maneuvered between the oncoming traders, squeezing between two flatbeds passing by. As Duncan got to Rose, the left-behind guy's wagon was making its way through the main gate.

To everyone's surprise, nothing was pulling the wagon — nothing that they could see, anyway. Duncan gripped the hilt of his sword as he anticipated a fight.

Rose turned to Duncan. "How's that wagon moving? I don't hear a motor."

"And you won't," Duncan declared. "All the fuel in the world is gone…as far as I know. Unless they've hoarded it and now want to flaunt it in everyone's face. I'd say it's being powered by something else. Whatever it is, it's making me uneasy."

"Hmm, I agree," Rose replied as her gaze was torn away from him and back to the wagon.

When the wagon stopped, a side door opened. A man who looked to be in his fifties stepped out. He wore a dirt-stained dress shirt and slacks. Rose watched as he beamed a fake smile at her, making her believe he could've been a politician at one time in his life.

"My sweet sister, is this Melona?" the man asked in a jovial sounding voice.

"It is and my name is Rose Macready," she stated, not bothering to hide her dislike for the stranger. She elbowed Duncan when he snickered at her. "I'm the one who runs this village, and I'm not your sister!"

"Definitely not sweet either," Duncan muttered under his breath, making Rose quickly glare at him.

"What business do you have here in my village…mister?" Rose asked.

"The name is Sully, and I'm here to do what I've always done my whole life."

Rose tensed. "And what might that be, Sully?"

"To spread the good Lord's word and help absolve others of their sins so they may — "

"Blah, blah, blah!" Duncan blurted out. "These are good people who have their own spiritual beliefs and have no need in the crap you're peddling!"

"It's not crap!" Sully answered back, his face reddening with anger. "How dare you say such things about the word of God! His word is law, and it's my calling to bring as many of his wayward sheep back into His flock, heathen!"

"Your one God has already done that or have you forgotten? What happened on that day? Did you miss the bus to Heaven…maybe not answer the door? Why did He see fit to leave you behind?"

"I…uh…don't know!" Sully stammered, trying to control his temper. "It's not my place to question God's will. If you ever want to go to the Promised Land and see your loved ones, you won't question Him. Why He should spare all the pagan heathens of this world is beyond me."

"Maybe your God believes that our kind should inherit the Earth instead of the meek," Duncan goaded. "Makes sense to me. Most wars and atrocities have been done in your God's name."

"Your people should've been exterminated long ago!" Sully snapped. "Christ has returned, and He will clear the world of your filth!"

Duncan snarled as he moved forward, but Rose put a hand on his shoulder, stopping him. "Okay, that's enough dick-dagger fighting. Sully, you can use the proclamation platform and say your peace. We don't want any trouble here. Be warned, though. If you get any notions of starting a lynch mob, Duncan here will hang you first. Is that clear?"

Sully's anger seemed to ebb, but he never took his gaze from Duncan. He took in a deep breath. "That's an acceptable proposal, Mrs. Macready. You just keep that brute away from me, and I promise I won't cause any trouble here."

"It's *Miss* Macready, but you can call me Rose."

Sully slowly nodded as he leered at her with a lustful gaze, causing Duncan to growl irritably, deep in his throat. The man headed back into his wagon.

Duncan turned and walked away, so Rose followed along beside him, trying to keep up with his brisk pace. He seemed ready to explode, and she was worried he might do something rash.

"Did you really need to goad the man?" she asked.

"Yes!"

"Hmm, if I didn't know better, I'd say you were hoping to take his head off just for the hell of it."

No response.

"That wasn't what I had in mind when I asked you to greet the man. I wanted to keep things peaceful. My people need to feel safe when they go about their business."

Still, no response.

"Gods, Duncan, would you say something? I'm getting tired of having a one-way conversation here."

"I learned long ago to keep my mouth shut when a woman is ranting, and you're ranting," Duncan said with a smirk.

Rose fumed as she jumped in front of him, stopping him in his tracks. She stuck her finger in his face and growled, "Oh no, you don't! I'm not letting you get off that easy. I've never seen you pick a fight before, and it seemed to me that was what you were doing. Why did you provoke him?"

Duncan sighed as his shoulders slumped in defeat. "I was testing him, that's all…nothing wrong with that. I wanted to see what he would do if someone challenged him and his beliefs. I was just making certain he would stay peaceful."

"That wasn't a test; you were out to start a fight."

"True, but…" Duncan paused for a moment as Sully walked past them. "I don't trust him, that's all."

Rose furrowed her brow. "Why? What has he done other than arrive in a wagon painted with crosses all over it and powered by a motor that we can't hear?"

Duncan squinted against the sunlight as clouds parted a little. "Just forget it. Forget I ever said anything about this."

Rose put her hands on her hips, giving him a firm look. Duncan rolled his eyes and tried to move past her, but she blocked his path with each step he took.

"I can do this all day, Duncan," Rose threatened. "If there's something you've heard about this guy, I need to know, so I can protect my people." Before he could bull past her, Rose took Duncan's hand and softly added, "You can tell me anything."

Duncan shifted from foot to foot. "I don't fully understand it myself. I don't know why I don't trust him." When he saw she was still waiting for an answer, he sighed heavily. "I really, really don't trust the guy, and I don't know why."

"Like a gut feeling or instinct?" Rose asked with a quizzical look.

"No, I know exactly what those things are, but this feeling is something different. It has plagued me my whole life. And ever since the firestorms, it's only gotten worse. It's like something inside me, you know, and it's screaming, 'Don't trust him' or 'Bad person'. When I begin to feel like that, the person tends to do something terrible."

"And what did it scream when you saw Sully?" Rose asked, although now she feared the answer.

Duncan looked past Rose and saw Sully up on the proclamation platform, spewing his moral beliefs and preaching about repenting and redemption to those who walked by. There was a small cluster listening to what the man was saying. After all, they had no other form of entertainment today. None of the villagers, though, seemed enthralled with his passionate chatter, which only gave him more fuel to keep going.

Rose noticed that Duncan's hand had slithered around the hilt of his sword. He seemed to be listening intently to the man's words. As his face tensed, and the muscles in his jaw ticked, Duncan's cobalt eyes appeared to grow even darker. "Duncan, what do you hear?" she asked as she squeezed his hand.

"Death. That's what I hear." He noticed that Rose shivered. "Rest assured, while I'm on wall duty, I'll be keeping a close eye on our guest. Now, if you're through interrogating me, I've got a job to do. It appears I'll be watching two fronts today." Duncan pulled his hand free from her grip and walked towards the wall, turning his head to glare at Sully.

She watched Duncan go for a moment longer before walking towards the area of the village known as "trader alley". Sauntering between the traders and villagers, she greeted each person and made sure that the men took notice of her with some flirtatious words and movements.

What better way to get trade items for nothing, especially if the men were showering her with gifts to show their affections? She stifled a laugh as she wondered if it would be worth the trouble to go skyclad during peak trading days. Just imagine how many of these poor saps would give away everything they owned just to have a glimpse of her naked body. It was a cruel thought because that would be all they would get from her. They could look but not touch. But men are men, and they always would be.

As the first few raindrops began to fall, Rose started to ponder what was going on inside of Duncan's head. This was the first time he had ever spoken about himself in terms of having any supernatural abilities. She had them, but she had never considered that Duncan had them also. She wanted to know more.

Duncan was a man, but he was also a puzzle to figure out. Rose did enjoy putting puzzles together — and taking them apart. Once you set the right piece in its proper place, much will be revealed. If he did have supernatural abilities, other than a warning voice, Duncan had never let on before, which got Rose to thinking: What if Duncan doesn't know what he has?

He didn't talk about his past or family ties. All Rose really knew about him was that he had a wife, and she had been reaped by the grim reapers during the firestorms. But there were more layers to that relationship. If Duncan does have supernatural abilities, she thought, it would be in my best interest to discover what Duncan really is. How do I start, though?

She looked in the direction where a row of wooden huts sat. The villagers used them as shelters. They were just big enough to house three people if needed and were furnished with a small dining table, chairs, cots, and a fire pit for cooking. They were decorated and outfitted by the occupants to suit their needs. There were bigger huts on the other side of the village for larger families.

Being the founder of Melona, Rose took pride in her extra-large place and lavished it with an actual queen size bed. She had a black satin bed set, several dressers, and two armoires filled with her favorite elegant dresses. She also had a free-standing jewelry cabinet with a vanity mirror and two fire pits: one for cooking and one for brewing potions and herbal remedies.

Why rough it when one could live in style was Rose's mantra. She made it clear to everyone that they could have whatever they wanted, as long as it didn't create problems within the village. If someone wanted a bigger place, they couldn't just take it by force from someone. They had to build their own, just like everyone else.

Off in the corner of the village was the smallest of all the wooden huts. It had been built by Duncan shortly after Rose convinced him to stay. She glanced up at the wall as she walked, keeping a trained eye on him. He was sitting sideways on an old, wooden crate so he could watch the surrounding area outside the walls and discreetly keep an eye on Sully.

Duncan saw her and gave her a two-finger salute before glaring at Sully again. The zealot was stomping around on the proclamation platform, dramatically waving a weather-worn copy of the Bible. He wore a bright yellow rain poncho now and had gold trim bifocals perched on the bridge of his nose. "Heed my warnings, good people of Melona!" he cried out. "There's little time left for any of us in these dark days. Turn away from the sins of this world and come with me as I spread the teachings of the one and only God!"

"One and only God, you say?" someone in the audience asked.

"That's correct! There's only one true God, and He will lead us all to salvation!"

"What's His name?" a young lady asked.

Sully's cheeks flushed red. Stammering, he replied, "He...uh...has no other name than God or our Lord and Savior. Why would you ask me this?"

"Because I know the names of all the Gods and Goddesses I pay tribute to," she replied. "I was curious to know the name of your God. Does anyone know His name?"

Laughter and more questions came at Sully. "Does He come down and talk to you personally?" one man asked. "How does He feel about all the atrocities done in His name?" an old lady shouted.

Sully's face reddened with anger and contempt. These people are just harassing me, he thought. Rose passed by quietly, having a difficult time holding back her own laughter. Finally, Sully barked out, "There's no hope for you godless heathens! Your days of fun and ignorance will come to an awful end sooner than you realize!"

"Godless? I know many deities!" a young man called out and crossed his index finger over his middle finger in a superstitious effort to *not* bring down the gods' vengeance on him. "You say heathen like it's a bad thing. If you wish to live a ridged life from a dogmatic, religious point of view then that's wonderful because that means more fun for the rest of us!"

Several tendrils of lightning streaked in the sky above, and the rain fell out of the clouds in a sudden downpour. Sully marched off the platform, muttering under his breath as the small crowd started dancing around in circles with their arms in the air, thanking their gods for the rain. A few removed their wet clothes, making Sully even more uncomfortable as he fled back into his wagon.

Rose made her way past some of the villagers who ran for their huts. She glanced over her shoulder one last time at Duncan. He was still sitting on the old, wooden crate, despite the downpour and lightning, now keeping a watchful eye on the area outside the village.

She grabbed the door handle and hurried into Duncan's hut.

Chapter 5

Rose leaned against the door for a moment to catch her breath. She grabbed handfuls of her thick, raven hair and started to wring it out as she surveyed Duncan's hut. She knew he was a simple man, but this place was practically a janitor's closet. Scratch that, she thought, a janitor's closet actually had space for supplies.

Duncan hadn't built his hut for comfort but for shelter only. She bent over and then quickly flung her hair over her head in one, big flop-smack on her back. Scrutinizing the hut, Rose saw Duncan had a tattered sleeping bag rolled up on the floor, and next to it was the backpack he wore whenever he travelled. She quickly searched the backpack. In it was his only change of clothes.

Both backpack and sleeping bag were stashed beside the door—probably in case he had to bug-out quickly, she thought and felt a disconcerting tremble. She quickly shook it off. Old habits of surviving on the road seemed to stick with the man, but it struck Rose as odd that he would still feel the urge to run, especially in a well-protected village.

Did Duncan have plans to leave? That thought troubled her, and she tried to throw it off as she snatched up the sleeping bag, examining it closely. She stopped. "Duncan, I don't want you to leave," she muttered to the empty room. She thought about how lonely she would be without the man and sighed heavily. "Oh, stop it!" she ordered herself. She turned her attention back to the sleeping bag and crinkled her nose at the different odors that assailed her nostrils.

"Good gods, what road kill does he sleep with?" Rose cringed as she peered into the opening.

This sleeping bag should be burned! Only, the fumes that would emanate from it would probably kill most plant and animal life for miles, she mused with a smirk. She hesitantly reached in and plucked several loose strands of Duncan's strawberry blond hairs out of the bag and tucked them into a hidden pocket in her dress.

Placing the filthy sleeping bag back on the straw-covered dirt floor, she rolled it up the best she could while holding her breath. Why wouldn't Duncan barter for a different bag? Rose stood up straight and looked at the rest of what the man called home.

He had a small fire pit with a cast iron skillet and cauldron for his cooking needs, and setting next to it was a serving spoon and long fork. The countertop that most people had in their hut was missing, but in its place was a five-gallon bucket with dirty water in it, a wash cloth and a scrub brush for cleaning.

"Duncan the minimalist," Rose muttered as she walked towards the door. She couldn't help but glance back at the contents of the hut. She shook her head sadly and tsked her tongue. "You could live so much better than this, you silly fool."

She opened the door and looked in the general area of the wall where Duncan had positioned himself. He still sat on the wooden crate, ever vigilant, watching the landscape despite the heavy downpour.

Thunder rumbled from above as lightning brightened up the sky for a moment. Rose made a mad dash towards her own place, water splashing and mud spitting up with each of her long strides. She kept a hand against her concealed pocket so none of Duncan's hair could escape as she ran.

The village was flooding a little in areas; the bulk of water came from the creek itself, although the deep ruts created by traders' carts channeled the runoff toward the open gates and into the village. All the traders were huddling under the storage building, their carts still out in the open. Rose didn't see Sully among the crowd of people, but she figured he was taking refuge in his holy-roller wagon.

There were villagers still out dancing skyclad and having a great time celebrating the rain when Rose got to her over-sized hut. She grabbed the handle and pushed her way inside where it was warm, dry and…not a closet. She looked down at her wet clothes and shivered from the cold. Walking over to her altar, she placed Duncan's hairs in a cast iron cauldron. She needed them to use as a key ingredient to her divination potion, but first things first, though.

Rose wanted to be dry, so she began removing her soaked clothes. She sat down on a green, plush, cushioned chair and tugged off her calf high leather boots. Rose slipped her fingers inside the sleeve of her glove and rolled it down slowly. As much as she wanted the wet garment off, she did enjoy the feel of silk gliding over her skin. Her eyes rolled back in her head at the sensation of her other silk glove coming off.

Reaching behind her back, she unzipped her dress. As she stood up, she wiggled and tugged the full length garment off her cold, wet body. It pooled at her ankles, and Rose stepped out of it. Picking up the wet dress and the long sleeve gloves, she draped them on a drying rack that stood near her fire pit.

Rose walked over and snatched down a couple of towels and a red bathrobe. She sat down on her queen size bed and wrapped one towel around her rain-soaked hair. A burning question kept repeating itself in her mind: What is it about Duncan that makes him have a supernatural ability and not know anything about it?

When it came to the supernatural, Rose believed that knowledge was the key to everything. Whether it was how to fight an enemy or how to use magic to help the environment, knowledge was paramount. She had an exceptional talent; she could commune with animals and even nature itself, and they spoke back to her telepathically.

Rose did her best to conceal most of her paranormal gifts from others because magic took a hard toll on her mentally and sometimes physically. She sighed, remembering springtime; she had to use her own blood on the seeds her villagers used to grow their crops. That was the secret of how Melona always had an abundance of fruits and vegetables year round.

Once she was satisfied her body was dry, Rose stood up and slipped the bathrobe on. Not bothering to tie the belt, she walked over to her altar. She sat down on her plush chair that was next to the altar and pulled a small, wooden jewelry box over to her. The box was where she kept an assortment of her dried herbs and small bottles of liquid concoctions.

Rose thought for a moment as she perused her ingredients, trying to decide what combination this new potion would call for since she'd never actually made a potion for this purpose before. Would the results be instantaneous? Would the spell work gradually for days on end? She didn't know.

One thing was certain, though: if Duncan could be shown how to use his abilities and hone his natural skills, he could be a great asset to her. It would also be nice to talk with someone who actually possessed supernatural powers, like herself. Most of the villagers had their own spiritual beliefs, but none of them had outwardly shown any gifts like the ones Rose possessed.

Am I so desperate and lonely that I must drag someone into this path with me — this path that can be dangerous and full of scary potholes? Maybe I just like Duncan well enough that I want him to be a badass? She sighed.

Duncan was a private man who would prove to be difficult if she tried to explain and teach him straightforwardly, especially since he didn't trust anyone...not even her. And that was all due to the screaming voice inside his head telling him more about others than he wanted to know.

Rose pulled out a small jar that held water from the well. Water from different sources had very different "personalities." Water from the creek didn't seem to be as potent in spellwork as well water. And sometimes direct rainwater was totally useless — probably from so much contamination.

She glanced inside the jar at the well water, making sure she had enough; she would use it as part of the liquid base for her potion. Her concoction was going to help her divine what Duncan was, so she grabbed out some alder from the box. Feeling it needed to be enhanced, she plucked out ambergris and a few arnica flowers to aide her psychic energies. There were also dried and diced vanilla beans for prophetic dreaming, ginger powder to give it more magical power, and crushed garlic cloves because of its tendency to enhance all the other herbs it mixed with, making them stronger.

Rose glanced at her selection and knew she should add some dried sage to the mix because it had a variety of magical properties. The one property she wanted was wisdom. Knowledge is power and that is what she sought, after all.

She put all the herbs in a ceramic mortar and ground them together with a stone pestle. As she worked, she muttered a prayer to the Earth goddess to put Her blessings on her work in hopes that the potion would do its intended job and not kill her. That was always important, especially when dealing with different herb combinations for consumption.

Rose had her share of miscues in that aspect, but she was alive and that's all that mattered. She put her grinding stone down and poured the water into the potion. She pulled out a small knife from the jewelry box and gave her right index finger a prick. She milked her blood from the cut and then used her finger to stir the contents together. Her blood would help bind the potion and its magic to her so she could better control the flow of information that she would hopefully receive.

As she stirred, Rose grabbed Duncan's hairs she had taken from his hut and put them into the mix. "Can't forget the main ingredient," she muttered. Her last act in making the potion was to add LSD for visions and a DMT mix to speed up the process. As soon as the hallucinogenic items were stirred in, she took a deep breath.

Picking up the potion, she drank down every bit of the concoction. It didn't take long before she doubled over, clutching her stomach and hoping like hell that she wouldn't throw up. Rose was pretty sure it would taste even worse the second time around. As she slid down on the floor, still clutching her stomach, she crawled slowly over to her bed.

"Fuck…guess you should've…ate something first, huh?" Rose moaned as the cramping intensified along with the nausea. Her breathing became more labored as her body broke out in a sweat. She managed to crawl into bed, curling herself up in a fetal position as more waves of nausea hit full on. At least the cramping is letting up slightly, she thought and moaned involuntarily. Tears streamed down her face as she worked to control her breathing. Slowly, she slipped into a meditative state and was able to block most of the discomfort from her mind.

As she delved deeper, her mind's eye started to focus more, but it became intense as vibrant colors and shapes bombarded her vision. Rose felt an overwhelming rush of psychic and magical energies flooding into her brain. Before it got to be too much for her to handle and her synapses fried, Rose focused all her energies, ordering them to obey her commands and show her more of Duncan and his magical abilities.

"Show me what I wish to know; show me Duncan Morgan!" Rose mentally commanded.

In a flash, more and more energies tumbled through her mind. Suddenly, Rose saw the silhouette of a man, but he looked nothing like Duncan as far as she could tell. Then another silhouetted figure appeared beside the man. This one had more of a feminine feel to it. The female figure began to bloat around her abdomen which confused Rose for a moment, but then it hit her. Were these two people Duncan's parents?

Then a female voice spoke to her; it was both melodious and demanding as it commanded respect. Rose could hear the voice as she felt herself drift off into a dream state. *"As you sleep, more shall be revealed to you, whether you like it or not. Sleep now!"*

Chapter 6

Duncan sat idly at his post, the rain pouring down even harder now, and it chilled him to the bone. He tugged his old coat closer to his body and shivered. His jeans were soaked through and through, and so was his dark brown, long sleeve shirt.

Looking out over the wall at the surrounding forest, he noticed movement here and there. Fucking Chouls! They lurked, ever watchful, in the forest or among the tall rows of corn waiting for an opportunity to feed on some unsuspecting traveler.

Duncan wished he could go down there and clear out the forest of these loathsome creatures but any attempts at engaging the ghouls could be his last. Their intelligence and ability to communicate non-verbally caused a simple fight to turn into a feast. He had seen that scenario played out way too often during his travels. Invariably, people would want to show off just how badass they were and before they realized it, they were surrounded. He shuddered, remembering screams of terror and pain that had always followed the fight.

Duncan's hand gripped the hilt of his sword as he tried to keep his mind preoccupied. A busy mind didn't notice the cold as much. He looked over his shoulder at Sully's holy monstrosity of a wagon. Suddenly, the *voice* in his head screamed out, "*DEATH!*" A shudder snaked through his body like some great, devouring worm, and he gasped, trying to calm his raging heart.

He wasn't certain from where exactly the voice had come, but Duncan often used it to his advantage. It had kept him alive on the road on more than one occasion. The burning question in his mind was *why* he had it in the first place. Did it come from the stress of the Christian apocalypse, like a mental break down? That seemed plausible to him, except it wasn't a typical psychotic break. It was quiet and not constant.

Over the years, Duncan had made a few friends who had been schizophrenic. He had seen how they struggled on a daily basis with the chaos that plagued their minds. He saw the heartache and pain it caused their families and loved ones. Just the memory of those people tugged at Duncan's heart. He had done the best he could to be a friend to them when all others wouldn't. He had often wondered if his sympathy for them was because he felt a kinship with them — after all, he heard a *voice* too.

Duncan glanced down again at the forest as a feeling of unease crept into his mind. "What are you bastards up to?" he muttered. "What are you waiting for?"

"Probably a lone trader, easy to kill."

Duncan whipped his head away from the forest and gazed at Alex in surprise. Alex put his hands up to show he wasn't a threat, which puzzled Duncan.

"Easy there, big guy!" Alex said in a soothing tone. "I come in peace, and I'd appreciate it if you would sheathe your weapon."

Duncan glanced down. To his surprise, his sword was in his right hand, and its deadly tip was pointing at Alex's stomach. Why did I do that? I don't recall unsheathing my sword. "Sorry about that," Duncan muttered, feeling embarrassed and confused. "I'm a bit on edge at the moment."

Alex grinned. "Really? It doesn't show."

"Next time, don't sneak up on me like that." Duncan stood up and rammed his sword back into its sheath which hung from a dirty rope that served as his belt. "I just about made you into a Choul happy meal."

"Aw, don't be like that! You mean you would rather feed my dead body to those things than give me a proper burial?"

"Yep, because I'm lazy like that. I don't want to hurt my back digging a damn hole for your sorry carcass. It would be pointless to do so anyway. The Chouls would eventually smell your rotting flesh, dig you up and eat you."

Alex's jaw dropped as his face paled. "What? No fucking way! You're kidding me, right?"

"On which part? Me being lazy or the Chouls digging you up?" Duncan asked with a sly grin.

"The first one, of course! Why wouldn't you want to bury me?" Alex was a gangly, redheaded twenty-year-old who might have been one hundred and forty pounds dripping wet…maybe. He was a tall bundle of energy who made the rounds on the wall twice as fast as everyone else.

Duncan had often wondered if the kid was working off energy and shirking his duties. Yet, every time he questioned Alex about what he'd observed, the kid pointed out things that Duncan had missed, such as how the birds had gone quiet, meaning ghouls were nearby.

Duncan put his hand on Alex's shoulder. "My friend, is that what you would do? If someone you knew died, would you bury them?" Alex quickly nodded, so Duncan went on, "Then you would be digging your own grave, especially if you were out in the wilderness and not here in the safe confines of this village."

"What do you mean?"

Duncan looked over his shoulder at the village below them. "This is a luxury, being in a place like this. Out there in the real world, though, you have to make hard choices about things that will go against every moral fiber of your being. If you stop to dig a grave, you would become so wrapped up in the task you won't see or hear the Chouls that are creeping up behind you as you dig away."

Splashing from beyond the walls caught both Alex and Duncan's attention. They both looked down and saw the ghouls were on the move, heading towards the main gate. To Duncan, the ghouls resembled ants marching in a single file line. "What are those things up to?"

They both ran along the top of the wall, trying to get a better view of the situation. Duncan yelled out as loud as he could to the other guards, "We got ghouls at the gates! Everyone to the gates!"

Once they got to the wall with the entrance gates, Duncan saw the ghouls standing there. They weren't banging on the big double gates, as usual, or even trying to climb them, which they often did. The ghouls stood a good ten feet away from the gates, waiting with all the patience of the dead.

"What are they doing, Duncan?" Alex asked, frantically.

"I don't know. Whatever it is, it can't be good for any of us," Duncan replied. Another guard at the opposite end of the village cried out, "More ghouls are over here as well!"

"What are they doing?" Duncan yelled back.

"Nothing! Just standing there, being creepy as fuck!"

Duncan could see the villagers looking around, fear in their eyes, as many of them gathered together for strength and safety. These are good people, Duncan thought, not a fighter like me! They shouldn't have to live in fear. Just then, a familiar voice started shouting, using an old bullhorn to carry his message.

"This village is filled to the brim with heathens and sinners!" Sully snarled from the proclamation platform. "I've tried my best to convince you people to turn away from your wicked ways, but now it's too late for all of you!"

"Alex, come with me!" Duncan barked as he ran for the nearest ladder. "We need to take him out!"

"Why? Other than being a religious prick, what has he done wrong?"

"He's a crazy zealot. I'm afraid he's going to do something rash! Move your ass!"

As Duncan got to the ground, he could hear Sully continuing on with his malicious ranting. Duncan slowly stalked closer to the religious man. His words were unnerving some of the villagers, making them nervous, which made Duncan furious to no end.

"This village has to be cleansed of all the sinners that reside in it. The good Lord Jesus has sent me on this quest, and now you all shall parish by his mighty weapon!"

Suddenly, several villagers screamed. Duncan whirled around and couldn't believe what his eyes were seeing.

Ghouls!

Ghouls were crawling out from under Sully's wagon! Was that how he made his wagon move without a motor or animals?

"Everyone to the courtyard!" Duncan roared. "Ghouls are within the walls!"

"The ghouls shall feast on your flesh and drag your souls down into the fiery pits of Hell!" Sully cried out. "Open the gates and feast my fallen brothers and sisters! I shall lead you all to the ones you must smite with your teeth!"

Duncan stared in horror as he saw Sully remove a small box from a pocket in his white robe. The zealot held the box in his hands and grinned maliciously.

"No!" Duncan screamed and ran at the man. He suddenly stopped as he realized he would never make it to Sully in time.

With his thumb, Sully pushed a red button on the box.

BOOM!

Chapter 7

Duncan threw himself behind the nearest trader cart while the villagers scattered or dropped to the ground. Chunks of rock and mortar flew through the air like missiles. The explosion took out a portion of the south wall, leaving a massive hole where several men, who were on guard duty at the time, lay battered and broken on the ground.

As the dust settled, Duncan saw the ghouls coming through the gaping hole in the wall and dragging away the guards' bodies. More screams sounded out and Duncan looked behind him. Other ghouls were heading over to the main gate. To Duncan's horror, the ghouls were grabbing for the wooden planks to unlock the entrance gate. They had formed a line to protect several other ghouls that were tasked with the job of opening the big double gates.

Alex and several other armed guards had made their way to the main entrance, but it seemed none of them were having much luck breaking the ghouls' line. The guards were slicing and hacking away, but the ghouls seemed to move in unison, not getting cut at all.

The villagers had scattered in terror, trying to make their way to their huts as more ghouls poured in from the south wall. Duncan resumed his angry march towards Sully. The man had a look of pure bliss on his face, which only infuriated Duncan even more.

Two ghouls rushed towards him, but Duncan made a swiping arc with his sword and took the head off the first one and nearly beheaded the second. He took the steps that led up to the proclamation platform two at a time with murder in his cobalt eyes.

"Judgment is upon your disgusting village!" Sully snarled through the bullhorn, and then his gaze locked on to Duncan. "Time to die, you pitiful wretch!"

Duncan swung his sword and chopped Sully's bullhorn in half. Thrusting his blade into Sully's chest, he twisted it. The man dropped down to his knees and clutched his chest as Duncan yanked his sword away.

"Your death was too swift of a punishment for you, Sully!" Duncan hissed as he turned his attention back to the swarm of ghouls. He heard the tell-tale sounds of creaking that the main gates always made, which meant the ghouls had opened it. The village was now truly lost.

Duncan felt dazed as his jaw suddenly seared with pain. He staggered and turned, trying to see who had hit him. Bewilderment struck Duncan harder than the punch had. Sully stood there in a fighting stance, his fists clenched and blood oozing out from his chest wound.

"Stabbing an unarmed man, that's not very sporting of you, Mr. Morgan!" Sully grinned.

"I consider your ghouls to be weapon enough to justify it, you son of a whore!"

Sully jutted out his chin in pride. "You can't kill me; the Christ has made me pure and immortal. There's nothing you can do to—"

Duncan swung his sword and cleaved off Sully's head with one strike. The man's body dropped in a bloody heap at Duncan's feet. He grabbed Sully's head by the hair and looked at it for a moment, waiting to see if he would run his righteous mouth again but nothing happened.

At that moment, he felt several hands grab him from behind. Duncan spun out of the ghouls' grasp. He swung Sully's head around, using it as a weapon to smash into their faces. The ghouls backed away, staring at the head. Duncan moved it back and forth, like it was some sort of macabre metronome. To his surprise, the ghouls watched it intently as if waiting for instructions from it.

Screams of terror and anguish assailed Duncan's ears as one by one the villagers were being eaten alive in their huts and out in the compound. Duncan felt the hairs on the back of his neck stand up as he felt more ghouls coming up behind him.

He turned and saw at least eight of them surrounding him but none made a move at him. They merely stared at him, their mouths quivering for flesh. Chills ran down Duncan's spine as he stared back at them. He didn't trust that they would stay unmoving for long.

Perhaps when Sully's head grew cold, they would notice he wasn't alive. Duncan pulled off his rope belt and lashed Sully's head around his waist. Expecting a fight, he moved towards the stairs. To his surprise, the ghouls all parted, like the Red Sea had done for Moses.

Duncan chuckled inwardly at the irony of that thought as he swiftly bounded down off the platform. He kept his sword out and a hand on Sully's head, not wanting it to fall off and roll away. He decided to try and get to his hut, figuring to grab his gear and make a run for the forest.

Anywhere was better than staying here!

Ghouls either reached out or lunged for him but none actually touched Duncan. "I guess you're not a total useless dick after all." Duncan smiled as he patted Sully's head.

Pandemonium raged throughout the village. Duncan saw people dragged from their huts and ripped open. He saw other ghouls stepping out of huts with blood covering their faces. Most had bits of flesh and entrails stuck in their teeth.

The main gates were no longer guarded, and the guards who had defended it were now on the ground being devoured. "I'm sorry, Alex," Duncan muttered remorsefully for the dead man. "You fought well and did your job." As anger filled his thoughts, he took out his fury on any ghoul that stood idly by as he passed them, lopping heads off left and right.

The door to his hut had already been broken down, and several ghouls were waiting for him to return. Duncan paused, flinching when he saw them. He let out a pent up breath when none of them made a move to attack him. Quickly deciding to send them back to their graves, he sliced their heads off one by one. He wiped his blade clean on one of the ghoul's tattered jacket.

Duncan laid his sword down on the straw-covered, dirt floor of his hut and grabbed his sleeping bag. He tucked it into a set of straps on his backpack. Opening up the backpack, he pitched in his cast iron skillet and pot, as well as his utensils. He then zipped up the backpack. As he slipped it on his back, Duncan picked up his sword and stood up straight, looking around at his small shack for anything else he might need during his escape.

"Crap!" he growled. He had almost forgotten his most important gear. He hurried to a flat rock near the fire pit and lifted it up. A small tackle box filled with an assortment of lures, baits, and hooks was in a hole under the rock. Along with the box were a collapsible fishing rod and reel and also a crossbow with hand-carved bolts made during his years on the road.

As he pulled his backpack off again, he stowed his fishing gear inside it, plus his crossbow bolts. The bolts wouldn't do any good against the ghouls, but they were great for wild game. He slung the crossbow on his back and slipped his backpack on again.

Life on the road—ready or not, here I come *again*, Duncan thought bitterly. He hurried towards the doorway with a grim look on his face and saw more ghouls wandering around outside. Duncan paid no attention to them as he walked between them.

He unclipped a small canteen from his rope belt and strolled over to the village well. Better fill it up before I go, Duncan thought as more ghouls glared at him...and Sully's head. He had a sneaking suspicion that his camouflage wasn't going to last much longer, but he decided that he would worry about that when the time came—when he was far away from this place.

More ghouls wandered up to the proclamation platform, probably drawn there by Sully's headless body. Duncan quickly ladled water from a small, wooden bucket into his canteen, only stopping long enough to take a few gulps before hooking it under his belt.

He turned around and headed for the hole in the south wall, planning to leave Melona far behind. As he went, he recited over and over the mantra he had made up long ago while on the road: "When the ghouls come, I'm done!"

Going south would lead him to a flooded creek. The raging water would make it difficult for the ghouls to cross if they decided to give chase. Duncan took long strides, hurrying toward the destroyed wall. Every so often, though, and for some reason he couldn't explain, he would glance over at the other huts in the village. All the doors to the huts were broken down or ripped off their hinges, save one.

And that one hut belonged to Rose.

Duncan stared at it for a long moment, uncertain as to whether he should make a run for it or risk his neck for the sorceress. As he focused on her hut, the strange inner voice inside his head spoke to him.

SAVE HER!

Duncan scowled as he looked up, attempting to see his own forehead. "Thanks for trying to keep me safe, you sorry-ass mystery voice," he growled sarcastically. He knew he would never get any peace from it, so he begrudgingly turned and ran towards Rose's hut.

He sliced and hacked his way to it mainly because he wasn't sure just how much protection Sully's head would give the both of them. She may be a sorceress, but unless she could chop heads off with those magical powers, Rose would be defenseless against a swarm of ghouls. And for some reason, that only angered Duncan even more.

"Great," he growled, "I'm on babysitting duty."

Already he could see more ghouls banging on Rose's door. Her doors were stronger than everyone else's, but like all the other doors, hers could only hold out for so long.

The ghouls were pounding and clawing at the front door, leaving streaks of black ichor from where their fingernails had ripped off. Duncan pushed passed the ghouls that were too slow to move or take notice of him.

What the hell was that bitch up to? Had she escaped already? No, Duncan thought, I would've seen signs of Rose either casting her magic for protection or barking out orders to the guards. If Rose was still in there, then why hadn't she come out to see what was going on in her village. Hell, the explosion alone should have alerted her that something had gone horribly wrong!

As Duncan got within ten feet of Rose's hut, the hinges finally pulled away from the doorframe. As wood splinted and cracked, Duncan sprinted as fast as he could to stop the ghouls from flooding into Rose's huge quarters.

Duncan hacked and cut off heads and legs, but it seemed like there were just too many ghouls for him to deal with and get to Rose in time to save her. "Stupid, fucking voice! Why do you want me to save this spoiled, little brat anyway?"

Like a clogged sink with water backed up in it, the doorway that was overrun with ghouls finally gave way, and Duncan, along with the ghouls, spilled into Rose's gigantic hut. He couldn't believe what he was seeing. Rose was passed out on her queen size bed, wearing only a bathrobe that was barely covering her.

"This is going to be interesting, indeed," Duncan swore sarcastically.

Chapter 8

The ghouls were encroaching on Rose as she slept quietly in her bed. For the life of him, Duncan couldn't understand why she hadn't been startled awake by the noise. "Rose! Get your ass up!" Duncan shouted as he maneuvered his way to her, chopping off heads as he moved. "Rose, damn you! Fucking wake up. You're going to get us both killed!"

Several ghouls, their mouths salivating out a thick, green drool, pawed at Rose before grabbing her ankles and yanking her body towards them.

SAVE HER!

Duncan bull-rushed forward and knocked the ghouls down on the ground. He lost his balance and fell face-first on top of Rose. Finally stirring awake, she glared up at Duncan through bleary eyes.

"Duncan! What the fuck are you doing in my quarters! Get off me right now, you nasty freak!"

Rose wanted to scream more at him, but Duncan clasped his hand over her mouth. She bit him. "Look around you," he screeched out in pain but kept his hand over her mouth. He forced her head to turn. "Look, damn it, and stop biting me. I'm trying to save your ass!"

Rose's face paled when she saw that her beautiful home was swarming with ghouls. She squirmed, trying to wiggle free from under Duncan, but he wouldn't let her up.

"Do you have a sword?" Duncan whispered as he removed his bloody hand from her mouth.

"It's under the bed. What's happening?"

"No time to explain. Just grab your boots and sword. I'll lead us to safety."

"I want to know — "

"NO FUCKING TIME, ROSE!" Duncan screamed out in frustration as he rolled off of her. She reached down and pulled out her katana sword from under the bed. She looked down and saw her stomach was covered in blood. Looking up at Duncan as he scrambled off the bed, she frantically asked, "Were they…eating me?"

"No, but they were about to." Duncan swung his sword and took off another ghoul's head. He retrieved her leather boots and pitched them at her. "Hurry. I don't know how much more time we have."

When he turned around to face her, she got a better look at him. "What the fuck is that?"

He looked down at the preacher's head, still held at his waist by his rope belt. "Sully makes for a good deterrent against the Chouls."

"Huh?" Confused, Rose squeezed her feet into her boots and tightly cinched up her bathrobe. She quickly pulled her katana free from its sheath and swung away at the nearest ghoul, spilling its stomach contents on the floor. The ghoul looked down at its abdomen.

"Aim for the neck, woman! Those cuts will only tickle them!"

"Hey, I just woke up. Give me a break, will you?" Rose hacked off the ghoul's head in one clean swipe. "I need some of my better clothes; make a hole for me—"

Duncan grabbed Rose by her wrist and ran through the doorway, dragging her in tow. She wanted to protest, but several hungry ghouls' stares made her think twice about it. Seeing Sully's head on Duncan's rope belt, the ghouls parted, allowing Rose and Duncan to run towards the north entrance gates.

From somewhere behind them, they heard a blood cuddling scream. Despite their best efforts not to, they both looked back in the direction of the scream. The sound came from one of the ghouls!

Kneeling beside Sully's lifeless body, a ghoul shook it as if hoping the man would spring back to life. It wailed once more before casting its sickly, green eyes at Duncan and Rose. It extended its rotting arm and pointed at them. "False ones!" it shouted to the others. "Deceivers…eat them both!"

Duncan yanked Rose forward as the ghouls marched after them. He used his sword and cut away at the part of the rope holding Sully's head, letting the bloody mess drop to the ground. "Good riddance," he growled.

Suddenly, a group of about twenty ghouls appeared at the entrance gates. Duncan whirled in the opposite direction, slinging Rose around with him. They ran toward the hole in the south wall until they came to the flooded-over creek that ran through the back of the village.

They stopped and stared at the creek, made dangerous by today's torrential downpour. The creek had long provided the vital, life-sustaining water for the villagers, and Rose knew it well. Many times she had prayed at this creek, thanking the gods for it.

She looked back over her shoulder and saw that the ghouls were coming faster and would soon overtake them. "Let me go," Rose panted. "I can slow them down!"

Without question, Duncan let go of her hand, which surprised her. She stepped closer to the creek. Her eyes flared as she mentally commanded the water, *"Give us safe passage and slow the ghouls down, please!"*

Duncan's jaw dropped as the creek parted. On one side of the newly-created path, the water rose straight up into the air as a standing wave, and that wave was getting taller by the second. On the other side of the path, the water still raged down the creek bed, leaving a dry — not damp — creek bed. "Holy Moses!" Duncan exclaimed.

"Hurry, it won't hold much longer!" Rose warned as she scurried across the dry creek bed toward the south wall.

Duncan darted forward toward the other bank as several ghouls lunged for him. As he stepped onto the other side of the creek, he looked back. Several ghouls were right behind him. At that moment, the standing wave broke, and water slammed back down into the creek bed. The ghouls were swept away downstream. As more arrived at the creek, a few attempted to swim across toward Duncan and Rose, but the raging water was unrelenting, and they too were dragged away.

Rose sat down on the ground. She grimaced as she used her sword to cut her hand. Duncan grabbed her by the arm, trying to stand her up, but she yanked free of his grip.

Confused, Duncan scowled. "You do realize that we aren't out of this mess yet, right?"

"I do and that's why I need you to keep them off of me." She slapped her bloody hand on a small patch of grass and added, "If you can manage that, then we both might make it out alive."

Duncan looked towards the hole in the wall and saw the ghouls bunching up, trying to prevent them from escaping. Several smaller clusters broke off from the main group. Duncan figured their intent was to come at him and Rose head on, maybe flanking them as well. "Nowhere to go," he growled. Leaning down, he snatched up Rose's katana.

"Come on, Chouls!" Duncan roared out as the first wave of ghouls charged forward. "Dinner is served." He twirled both swords and readied himself for a fight. "Except this meal has teeth that bites back!"

As Duncan hacked and slashed, Rose focused all her attention on the patch of grass that she had just bloodied. Her eyes glowed with energy and her long, raven hair floated up ethereally despite the downpour of rain. *"I call out to all of my plant friends! I ask for your aid in helping me and my companion escape from harm! I give my energies as well as my blood to you as payment for this task."*

Duncan decided that if he couldn't behead all the ones who got close, he would go for the legs instead. It may not kill them, but it sure as hell would slow them down, he thought as he swung the katana at a downward angle. The blade cut through one ghoul's leg like it was nothing. He quickly swung his own sword at the neck of another oncoming ghoul.

Suddenly, the ground gave off a strange vibration, shaking a little. Duncan figured it must've been an earthquake or maybe lightning had just struck the ground somewhere nearby. He was too preoccupied to care at this point. As his adrenaline ebbed, though, exhaustion took its toll on his body.

The ghouls attacked in wave after wave, harassing him just enough to make him fight for the ground he was protecting. Son of a bitch, Duncan thought as it dawned on him that the ghouls were trying to wear him down. They were waiting for him to make a mistake and become easy pickings. The dead had all the time and patience in the world, and they didn't need to rest. They also didn't need to catch their breath during a battle, something Duncan desperately desired to do.

"Hurry up...Rose! I'm good...but not...immortal...like them!" Duncan croaked, severely out of breath.

"Hang in there, Duncan. Help is coming!" Rose replied in a monotone voice, swaying back and forth in a trance.

Duncan grunted in frustration. He wondered what kind of backup she was calling for. "What the hell is taking them so long? You calling up an army of snails and slugs?" As Duncan laughed under his breath at the thought of a gastropod army, he felt a pair of hands on his arm. Pivoting around, he saw a ghoul had him. He thrust his knee into the ghoul's abdomen and followed up with a slice to its exposed neck.

Duncan staggered back a couple of steps and took in a deep breath before resetting his fighting stance. More vibrations came, but this time they were stronger and closer. It had to be an earthquake.

Rose stood up and wiped her hands on her bathrobe. "Time to kiss these dead fucks goodbye. Stand back and watch."

Duncan backed up and stood beside Rose. The ghouls marched in unison towards them with their arms extended out in front of them, their mouths gaping open. Duncan tensed and gripped the swords tightly. Rose touched his forearm gently and whispered, "Trust me, Duncan, okay?"

"Against all this? I can't, Rose!" His breathing came in quick, shallow gasps, and he readied himself to go down fighting.

The ground between Rose and Duncan suddenly exploded. Dozens of creeping vines shot out of the soil. The vines were a vibrant green, almost glowing, and two times their usual size. The vines slung themselves around some of the ghouls, wrapping them up and pinning them down to the ground. The ghouls that weren't pinned down got corralled and herded over to the creek, where the vines shoved them into the raging water.

"When are you going to learn to trust me?" Rose took her katana from Duncan and sauntered over to the hole in the wall and went through.

Duncan grumbled as he followed her, stepping with care on the loose chunks of rock and avoiding the splintered razor wire that jutted up like thorn brush. "It will take more than a few magic tricks to earn my trust, sorceress. We aren't out of this yet; the others are on the move. I'm not sure we can make it to the forest quick enough."

"Tired already?" Rose asked as she kicked a downed ghoul in the head. "Someone needs to work on his stamina, especially if he plans on keeping up with me."

Duncan snarled, "Damn it, woman, I've been fighting all this time. I wasn't sleeping in my bed or playing in the dirt!"

"Aww, poor wittle Duncan, boohoo! Should I bake you a cookie or draw a hot bath? Will that make it all better?"

"I'm warning you, Rose. Don't poke at me right now. I'm not in the mood for it!"

"Oh, what will you do to me? Spank me for being bad?"

"Keep it up and I might do it!"

Rose grinned as she looked over her shoulder. "Here's a little motivation for you to catch me, big boy." She flipped up her bathrobe, revealing her curvy ass. "Come and get it, Duncan...if you're man enough for it!"

Duncan stopped dead in his tracks, his gaze falling on her bare ass as she made a run for the forest. She didn't bother to cover herself up again but let it all hang out as she ran. The sight of her elicited a lustful growl from him.

"I heard that!" Rose called over her shoulder and laughed.

Duncan rolled his eyes as he sprinted after her. "If she wants to play with fire, I'll burn her ass."

More ghouls came around the sides of the village walls, their moans giving Duncan more than enough motivation to run. He could sense their unblinking stares on him, and he felt something violently surge up inside his body. In this haze of confusion, Duncan tripped over a tree root and went face-first into a mud puddle.

Rose looked back and gasped. "Duncan! Get up!" she shouted frantically. "They're almost on top of you!"

Duncan flipped over on his back, wiping the mud out of his eyes as he did. When he saw that the ghouls were within reaching distance, he cried out in surprise. Frantically, he crawled backwards on his elbows, trying desperately to get away from them.

His crossbow was still on his back and unreachable in his situation. Trying to lunge to at least a sitting position, he realized to his horror that he couldn't move. He was snagged on something in the mud, making it impossible for him to get up. Panic set in as he hysterically tried to remove his crossbow, but the strap was at an odd angle and pressed tightly against his chest.

Rose looked around for anything she could use to distract the ghouls, maybe lure them towards her. She couldn't let Duncan die that horrible death after he chose to save her. She soon learned that screaming at the ghouls did no good. They ignored her and concentrated on Duncan.

As cold as it felt to her, Rose focused a ball of energy in her hand with the intent to kill Duncan. "Better that he die quickly by my hands than be eaten alive!"

Just then, several ghouls reached down and yanked on him. The crossbow strap snapped as the ghouls grabbed him out of the mud. One ghoul got hit in the face with the strap. It leaned in and spoke to Duncan, the stench of death and decay assailing the man's nostrils. "Heathen! You will…be cleansed…of your flesh. Our judgment…is final!"

More ghouls swarmed around him, preventing Rose from getting a clear mercy shot. Sheer terror flooded Duncan's mind as he saw all the decaying faces leaning forward, their maws chomping feverishly. He screamed in anguish as the first of many bite-sized amounts of flesh and muscle were ripped and torn away from his body. Tears streamed down Duncan's face. As the pain intensified, he felt that same strange, violent surge building up inside him again, this time to the point of explosion.

He wanted to close his eyes and never open them again but, unfortunately for him, that strange surge of pressure forced them wide open. Awash with a bright, white light, Duncan let out a high-pitched cry.

Rose saw the flash and instinctively took cover behind a nearby boulder. The heat from the light took her breath away, but before she could close her eyes, she saw the white flash had specks of other colors, like red and purple in it.

As the last of the white light dissipated, Rose looked around at her surroundings. Scorch marks covered the ground everywhere. She stood up and touched the nearest tree. Despite being blackened and scorched, it was cool to the touch, and she could see that it wasn't that badly damaged from the blast. Turning around, she looked towards Duncan.

Rose was taken aback by what she saw. No ghouls anywhere, only ash and black scorched marks were on the ground as if a bomb had just gone off, and Duncan was at ground zero. He was on his back, halfway in the crimson mud puddle, convulsing and twitching.

With her katana in hand, Rose made her way to Duncan. As she went, her eyes darted all around just in case there were any surviving ghouls nearby wanting to pounce on her. As she dropped down on her knees beside him, she cupped her hand over her mouth to stifle a gasp. The ghouls had inflicted horrible injuries on his body. Rose laid down her katana and grabbed Duncan under his arms, pulling him away from the puddle. He was cold, probably from the blood loss. Normally, bites from the ghouls didn't let much blood escape the body because they wanted their victims to remain alive as they devoured them. They produced a green crud that oozed from their mouths as they bit people. That "ghoul-crud" as it was often called seemed to coagulate the blood flow around the bite areas.

One could survive a ghoul bite or two, but their mouths were filled with bacteria that caused infections to spread throughout the body.

She grunted as she struggled with his limp body, her feet slipping in the slick mud and losing traction. Duncan was still breathing which Rose was glad to see, but she knew he was in a world of pain. He needed his wounds tended, and the only way she could do that was to take him back to the village.

Rose looked back at her beautiful village. Ghouls were moving around, going into huts and setting the doors back up; they even took the time to close the main gates. They were making Melona look normal, like nothing had happened. The next group of traders would walk into the village like cattle going to slaughter.

"Fuck!" Rose looked down at Duncan and then back at her village. She had to do something to warn people of the dangers that awaited them inside the walls. But how? She didn't want to leave Duncan out in the cold rain, all alone and vulnerable to another ghoul attack.

Chapter 9

An intentional rustle of leaves to her right let Rose know one of her wolves was nearby in the brush. She could make out its face and knew it was the alpha of its pack. She was a fairly large wolf, and her short, black fur that was speckled with gray hairs covered her muscular body.

"Duncan is hurt badly," Rose mentally told the animal. *"Watch over him while I make a warning sign for the village."*

The wolf gave a slight nod and then came forward with five more wolves trailing after her. The pack formed a protective circle around Duncan, keeping a watchful eye in every direction.

Rose snatched up her katana and stood, thanking the wolf pack for their aid. Walking towards Melona, she looked down and saw the alpha wolf softly padding alongside her. *"I asked you to watch over him, not me. He needs you more than I do!"*

No response.

"Fine! Come along if you must. You listen about as well as all the males I've known."

The wolf growled slightly which made Rose smirk. As she snuck along the outside wall, she looked around for anything she could use as a warning sign. She would've had the creeping vines encase the whole village, but she didn't want to use her magic unless it was absolutely necessary. Magic took a hard toll on her body physically.

Think, Rose, think! Drawing a blank and being soaked like a drowned rat wasn't getting her anywhere. She grunted as she summoned a magical flame in her hand. Creeping up to the main gates, she carefully burned her warning into the wood.

Even with the alpha wolf at her side, Rose's eyes kept darting around, searching for the ghouls. She wouldn't be taken by surprise again! She thought about Duncan lying unconscious in the wet grass. "A near happy meal for the ghouls," she whispered, and the wolf glanced up at her. Okay, she thought, why am I lamenting about Duncan? I'm in more danger than he is at the moment.

Rose focused on her magical flame, trying to spell out the words "GHOULS INSIDE!" and not alert the blasted creatures to her presence. It was difficult because the wood was burning, creating an odor, and the ghouls had a better olfactory system than the wolves.

Rose could barely hear the ghouls sloshing around in the mud inside the village. None of them spoke or made any grunting sounds, but then again Duncan had mentioned that they could commune telepathically. For all she knew, the ghouls could be setting up an ambush for her, and she would never see it until it was too late.

As she finished her warning, she noticed her blue flame kept sizzling. It wasn't the rain causing the sizzle. Water made fire *hiss* on contact, not sizzle. Whatever it was, it was thick and green.

Rose blanched as realization hit her, and she frantically looked up. A gangly female ghoul stared down at her with hunger in its putrid eyes. The flame died out as Rose stumbled backwards away from the gates.

The female ghoul leaped down at her, just missing her with its outstretched hands. As it sprang to its feet, Rose steadied herself and unsheathed her katana. The wolf lunged at the ghoul, biting down on its leg. The wolf slung its head back and forth violently, ripping and tearing at the creature's leg. Rose seized the opportunity and lunged forward, swinging her sword like a baseball bat at the ghoul's neck.

The katana did its work, and the severed head fell to the ground, wobbling as it rolled in the mud. As the ghoul's body dropped, Rose stifled a happy squeal. The wolf lumbered over and used its snout to push the decapitated head towards her. She frowned. "What are you doing?" she whispered. The wolf again pushed the head toward her. Suddenly, Rose's lips formed an O-shape, and she understood.

"You want me to use the head as part of my warning?"

The wolf nodded slightly, so Rose picked up the ghoul's head by its matted, sticky hair. The odor that wafted up from it nearly made the sorceress empty the contents of her stomach. She gagged as she ran to the main gates and set the head down beside them.

Rose put her hands on her hips, thinking as she looked at the gates and the severed head. She created the blue flame once more and went to work on the spot just above the "I". The flame burned into the wood so deeply that she feared if she wasn't careful, it would burn a hole clean through the gate.

When she was finished, she stopped and extinguished the blue flame. Bending down, she grabbed clumps of mud and slathered them in the hole the flame had just made. She then snatched up the severed head and wedged it snuggly into the hole. The head oozed a nasty black ichor from its neck, but she felt confident it would stay in place. She backed up and gave her handiwork a nod of approval.

"That's one way to dot your "I's"; Rose giggled inwardly as she hurried away from the gates.

She leaned down and rubbed the wolf on its head and scratched behind its ears. The alpha growled contentedly, and Rose could tell she liked it. Now that she had finished her warning to future, unsuspecting traders, she needed to figure out how to get Duncan somewhere safe so she could tend his wounds. He needed food and water…and possibly a bath, if he was lucky.

As she stood there thinking about how to move Duncan, the alpha wolf sat down and silently watched Melona's walls for ghouls. Rose kneeled down beside Duncan. To draw more blood, she squeezed her palm that she had cut earlier. A small amount of blood trickled out, but it was enough for what she needed. She placed her bloody hand on a patch of grass.

"*Grass and vines hear my call. I need some of your leaves and stalks — whatever is green that you can spare. Your roots and rhizomes will not be needed. Receive my blood as payment for what I ask of you. My friend Duncan is severely hurt, and I need a way to move him to safety. If any of you will come to my aid, I will greatly appreciate it. Thank you.*"

Rose sat down and took Duncan's hand in hers, squeezing it gently. He was still twitching and shaking but not as violently as when it had first started, which gave her a small glimmer of hope. Then again, Rose wasn't a doctor, and he was neither a plant nor an animal.

The ground vibrated beneath her, and she watched as creeping vines slowly pushed their way out of the earth and awaited Rose's instructions. "Thank you for helping. Will you please weave a mat for my friend here?" She concentrated, letting her mind visualize what she wanted. That way, the plants would know exactly how to make a mat, something they wouldn't have known how to do otherwise.

The vines moved in unison, crisscrossing and overlapping each other. "Oh," Rose added, "and I'll need a sturdy strap on the mat so I can easily drag him around until he gets better." Again, in her mind, she pictured what she needed.

Grass quickly squeezed through the slits of the mat, making more of a cushion for Duncan to lie on. As the vines and grass finished making themselves into a make-shift gurney, Rose knelt down and inspected it. Each of the weaves was tighter than she could have done herself. She pulled out her katana and said, *"This is more of a blessing than I expected to receive from you, my friends. Thank you."*

Rose cut the vines with one quick stroke of her sword to separate them from their roots. She sheathed her sword and grabbed hold of Duncan's clothes, tugging at him, trying to move him onto the gurney. The wolves stood up and gently bit down on his clothes, giving them small yanks to help her.

Duncan groaned and half-heartedly flailed his arms and legs. A thought occurred to Rose, causing her to stop and hold her breath as she watched him. She hoped he didn't think the ghouls were still swarming all over him. Sighing heavily, she gave one last tug to get Duncan all the way on the gurney. When he was finally situated the way she wanted him, she reached down and pulled on the gurney's strap.

The mud was slick, and she slipped and fell on her ass. As mud splattered all over her, Rose crinkled her nose. "Your dead weight better be worth all this hassle," she snarled in frustration.

She watched him for a moment, guilt creeping into her mind. "Sorry, Duncan," she muttered. Reaching down, she squeezed his hand but got no response but tremors. He wasn't shaking so much now, but his body still jerked into a spasm every couple of minutes.

Now that he was situated on the gurney, Rose lifted her head, closed her eyes and mentally called out, "*To any of my four-legged friends, I ask for the aid of a strong back that can carry me and my injured friend to the safest part of the forest. Help us please and I'll give you tribute in food.*"

Rose knew she had nothing readily available to give whatever animal came her way, but she could encourage plants and seedlings to grow faster, more luscious.

She crawled over to Duncan so she could examine his wounds more closely. I might as well pass the time by doing something productive, she thought and removed his bug-out bag from his back. His bites looked inflamed, and the ones that were still bleeding had a stinking odor to them, which meant *ghoul infection*, as it was called, had already set in.

But it was the bleeding that frightened her the most—it wouldn't stop! If all his bites are like this, maybe I should kill him and put him out of his misery, Rose thought bitterly. Her heart ached for him. He was in this mess because he had chosen to save her.

Suddenly, she saw a way to stop his bleeding. Duncan still had some of the green ghoul-crud on his body. "Thank goodness for small favors," she muttered.

She figured she could use the ghoul-crud to stop his bleeding. With a disgusted look on her face, Rose crinkled her nose and ran her hands through the remaining sickly, green crud on him, scooping it up. She began applying it to his bleeding wounds.

More than once, Rose had wondered if the ghoul-crud really acted as a coagulant or if it was just an urban legend. Now, though, she watched the crud and prayed the stories about it were true. She suddenly gasped. She could hardly believe her eyes.

The stories were true; the ghoul-crud was a coagulant! Duncan's bleeding stopped instantly upon contact with the green crud.

Still, the stories never mentioned anything about bite victims having convulsions or even tremors. Over the years, she had seen people who had been bitten by the ghouls and escaped. She'd never seen the convulsions — just infections and a lot of pain too.

Rose heard the sound of slouching, heavy footsteps coming from the forest to her left. It was a large ox with horns as big as Rose's thighs. She stood up and splashed through the mud puddle, greeting the giant beast. She stroked its head and neck, murmuring, "Thank you for coming. I don't have any food right now, but I promise I'll make the grasses taller and more abundant on our long journey ahead. If this isn't what you want then you can go. I'll understand and wait for another creature to come."

The ox nodded and licked the side of Rose's face, leaving a thick, slimy trail from the wake of its huge tongue. Rose smiled as she crinkled her nose slightly and said, "Thanks…I guess."

She walked over to where Duncan was and called for the ox to follow her. It lumbered slowly, kicking up mud and water as it maneuvered its massive body into position. Rose grabbed the long vines and looped segments of them around the ox's horns, leaving enough slack to make a reign for her to hold on to as she rode on top of the beast.

The wolf pack scattered and ran back into the forest.

"Okay, big boy, let's get out of here," she commanded. "Hopefully, we'll find somewhere safe and possibly dry." As the ox lumbered towards the forest, Rose constantly looked behind her, making sure Duncan was safe and hadn't rolled off the gurney.

She wrapped her rain-soaked bathrobe close to her body as she sensed someone was watching her from somewhere. She nervously glanced around, trying to determine if the person was human or ghoul but failed. Whoever he was, he gave her the creeps!

Chapter 10

An ominous structure stood in the middle of the barren desert now known as the ocean sandpits. From its aesthetic features, the huge building seemed out of place in the desert. The massive walls surrounding it were covered with ancient sigils that no human alive could decipher because they were from a language that had never been spoken on Earth.

Each individual sigil had an iridescent shimmer, like it was part of the walls but still not of this dimension. Vine tendrils made of gold and silver clung to the walls which had been erected from gigantic, uncut marble slabs.

The main courtyard and palace were made of gold and didn't have a speck of dust on them anywhere, despite all the sand. People walked around here and there, but most of them were either training to fight with weapons or going to services to hear the teachings of *"Jesus"*.

The message of Jesus was simple and clear: All who worshiped him would be granted immortality; once the sinners who followed the ways of Lucifer were punished and purged from Earth, the whole world would belong to Jesus' followers as a reward.

Jesus walked among his disciples, observing each one with a sense of pride swelling inside his chest. Both men and women were fiercely training with swords and shields while another group was mastering the power to control their fallen warrior brothers and sisters, the ghouls.

Each person was different in some way when it came to commanding the dead, either through verbal commands or, in some cases, telepathy. As with any kind of training and conditioning, the ghouls always needed a target. Every day, a child was brought out of the palace's dungeon and used as training fodder.

The children had been reaped along with their parents during the days of the firestorms. It had been proclaimed by Jesus that all children were to be removed from their shackles by their parents so they could be part of what he called the Fallen Warriors of the Light training sessions. This was to be a way for the parents to show true devotion to their Christ. Once a day, the children who weren't sacrificed to the ghouls were forced to clean every inch of the palace and the main courtyard.

Today, the sun shined brightly in the sky, despite the dark, ominous clouds on the horizon. When any of the disciples noticed that Jesus was walking amongst them, they would fight harder and get more deadly with their blows.

Jesus smiled brightly and waved at everyone, sucking up all of his warriors' passionate love and devotion for him. Overseeing the warriors' training were two angels, Xaphan and Wormwood. They also enforced the decrees Jesus proclaimed for his people. Both angels gave a respectful bow as Jesus walked up to them.

"How are my sheep faring on this day, Xaphan?" Jesus asked.

"Same as every training session," the angel replied, his voice both melodious and gruff. "They fight and stab each other." Xaphan was a large angel who wore only gold plated boots and dark fur shorts that were made from yak skin.

A massive sword was strapped to his back, between his translucent wings. He had long, flaming red hair and a muscular chest. His skin had a dark bronze tan, and he had angelic symbols tattooed on various parts of his massive body. Xaphan gripped a staff in his beefy right hand that was nearly as tall as he was. It too had angelic sigils etched into it that would glow with power and then pulsate.

"There are a few who do standout, but it's your call as to whom you wish to promote for fieldwork," the other angel Wormwood added, his voice sounding like an ailing cat. His body and attire when compared to Xaphan's were in complete contrast. Wormwood wore several layers of tattered robes made of stained, dirty fabrics while having a sickly green/brown cloak on his back.

He was bald but had a dark complexion, like he was from the Middle East or some other desert region, and the boots he wore had the same sickly green/brown color as his cloak. The angel was far from the picture of perfect health. He looked emaciated and none could figure how he had the strength to walk around, let alone help train the humans.

"Good to hear, Wormwood," Jesus told him. "I believe we will need someone to step in and fill the void that has opened up."

Wormwood's eyes glowed as he gazed at Jesus. "I see." He leaned in closer. "Are you well, old friend? You appear to have lost some of your...*vitality*." His grin was more of a sneer.

"I'm fine, Wormwood!" Jesus glared as he growled at the angel. "Do not question my health, or I'll tear your nasty wings from your back and feed them to you!"

"My apologies...*Jesus.*" When Wormwood said the name, he threw back his head and laughed.

Afraid the humans were listening to them, Jesus gasped and glanced around. Glaring at the angel, he growled, "When you say the name Jesus, say it with respect!"

Wormwood shrugged and gave Jesus a deep bow, chuckling quietly as he did. "May I spread some pestilence over the warriors?" he asked with a twinkle in his eyes. "It feels like it's been ages since I've used my powers."

"Why would you do that?" Xaphan asked in a disgusted tone. "You could kill them!"

"Nonsense," Wormwood replied with amusement in his voice. "When has an immortal ever died from a disease? It would only make them sick for a few days. Sweet little Purah would enjoy the sorrow it would cause."

Jesus rubbed his beard.   "No! This is a holy place; I won't have you defiling it with your putrid sickness! Speaking of Purah, have either of you seen her today?"

Both Xaphan and Wormwood flinched and looked at each other nervously. Finally, Xaphan spoke, "No, she wasn't in her room when I looked in on her this morning. Someone said she wasn't anywhere on the grounds."

"Purah's a big girl; we aren't her keepers." Wormwood pointed at Jesus with a knowing look. "You knew the risk of bringing her into the fold."

Wanting to head back to his library, Jesus pushed past the two angels and started to stalk off. From behind him, he heard Wormwood call out, "Oh by the way, Penemuel is waiting for you in your chamber. Maybe you can send him to find our wayward Purah. Give him something important to do instead of that writing crap."

Jesus stopped abruptly and turned around. With a menacing look in his eyes, he walked back and got in Wormwood's sickly face. "We all have our parts to play in this world on which we now live. Xaphan cleansed the planet with his hellfire storms; you brought about death with your plagues and pestilence on the land; Purah gathered our warriors and raised the dead." He nearly spit out the words.

"Penemuel's work is the most important of all. He wrote how this whole End of Days scenario should play out." He grimaced angrily and moved even closer to Wormwood, which caused Xaphan to back away a few steps from the angel. "You both know my role and never forget it! I could easily cast out and destroy both of you with just a mere thought. Remember, Wormwood, you're treading on thin ice!"

"That may be the case...*Jesus*," Wormwood replied as he stuck out his gaunt chin in defiance. "You may have the power, but you can still be killed like the rest of us." He heard Xaphan gasp in horror. "I'm not afraid of you. My sickness can affect you any time I want it to—even *after* I'm dead!"

With rage in his eyes, Jesus backed away from the two angels. He turned and stormed off towards his library. Xaphan grabbed Wormwood's arm and growled under his breath so none of the warriors could hear. "Why did you have to do that? He could kill you with all the power he has at his command now."

"He has an ego that has grown ever since the days of old, when the End of Days plan was first concocted. Our brother needs to be reminded that he's still one of us, despite the powers he has garnered over the years. I don't care what his *name* is now! He can call himself anything he wants, but he's still the same old *pretender* he's always been!"

Jesus fumed as he moved through the palace halls, wanting nothing more than to destroy Wormwood for his defiant attitude. That would make things more difficult, though, and he would have to tend to the humans more than he wanted. Although, it might be worth the headache, he mused.

Wondering what Penemuel wanted, Jesus turned left and walked up a long flight of stairs. Once he got to the top, he waved his hand, and two huge double doors opened into an antechamber that had several hallways connected to it.

He walked down a narrow corridor that had multiple paintings of his visage and several full body portraits. Each painting came from a different time period, and each one had the same thing in common: They depicted Jesus as having perfect, porcelain skin and ageless youth.

As he neared his library, one of the two guards stationed by the door opened it for him. Jesus smiled. "Thank you. You may go but do return in an hour. I don't want to be disturbed."

"Yes, my Lord!" both of the guards replied with a look of awe and jubilation on their faces from being in the presence of Jesus.

He gave a wave to dismiss them as he entered his library but noticed that they stayed to watch him go inside. He slammed the door shut and waited by it to make sure the men had gone.

Jesus' personal chamber was an expansive room with iron sconces that held the huge candles that helped to light up the area. The floor was covered with several large, ornate rugs that were adorned in angelic sigils. The walls also had paintings that depicted him in a crucifixion, a resurrection, and him in several images of the End of Days.

One painting, Jesus liked best, was of him and his disciples sitting at a long table, feasting on food and wine while the floor beneath their feet was cut out to reveal it was supported by the slain bodies of the last sinners of the world.

From across the room, a voice called out, "In the name of the Creator, must you look like that *all* the time, Sorath?"

Jesus glanced over at the angel sitting in a wingback chair. "You know I must, Penemuel. Remember, you penned this elaborate ruse for the humans, and I must keep up appearances." His body shimmered and shifted its form into an angel.

Jesus, or rather Sorath, stood tall at six and a half feet. His body was now covered in a crimson armor with a massive sword strapped to his back. The fallen angel had perfect, porcelain skin and an air of regal nobility, just as the paintings showed. He had long, black hair and eyes to match his armor. Flexing his wings to their full span, he glowed with celestial energy and lit up the room.

"Yes, I know I wrote it, but you look better like this, brother," Penemuel said.

"Get to the point already," Sorath growled. "What do you want?"

"I was curious to know if you felt a shift of power today...like a disturbance from somewhere?"

"No, I only felt the loss of some of the undead as well as one of their handlers."

Sorath watched Penemuel steeple his fingers underneath his soft chin. He walked towards Penemuel and sat down across from him in a wingback chair. He didn't like when the fallen angel was like this, all contemplative, because it usually meant he was plotting something.

"Speak your mind, Penemuel. I can see the wheels of thought spinning as if you are writing another grand story."

Penemuel gave him a toothy grin and stood up to pace around the room, an old habit he had whenever he was in the midst of writing. As he looked down at the floor, Penemuel asked, "Did this loss occur an hour ago?"

Sorath thought for a moment. "Yes, it did. What does that matter?"

"Hmm, that would be roughly about the time I felt the disturbance. There is no such thing as coincidences in the universe."

"You believe there's a connection to the two? Someone or something caused it?" Sorath watched Penemuel with suspicion.

"The force that was unleashed today was powerful enough to be considered a volcanic eruption, but now that you say that some of our flock—"

"*My flock*, you mean," Sorath growled.

"Of course," Penemuel replied as he rolled his eyes. "If some of *your* flock did perish, that would rule the volcano theory out."

"Because why would my flock be near a volcano in the first place? No one would be able to inhabit that kind of location for long."

"Precisely!" Penemuel exclaimed as he pointed at Sorath. "I suggest we dispatch a scout to check out the area where the disturbance occurred."

"Why didn't you go out there yourself?" Sorath narrowed his eyes at the angel suspiciously. "Or have you already done that? Do you know exactly who the murderer of my flock is?"

Penemuel stopped in the middle of the room and shot Sorath a surprised look. He watched as Sorath grew angry. "Of course I checked on it myself. I had to confirm what I found was somehow linked to you by asking if you felt anything."

Sorath's anger did not fade. It stayed just under the surface, festering. Whenever Sorath felt the loss of his flock, whether it be the living or the risen dead, it wounded him, like pieces of energy were being violently ripped from his body. The pain never seemed to ebb, and Sorath was constantly on edge. He used his disguise as Jesus to help mask his emotions, but lately that hadn't been working.

"Give me one good reason why I shouldn't kill you for toying with me?" Sorath scowled.

"After seeing the site of your warriors' slaughter, I feel you may need my aid in taking this being down."

Sorath raised one eyebrow, his anger ebbing slightly. He eyed Penemuel closely, trying to read him in case he was lying.

With a serious look on his face, Penemuel clasped his hands behind his back. "Who or whatever it was, the being beheaded an elite master named Sully and then vaporized a large cluster of the risen dead warriors."

Sorath shot up out of his chair. "What?" he exclaimed. "Vaporized?" He grabbed Penemuel by his arm. "How is that possible? No one on this pitiful world possesses that kind of power! Are you certain of this?"

"To be one hundred percent certain, I'll require Purah's assistance."

"She's not here," Sorath said as he let go of Penemuel's arm. He stalked over and opened the French doors that lead out onto the balcony. Walking outside, he leaned against the gold railing with his arms crossed and looked out over the wasteland.

Sorath never feared anyone seeing him in his true form out here because he had a magical ward placed here on the balcony to give the illusion that he was still "Jesus". He was a strong and powerful fallen angel, and with his disciples worshipping him, he felt invincible. Purah's absence, though, made him uneasy.

He had always felt sympathy for the petite fallen angel. Her memory issues had come about through a curse heaped upon her during a rather vicious battle. Purah was a powerful female in her own right. As broken as she was from her fall from Grace, she could unravel everything Sorath and the others had worked so hard to build.

"Not here?" Penemuel asked as he stepped out onto the balcony and stood beside Sorath. "She's off her leash and wandering the world?" He sighed. "Pity, I was hoping she could help me figure out who destroyed her creations."

"You must go and find her at once, Penemuel."

Penemuel sneered. "Why me? Wormwood or Xaphan could easily do this. I'm guessing they've graciously declined babysitting duties for the day."

Without warning, Sorath turned, grabbed Penemuel by his neck, and kicked his feet out from under him, slamming him down onto the floor of the balcony. The fallen angel struggled to get free, but Sorath used his knee to pin one of his legs down while restraining his left arm.

He leaned close, his crimson eyes blazing brightly with fury. "You will either find Purah now," he growled coldly, "or I shall rip your wings off, break your arms and legs, and then I'll take flight with you and drop you to the Earth from the stratosphere. So choose wisely, brother."

As Penemuel choked and gasped for air, Sorath squeezed his neck even tighter. He yanked the fallen angel up slightly and hammered Penemuel's head against the floor.

Seeing black spots before his eyes, Penemuel felt warm liquid running down his neck. Sorath let go of Penemuel's throat and flipped him onto his stomach. As he grabbed Penemuel by his wings, the fallen angel croaked out, "Stop! Don't...do this! I will find...her...for you, brother." He coughed as Sorath loosened his grip slightly. "Without my wings, it would take...me forever...to find her."

"True," Sorath replied as he shredded the inner tendrils of Penemuel's wings. "I want you to have a reminder of what you'll lose as you fly during your search for Purah. Never anger me again!"

Penemuel felt the energy from his wings suddenly extinguish as if someone had blown out a candle, and he screamed in pain.

Sorath let go of him and stood up, walking back to the balcony rail. He felt the tension and anger slowly fade.

The horror of what Sorath had done to Penemuel covered him like a shroud covering the dead. He would still be able to fly, but it would take a lot more effort to keep him in the air. And with each stroke from his wings there would be accompanying pain.

Maybe I would be better off without any of them, Sorath mused. Penemuel's groans caused him to look down at the fallen angel, struggling to lift himself up.

Desperately trying to regain his balance, Penemuel stood and gripped the railing for support. The pain was still horrendous, and he grimaced each time he flexed his wings. Waiting until Sorath had turned his head to look out over the wasteland again, Penemuel glared hatefully at the fallen angel's back.

"Leave now and don't return without Purah," Sorath growled without looking at Penemuel.

Penemuel forced himself to be pleasant. He certainly didn't want to anger Sorath again — not until he had healed. "With pleasure, my brother!" Inside his head, though, he growled, *One day, my blade will be your downfall.* He took flight off the balcony and groaned in pain as he did.

"If you fail at this task," Sorath called out as Penemuel clumsily flew up, "I won't be so generous with you next time."

As Penemuel flew away from the golden palace, Sorath's mind dwelled on how his fallen brothers had been behaving lately. First, Wormwood challenged and defied him; now, Penemuel was hiding information from him, which meant he was plotting something; Xaphan appeared to be aligning with Sorath, but that didn't mean he wouldn't help the others stage a coup. The only one Sorath felt he could trust was Purah. Even if the others tried to have her conspire against him, she would forget the whole thing and be useless to them.

Sorath now wondered if that was why Purah was missing. Did they kill her or did she set out on a quest for them, knowing she would forget and lose her way. That would explain why Xaphan and Wormwood flinched when he inquired about her earlier.

He shook his head, trying to push the paranoia out of his mind. "I'm a god," Sorath said aloud. "My fallen brothers are jealous of me and wish to take my crown." He sighed heavily. "And it is a thorny crown too!"

A loud knocking on his door snapped Sorath back into reality.

Chapter 11

Sorath knew it was one of the fallen angels knocking because all the humans were too timid to pound on his door like that; they were too afraid to disturb him. He called out over his shoulder, "You may enter."

As the door opened, Sorath could sense that it was one of his fallen brothers but didn't bother looking to see which one it was. He knew it wasn't Purah because she had a habit of entering without knocking, and her excuse was that she was exploring. She was the one bright light in this world that Sorath actually cared about.

"Is Penemuel on his way to find our wayward sister?" Xaphan asked as he approached the balcony.

"Yes he is…" Sorath's voice trailed off as his thoughts brought him back to his earlier musings.

As Xaphan stepped out onto the balcony, he noticed Penemuel's fading energy tendrils at his feet and kicked them aside. "Must you do that to our brother?" he asked as he leaned his back against the railing. "It will be more difficult for him to find Purah, especially since it's been eons since he's been injured like that. He isn't a fighter like the rest of us."

Sorath glanced at Xaphan but didn't say anything to him. He turned his head and stared down at the courtyard below. Maybe it's time to cut all ties with my fallen brothers, he thought. Sorath knew that both Xaphan and Wormwood had a psychic connection stemming back to the days when they created the apocalypse. That connection made it easier for them to coordinate their assault. If he attacked Xaphan now, he would call out to Wormwood for aid. He could be trusted to do that much.

They had all done their jobs and served their purpose, but now their services were no longer required. As for Penemuel, he will die too for there were no more stories to be written, and he was useless in a fight. Sorath ignored Xaphan as he turned around to look blankly into his chamber, his hands cupping the back of his neck.

"Are you alright, brother?" Xaphan asked as he reached over and touched Sorath's elbow.

As swift as lightning, Sorath snatched Xaphan's arm and unsheathed his own sword at the same time. He instantly slashed the sword down on the fallen angel's back. Grinning viciously, he removed the sword from Xaphan's back and severed his wings.

Xaphan howled in pain as he dropped to his knees, trying to reach around for his own sword. Sorath hoisted Xaphan up by his arm and flung him into the chamber. The fallen angel crashed into the far wall with a bone shattering thud, leaving him dazed. His staff rolled out of his hand and across the floor, out of his reach.

Sorath took to the air and flew head on at Xaphan. As he closed the gap between them, he sensed Xaphan calling out to Wormwood, and it made Sorath grin like a madman.

Sorath took Xaphan by his neck and lifted him up off the floor like he weighed next to nothing. As Xaphan gasped and wiggled his body to get free of Sorath's vise-like grip, he choked out, "Why…why this…betrayal?"

"You are of no use to me," Sorath answered as he plunged his sword into Xaphan's heart. The fallen angel gasped as blood bubbled out of his mouth. Sorath removed his sword and dropped Xaphan, letting him fall to his knees. He raised his sword high and added, "Rest well, my brother." He brought his sword down and cleaved off Xaphan's head just as his chamber door was flung open by Wormwood. Xaphan's massive body turned to ash as it burned away by an unseen fire.

"Looks like the would-be King of Mankind has decided not to share his spoils after all," Wormwood growled, spitting on the floor in disgust and anger. "Unlike poor Xaphan, I won't be so easily dispatched!"

Sorath eyed Wormwood intently as he twirled his sword around. Wormwood slowly stalked around the room, circling Sorath, never taking his sickly, green eyes off him. From behind his back, Wormwood retrieved a weathered, double-edged axe, its edges covered with a sickly, green crud that oozed from it.

Sorath charged Wormwood at full speed, bringing his massive sword down hard, aiming for his head. Wormwood, though, was able to fend off each blow that he swung.

"You're good, Wormwood, but you'll not be leaving here alive."

Wormwood chuckled. "Stop boasting. Let's see if you have what it takes to make that fantasy a reality."

Wormwood swung his axe at Sorath. It missed the fallen angel, but the sickly, green crud was flung off the blade, and it splattered onto Sorath's cheek. Searing pain coursed from his cheek as the crud ate away like a putrid acid at his flawless, porcelain-like skin. Through bleary eyes, Sorath could see Wormwood grinning, showing those rotting teeth of his as he stalked closer, readying for the kill.

"I see you plan on using your disgusting fluids on me, brother."

"Why shouldn't I?" Wormwood snarled as he swung his axe, sending more of the green crud at him. "I'm fairly certain you didn't give poor Xaphan much of a fighting chance. You will suffer before you die!"

"Now who's the one boasting?" Sorath taunted as he shielded his face with his armored forearm. "I'm still waiting for you to make good on your threat, but you have yet to make contact. I believe you're scared."

"Nonsense, it is you who fears me, dear brother." Wormwood swung his axe with a bone-jarring strike that made Sorath drop his sword. Wormwood seized the opportunity and reached out, grabbing Sorath and holding him tightly. He dug his bony fingers under Sorath's armor and released his plague-pollen directly onto the fallen angel's skin.

"Feel the burn, brother!" Wormwood mocked as Sorath struggled to get free. "Now you will suffer!"

Sorath grimaced and then let out a bloodcurdling scream as the plague-pollen ate away at his skin. Wormwood dropped his axe to the floor and placed his hands on each side of Sorath's face. He smeared more of the pollen over every inch of uncovered skin. Flesh and muscles melted away like ice under hot water. Sorath dropped to the floor, clenching his body as there was nothing he could do to stop the burn.

Wormwood watched with joy as Sorath writhed in agony. He grabbed his axe up off the floor and let it lean against his shoulder as he casually strolled over to Sorath. "As I said earlier, my sickness still affects you. Your suffering shall be tenfold before I let you die."

Wormwood brought his leg back and kicked Sorath in the chest and abdomen. Even though Sorath wore his armor, the pain from each kick felt like he was naked. Most of his skin was eaten away now, and the metal armor touching the raw places seemed like salt on a wound, only worse.

Pink liquid seeped from Sorath's armor, pooling on the floor beneath him, making it difficult for him to get up. Wormwood grunted loudly as he kicked Sorath under his chin, sending him skidding across the floor towards his favorite chair.

"Is it time, brother?" Wormwood mocked as he closed in. "Shall I grant you mercy?"

Despite his body screaming out not to stand, Sorath pulled himself up using the chair. He turned to face Wormwood and saw he held his axe in both hands, readying to give the final death blow. Sorath bent forward slightly so Wormwood could get a clean cut.

"As you wish, my brother," Wormwood said, moving himself into position. "Any last words — that is, if you can still speak?"

Sorath put his arms out to help balance his unsteady body. It was then that he saw it, only five feet away from him. He croaked out, "Make your blow now...or you...might die...instead."

"Die? Me?" Wormwood threw back his head and laughed. "I think my pollen has eaten away at your brain." Wormwood chuckled. "If that's the case, then I have no choice but to grant you mercy."

As the axe started its descent toward the fallen angel's neck, Sorath silently willed the object to come to him. Xaphan's staff instantly flew through the air and into his hands. He pivoted and blocked Wormwood's killing blow.

Wormwood had an astonished look on his gaunt face, and Sorath used this small distraction to push the axe away. He aimed the tip of the staff at Wormwood's chest. A deadly fireball shot out of the staff, and the blast sent Wormwood tumbling across the room, where he landed hard on the floor.

He rolled over, gasping for breath and clutching at his chest. He saw a sight he'd never seen before…he'd never thought possible. Sorath was standing before him wielding not only Xaphan's staff but Wormwood's axe as well. Sorath's skin was glowing brightly, and it was regenerating rapidly. His crimson eyes were blazing with power, and he was hovering slightly off the floor, without the aid of his wings!

Wormwood knew then he had miscalculated Sorath's power. He wanted to flee, but he couldn't stand. Not only couldn't he stand, but he suddenly found that he couldn't move at all. Even his wings couldn't respond to his commands. He was paralyzed! Sorath had to be doing this to him!

"This is not possible!" Wormwood squeaked out in terror. "None of us can wield another angel's primary weapon, let alone use it! How are you regenerating so damn quickly?"

As Sorath pointed the staff at him again, he tried to brace himself for another impact, except he was still paralyzed. Without warning, Wormwood's body lifted off the floor. He was levitating! He now knew his time was up because Sorath had complete control over his body.

Sorath floated effortlessly over to him, reveling in his powers to control other fallen angels and their weapons. Once he got within arm's reach, Sorath stopped and glared down at Wormwood with distain, like he was gazing at a human.

"All this is possible," Sorath crowed with pride, "because I'm no longer a fallen angel like you or Xaphan. I'm better and stronger. With the prayers and tributes I get from my immortal followers, I am more like a god now. I'll grant you the mercy you wanted to grant me."

Sorath stepped closer to the paralyzed fallen angel. He raised Wormwood's own axe and with one swift stroke, Sorath cut off his opponent's head. He let the head stay frozen with the still levitating body as the unseen flame consumed it, turning Wormwood into a sickly, green ash.

Sorath lowered the staff and let Wormwood's remains fall to the floor. He then lowered himself back down. This was the first time he had ever tapped into this energy, and it made him feel invincible. Wormwood was right; he shouldn't have been able to regenerate so fast. To look at Sorath, you would never know that just five minutes ago, he had no skin on his face and nearly no muscles either.

He walked over to where most of his skin and blood mixture had pooled on the floor, and he pointed Xaphan's staff at it. The tip glowed with energy as he focused on the bloody mess, making it turn into ash also.

Sorath smiled as he walked back out to his balcony to gaze down at his devoted warriors. The rushing patter of footsteps alerted him that his guards were returning to their post. When they saw the door was wide open, they rushed inside. They looked frantic at first, but then they saw Sorath in the guise of Jesus and dropped down on their knees.

"My Lord, are you all right? It looks like a fight happened in here! Are you hurt?"

"As you can see, I'm fine. I need a servant to come in here and tidy up this room for me. Can one of you arrange that?" the phony Jesus asked with a loving smile.

"Of course, right away, my Lord!" one of the guards cried out as he rose and ran for the door.

Sorath, still in the guise of Jesus, motioned for the other guard to rise and resume his post as a sentry outside the door. Sorath walked out of the room and down the corridor. It was time to appoint a new leader to take Sully's place. He would also have to figure out who killed the man and vaporized his fallen warriors.

He wondered why he hadn't interrogated the two fallen angels to find out if they had something to do with Purah's absence. He half shrugged as he opened the double doors to go down the stairs. Even if Penemuel doesn't find her, he thought, she'll show up soon enough. But if any had harmed her in any way, he promised to make their deaths more painful and excruciating than what Wormwood and Xaphan had gone through.

Chapter 12

Deep in the forest, the canopy was just thick enough to shield Rose from the worst of the rain. During their trek, she had made multiple stops to pick the medicinal herbs that grew along the way and to dress Duncan's bite wounds with thick poultices. Each bite had an angry red tint and more than likely was festering into a full blown infection.

Duncan was no longer twitching or convulsing, but he made more grimacing faces. He was in pain, and there wasn't much Rose could do for him at the moment. She caught herself glancing back at him more than usual, and it wasn't to make sure he hadn't tumbled out of the gurney.

As the ox trudged through the foliage, Rose scanned the area for more ghouls. If a pocket of them were hiding out here, Rose would put up a fight, but she knew she wouldn't win. Sure, she had the pack of wolves that would fight and die for her, but the sheer number of ghouls could trump them with ease.

As the eerie feeling that she was being watched grew stronger, the hairs on the back of her neck rose. Was it the ghouls? She dismissed that thought right away because she had faced them on more than one occasion and had never been this unnerved by them. It was true that she feared them, but the feeling Rose had now was that she was being hunted. She was prey!

As they made their way up a steep incline, Rose heard rustling from somewhere to her right. She anxiously looked around and counted all the wolves that were escorting them. All were accounted for. Why hadn't the wolves sensed her hunter?

Whoever was following them was letting her know they were nearby, which only increased her anxiety. As they crested the hill, Rose could see a vast meadow covered in clovers and daisies. Off in the distance, a small opening to a cave beckoned them.

She urged the ox onward, heading towards the cave. As her paranoia worsened by the second, she cast a watchful eye over her shoulders. How had Duncan managed being on the road for so long? Rose wasn't use to roughing it.

Even in the early days of the firestorms, she had lucked out and ended up with a large group of people who were looking for a safe place to stay. Rose told them of an old rundown farm that she knew was in the area. It was secluded and, more importantly, already had most of the resources they would need, like a running creek and several water wells.

She told them she excelled in growing fruits and vegetables and could ensure they would have them year round if they could aid her in creating several underground greenhouses. With a lot of repurposing and labor, they created Melona and had more than enough food and water to consume.

Rose glanced up at the thunderheads and shivered. It was almost dark, and she was cold, soaking wet, and practically naked. Yearning for her fire pit and her queen sized bed, the lack of comfort and safety crept into the back of Rose's mind, and she considered turning around and trying to reclaim her beautiful village.

She mentally slapped herself back into reality as they neared the entrance to the cave. How could I take out all the ghouls on my own? My magic's good, but it can't incinerate the ghouls the way Duncan's had done earlier. Rose glanced back at the man — the stranger, really. She didn't know anything about him other than his wife had been reaped by the grim reapers. Now, as she thought about the deadly light that had come from him, she realized she must find out everything about him — for her own safety, if nothing else.

Again, she felt someone stalking her from the shadows.

As the ox stopped at the cave's entrance, Rose dismounted and unhook the reigns so the animal could roam free without the extra burden of the gurney. She affectionately patted the ox's head. "See? There's plenty to eat for you. Go graze and thank you for your help."

The ox nuzzled against her and licked her face. Rose crinkled her nose in disgust as its tongue left a trail of thick saliva on her face. "Thanks," she said half-heartedly.

While Rose grabbed the straps to the gurney, several of the wolves entered the cave to check it out, making sure it was safe. Wanting to walk backwards as she pulled the gurney, Rose turned her back to the cave and faced Duncan. She pulled, but the gurney didn't move. Determined to get him inside the cave, she dug her heels in the soft, rain-soaked ground and pulled with all her strength. The gurney moved, but it was a slow tug-of-war game, and though she was the only one pulling, it felt like the gurney was winning.

The wolves emerged from the cave unharmed and beckoned for her to enter. She tugged Duncan forward toward the opening. Relieved to know the cave was safe, she couldn't help stopping at the entrance and looking back at the trees. Her unseen stalker was out there somewhere. She could *feel* him!

Whoever he was, he had kept up with them just enough to not be seen. Yet, the hunter had also made it a point to let her know he was still on her trail. One of the wolves brushed up against her leg, and she looked down at it. Why hadn't the wolves sensed her stalker and gone after him?

Once she got a better footing inside the cave, it became easier to drag Duncan a good twenty feet from the entrance. Even though it was darker, it was also warmer in the back. She dropped the straps and bent over to catch her breath. Pulling him had been exhausting.

As her breath came easier, her thoughts kept returning to the stalker. The more she thought about him, the angrier she became, and she stormed out of the cave. Determined to find out who he was and what he wanted, she stood with her hands on her hips and glared around at the various places a person could hide.

She didn't give a damn if she called out a horde of ghouls. At least she would have her answer. Did this person mean to harm her? Rose unsheathed her katana and held it as she steadied herself for a fight.

"Alright, you son of a bitch, show your cowardly ass right now! I know you've been following us, so if it's blood you want, then I'll gladly make you bleed!" She took a few steps toward the clump of cedar trees to her left.

Suddenly, Rose felt the hairs on the back of her neck rise up as a cold shiver stomped down her spine. Whatever he was, he was trying to instill her with fear. She did all she could to stand her ground in the pouring rain, but her mind was screaming at her to flee.

The pack of wolves surrounded her, forming a protective circle which gave Rose a little more courage. She heard a whipping sound of fabric that came from somewhere behind her. She whirled around, but no one was there!

As several of the wolves let out low growls, a masculine voice sounded out, and his cadence made her blood run cold as ice. "Interesting choice of words, heifer. I do love a good game of bloodletting. Of course, it won't be *me* losing *my* blood."

Rose looked up. A man squatted on top of the cave's entrance like a gargoyle guarding a church. He flashed a wicked smile at her, making her pulse speed up, and shivers bump down her spine.

She glared angrily at the guy. "Who the fuck are you calling a heifer, asshole? I should gut you where you stand!" When she got a better look at him, she gasped. "Wait…what the hell are you?"

The man, if he could be called that, wore a weather-worn, black duster jacket. His black jeans ended with black climbing boots, and he had on a black t-shirt with writing on it in white letters: "*I survived the apocalypse, and all I got was this lousy shirt!*"

Too much free time on this jerk's hands, Rose thought as she cocked an eyebrow. He had pale skin which made Rose wonder if he hadn't gotten out in the sun much. His black, slicked back hair made his pale skin seem even whiter. He cut his steely eyes at Rose's neck which made her unconsciously cover it with her hands, much to the delight of the stranger because Rose's bathrobe had suddenly opened up, exposing her nakedness.

"Are you offering more to me than just your blood?" The stranger chuckled. "If so, then by all means show me more of that exquisite body. Perhaps you prefer for me to undress you? I always loved gifts that keep on giving."

Rose gasped as she looked down and saw there was nothing hidden from this stranger. She quickly tucked her robe against her body the best she could and snarled, "In your dreams, creep! Why are you following me? And who are you?"

"You presume too much, harlot," the stranger replied. "I'm after the one who resides just beneath me. I've been watching him for a few days now, but he appears to have gotten his sorry ass hurt. Such a pity."

"He didn't get hurt on purpose! He was trying to save both our asses but got swarmed by those damn ghouls. Still, you've been hanging back and watching. You know what happened back there, right?"

He nodded but didn't say any more. "You got a name?" she asked. "Or should I keep calling you creep?"

In less than a blink of an eye, the stranger was standing behind Rose, and her katana was now lying on the ground next to where she was standing. The wolves lunged and missed him as he moved back to the top of the cave—with Rose in his arms!

Rose threw her elbow into the stranger's ribs several times, but it didn't seem to faze him. He laughed as he held her close to his body and inhaled her scent. "You smell delicious!" he murmured. "If you don't call off your precious pack, I'll blood them all."

"You wouldn't dare!" Rose bit out defiantly, but fear was swelling throughout her body because she knew he would...and could.

"I'm a vampire, and I've proven to you that my speed is fast. I can kill even faster than that. Call them off or I'll kill them and drain you slowly, so you can watch them die. They won't go quickly either!"

Rose knew he was telling the truth. That wasn't speed he was using; this fucker could teleport! No wonder he was able to keep up with her and not be seen at the same time. He was probably using the trees which would explain why none of the pack knew he was there.

She sensed the alpha female sneaking up from behind while the other wolves attempted to climb from different angles. None were getting closer. Distraction was their plan, but even that wouldn't work against an old predator as fast as he was.

"Stop!" she called out to her wolves. "Don't hurt him! I'm okay, guys!"

He glanced over his shoulder and commanded, "You heard the lady. Back off, fur balls, or she'll die first!"

Rose knew he wasn't threatening her but, rather, the alpha female behind them, poised to strike. Rose pleaded to the alpha mentally, *"Don't do it. He will get you before you can get a piece of him. Trust me, and do as I wish...I want to keep you all safe and alive."*

The alpha grunted and snapped her teeth at the vampire as a way of showing she didn't like the idea of not attacking him. She moved away a few feet from him where she could watch him closely.

"That's better. Now that we have this cave all to ourselves, shall we get to know each other?" He licked Rose on her neck slow and softly. "I can think of a few ways to pass the time."

Rose shuddered under his influence, but she somehow managed to push him away and put a little distance between them.

He shrugged his shoulders. "Your loss, harlot."

"Stop calling me that! My name is Rose. Rose Macready. Keep it up and I'll burn you to ashes so badly that you'll wish you had stepped into direct sunlight to burn up quicker!"

He snorted. "I didn't know your name and seeing that you're dressed like that, I could only assume Duncan was saving a precious chamber partner. Besides, the sun doesn't burn my kind, that's a myth told by humans so they can feel safe during the day."

"I see. Do you have a name or should I just call you Edward?"

He crinkled his nose and sneered. "Eww! How dare you compare me to that fictional, sparkling, goofball! He doesn't hold a candle to the real deal, nor could he be man enough to be one of us! You will call me—"

"Dracula? Lestat?" Rose teased. "No...wait! I've got it!" She grinned. "Nosferatu!"

The vampire looked pissed. Finally, he calmed down as he thought about what she had blurted out. He gazed at her while tapping a finger to his chin. "Good names but mine is actually Devlin. Be thankful I like you. I don't take kindly to being interrupted by complete strangers."

"Ah, I guess flashing my goods helped sway you from ripping my throat out?"

Devlin gave her a hungry stare. "Indeed."

"So why are you stalking Duncan? What did he do to you that would make you want to kill him?"

Devlin looked appalled by her words. He put his splayed hand on his chest over his heart. "You think I want to kill Duncan? Why on Earth would you think such a thing?"

"Because you're a vampire, and you've been stalking him all day now," Rose hissed irritably with her hands on her hips.

"Yes, I can see how that looks from your perspective. I'm completely innocent of these charges, and you wound me, Rose." He suddenly threw his hands up in the air as if he was surrendering. "Okay, you got me. The stalking part is true, but that's what I do."

"How come I haven't seen more of your kind around?"

"Would it make you feel better knowing that there're vampires roaming the world…along with ghouls?" He chuckled when he saw her frown. "We stay hidden from everyone because it's safer that way. It's also easier to kill our food." He grinned as her brows knitted together. "Before all hell broke loose, it was easy to feed because no one feared the darkness. Several centuries ago, people feared the dark. Of course, their dark was very dark."

"What do you mean?"

"People had nothing but crude lanterns to dispel the darkness. Just before the apocalypse, though, people had all kinds of things to light their way. Their dark wasn't very dark."

"So, your kind was with us…but hidden?"

He nodded. "Did you announce to the world that you were a sorceress?"

"No, of course not! Religious zealots would've burned me alive."

"My point exactly. The world is more open to you than it would be for my kind, but I know eventually my kind will come out of the closet…so to speak. Let's face it; you are our favorite meal." He grinned when she frowned. "Speaking of meals, may I go see Duncan?"

"As long as you can get me down." Rose and Devlin were instantly on the ground by the cave entrance. He was holding out her katana for her to take.

"Fuck, you're fast!"

Devlin motioned for her to go into the cave first. After he made his move to walk behind Rose, the wolves growled at him.

"It's okay," she called out mentally. *"He knows Duncan, but if he makes one false move, he's all yours."*

"Good girl, keep them on that leash if you want them to live," he announced as he slapped Rose on her ass.

She turned to confront him, but he wasn't there. When she heard him laughing farther back in the cave, she marched in after him. "That's a free one. Next time, I'll roast you alive, you fucking prick!"

Devlin let out a belly laugh, and the echo from it boomed throughout the cave. Rose ambled her way towards Duncan and Devlin. From what she could make out in the dim light, the vampire was now squatting beside Duncan, carefully examining him. He looked from Duncan to Rose and back again several times before asking, "What did you give him for pain? His heart is racing, and his blood pressure is skyrocketing. He's needlessly suffering."

"The only things I gave him were the herbs for the poultices that cover his wounds. All my good stuff is back in my village…but it's overrun by ghouls now."

"You could've given him some of those herbs orally!" Devlin hissed. "It might not be the most effective way, but it would be better than this!"

"Hey, cut me some slack! I'm doing the best I can with what I have to work with here!"

"Poor man would've been better off if you hadn't destroyed all those ghouls with your magic. If you can do that, then why haven't you gone back to your village and cleaned them out?"

Rose looked at Devlin like he had grown an extra head. How could he think it was me if he was watching us so intently?

She angrily got up in his face, wanting nothing more than to slap that accusing glare off his smug mug, but she knew that would only hurt her hand. What little she knew of him, she figured the slap would just turn him on. "How can you say I did that? I sure as hell didn't do that; I'm not that powerful!"

Devlin gazed into her eyes. "Then who did it? From my vantage point, all I could see was you making magic in your hands and then BOOM! That flash of light blinded me for a few minutes. If I hadn't ducked behind a boulder, the intense heat wave that followed would have incinerated me too." He glared at Rose. "You unleashed your spellwork! No one else, just you!"

"It wasn't me; it was Duncan!"

"Him?" Devlin chuckled. "That man hasn't got a shred of magic in his entire body. And you want me to believe he blew those ghouls away?" He laughed at her.

"If the blast came from me, why is Duncan not scorched or burned?"

Devlin abruptly stopped laughing when he realized that what she said had merit. He knelt down beside Duncan's body and inspected him closer. Devlin sniffed Duncan's clothes. He found a little hint of residual magic but no burnt odors.

He looked up at Rose with concern and said, "He's different. I can tell just from his scent. But to truly understand, I will need…"

"What?" Rose demanded.

"His blood."

Chapter 13

"Don't you dare bite him! Duncan's been through enough as it is and—"

"Rose, please. Would you stop judging me? Just a scratch is all I require. I have more self-control than you realize."

"And I'm supposed to take your word for it? Hell, I don't even know you!"

"I haven't ripped your throat out yet…and I'm famished too," Devlin replied as he licked one of his fangs.

Rose put her hand on her carotid artery in her neck as though she could block his senses from it and keep his hunger from growing. She hated not being able to read the vampire. He was both handsome and deadly at the same time, and she was concerned that she might say the wrong thing to him. If she did, he'd be on her before she knew it, drinking his fill while draining her blood until she was dead.

For some strange reason, that thought aroused her. It could be an erotic but dangerous game to play. Maybe I could nick my neck with my katana and let my blood stream down my body. I could take off my robe. The blood could stream over my nakedness. That would probably entice him to lick my body and explore all of me with those rough hands of his. Maybe I should let him take off my robe…let him peel it off my naked body. He could kiss and caress wherever he wanted, taking full possession of me.

Suddenly, Duncan groaned, and Rose shook herself inwardly, bringing her thoughts back to reality. She saw Devlin eyeing her intently, his mouth gapping open in disbelief.

"What?" Rose cautiously asked.

"Must you do that now?"

"Do what?"

"Fantasize about me!"

Rose gasped. "I wasn't doing that! Is that all you can think about? Sex and blood?"

Devlin flashed a toothy smile at her, his fangs lengthening and looking wicked and deadly. "Those are my two favorite subjects. Don't play dumb with me, Rose. You're too smart for that, so stop selling yourself short. Besides, your body is betraying you as we speak."

Rose blushed. "That bad, huh?"

"Not really, I love your scent. It's intoxicating but also distracting. Before I get ahead of myself, duty calls." Devlin lifted Duncan's arm and ran one of his sharp fingernails against the top of the man's hand. As blood trickled out from the cut, Devlin raised Duncan's hand to his lips. He lapped up the warm, salty liquid, flicking his tongue in and out of his mouth—like a snake. He looked up at Rose as he lowered Duncan's arm. Cocking one eyebrow, he gave her a bloody grin.

Rose gasped at the sight and turned to look at the rock wall, trying to get what she'd just seen out of her head. "Duty calls," she reminded. "What did you find out from your little test?"

As Devlin stood up, his eyes rolled back in his head. He swayed back and forth, like he was about to collapse. Staggering to the wall for better support, Devlin leaned against it. He was quiet for a long time before finally opening his eyes. "Whoa!" he exclaimed. "Blood is so intoxicating. What a rush!"

Rose sat down beside Duncan and wondered if the vampire planned on taking more than he just had. She stole a glance at him. Devlin looked high; his eyes had a glazed look in them. When she remembered that it was Duncan's blood he'd gotten stoned on, she revised her impression of him. He definitely didn't look sexy anymore!

Rose had one hand on her katana, ready to strike if Devlin made a move to bite Duncan. She looked down at the man as he lay near death. Had he not stopped to rescue her from the ghouls, he'd be fine right now. She reached over and smoothed his strawberry blond hair. He was burning up with fever, and he moaned in his sleep. "What did you discover?"

Devlin sighed. "His blood tastes the same as it did before, but now it's flooded with magical energy."

"Wait, you knew what Duncan's blood tasted like before tonight? You mean you've bit him before?"

"Yes and no, Rose." Devlin slid down the wall to sit beside Duncan. "We met a few years ago. He stumbled upon me feeding. Duncan was bloody and battered, like he had just left a barroom brawl. You can imagine how that went."

"Let me guess? He attacked you."

"No, he didn't. That surprised me too because he saw me feeding. I've gotten careless a few times when feeding and had to end up killing a witness. Invariably, they'll call me the spawn of Satan or a demon. Then they try to stab me in the heart."

"So, is that true that a stake to your heart can kill you?"

Devlin's eyes suddenly twinkled. "That would be telling too much, especially to someone who's eager to test it. Many have tried and failed. I'd hate to kill such a beautiful lady as you, Rose."

"It will take more than a compliment to win me over. I'm not that easy and many have tried their luck and played their games too."

Devlin chuckled. "And yet just a few minutes ago, you were mentally throwing yourself at me."

"Hey, a girl can have a fantasy or two, can't she?" Rose protested, but it came out whiny.

"Yes, indeed, because I've been having many about you, Rose." Devlin grinned.

Rose blushed as she fanned herself. "Okay, horn-dog, enough about sex. Tell me more about what kept you from killing Duncan."

"Sex is my favorite subject, and I do excel at it. Care for a demonstration?"

"Devlin!"

The vampire laughed. "Okay, okay, another time then." Rose glared at him, and he pressed on, "As I said, Duncan found me feeding, but he didn't attack me like everyone else. He stood there with his hand on the hilt of his sword and stared at me. It was like he was waging a war with himself as to what to do about me, and then he surprised me with his decision."

"What was that?"

"He shrugged his shoulders and walked past me, as if I were something he'd seen every day and accepted. Hell, he didn't bother to touch his sword anymore, like he knew he was safe."

Rose thought about that. It seemed plausible that Duncan was listening to that inner voice he had spoken about earlier today. Was that why he hadn't attack the vampire? He did say that the voice started shortly after the firestorms occurred, so it stood to reason that he paid attention to it when it warned him about a dangerous person. Did it go the other way? Letting him know a person was good too?

Devlin stared at Rose and asked, "You know something, don't you?"

"Maybe, but until he wakes up, I can't confirm if my suspicions are true."

"Tell me…please."

Rose saw that he was genuinely interested, probably because this was a puzzle that he couldn't figure out on his own. She wasn't sure if she should tell Devlin about the voice in Duncan's head. Maybe Duncan would see it as a betrayal of his trust. Duncan tolerated her, but he hadn't fully accepted her into his tiny circle of trust. Rose bit at her bottom lip in uncertainty, but then she felt a hand on top of hers. Devlin's hand was colder than most hands, but it also felt comforting and inviting.

"Duncan may hate me forever if he finds out I've told you this. He doesn't trust me that much."

"I know of his trust issues, and they run deep. If he's told you something of a sensitive nature then he must trust you more than most people. Seeing him in this condition and how you've cared for him, I can't say I blame him for confiding in you."

"Can you see why I'm so…hesitant to tell you?"

"Yes, and I shall press no further, Rose. Someone like him deserves a friend like you. Life gets lonely when you fear to trust others with your most precious secrets."

"I assume you didn't let him leave when he walked away?"

"No, I didn't. I tried to scare him and make him fight, but Duncan didn't rise to my bait, not once. He wasn't afraid…just apprehensive around me. He finally got tired of my antics and told me to piss off and go bite someone who cares. I think I nearly died a second time from laughing so much. His mood lightened up slightly, and we talked awhile, traded war stories from what we'd seen on the road. I gave him a heads up on where safe passage from the ghouls was. I actually wanted him to be safe in his travels." Devlin grinned. "But I charged him a small price for the information."

"His blood?"

Devlin nodded. "He wasn't thrilled with the idea of me biting him, but I told him that I would take the blood from one of his many open wounds. Even then, he wasn't sure. Finally, after much negotiating, he begrudgingly agreed to it." Devlin paused for a moment, remembering that night. "What I tasted then is the same as I tasted a few minutes ago. Only now, though, Duncan is teeming with magical energies, the likes I've never seen in my lifetime. And I've lived a long time too!"

"Why did you want his blood?"

"Trade secrets, love. I don't go around telling everyone my business. No social media for me, even when there was social media. Some things you take to your grave—or coffin— okay, you get my meaning, right?"

Rose nodded as she let go of Devlin's hand and gently caressed Duncan's arm. Now her suspicions were confirmed. Duncan was a magical being and though it was latent inside him, it was now coming up to the forefront, wild and untrained. That could be dangerous if he couldn't harness and control it.

Still, Rose wondered what Duncan was and what abilities he possessed. He wielded energy that was powerful enough to vaporize a small horde of ghouls and had an inner voice that kept him safe. What else didn't she know about Duncan?

Rose stood up and walked slowly towards the cave entrance, pondering on this new development. One channel open to her was to sleep on it and see what revelations came to her in her dreams. Most of her dreams, though, were open to interpretation. She had tried to dream about Duncan at Melona, but she had been interrupted by the ghouls. Even with the help of the potion she had drunk earlier, the images were hard to sort out, let alone make any sense of their meanings.

Rose hugged her arms around her stomach as she neared the entrance. The storm was raging, and the wind had picked up drastically. The wolves were all huddled up at the entrance, keeping each other warm while watching for any possible threats.

Would the vampire leave her alone as she slept? Could he really control his primal urges? Rose still didn't trust Devlin, but he was growing on her. He was handsome for an old, dead guy and deviously clever, but would he risk his own life to protect them while they slept? Maybe he would simply say, "Fuck this!" and teleport to safer grounds. Rose disliked that thought.

It wasn't that she was incapable of taking care of herself and Duncan. Rose was flat out scared that she would go to sleep and wake up like she had earlier, with Duncan on top of her and surrounded by ghouls, except it would be the ghouls on top of her tonight—eating her!

"Rose?"

Rose turned toward the vampire. Had she heard a hint of panic in his voice?

Duncan!

Something was wrong with him, and she knew it. Rose ran towards Duncan, not caring that her robe was fully open and flowing in back of her like a cape. She dropped down on her knees, inspecting Duncan's body for signs of distress. He was breathing, but he was still grimacing like he was in pain.

"What's wrong with him?" she demanded. "Better yet, what's wrong with you?"

The vampire had a look of astonishment on his face, his mouth gaping open. Even his breathing was more shallow and quick, like he was a kid on Christmas morning. Rose looked at him curiously as she cocked her head to the side and patiently waited for his answer.

Devlin gently raised Duncan's arm by holding his hand. "Do you recall me cutting him and taking his blood from this hand?"

"Yes, of course. I was here or have you forgotten my protests? Do vampires get senile as they age?"

"Rose, stop being a smartass and look at his hand!" Devlin exclaimed, but it sounded like his excitement was dampening down anger. He turned Duncan's hand so Rose could inspect it.

She gasped, staring at the site where the vampire had taken the small amount of blood. "Where's the cut?" she insisted. "What happened to it?"

Devlin smiled at her. "Healed and without a trace of a scar. Trust me; I've been looking at his hand, and that fresh, pink skin is *new* skin."

"And the bite marks from the ghouls? What do they look like?" she asked in a small voice and shivered.

"Look," Devlin urged her and lifted Duncan's shirt.

She leaned over and inspected the man's chest, squinting down at him as she tried to see him better. Even in the shadowy cave, Rose could see that Duncan's bite wounds had started to heal.

"He's healing throughout his entire body," Devlin assured her. "That may be why he's in so much pain."

"I would think a magical form of healing would be less painful."

"There are many forms of healing, and I imagine he's going through multiple ones as we speak. From ancient times, pain has been associated with healing. Who knows what that magical energy is doing on the inside of him, right?"

"Oh, I didn't think of that. I wonder what he will feel when he comes to." Rose turned her head in guilt as she added, "Hopefully, no pain at all."

Devlin's lips parted as he looked at Rose's teary eyes. He maneuvered over and sat down beside her, cupping his hand under her chin so she would look at him.

"What's with the guilt?" he asked softly with concern in his voice.

"This is my fault, damn it!" Rose shot to her feet. "He wouldn't be in this condition if he had saved himself and…and…"

"Left you behind to die?" When Rose nodded quickly, Devlin added, "Come now, Rose. Do you really believe he would've done that to you? He's more honorable than that. I should know because I've been watching him. Today was no different."

Rose sniffled. "How so?"

"What I saw today was your village overrun with ghouls. The villagers didn't have a snowball's chance in hell to escape alive. Duncan had every opportunity to escape, but he hesitated when he looked at your hut. Duncan didn't want you to die."

"But Duncan doesn't think that much of me. He likes to tease, and we banter with each other. That's all. He's not tied to me."

Devlin pulled Rose close to him and held her tightly. She inhaled his masculine scents that wafted into her nostrils—forest, earth, and copper, she thought. He was a vampire and fed on blood; that accounted for the coppery odor.

He seemed as if he genuinely cared about how she felt as he ran his fingers through her damp hair. Leaning in next to her ear, he murmured, "Don't sell yourself so short, Rose. Any man who is as good as Duncan would have many reasons to want to be tied to you. You're smart, attractive and full of fire. You can take care of yourself...and him."

"Why would that matter to any man? Look at me now. I'm a fucking wreck with barely anything on my back expect this flimsy robe. What good am I to anyone like this?"

Devlin grabbed Rose by her arms and put his forehead against hers, looking into her eyes. She found it difficult to look back at him, so she averted her eyes because this was too much for her to take.

"Look at me, Rose," Devlin ordered softly. "Look at me, please."

Rose looked at him, her heart and head feeling like they were overflowing with emotions. Why did he care so damn much? She could see he hated seeing her like this. Quite frankly, Rose hated for anyone to see her in this state. She was brought up to be strong, to never show any signs of weakness, and crying in front of others was definitely a weakness. She glanced around, looking for an escape route so she could hide and let out these overflowing emotions, but Devlin wasn't budging.

"Any man would see qualities in you that would cause him to think he wouldn't have to carry his load as well as yours. He would see you as an equal because you bring so much to the table that you could compliment what he has, which makes for a good partner. You would be a good partner for any man who is worthy of your time and energy, whether he be a friend, a travelling companion...or a lover."

Rose's breath gasped at the word, *lover*. Why are Devlin's words affecting me so much? He probably wants to disarm me with sweet words and then disrobe me with tender caresses.

"Tell me the truth, Rose. How long has it been since you've been with a good man?"

She gasped again. He wanted her! And she wanted him. She didn't want to seem too easily slain by this gorgeous, undead beast's charms, so she decided to take control of the situation. She would treat him like all her other suitors who breezed into Melona. If I'm going to play with this scorching fire holding me, I might as well get burned.

"You mean sexually?" Rose raised an eyebrow provocatively. "Why? Are you offering?"

Chapter 14

Devlin let out a low growl. "Yes…and no. You misunderstand me. What I meant was how long has it been since you've had a good man as a friend, companion, or a lover? Though now you've got me curious about the last one."

Misunderstand him? I doubt that, she thought. "If I start answering your questions, then you need to do the same for me. If you want me to be honest and blunt, I can be that. But I expect the same from you. What do you say to that, Devlin?"

Devlin straightened up as he let go of her. "I can do that also, but there are certain things I can't discuss for survival reasons. If it's what I consider a secret thing, I will say that the subject is closed. Is that a fair compromise?"

Rose nodded. Suddenly, guilt crept into her mind. I should be tending to Duncan's wounds and making more of the medicinal poultices for him. Water! Rose thought with a panic as she hunted around for anything that she could use to serve it to Duncan. There were no cups in the cave. Perhaps a curved rock would work.

"What are you doing, Rose?" the vampire asked, a hint of annoyance in his voice.

"What does it look like I'm doing? Duncan needs water, and I'm not sure if there's anything in here that I can use."

"Like a canteen?" Devlin asked. He reached for something in the shadows.

"Yes,—hey, where did you get that?"

An amused look washed over the vampire's face as he shook the canteen in his hand, letting Rose hear the water sloshing inside it. "From Duncan's backpack. The canteen was full of water, so I took the liberty of giving him a few sips."

"Really?" Rose asked with confusion. "When did you have time to do that?"

"While you were over there by your furry friends. He's really good about packing his bag with all the essentials for being on the road."

Rose felt her cheeks heat up. Why the hell didn't I think to look in his bag?

Devlin unscrewed the lid and handed it to Rose. "Drink up. You need it as much as he does."

Rose took a few swigs. "Thanks, I'm fine."

"You're flustered and tired. What you need to do is relax."

Rose snorted as she handed Duncan's canteen back to the vampire. "Oh, like that's easy to do. I'm stuck in this wretched hole in the ground; I'm wet, cold and have no bed to sleep on. Unlike you, I will need both food and water to sustain myself. Plus, I have to care for Duncan!"

Devlin smiled. "Sorry that you can't be perfect like me, but rest assured you won't starve. Duncan does have food in his bag."

"Probably trail mix and energy bars. I want something better like apples or peaches or — "

"Like you had back in Melona?" When Rose nodded, he added, "Then don't go anywhere, I'll be right back." Devlin vanished right in front of Rose. She gasped, startled. Teleporting was a skill she hadn't seen, and it would take her mind time to wrap around the fact that someone could actually do it.

She looked down at Duncan. Again, guilt hit her full swing for being so selfish. This man had a bug-out bag packed, ready for life on the road. Here I am whining that I prefer fresh fruits to what he has to offer. Hell, he risked his damn life to save my ungrateful ass. Now what he had packed away for himself, he'll have to share with bitchy ol' me.

Rose was used to the finer things in life. Now, though, it was time to put her big girl panties on and suffer like everyone else around her, except she didn't have any panties.

A pop of air and a whisper by her ear startled Rose to the point of stumbling. She tripped over Duncan's body. Before she hit the ground, an arm was around her waist, lifting her up backwards. Devlin pulled her to him until her back was snug against his body.

He chuckled. "Sorry, I didn't mean to frighten you."

"Can you really blame me? I was nearly eaten alive today. Give me a better heads up next time you pop in here, you dumb shit!"

Devlin held her tightly against him, her ass pressing against his male member. He sighed slightly, letting her curves settle against his rock hard body. Rose struggled for a moment but then he reached around and produced a juicy red apple, gently pushing it in her face.

All her cares seemed to blow away with the wind. "Where did you get this?" Rose purred as she took a bite, not bothering to take the apple from Devlin's hand. He didn't seem to mind at all.

"I plucked them from your own orchard."

"You didn't have to do that. I was being selfish and bratty about Duncan's supplies."

"It was no trouble at all, Rose," he said softly. "Now let me take this wet thing off of you so you can feel warmer."

Rose looked over her shoulder at him. "You're just dying to take my robe off, so why not, right?"

"I've already died once; this is purely for survival reasons." Devlin grinned and then added, "You will get hypothermia if you don't get out of those wet clothes." He pointed to a spot in the cave. "If you'll make a small fire right there, I can drape your robe over that rock to dry it out."

Rose nodded but kept an eye on the vampire. She didn't fully trust him but, then again, Devlin had been on his best behavior. He could have easily subdued her and took whatever he wanted, and there would have been no stopping him, but he hadn't.

She closed her eyes and made a small, red flame appear in her hand. Letting it drop on the ground, it stayed there and didn't go out. It would flicker with the air that passed into the cave, but nothing more. If Rose wanted it to get bigger or extinguish itself, she could *will* it to happen.

Rose felt Devlin's fingers as he gently tugged at the bathrobe, slowly peeling it away from her body. She shivered as he let it slip down her back, allowing it to softly caress her damp skin. Naughty vampire, she thought but wasn't about to tell him to stop.

As her arms were freed from the wet sleeves, Devlin moved from behind Rose and draped it delicately over the jagged rock by the flame. With it off, Rose felt the warmth from her fire as it heated up the cave.

Devlin turned around and got a full eye view of a skyclad Rose. He stood there as he ran a hand over his mouth, appreciating what he was seeing. Rose put her hands on her hips as she asked, "Is this what you were hoping to see tonight?"

"It is," Devlin's voice came out hoarser than earlier, "and so much more."

Devlin beckoned Rose to him with the apple she had taken several bites from already. She sauntered towards him, making sure that he would see everything. Snatching the apple from his hand, she turned around to show off her bare ass. Rose smiled in between bites as she heard him groan with lust.

"Like I said before, thanks for the apple. I figured I might as well pay you with a little peepshow for the time it took you to gather it."

"Who said I only brought back one?"

Rose turned around and saw Devlin had his wicked grin on full display. His fangs were as fully erect as his own male member that strained to be released through his black pants.

"If you want more food, then you'll have to come and get it." He spread his black coat open to show the bulges in the pockets.

Rose's mouth gaped open. How much fruit did he grab for me? Suddenly, her body was pulled to Devlin until she was mere inches away from him. His fiery red eyes locked on to hers in a possessive way, like he was claiming her and no other person in the world mattered. Rose felt him wrap his thick coat around her body as he tugged her next to him. She felt the hard bulges the fruit made in his coat, and then she felt his rock hard member bulge too.

Devlin held on to her as if she might run away. "Let's sit down and get you all warm and cozy by the fire, shall we?" She nodded as he lowered them both down to the ground. He adjusted his legs so she could sit on his lap and still be able to face him.

Rose leaned in toward Devlin's body and inhaled his scent as it wafted up. She got a sense of calm and safety in his embrace and wondered if this was a normal way to feel about a complete stranger. Was this feeling all hers or did the vampire release some sort of pheromone to make all his victims more willing and suggestible?

Slowly and methodically, Devlin ran his fingers through Rose's hair as if he was playing a musical instrument, and he was the only one who could hear the music being played. She gazed up at the vampire and saw that his eyes were closed and that with each stroke, he was inhaling.

Okay, that's different, she thought. Rose wondered what she smelled like to him...besides dinner and sex. Was he worth getting to know or should she play him like all the other male suitors that had breezed through Melona? The fire was a good comfort but so was being close to Devlin. Just the smallest gestures like running his fingers through her hair or willing to go to her orchard and gather food for her spoke volumes about him.

"What are you thinking about?" Rose whispered.

"Food. Care to donate to the cause?" Devlin grinned mischievously.

"I'm being serious, jackass!"

"So am I, Rose."

Rose felt a chill creep down her spine.

Could she run away? No, she decided, his quick reflexes and teleportation would make the effort on her part a waste of time. Devlin hugged her close to his body, trying to calm her, but Rose wasn't having it.

"Is that all I am to you?" she demanded. "A walking, talking happy meal?"

"No, you're so much more to me than that. If you weren't, I'd be feeding on you without a care in the world. Even your naked body wouldn't have stopped me. How many times do I need to say it before you will understand that I'm not here to hurt you, Rose? Sure, I'd love to get a taste of your blood, but now is not the time for that."

"Not the time?" her voice squeaked out in horror as she shivered again. "With comments like that, how can I believe you won't do it when the time *is* right? How can I trust you?"

Devlin sighed. "Yet again, you misunderstand what I'm saying. To me, you're food; that much is true. You are also a treasure worth keeping safe from harm. I don't want to hurt you, Rose. If that means I must travel roads with you and never see another human to feed on. So be it, I would starve for you, Rose."

She stopped her struggle as she gazed up at the vampire. The look in his eyes said it all. He was being honest, though she couldn't imagine what his hunger for blood was like. Quite frankly, she never wanted to find out. She doubted that there would be a road where there were no humans to feed on.

"You wanted me to be open and honest when you asked me questions, didn't you?" Devlin asked with a knowing gaze. "Please don't take what I'm saying lightly. The need for blood is a terrible but necessary evil for me to sustain myself. Think what it would be like to be starving for weeks on end and having your succulent orchard in front of you, but it's just out of your reach. Now times that by ten and that's how bad the hunger gets for me on a daily basis."

"But why would you torment yourself when you could have my blood for the taking? It's not like I could stop you."

"Oh, but you could and already are; you just don't know it, Rose." Devlin turned his gaze away, looking at her fire.

Rose snorted. "Really? Am I protected somehow? How is it that I'm stopping you from ripping my throat out and taking your fill? I'm not wearing anything, except you for the moment, so what is it that repels you?"

He didn't look at her. He spoke, sounding like he was far away and lost in a memory. "I've been watching your village for a while now and was waiting for the opportunity to speak with Duncan alone and away from prying eyes. That meant I couldn't just teleport my way into your lovely village. As I watched, I saw you on many occasions dealing with traders and being the strength for others within the walls. I saw a woman who demanded respect and who could handle herself without the need to hide behind others. I could hear some of the lewd, sexual remarks about you made by the traders, and it took all my self-control not to pop in and rip out their throats."

"Feeling a little jealous, were you?" Rose smiled, but he never looked her way.

"I wanted to protect you from the world, but I felt that wouldn't be possible…or even necessary. You have Duncan, and I knew he would watch over you because he's a good and honorable man. He'll never cause you any harm. I wanted to ask him about you but knew he wouldn't say anything, other than your name and what you do. He's a keeper, Rose."

Rose felt butterflies growing in her stomach. "You sound so sad when you say that. Why's that, Devlin?"

The vampire finally looked at Rose. "Because you're a treasure to behold and loved like no other woman in the world. You would make this life worth *living*."

Rose gulped loudly, now worried that the vampire was thinking about the two of them together. She noticed Devlin was shifting his body, and she felt his throbbing member poking her ass. He was turned on. It was then that she realized she was too. "Do you want me to move so you can sit more comfortably?" she asked, but hoped he would say no!

"I'd rather be uncomfortable than see you wet and shivering from the cold."

Score! Now to play, she thought. "Is the *hard* rock under us making you uncomfortable?" Rose gave Devlin a beguiling smile and a wink. He let out a low, sexy growl.

She wondered just how much he could take with a beautiful, naked woman in his lap and still remain a gentleman. You're playing with fire, Rose, she reminded herself. Keep it up and you'll get scorched. Devlin's red eyes were mostly locked on to her eyes. Every so often, though, he would glance down at her neck. Rose bit her lip as she careened her head to the side, exposing her carotid artery to the vampire.

Devlin's breathing got heavier and his voice more raspy as he whispered, "Rose, you're making things difficult. Why must you play this dangerous game with me? I told you I wanted to keep you safe. How can I, when you make me want to…"

Rose caressed his chest, slowly making her way down to Devlin's pulsating shaft. She grabbed it forcefully to get his attention and began rubbing it through his pants, grinding it against the fabric.

Devlin felt her slide off him just enough so she could use her other hand to cup his swollen balls. His eyes rolled to the back of his head as his eyelids fluttered rapidly.

"What do you want to do to me now?" Rose purred against his chest as she nipped at his nipple through his shirt. "I'm doing my best to behave. I trust you'll do the same?"

"W-What?" Devlin muttered out incoherently.

"If I'm going to be able to trust you," Rose murmured by his ear as she stroked him hard and fast, "then you have to be on your best behavior, even now."

"Rose...please, don't..."

"Don't stop? Not a problem, big boy. Here, let me help you out." She chuckled mischievously as she unfastened his pants and tugged at the zipper. She coaxed Devlin's hot, throbbing member through the slit in his boxers. Rose had a firm grip on his big shaft and twisted it gently as she stroked it in a rhythmic movement.

Devlin buried his face against the wall, torn between ecstasy and lust, as his hips bucked uncontrollably with each stroke Rose gave him. He clenched his hands into fists, digging his sharp fingernails into his palms as he tried to maintain control. With his eyes closed, Devlin grimaced as he mentally repeated the same mantra over and over again: *Stay calm, remain in control! Stay calm, remain in control! Stay calm, remain in control!*

Through the foggy haze in his head, Devlin could barely hear Rose asking him a question. The blood that coursed through this wicked woman's veins screamed to be tapped. He could hear her heart racing in tune with his own.

"So…how long has it been since you've been with a good woman?"

"Too…long, Rose…" he bit out as he gasped for air.

"I hate to break it to you, but you're not with one now," Rose purred as she leaned down and kissed his crown, licking the pre-cum from his tip. "I'm a bad woman to be with. Hmm, how long has it been since someone has sucked on you, *vampire*?"

Did he hear her right? Was she going to suck his blood? He looked down and saw a sight that nearly sent him off the deep end. Rose was no longer covered by his jacket. Her arms rested on his legs as she worked his member over. On her knees, her curvy back bowed, and her butt jutted up in the air, causing him to be mesmerized by the slightest movement of her ass. Through the cobwebs of euphoria, his mind screamed, *Rose Macready is a Goddess!*

She lifted her head momentarily. "It's time for this lovely piece to get the Rose treatment."

"W-what…Rose…ooh….ughhhh!" He moaned out as Rose slid her tongue along his tip and shaft. Once it was wet enough, she gently blew on it, making him shiver. She licked more—a lot more! He bucked his hips, wanting to fuck Rose's mouth, but she leaned down on his legs, keeping his thrusts to a minimum.

Devlin's fangs grew longer as the need to feed built up inside him like it had never done before. *If I could have a small taste of her, I could be — NO!* he mentally screamed. At war with himself, he felt the hunger inside him gaining ground with each passing second.

He looked down just in time to see Rose fully envelope his throbbing member into that sweet, wet mouth of hers. *Fucking heaven!* Devlin did his best to control his bucking, but even that wasn't possible. *How did she manage to take complete and utter control over my body?*

"Mm," Rose purred as she hummed, vibrating his member with her mouth. She raised her head for a moment, sliding Devlin's throbbing member out of her mouth, teasing him. "Delicious!" she pronounced and grinned mischievously. "I'm feeling a bit greedy. I think I'll take more of you. What do you say to that, *vampire*?"

As Rose took Devlin's member fully into her mouth, his eyes shot open. There was no longer any white in his eyes, nor could his irises or pupils be seen. They were consumed with a blood red tint as both his lust for blood and her were neck and neck in a heated race to see which one would come out on top.

Rose bobbed her head as her lips stroked Devlin's member, wanting to make him explode. *How long has it been since he had a proper release,* Rose wondered. *Longer than me, I'm sure.* She felt his member swelling up to its max, his veins bulging everywhere along his shaft. She knew it wouldn't be much longer before he exploded his seed like a geyser.

Devlin snarled and contorted his body as the heavy pressure built up for a climax. Along with it, he could feel his blood lust building just as strongly.

In a panic, Devlin yanked back the sleeve of his coat and viciously bit down on his own forearm, his fangs piercing his skin and muscle like they were nothing. He drank his own blood to help sate his hunger, but it was only a temporary fix, and Devlin knew it.

He hoped that Rose would be too distracted by her wicked fun and wouldn't notice he was draining himself. It was degrading to do this sort of thing—an old survival trick he'd learned long ago when food was scarce. As bad as it looked, Devlin wanted her to fully trust him. He wouldn't harm her, so he chose to harm himself.

His blood lust ramped up as shockwaves of euphoria and lightheadedness slapped him back into reality. He was in the throes of ejaculating. Devlin let go of his bloody forearm and screamed as he bucked his hips like a maniac.

Rose watched with glee as he sprayed his cum over both of them. It felt as hot as lava and would burn her core just as easily if she let him inside of her.

A bright light from her right caught Rose's attention. She knew it wasn't her fire because it sat to her left and was flaring and burning brightly with the passion she got from handling Devlin's member. Her fire looked like a candle flame compared to this new light source. Was someone coming, besides the vampire? Rose thought about several different spells she could cast...just in case.

She looked over at the new light. It was Duncan! He was glowing brightly with a vibrant purple glow all over his body. Not only that, but he was floating in the air!

Rose let go of Devlin and stood up as best she could, padding over towards Duncan. As she neared him, she could tell the light was coming from his body. She sighed in relief that it wasn't someone's spellwork attacking him. Rose reached out and let her hand touch the purple glow. It gave her a sense of calm and peace, like she was in another plane where nothing could harm her. The horrors of this world seemed to melt away.

As the glow dissipated, Duncan's body lowered itself back down to the ground. Rose stood there dumbfounded as yet another piece of this mysterious man had come to the forefront. What was Duncan becoming and why now?

A sharp shifting of feet from behind caught her attention. She knew it was Devlin and turned around, casting a beguiling smile at him. Her smile vanished instantly!

Devlin had his pants down at his ankles and blood dripped from his left arm. It was his blood red eyes, though, that sent terror into her heart and panic into her head.

"Rose," he snarled as his fangs dripped with his own blood. "Forgive me…but I must feed!"

He lunged at her!

Chapter 15

Rose stumbled and fell, hitting her head hard on the rocky ground. Devlin draped his arms around her midriff and pinned her down. Rose blinked her eyes as she tried to rid her vision of little, black spots. Dazed, she wondered why she was on the ground and what that hissing noise was that she heard. She felt sharp, stabbing pains on both sides of her abdomen, which made her look down. To her horror, Rose saw a monstrous creature clawing its way up her naked body, its red eyes full of hunger and malice.

Devlin!

His mouth was bloody as his lips scrunched back, revealing those long, deadly fangs. Has he been feeding on me? Is that why I feel so out of it? Rose tried to squirm and crawl away on her back, but Devlin yanked her towards him, refusing to let her escape. As he loomed over her, his bottom jaw quivered with anticipation. Rose kicked and punched him, but nothing she threw at the vampire fazed him. Devlin slid his hips between her thighs and roughly grabbed her by the back of her neck, yanking her up to his face.

Desperation and panic rushed through her mind as she wildly flailed her arms at him. Stupid woman! Why did I tempt this guy? I knew what he could do to me. There's no stopping this freak!

Devlin took a deep breath, inhaling Rose's scent as he licked his sharp, clawed fingers clean. Is that my blood? Oh gods, Rose thought, it *is* my blood, and he's lapping it up like…food! She blanched, knowing what was coming next. Devlin leaned down and slowly licked her neck, tracing her carotid artery with his tongue. Shivers sped throughout her body.

"Rose…" Devlin's voice sounded like death itself, "you taste…divine…"

Rose whimpered as tears rolled down her cheeks. She was helpless under Devlin's assault. What will it feel like having my skin ripped away from my throat?

He put his forehead against hers and let his blood red eyes stare down into her teary ones. "Help me…Rose!" he begged. "Stop me now…before I…hurt you!"

"I can't!" she squeaked out, her voice quavering with terror. "Don't make me suffer. Just kill me and get it over with!"

At war with himself, Devlin roared and snarled. He was like a starving madman who hadn't eaten in three weeks and was tied down to a chair, being forced to gaze at a perfectly cooked steak with all the fixings. He was doing all that he could do to resist biting her. Trying to stay true to his word, he didn't want to hurt her, but he was losing the battle fast.

"Get me off you, Rose! Use your magic!" Devlin growled as he dove towards her neck, his fangs growing longer and sharper.

She closed her eyes, trying to come up with a spell to knock him off her body, but she was too late. Rose felt a slight nick in her neck and then...nothing. Even Devlin's weight was no longer burdening her.

What happened? Rose wondered if she had instinctively cast a spell out of fear and didn't remember doing it. She opened her eyes, wildly looking around for Devlin. The only sight in front of her was a pair of legs that stood over her. She noticed that there were patches of cloth missing from the pants, ripped or bitten out instead of cut...

Duncan!

Rose saw Devlin picking himself up off the cave floor, the wolves encircling him. He tenderly rubbed his jaw, as if he expected it to be broken. What had Duncan done to the vampire? She scrambled to her feet and cowered behind Duncan for safety. Leaning out around Duncan, she watched Devlin as he recovered.

"Thanks, Duncan!" the vampire mumbled. He forced his hand into his mouth and bit down hard on it.

Rose felt queasy watching him feed on his own blood, but she wasn't about to look away. The more he drank, the clearer his eyes became. He turned and faced the wall, refusing to look at them. "I'm sorry, Rose. I've failed your trust. I must go now and feed. Forgive me, Duncan."

Rose saw a tear run down Devlin's cheek. It was red like blood, and his eyes were changing back to those terrifying blood orbs. Without warning, he vanished without a sound.

Duncan's body relaxed as he let out a pent up breath. He walked over and sat down on a nearby rock with a multitude of emotions streaking across his face as he quietly sat in deep thought.

Rose wasn't sure whether to approach him or leave him alone, so she decided to sit down on the gurney. The wolves loomed up around her, wanting to protect her. She was surprised that none of them had attacked Devlin while he was on top of her but, then again, maybe they were afraid of the monster.

Confused, Duncan glanced around at his surroundings. It was then that he saw Rose's robe splayed on another rock near a fire that had no kindling keeping it going.

Duncan snatched the robe off the rock and held it in his hands with care, as if he were holding a baby. He put it up to his face and inhaled, his eyes fluttering. Rose watched him intently and realized that if she was going to figure out what was going on with Duncan and his new magical abilities, she had better do it quick, before he got all secretive again.

She tactfully started her questions — a couple of easy ones first and then she would get to the meatier ones. "Why are you sniffing my robe? You got some sort of fetish I should know about?"

Duncan chuckled under his breath. "It's…" He stopped, trying to say what he couldn't. Finally, he shrugged. "No, you wouldn't understand. You'd just think I was crazy."

"No I won't," Rose snapped back. "Why would you think I'd be so judgmental of you?"

"It wouldn't be the first time, Rose. Have you forgotten already?"

"Just tell me!" Rose insisted, frustration thick in her voice. "You're the second person who's sniffed me today, and I'd like an answer as to why!"

Duncan clutched the robe to his chest, as if he didn't want to give it up. He wouldn't look at her. He just stared down at the ground. "Do you recall what happened to me? Before I woke up in here, I mean?"

Rose answered uneasily, "Yes…"

"It's like a blur to me, but I do remember being overwhelmed by the ghouls and screaming for my life. The thing I remember the most about that moment was the odors: death, putrefaction, grave-breath, rotting cloth. Even that green crap that drips from their mouths smelled worse than all those combined."

He lifted her damp bathrobe once more and inhaled it. As he lowered it into his lap, he smiled. "Breathing in the scent from this simple fabric gives my mind peace. After all those horrible things, I'm still alive and well. It's like breathing in sunshine and roses after a fresh spring rain…the kind of scent I could enjoy being around forever."

All of Rose's frustrations melted away as her lips parted in surprise. She crawled over to Duncan. He seemed different to her. Should she tell him the ghouls had taken several large bites out of his flesh? Would he be mad at her for withholding that from him, even though it was to protect him? More than likely, Duncan despised secrets and lies. How could she bring it up without setting him off in a panic attack or worse, a mental breakdown?

"What else do you remember?" Rose asked as she leaned on his knee, looking up at him.

Duncan grinned. "I recall a certain sorceress flashing her ass at me and making a promise I intend to keep right now!"

Rose felt weightless as Duncan heaved her up off the ground and draped her over his knees. Wow, when did he get this strong? How much had his body changed while he was unconscious?

Duncan placed one hand firmly between her shoulder blades and then he proceeded to gently swat Rose on her firm, curvy ass. "You've been a bad girl."

"Hey!" she protested. "I recall you never did catch up to me—OUCH!"

"Doesn't matter if I kept up, you were being bad, so now I must follow through. You offered this beautiful bounty and now I'm claiming my prize!"

"OUCH! DUNCAN! NOT SO HARD!" Rose cried out.

"What are you talking about?" Duncan asked, feeling confused. "I'm barely tapping you."

"The hell you are! I think my ass is bleeding!"

He reluctantly removed his hand from her backside and saw that he had left giant welts on her in the shape of his hand. He grazed his fingertips over them, making Rose jump and groan in pain. Panic flooded Duncan's mind as he let go of her.

She threw herself off of him and backed away, trying to rub her butt. Each time she touched her backside, though, she flinched and cringed with pain. "If I had known you were a sadist, I'd never have offered myself up to you, asshole!"

"Rose!" Duncan's voice shook with fear. "What's happening to me?"

"What's happening is you're being an abusive dick!"

"No, I'm not!" Duncan pleaded. "Something is really wrong with me, and I'm...afraid."

She rolled her eyes. "Afraid? Afraid of what, Hercules?"

Tears rolled down Duncan's cheeks. "I'm afraid I may hurt you and not know it. I don't know my own strength anymore! I seriously thought I was lightly tapping you!" Rose let her next insult die in her throat as he added, "I'm strong. So strong that I lifted you up like you weighed as light as a feather. I kicked Devlin in the jaw with little effort, but he went flying across the cave away from you."

Rose stared at Duncan and saw that he was visibly shaken. She wondered if it would be a good time to bring up other changes in him that she had witnessed. Meekly, Rose stepped forward and embraced Duncan. She felt his body tense, but then he relaxed. She found herself running her fingers through his thick mane of strawberry blond hair.

"I want to hold you, Rose, but—"

"I understand," she said softly. "I've noticed other changes in you as well."

"Like what?" Duncan leaned more in toward her, but he held off hugging her, fearing he might crush her.

"I'm hesitant to say right now. Seeing that you're in a fragile state—damn it, Duncan, if you accuse me of having secrets or lying to you, so help me, I'll beat the shit out of you!"

He lifted his head to look into Rose's eyes. They sparkled whenever she got emotional and now was no different. She looked tired, though, and needed her rest. Had she even slept since getting them into this cave? How did Devlin figure into all of this? Duncan sensed that Rose was hiding something from him, but at this point he didn't care. He had many questions of his own and wondered if she would be honest with him.

"If I can't handle it, then that's on me," he told her. "I have a lot of gaps that need to be filled in."

"You and me both," Rose huffed, thinking about the death light he had produced to burn the ghouls with.

"Then ask away, Rose. I did promise to explain everything to you back in Melona."

Rose nodded in agreement. Melona would be a good place to start. As far as she knew, her village had been overrun by ghouls and that, somehow, Sully was involved with it because Duncan had worn the guy's head like a trophy around his waist.

Wrapping her arms around Duncan's neck, she sat on his lap, wincing as she settled down.

Duncan gave her a sad look. "Sorry. You sure you want to be this close to me?"

Rose nodded. "I trust you, Duncan Morgan. You're a good man. You poke fun and tease me, but you've never tried to hurt me or do me wrong."

Duncan smiled. She was a powerful sorceress and a good leader for her village. It was a shame that none of her people got out alive. He wondered how she would take the news.

"Tell me what happened to my beautiful village and spare no details?"

He explained how the events started to unfold. He described how the ghouls had gathered at the main gates, as well as the southern wall, just waiting, like they were waiting for orders. He told her how Sully had pushed a button on a small box, causing the south wall to explode, making a hole for the ghouls to get inside.

"Good gods!" she exclaimed as she heard the story. "He brought some of the ghouls into the village, hidden inside his wagon?"

"Yes, and Sully was somehow able to control them. It's like he was a general, and they were his foot soldiers. He had them coordinate an assault on the entrance gates; they removed the planks that locked them shut."

"And you're sure Sully had this ability to control them?"

"Yes, that bastard stood on the platform and preached about how we were all sinners and needed to be cleansed by the ghouls—the weapons of the Savior."

Rose shuddered at the thought. As if the ghouls weren't scary enough on their own, now there are people in the world like Sully who could order them around. How was this possible? Weren't they controlled by whoever set the Christian apocalypse in motion, someone other than their God?

"Was that when you went after him…Sully, I mean?"

"Yes," Duncan said simply.

"I hope you made him suffer!" Rose hissed, bitter about how her home and livelihood had been taken away from her.

Duncan shrugged his shoulders as he looked out at the rain, wondering if it would ever let up. He rubbed his chin stubble as a way to keep from holding Rose like he wanted to. She was beautiful in every sense of the word, but Duncan was a married man and had made a promise to his wife that he would be faithful until death do them part.

His wife may have been reaped five years ago, but in his mind that didn't mean she was dead. Duncan had many opportunities to stray, but he had never been unfaithful to Pamela. If Sully had been reaped and returned, wouldn't it be possible that his wife could return as well?

He sighed and told Rose the rest. When he was finished, he looked down at her. "How the hell did I get eaten alive if I'm still here talking to you?"

"What do you remember?"

"I fell down...I tried to get away...the ghouls were all around me. They lifted me up and were—oh gods!" Duncan's face paled as terror set in. Rose jumped up as he scrambled to his feet. He paced up and down in the cave, clenching his fists. "No, no, no! That didn't happen!" he suddenly blurted out. "How could I live through that? It's impossible! I...I should be dead!"

"But you're not dead, and that's the best part," Rose insisted. "You didn't die saving my sorry ass."

"But I'm not hurt, Rose! I'm not in any kind of pain. I can remember those nasty teeth biting down and ripping my flesh and muscles like I was a walking, talking meatloaf!" Duncan frantically looked down at his body, noting for the first time his shredded clothing and the poultices.

"I was ready to save you from that fate," Rose said softly and shuddered. "I mean, I was ready to kill you, to put you out of that horror, but—"

Duncan looked at Rose with surprise. "So that was your magic I felt in my body? I hate to tell you this, but your mercy spell sucks balls! All it did was force my whole body to vibrate. I felt like a great pressure was going to explode inside me, only it never did."

"I hate to burst your bubble," Rose admitted, "but the magic you felt wasn't mine."

"Oh, so who saved my ass back there then? Did he survive because I'd like to thank the guy?"

"Yes, he did survive," she said softly. "I'm staring at him right now."

Duncan looked over at Rose, wondering if she was messing with him. The grim look on her face, though, told him that she was dead serious. How was this possible? I've got no more magic in me than a rock.

He hurried over to Rose and got inches from her face. "You've got to be shitting me, right? How can I do magic when I don't have any talent for it, let alone know how to wield it?"

Rose gazed into Duncan's confused, watery eyes. There was a tidal wave of emotions inside those cobalt eyes of his, ready to sweep her out to sea if she couldn't give him a proper answer.

Rose placed both hands on his chest and gently caressed him. "I wouldn't lie to you about this. I thought I'd lost you to those monsters. They swallowed you up in that massive horde, and I couldn't release my kill-spell on you. But as it turned out, I didn't have to. You screamed and screamed and then a blast of hot, purple energy came out from inside the horde. The only one in there with the ghouls was you, Duncan."

"Was that when you got me away from them?"

She shook her head. "The energy you released vaporized all of them. Only ashes remained. You were on the ground shaking like you were having a seizure or something."

He grabbed a patch of poultice and began pulling it off his skin.

She watched intently, not sure what they would find. Once Duncan cleared away the last bits of the poultices, Rose let out a sigh of relief while Duncan looked on in amazement. There were no bite marks or any other signs of injury on his body. His wounds had only fresh, pink skin over them. Rose ran her fingers over a place where a wound had been, noticing that it was firm and tight. There were no holes underneath his skin!

"My god, Rose, what were these poultices made of?"

"A combination of herbs that I found in the forest. They're an antiseptic and good for healing. Don't get your hopes up that I'm some grand miracle healer. My poultices didn't do that," she insisted and pointed to the new, pink skin over one of his many wounds. And that brings us to another thing you can do."

"And that is?" Duncan asked cautiously.

"You now can heal yourself quickly. From the looks of this," she poked at the pink skin, "you can regenerate new tissue too."

"This is getting to be too much!" Duncan said as he backed away, rubbing his head.

She watched him as he began to pace again. Duncan had been as ordinary as a man could be. Now, though, it appeared his life had changed as if someone had flipped a switch. Before today, he only had an inner voice he listened to that kept him safe. Now, he had super strength. He could heal his wounds and regenerate new skin, even when unconscious! And where did that ghoul vaporizing ability come from?

Rose pondered all of these pieces of the Duncan Morgan puzzle, and still the picture was incomplete. She knew that there had to be more pieces to come, and Rose felt like a novice magic user compared to Duncan.

"I gotta get out of here," Duncan said suddenly. "I need to take a walk."

"It's raining," she told him.

"I don't care. I've got to get some fresh air!"

As Duncan walked past her, Rose noticed that his physical build had been altered as well. As long as she had known him, his body had been lean and fit. Now, his muscles appeared to bulge out like he'd been lifting weights for years. Duncan's body looked defined and sculpted as if his shredded clothes were feeling the strain of his new physique.

Add the body of a god now, Rose thought jokingly. She suddenly quit laughing inwardly when she realized that thought might not be that far from the truth. This transformation of his physical body was not natural. How had that been achieved in such a short amount of time? Maybe that was why Duncan appeared to be in so much pain when he was comatose. Devlin did say that his body was performing multiple healings. Rose could count his new physique as one of those healings. To her, that would explain what he was now becoming. She stopped and stared after him as he walked out of the cave.

So what was Duncan becoming?

Sleep would hopefully be the key to unlocking the answer to this mystery. The concoction she had taken earlier today still sat heavy in her stomach. She could feel it calling to her to rest and let it take hold over her curious mind. The one place in the cave that looked comfortable to lie down on was the gurney she had made for Duncan. Rose figured he wouldn't mind if she slept on it since he had his sleeping bag with him.

From behind, Rose heard a swift rustling of clothing and a masculine voice clearing his throat to get her attention. She turned around and saw the vampire standing between her and the cave entrance.

Devlin held up his hands in a non-threatening way. "It's okay, Rose. I mean you no harm. I'm sorry about what I almost did to you earlier."

Rose noted the red orbs that were his eyes now looked normal…human. Even his fingernails looked more human than the monstrous claws that had dug into her sides. He seemed calmer which could only mean one thing: Devlin had fed on someone!

Rose shivered violently as she wondered how brutal and cruel he had been on his last "meal" since he couldn't have her. She thought about the horror his victim must have felt, knowing a vampire was taking their life. The thought of Devlin's fangs piercing her skin made her unconsciously put a hand up to cover her neck.

Devlin pursed his lips. "Rose, you need not fear me; the hunger has been sated. There's no call to cover that lovely neck of yours."

Rose snorted. "Ha! Could've fooled me! Just minutes ago, you were ready to rip me to shreds!"

"But I didn't, now did I?"

She shook her head. "That's beside the point. You tried and nearly succeeded. Hell, my sides still sting from where your claws used me as a pincushion! If Duncan hadn't awakened, I'm sure I'd be dead right now!"

"Rose, you injure me more with your words than with any weapon you could slay me with." Devlin pouted, "I tried to warn you, but you wouldn't listen to me, you naughty, little minx. You were not in any danger of being killed."

"I recall you lunging at me and clearly stating your intentions of feeding on me!"

Devlin sighed as he shook his head. "I tried to warn you before that. You never gave me a chance to explain that what you were doing to me was going to get you *fanged*."

"Yeah sure, and I'm supposed to believe that? I swear you—"

"Rose, shut your mouth!" Devlin growled with frustration and anger. He rubbed his face before adding, "Just once, be quiet and listen to what I have to say before you get all defensive and judgmental on me."

Rose stuck her tongue out and flipped him the middle finger, but she remained quiet. She glared at the vampire as she crossed her arms over her bare chest and made a waving motion with her hand for him to continue on.

Devlin grunted but remained calm as he smoothed back his slick, black hair. "As I said before, my two favorite subjects are sex and food. I love them both with a passion because life would be dull and painful without them." Rose cocked her eyebrows as if to say "so?" and he went on, "When I have sex, I have the urge to feed. Unlike the act of feeding for food, this need is for pleasure because I find it stimulating and erotic…as well as intimate on a primal level. If I were to make love to you, you would get *fanged,* but you would share in the pleasure of it because it can create multiple, explosive orgasms for the both of us."

Rose's jaw dropped, and disbelief streaked through her mind. Speechless, she stood there like an idiot at a Mensa meeting. Devlin further revealed the details of his vampiric, sexual intimacies.

"You made it difficult on me," he lectured her, "because you made it all one-sided. As a vampire, I have a need to reciprocate the pleasures so the hunger will stay sated. By doing this, foreplay and love-making can go on for a longer period of time. When the moment is right, I'll dip my fangs into your neck and wring out the orgasms like you never dreamed were possible."

"Big talk, Devlin. It sounds like male bedroom bragging to me."

"I lost your trust today; let me make it up to you."

"I know what I did was bad and stupid," she said. "The blame is on me for pushing you over your limits."

Devlin blushed. "Actually, you're right. In that state, I could've hurt you in more ways than you realize. I was in the state of mind to not only blood-rape you, but rape your body as well. That tends to lead straight into death! I would've done anything to prevent that from happening, but I might not have been able to stop. That's how serious this was for me. I almost succeeded too. I'm indebted to Duncan for his quick mule kick."

Rose leaned against the cave wall as the full weight of what her teasing had nearly caused settled over her. I nearly got raped and killed by a vampire, she thought. All because I was arrogant enough to put him in the same peg-hole as every other man I've come across in my life.

Bile rose up in the back of her throat, and her stomach threatened to empty its contents. Rose felt arms wrap around her and then realized she was in Devlin's embrace.

"I have a peace offering to give you," he said softly. "It's to make up for my lack of control."

"What? More fruits or maybe some wine?" Rose asked and smiled a little.

"I have those too, but they're not my peace offering."

"Spit it out, fang boy!" she insisted. "What have you got that will mend this bad blood between us?"

Chuckling, Devlin replied, "There's nothing bad about your sweet blood, Rose. What I have is the one thing you can't go without. I'm sad to give these to you, but I brought you some clothes."

Chapter 16

Duncan walked quietly in the downpour. I should be a dead man, just like the rest of those villagers I couldn't save. Why was I spared and not them? What's so damn special about me that I should deserve a different fate? Realizing he was suffering from survivor's guilt, he sighed heavily.

He had witnessed firsthand the outcome of ghoul attacks. Very seldom did people survive an attack by a ghoul horde, not if they stayed and fought. People who had been bitten by a ghoul and survived said their wounds never healed properly, and no matter what they put on the bites, the pain never went away.

Duncan sat down on a nearby moss covered rock and pulled one leg across his thigh. As he brushed more of Rose's poultice herbs off him, he noticed that his back wasn't hurting. Ten years ago, he had been working at a construction site as an electrician. He was on a ladder feeding wires into the ceiling when another guy walked into the room with a long piece of plywood. The man hadn't seen Duncan or the ladder and ran into them both.

He had lost his balance as one of his legs slipped between the gaps of the ladder rungs, breaking his leg and his fall at the same time. It also put a permanent pain in his lower back, but over the years he had learned to deal with it. The only time it gave him fits was if he sat cross-legged or any way other than having both of his feet firmly on the ground.

Twisting and turning, he tested his back. He smiled with the knowledge that he could once again sit and relax however he wanted without having to struggle to find a pain-free position. It gave him the notion to go running through the forest or maybe climbing a nearby tree. Duncan felt ten feet tall and bulletproof, like there was nothing he couldn't do. If his body healed itself this quickly, then what couldn't he do? For now, Duncan used the rain to help wash away any residual poultice herbs.

He looked up, and off in the distance he saw a natural waterfall caused by the rainstorm. It had washed off the rocky top side of a large embankment, and down below that was a small pool of runoff water that had pounded into a grassy area.

Duncan stood up and jogged over towards the waterfall, figuring it would make it easier to clean Rose's herbal medicine off his body. Too bad I don't have any soap or shampoo, he mumbled. He stripped off his tattered, wet clothes and carelessly tossed them on the ground. Happily stepping into the pool of water, he grimaced from the cold and shivered. He didn't care; the frigid water felt good on his body.

He took a step toward the waterfall, and the ground gave way, causing the grass below his feet to feel like a sponge. Duncan closed his eyes as he stepped under the cascading water, imagining that he was back in his old home with his wife showering together.

He moaned as he recalled that last night with her. He had just gotten home from work and discovered that Pamela was in the shower with the bathroom door wide open. The steam from the hot water fogged up the mirrors and the glass shower door. He stood there watching her silhouette swaying as she ran her bath sponge over her body.

He couldn't resist. He quietly stripped off his clothes and sneaked into the bathroom. Opening the shower door, he stepped inside, surprising Pamela by grabbing her from behind. As she screamed out in surprise, Duncan spun her around to show it was him.

She hit at him, although not very hard. "You scared me, goofball!" They stayed in the shower making love for a good twenty minutes. He sighed, happily remembering. Then, for some reason, Pamela's face and body slowly melted from his mind, and she was replaced by the image of Rose.

Guilt crept into his whole being. Surely there was nothing wrong with fantasizing about another woman. He found himself touching his erect member more than scrubbing down his body. As he did this, he got the feeling that he was being watched.

Duncan didn't care because it was either Rose or the vampire, Devlin. He wanted to get clean and wasn't going to be a prude around either of those two. Suddenly, Duncan froze. What if ghouls were watching and waiting for him?

He opened his eyes and warily looked around. No one was there, and the voice in his head was quiet. That didn't mean he wasn't alone though. He still felt as if someone was watching him. Duncan knew his sword was a few feet away, and he could easily grab it if need be. He quickly decided to draw the person out by turning his back to the forest and facing the embankment.

If they think my guard is down, then that should entice them to show themselves to me. He listened intently over the sounds of the falling water. Duncan wondered if it was Rose, Devlin, or the Chouls. Who else would be out here in the middle of the forest at night? Whoever it is, he thought, they're not going to like me if they're looking for a fight.

The snap of a downed tree branch caught his attention, but Duncan still made no move towards his sword. He turned slowly with his eyes barely opened so he could survey the area once more. Movement to his right was sudden and quick — too quick! Whoever it was, it couldn't be human!

Duncan bolted to his sword, grabbed it up, and prepared himself mentally for a fight. Whatever this thing was, it had crept up on him with the stealth of a…paranormal creature. With his heart pounding in his chest, he quickly turned his head, darting his eyes all around, hunting for any signs of the one hunting him.

"All right," Duncan snarled loudly, "you've had your fun. Now show yourself!"

The forest was quiet, with the exception of the rain and the waterfall behind him. Duncan felt like a fool standing naked in the water with his sword in hand. "Rose would so love to see this," Duncan grumbled, just above his breath.

He stepped out of the water. Wanting to reach down, grab up his clothes and get dressed, he didn't. Something inside him told him to stay on alert. Every muscle in his body tensed as he readied himself for this interloper.

Several tree branches snapped and fell harmlessly to the ground. Duncan looked over in the direction of the sound and saw a small figure sitting on a tree branch. He blinked his eyes and saw that this person wasn't sitting at all, but was hanging upside down and fiddling with its tiny hands.

Now that he saw the creature, the inner voice finally spoke up: *BROKEN SADNESS*. Duncan tried to glare up at his brain, muttering sarcastically, "Thank you, Captain Cryptic!"

The being finally looked over at him and must have noticed that he was aware of it. Suddenly, it waved at him! Confusion racked Duncan's brain, but he decided to wave back at the being.

It kicked itself off the tree branch and landed on the ground. Despite all the brush and tree branches under its feet, it made no sound.

So the noise it made was for my benefit, Duncan thought. Its way of knocking where there was no door. He leaned over and grabbed his tattered pants off the ground. They were soaked from the rain, but they were all he had, in the way of pants, and he was about to put them on.

He froze as a soft hand caressed his back. Each touch felt like electricity kissing his bare skin. He frantically looked toward the tree, but that creature was no longer there.

"You are beautiful to gaze upon," a soft, feminine voice spoke. "I should know because I've been watching you."

Duncan panicked, and he slipped in the slick mud, falling backwards into the pool of water. He scrambled to his feet and backed up. With his heart raging in his chest, he noticed that he had dropped his sword by the female creature's feet.

Damn, she was fast, he thought and cringed. She now had his only means of defense and could kill him if she chose to do so. The petite woman dropped down on her knees and looked at Duncan like he was some unknown creature to be studied. She wore a very old but stylish long, flowing, blue gown that matched her beautiful, sapphire eyes. She seemed sad, her eyes puffy with dark circles around them as though she had been crying.

"Why do you fear me? I'm not here to hurt you. At least, I don't think I'm supposed to. I don't want to hurt you."

"You startled me." Duncan flashed a sheepish grin. "I wasn't expecting you to be this close to me after you got out of the tree."

"What tree?" She looked confused.

"That one over there," he said and pointed.

The woman turned and looked toward the trees. Sighing heavily, she looked back at Duncan with a great sadness in her eyes. He lowered his arm and wondered what made her so sad. She was a beautiful lady and other than the dark circles under her eyes, her skin was flawless.

She slammed her right fist into the pool of water where Duncan was standing. The water violently shot up into the air like it was a geyser. "I can't remember! My mind is…broken, and I can't remember!"

Duncan realized that's what his inner voice meant when it said *broken sadness.* Obviously, the lady was having problems remembering things, and that might be where her sadness comes from.

Pity for the woman stabbed at his heart, but Duncan figured it would be good to get whatever answers he could from her before she forgot everything. Then again, she might be here to kill him and had forgotten it. With her speed, the battle would be over before Duncan knew he was in a fight.

"Calm down, my lady," Duncan said in a calming voice. "I didn't mean to upset you."

The woman looked up at him quizzically and then suddenly gasped, "Oh boy, you're naked! Are we lovers?"

Duncan stifled his own gasp and chuckled. How many men of lesser honor had taken advantage of this poor woman? Duncan shrugged his shoulders at her and replied, "I'm afraid not. You caught me here bathing. What's your name?"

"My name is Purah. If you're bathing, can I scrub your back?"

Duncan smiled and shook his head. "No, I'd just finished and was about to get dressed when I saw you."

"But you're still in the water. It looks like you're still bathing to me."

He was getting nowhere fast. "Why are you here, Purah?" he asked bluntly.

She looked around, her eyes suddenly full of tears. "Where is here? Why am I here? Are you sure we're not together in some way because I feel we are?"

"You're in a forest near the village of Melona. We're together because you just came here, and we met. That's about all I know."

Purah tilted her head as she gazed at Duncan. He wasn't sure what could be going on in her mind, but he figured she was trying to remember the two of them meeting here just now. He stood up and walked out of the water towards his clothes.

"You have the body of a divine one; did we make love here?"

Duncan snatched up his pants and tugged them on, noting that they were snugger than he remembered. He figured it had to be because they were drenched from the rain. Glancing over at her, pity welled up in his heart for her. She didn't know if they had made love or not. What an existence!

"No, we didn't make love, Purah," Duncan replied as he slipped on his shirt. It too was snug.

"Are you sure? Why else would you walk around naked in front of me?"

"I was naked because I was bathing. You've been watching me, so what's the point in me being modest in front of you? You've seen it all." Duncan smiled.

Purah stared blankly at him as he reached down and picked up his sword. Something about her didn't sit well with him. What exactly was she? He hadn't seen any fangs when she spoke, so he figured she wasn't a vampire.

 He sheathed his sword and stepped over to Purah, extending his hand to help her up off the ground. She took his hand and then suddenly started convulsing, like she was having a small seizure. Duncan cursed, blaming himself for her reaction.

He quickly guided her back down, laying her on her back. Uncomfortable with touching this strange woman, he immediately withdrew his hands from her. According to Rose, he didn't know his own strength, and now he caused convulsions! "What is happening to me?" he growled just above his breath.

He paced back and forth, considering on running back to the cave and bringing Rose out here to check on Purah. Rose knew a thing or two about medical treatments, but would she know how to deal with what this woman was going through? The sorceress took care of me, so why wouldn't she be able to do the same for her?

Before he could take a step to head back to the cave, Duncan noticed something else about Purah: She was glowing!

She groaned as she turned over on her stomach, and the glow was getting brighter by the moment. A blue haze of light shimmered all over her body. It pulsated in rhythm with each of her convulsions. She looked otherworldly, like she belonged amongst the stars and not down here on this hellhole called Earth.

Duncan was at a loss on what he should do. He finally decided to stay by her side and make sure she didn't flop over into the water and drown. He squatted down beside Purah. At that moment, he heard it. His inner voice screamed out, *TOUCH HER!*

Duncan immediately placed his hands on her. Purah's body stilled as her convulsions slowly dissipated. The blue haze of light shimmered around her body, until it swirled and faded into a dark hue of purple.

Am I causing this poor woman to suffer? How much more pain will I inflict on others? Duncan pulled his hands away from Purah to see what would happen. Instantly, she convulsed again. Duncan rolled his eyes and decided to pick her up and cradle her prone body in his lap.

"I'm touching her. Are you happy now?" he demanded of his inner voice. "Now tell me why I have to do this in the first place?"

No Response.

"Figures!" he growled. Duncan felt his inner voice could at least guide him a little better than this. What's the point of having it if it won't teach me or help me understand what the hell I'm doing?

What is that voice anyway, and what am I becoming? Duncan rubbed his hands along Purah's back to soothe her. Just then, he felt something odd. He gently turned her so he could examine her better. Through the purple haze, he saw that she had strange tendrils that were physically a part of her. They were all bunched together and teemed with energy. Was this the source of her great speed? What function, if any, did they provide her?

He looked back at the cave and wondered how Rose was holding up. She had been through a lot today. She'd lost her home, nearly got eaten by the ghouls, and then she'd almost became a meal for a vampire.

Duncan felt movement in his lap. He looked down and saw Purah had curled her arms around his waist and was gazing up at him, her sapphire blue eyes sparkling. He smiled down at her.

For whatever reason, she made his whole being heat up, causing a full body blush. What is she and why does she seem so comfortable with me?

It wasn't that he didn't find her attractive. Purah had a beauty that ran deep inside her. What held him back from pursing this mystery woman was a promise he'd made to his wife, Pamela. He had told her he would always be faithful to her. He rarely made promises, but when he did, he kept them or would die trying.

Over the years, people insisted that his wife had been *reaped* by a grim reaper and was probably dead. "You should move on with your life," they would tell him. "Find a girl and settle down with her."

The problem was that he had already found a girl and had settled down with her. Now she was gone. What if she came back? If he hooked up with another woman, and Pamela showed up on his doorstep one day, what would happen? He shuddered at the thought.

Pamela had not been a good woman or a good wife. She constantly bickered with him and fought over the littlest of things. When she wasn't doing that, she expected him to clean the house and cater to her every whim as she slept around with other men. It was Hell; he knew that. But he had made a promise that he would remain faithful and never leave her, and he wasn't going to break it.

His best friends, who Pamela didn't like, argued that he should leave her. They didn't understand how a promise could mean so much to him or how he would rather die than break one. But, then again, they broke their promises all the time.

One of his friends thought Duncan had mental problems, that the promise was some sort of OCD--Obsessive-compulsive disorder. Another friend thought that it stemmed from childhood traumas that he had forgotten. They all felt sorry for him.

If he discovered Pamela was really dead, then he would move on without having the burden of guilt weighing on his weary shoulders.

"Why are you so sad, Duncan?"

He looked down at Purah. "I'm not sad, just distracted and have lots on my mind."

"No, you're sad, and I can tell. I know sadness all too well. It feeds me and makes me stronger."

Confused, Duncan asked, "How can you do that? What kind of person would want to feed on misery?"

"I've been cursed; I made the ultimate choice long ago."

"What happened?"

"I went against the Will of the Creator and defied Him. He cast us out for our transgressions against Him. My curse was to do the opposite of what I did when I was in the Heavens."

Duncan wondered how long this lucidity in her memory would last. He wanted to know more and glean as much as he could from this Heavenly being before she shut down and forgot everything.

Wait! Was she claiming to be an angel, one that was kicked out of Heaven? That would explain the tendrils on her back; those had to be her wings. "Are you an angel?"

"I was…once, but no longer. I'm now considered a fallen angel. Most humans would say I'm a demon, but I'm not. Demons are different from us in so many ways."

"Did it hurt when you fell from Heaven?" Duncan asked and struggled to stifle a laugh. Wow, did I really ask that corny pickup line?

"Yes it did, and I'm still suffering from its affects. I will for the rest of my days. My wings didn't obey my commands, and I hit Earth, head first. That was when my curse began."

"Tell me about this curse?"

"It's an opposite or reversal curse. Whatever you once could do, you now do the opposite. I was the one who eased the grieving and suffering of Mankind, so they could transition and move on with their lives. Now I feed off the sadness and suffering of others. I gain strength and power from it, like tribute does for deities. The injuries I sustained have caused me to forget many things and conversations, and that frustrates me into sadness and tears. In a way, I feed off myself too."

"How is it possible for you to have a conversation this long with me and not forget?"

Purah studied on the question for a couple of minutes. "I can't say for certain, but it's strange that a mortal could cause my mind to feel normal once more."

"Lately," Duncan said, "I haven't been feeling so mortal. I'm changing, and I'm not sure I like it. Today I was being eaten alive by the Chouls. Yet, all my wounds have healed in a matter of hours. Does that sound like something a mortal can do?"

"That's impossible! Your body is too weak and fragile; it would never heal like that unless you were otherworldly like me."

"Otherworldly? No," he insisted. But there was some sort of connection between the two of them. He knew that much. He could feel it. Where had it come from, though, and why now? Did it have to do with the recent changes in his body?

"What's a Choul?" she asked.

He chuckled. "It's the name I use for those undead, Christian ghouls that prowl the land."

Purah looked saddened as her gaze went from his face down to his abdomen. Duncan wondered why she would feel so…ashamed. She hadn't marched the ghouls into Melona to "cleanse everyone's sins". That bastard Sully had done that. Duncan felt a sense of pride for slaying the man. He had been responsible for the deaths of a lot of good, decent people. Those people were just trying to survive and take care of their loved ones, and that Bible-thumping prick decided to come along and murder them all.

"Did the ghouls hurt you badly?" Purah asked but never looked directly at him.

"Yes. What's wrong? Why are you so upset?"

Purah looked up at him, her eyes pleading. "It's my fault you got hurt. Don't hate me for my role in it."

Duncan's heart ached for the little creature as he looked into her eyes. Her tears were about to spill out and mix with the rain. He ran his fingers through her silky, black hair while trying to soothe her.

"You had nothing to do with it. It was some asshole named Sully who—"

She gasped in surprise. "Sully's Fallen Warriors of the Light did this to you?"

Duncan felt a chill run up his spine. "You know Sully and his little army of Chouls? Why did he attack us?"

"It's what they're supposed to do. Their job is to cleanse Earth of all those who weren't taken to the Promised Land. Certain ones are chosen to lead a group of Fallen Warriors of the Light throughout the land and rid it of all the sinners and heretics who didn't give themselves over to Jesus."

Duncan was ready to ask his next question, but he felt he already knew the answer. If Sully was one of the many people who had been reaped, it stood to reason that Pamela was still alive also. Was she like Sully, a blood-thirsty murderer of innocent people? Was she the same manipulative, lazy, cheating bitch that he had once loved...and hated?

He wanted to know, but something inside him seemed to hold him back from asking. Bloody coward! Duncan chastised himself. Still, he needed to know if she lived or not. If she had died, then he would be free to be with someone else. Deep down, though, he believed that she was alive.

"Is that where you live, the Promised Land?" Duncan asked.

"Yes, I live there. Although to me, it feels more like a prison. I tend to wander off which annoys the other fallen angels because they're afraid I might get hurt or taken advantage of."

Duncan was about to ask her another question when he got interrupted by a loud, booming voice. It was both menacing and melodious at the same time.

"Hands off her, you loathsome, hairless ape!"

Chapter 17

Purah turned her head to see who had spoken. It was Penemuel; he hovered in the air a few yards from them, looking haggard, like he was hurt and had been flying around for a long while. His sword was drawn, and death sat in his angry eyes.

"A friend of yours?" Duncan asked but never took his eyes off the other fallen angel.

"It's Penemuel. He's here to take me home. He might try to kill you for being with me."

"Good," Duncan growled, eying the other fallen angel, imagining him as being on the same level as Sully. "I'm spoiled for a good fight!"

As Duncan's words settled into Purah's injured brain, she began to panic. "No! No, don't! You're no match for him! He'll kill you, and I don't want that to happen!"

"Then talk to him. Make him see reason."

Purah shook her head. "I doubt I'll remember why I went to talk to him. I…I don't want to lose you, Duncan!"

"Final warning, human! Let her go, and you might live to see the dawn…maybe," Penemuel hissed.

Duncan rolled his eyes. He lifted Purah up off his lap and set her on her feet as if she weighed next to nothing. He yelled back at Penemuel, "Keep your holy roller panties on. I'd rather not hurt you. There's no need for violence."

Penemuel glowered at Duncan as he hovered in the air, glowing brightly. His wings slapped back and forth, causing the plants around him to sway in the wind he created.

Duncan noted that some of the tendrils in Penemuel's wings were missing as if they were damaged. The fallen angel struggled to hover as he maintained his menacing appearance. If I can take out his wings, would that force him to fight like a man, Duncan mused as he plotted his attack.

No longer in physical contact with Duncan, Purah stared off into space, looking around like she couldn't recall where she was. Her memory had failed her once again.

Duncan side-stepped her to show the other fallen angel that he was no threat to her. Penemuel only glared at Duncan as he commanded, "Purah, come here now! You need to get away from that filth. I need you to help me figure out who destroyed your creations!"

Purah looked all around her, spinning several times before asking, "What filth? I don't see any filth here…just a lovely waterfall."

"I think he's referring to me as the filth, Purah," Duncan muttered under his breath, but she heard him.

"You, sir, are not filth. I can see that from here." As she stared at him, she smiled and breathed out a pleasant sigh. "For some reason, I feel so drawn to you."

"Purah!" Penemuel hissed, his patience waning. "You know better than to associate with humans! He could hurt you. I can't allow that to happen. I'm putting my life on the line to see that you are returned to the Promised Land safe and unmolested!"

"Humans?" Purah said, confused, as she looked around. "There are no humans here!"

Duncan glanced at Purah to see if she was mocking Penemuel. He saw in her facial expressions that she genuinely believed what she was saying. Duncan kept his sword sheathed, but his hand was firmly on its hilt.

Penemuel landed softly on the ground without making a sound. He cautiously walked up to Purah and looked her over. As he did, she reached behind him and snatched hold of one of the broken tendrils from his wings. "What did you do to yourself?"

Duncan watched intently, making mental notes, as Penemuel grimaced in pain while Purah tugged and pulled on the injured tendril.

She glanced over at Duncan and then up at Penemuel before saying, "Did our brother send you out to fetch me?"

"Yes he did, but I also have a task for you to perform."

"Oh, a task!" Purah jumped up and down, clapping her hands in delight, causing sparks to appear. "Why didn't you say so in the first place?"

Penemuel sighed. "I did, but you forgot again. This human has to die for touching you, Purah. You know this. It's tradition."

"No human has touched me — only Duncan there."

"He's the fucking human!" Penemuel roared, anger and frustration swelling in his chest. The trees shook from the force of his words. "Are you so blind that you can't see this creature for what he truly is?"

Purah placed her hands on Penemuel's chest as she looked up at him with pity in her sapphire blue eyes. "That's the problem. You don't see him the way that I do."

Just then, Rose and the vampire ran up to Duncan. "Devlin said…you were in…trouble," Rose gasped out, nearly breathless from running. "He heard…someone threaten you!"

The vampire glared at Penemuel, his fangs lengthening for a fight.

Purah looked over and saw the two strangers. She used her chin to point at Rose. "If that's the human you keep referring to, by all means, end her life. She's the only human here, Penemuel. The others are not human."

Penemuel snarled at the two newcomers. His sword flared a bright hue of blue, and it appeared to be on fire. He took to the air and flew as quickly as he could, aiming his sword at Rose's head, murder in his fiery eyes.

Feeling as if she was moving in slow motion, Rose attempted to unsheathe her katana. She barely had her hand on its hilt when Penemuel was practically on top of her, his blue-flaming sword reared back, ready to strike. She screamed and closed her eyes, waiting for the pain and knowing full well that she wouldn't have her katana out in time.

The next thing she saw was darkness, and her body felt weightless and light. Am I dead? she marveled. Is this what death is like? Is my soul flying away from this terrible world and into a better place? Her reality came crashing back to her as she heard cursing and felt a possessive hand around her waist.

"It's okay, Rose. You're safe for the moment," Devlin whispered into her ear.

Rose opened her eyes wide and looked around, her gaze finally focusing on the vampire. So that's what it feels like to be teleported. It was strange, for sure, but a lot better than having her head lying on the ground, her dead eyes staring at her own decapitated body.

She knew Devlin's murderous stare was meant for the winged prick. Questions were speeding through her mind: was that an angel who tried to kill me? What did I do to deserve death from a holy being? Who is that tiny bitch who told him he could kill me?

She saw that Duncan had his own sword out and was parrying the blows from Penemuel's enchanted sword. Duncan seemed to match the angel's speed with his own agility and quick reflexes, which frustrated Penemuel. Rose wanted to help Duncan kill the angel, but Devlin held on to her tightly. "Let me go, damn it! I can help!"

"No you can't," the vampire growled.

"Hey, I'm a big girl; I can take care of myself!" She squirmed and wriggled, trying to escape Devlin's tight hold.

"You'd be dead as soon as he saw you. I almost didn't get you out of there in time."

Rose glared at him. "Like you'd stand a chance against him yourself. I see that look in your eyes."

"I'd have more than a sporting chance against that creature, but I'm torn."

"Torn? Torn between what?"

Devlin finally tore his gaze from the fight and locked his eyes on to Rose. "I want to fight him, but I don't want to leave you here unprotected. You're stubborn, and I know you'd run headlong into the fight." He chortled as he added, "Don't deny it because that's how you are. I know you don't normally need protection, but in this case, you need to be protected from yourself."

Rose huffed irritably. "If I can't fight, and you're to be my chaperone, then let's go talk to that tiny twerp over there and see what she knows!"

Rose and Devlin turned toward Purah, and both of them gasped in unison. Purah was dancing around under the waterfall with her wings spread open. She looked like a little kid with her arms reaching up to the sky and grinning, seemingly oblivious to the fight that was happening thirty feet away from her.

Devlin sniggered. "I'm certain that one isn't quite right in her head."

"It doesn't matter; the little bitch will tell me what I want to know," Rose snapped as she rolled up her sleeves. "And if she doesn't, I'll beat it out of her angelic ass!"

Duncan and Penemuel slowly circled each other, their swords held high, ready to fight. Duncan wasn't exactly sure how he was managing to fend off Penemuel's attack, but he knew he had to strike a killing blow because his luck could run out fast. Is the guy toying with me? Is that why I'm doing so well?

Penemuel's grip tightened on the hilt of his sword as he swung a barrage of slashing arcs and jabs. To his surprise, Duncan blocked each blow.

"Your skills are par with mine, human," Penemuel said in mocking tone. "It's too bad that you're not as gifted with a sword as I am. But then, I've had eons of practice."

Duncan grinned. "Shut up and fight, wounded bird boy!"

Penemuel gasped at the word, wounded, and memories of Sorath shredding his wings' inner tendrils flooded his mind. He felt the pain again, the weariness from flying with only half-working wings. Once again, he felt the energy from his wings suddenly extinguish, as if someone had blown out a candle.

He hovered in front of Duncan, growling angrily. He wasn't growling at the man; he was growling at Sorath. And when he lunged at Duncan with an abdominal thrust, Penemuel was aiming at Sorath.

Swatting the angelic sword away as he side-stepped the blow, Duncan countered with a right hook to Penemuel's jaw. The blow staggered the fallen angel as he back-pedaled away from Duncan. He rubbed his jaw, surprised that this human's punch could actually hurt him. Over the years, he'd been punched by other humans, and the fight had always ended with the same results: a broken hand for the human and an unfazed Penemuel. He glanced at Duncan's hands and noted that he wore no gauntlet or protective gloves of any kind, and he appeared to be the one unfazed.

Penemuel twirled his sword as he hovered above the ground. He was determined to end this battle now since it was clear a fair fight with the mortal on the ground would be a stalemate.

He shot up into the air and swooped down towards Duncan, slashing away through his defenses and running his blade through his shoulder. Duncan cried out in pain and clutched his upper left arm. His skin felt on fire, and it grew hotter with each passing second. Again, the fallen angel swooped past Duncan, spinning him around. The blue, flaming blade found its mark just behind the man's knee, instantly dropping him to the ground.

Rose watched Duncan struggling to stand as Penemuel turned around to strike again, possibly a killing blow. She pushed herself away from Devlin and summoned fireballs to both of her hands. She had to time it just right or Duncan would be skewered by the fallen angel.

"Let them fly, Rose!" Devlin hissed angrily as he watched Penemuel gloat.

As Penemuel started his dive toward Duncan, Rose bit her lip, praying to the Goddess that her attack would find its mark. She flung both fireballs at the same time. One struck Penemuel's hand, disarming him, and the other one burst on his hip, flames engulfing his body. He abruptly landed and used his hands and wings to shove the flames off him. To both Devlin and Rose's surprise, the flames easily floated off the fallen angel's body, and were held stationary in the air.

Penemuel glared at her as he roared, "Your turn to burn, bitch!" He twisted his body and used his wings to cast Rose's own flames back at her.

She put her hand out to command them, but the flames wouldn't obey her. As the fire shot toward her, Devlin tackled Rose to the ground and covered her with his body. He grunted in pain as the flames passed over them, scorching his clothes and skin, but the vampire held on to Rose with everything he had. Once the fire was gone, Devlin teleported away without warning.

Rose scrambled to her feet. She looked over at Penemuel, who was still scowling at her.

"When I finish with this worm," he growled coldly, "you'll be the next to die."

Rose gulped, but she stood her ground defiantly. More splashing to her right caught her attention. Rose nervously glanced over and saw Devlin standing under the waterfall while Purah danced around him, splashing more water on him. He eyed her with annoyance as she bent over and splashed even more water on him from between her legs. He teleported back to Rose's side and growled, "No doubt about it, she's a few bags shy of having a full blood bank."

Duncan could feel that strange surge of energy flowing throughout his body once more. A little purple light caught his eye, and he looked closely at his injured shoulder. To his astonishment, his wounds were healing right before his eyes. Everywhere the purple light shined, it tingled in a good way. He felt the same sensation coming from his leg and now he wondered if he would be fully healed.

Penemuel stretched out his arm, and his sword flew effortlessly to his hand. He twirled it with an air of arrogance as he strolled up to Duncan. Turning his smug face down at the man, the fallen angel pointed the tip of his blade at Duncan's heart.

Duncan felt the surge of energy building within his body, screaming for an outlet.

"You fought well...for a mortal, that is. Alas, though, you were no match for me. Do you have any last words that I may write upon your gravestone?" Penemuel mocked.

"Yes, I do." Duncan clenched his hand tightly on the hilt of his sword. "I kicked an angel's ass!"

Penemuel grimaced with rage, which was the distraction Duncan needed. The man swung his weapon and bashed Penemuel's sword out of his hand with the loud clang of steel hitting steel. Duncan sprung up from the ground and gave the fallen angel an explosive upper cut punch.

Penemuel flew up in the air and landed hard on the ground about ten feet from where Duncan stood. As the stunned fallen angel rolled on the ground, Duncan charged at him. Was the purpose of this strange magic for fighting? He decided to test his newfound abilities, and he jumped.

Chapter 18

Duncan soared through the air effortlessly, feeling light as a feather. He instinctively knew he had command of where he would land if he focused on the spot. That's what he did. He concentrated on the ground right behind Penemuel as the fallen angel rose to his feet.

Duncan grabbed both of Penemuel's wings and, with one swift motion, he sliced them off with his sword. Penemuel let out a blood curdling scream as he dropped to his knees. The fallen angel reached behind his back in a panic, tears streaming down his face as realization hit him hard. A human had just grounded him!

Duncan let the lifeless wings drop to the ground as Penemuel rolled over on his back to face him. He crawled backwards away from the man, fear finding a home in his wide, manic stare. Duncan crept toward him with a grin of satisfaction.

He noticed that his newfound magical energy was demanding his attention once more, and he decided to let it guide him as to what he should do next. Duncan saw his arm extend out, and his hand open as if it waited to shake someone's hand. He frowned. "You want me to shake the angel's hand?" Duncan growled at his magic. He shook his head adamantly. "No way!" At that moment, his eyes locked on to Penemuel's sword, which lay on the ground off in the distance.

He heard his inner voice mentally command, *COME TO ME*, and Penemuel's sword lifted off the ground and glided its way to his hand. Duncan grinned as he pitched his own sword on the grass. He gripped the hilt of the angelic sword tightly. It was magnificent, like nothing he'd ever seen before.

He sliced it through the air. Suddenly, it thrummed with power — with a rhythm only he could hear. As he hoisted the sword toward the sky, the blade began to glow with purple flames. It was no longer Penemuel's sword; it now belonged to Duncan.

Rose and Devlin walked past Duncan and grabbed Penemuel by his arms, lifting him to his feet. He was still wailing in pain from losing his wings.

"Looks like you're the one who will be the next to die," Rose mocked with a smirk.

Devlin sniffed. "Hmm, I wonder what his blood taste like." He turned to Rose with a questioning look on his face. "Do angels have blood? I smell only energy from this creature, like he's a husk held together by energy."

Penemuel's face paled, and his mouth gaped open when he noticed Duncan holding his angelic sword. Words strained to roll off his tongue as disbelief muted his vocal cords. Finally, he squeaked out, "No! T-That's impossible! No one can wield our weapons but the rightful owners!"

Rose looked at Duncan and did a double take. Not only was the fallen angel's sword glowing purple now, but Duncan's eyes were blazing with the same purple energy. There was even a hint of purple light surrounding his whole body. What was he? "Man, his powers are growing faster than I would have thought possible," Rose said in awe. As he stood before them, Duncan's body showed signs that it too had grown in mass.

The vampire glanced over at his friend. "He's different, that's for sure," he agreed and chuckled. He immediately went back to thrashing Penemuel.

Duncan lowered the angelic sword as he stepped up to the fallen angel. He steadied himself so he wouldn't release the ever-building energy. It was so strong Duncan feared that it would be more powerful than what had vaporized the ghouls earlier, and he didn't want that fate to fall on Rose or Devlin.

He pressed the tip of the sword against Penemuel's throat and asked, "What makes you think you're so much better than all of us? You fly in here and threaten my friends, expecting us to roll over and let you get away with it? Give me one good reason why I shouldn't take off your head."

Penemuel gulped. "I know things…things that could be beneficial to you."

"I know one thing, you'd better answer all of our questions honestly, or I'll start hacking off body parts. I'll start with your feet and work my way up. Do we have an understanding or should I provide you with an example?"

"I understand." Penemuel's voice trembled with fear. He glanced down nervously at his own sword as Duncan poked him in his throat with it, causing blood to trickle out.

Devlin instantly swiped his finger through the trail of blood and lifted it to his nose, inhaling the scent deeply before he suckled on his finger. He crinkled his nose in disgust. "Meh, I've had better blood from a diseased rat. Now, where do you reside?"

Penemuel glared at the vampire but didn't make a move. He looked back at Duncan, wondering if he could still *will* his weapon. He focused intently on his sword but nothing happened.

Without warning, Rose smacked the fallen angel on the back of his head and snapped, "Devlin asked you a question, answer him!"

"My place is where one of the mighty oceans once thrived. We live in a golden palace known as the Promised Land, though if I don't return Purah back soon, I might as well be dead."

"That's your problem, not mine," Duncan said coldly.

"Actually, it will be your problem too because Sorath wants Purah at his side. He'll raze this world once more if she isn't returned to him."

"But," Rose chimed in, "I thought it was Jesus who caused all the destruction?" She frowned. "By the way, how did He destroy the world and reap all those people?"

"He didn't do either. Long ago, a small group of us fallen angels came up with a plan to screw over our Father, the Creator. Sorath had Xaphan unleash the worldwide firestorms, while Wormwood crept throughout the countryside spreading famine, sickness and disease. Purah, over there, was tasked with recruiting all the humans who had given their hearts to the Christ and took them back to the Promised Land. Once she was done gathering our holy army, Purah had to raise those who had died and add their names to the Book of Life. They would help rid the world of the undesirable humans who hadn't been collected…or couldn't be controlled."

Duncan's gaze went over to Purah. She sat on top of a large embankment, upside down with her head and back in the running water, her tendril wings flaring out every so often. Was that why she felt bad about him getting attacked and nearly eaten alive by the Chouls? The walking dead were here on Earth because she raised them from their graves. How could she be capable of doing all those things without forgetting before she could finish the job?

Duncan found it hard to believe, but Purah had said it was her fault and that she blamed herself. She looked like a free spirit, a child of nature, more than a bringer of the Christian apocalypse.

"Don't let her looks deceive you," Penemuel warned. "That one did all those things because Sorath enlisted her help. She has the ability to raise the dead from their slumber. She is bound to him as are the rest of us. We made this pact long ago."

"What exactly was this pact?" Devlin asked. He had stopped thrashing the fallen angel and now sat on a boulder, watching him.

"To aide Sorath in his bid to rule the world," Penemuel explained. "He wanted people to worship him as a god, under the guise of Jesus of Nazareth. I'm sure you're all familiar with the story of Revelations." He grinned with pride. "I wrote it."

"Where do you fit into all of this?" Duncan asked.

"I'm the one who made writing possible for you hairless apes. I gave Mankind that gift shortly after I fell to Earth, so I could influence him. As the prophets wrote their stories in the Bible, I added my magic and was able to make people read the Bible and get completely different messages from the stories. That's why there are so many religions and denominations in the world." He beamed a devious smile that oozed arrogance. "My greatest ability is to sway others with a few strokes of my quill pen. Many wars have been started because of me."

"Why would you want to do that?" Rose asked.

He shrugged. "I get bored easily, and I love to write. Why not entertain myself at someone else's expense? People never knew exactly how their feuds began, but in the end it didn't matter because they tended to annihilate each other."

"Let me guess," Rose sneered, "that was why you were cast out of Heaven."

"No, you pitiful excuse of a worm," Penemuel hissed. "We were cast down because we demanded that our Father love us above his hairless apes. He had become blinded to us and saw humanity as being in His own image, thus loving you more than us. When compared to you, we were second-rate citizens in His eyes."

"Oh, boohoo!" Rose said sarcastically. "Someone's got daddy issues and got kicked out of his house and now wants to throw a wittle fit down here on Earth. Grow up and get a life, you spoiled brat!"

Penemuel thrashed and struggled to free himself as he snarled at Rose. He yanked his arm free from her grip and slammed his elbow into her face. Rose fell backwards and found the fallen angel on top of her with his hands around her throat. Her eyes bulged as she tried gasping for air.

Devlin wrapped his arms around Penemuel's chest to pull him off Rose, but he didn't budge. Penemuel threw his head back and butted it into Devlin's face, stunning him.

"Spoiled brat, am I?" Penemuel growled down at Rose. "You know nothing of what you speak, and still you mock me? I'm going to enjoy watching the light leave your eyes— AARRHH!"

Rose coughed harshly as the pressure from her throat was suddenly gone. She rolled on to her side, grimacing as she rubbed her throat. Little black specks clouding her vision slowly dissipated.

Devlin knelt beside Rose and held her protectively close. She looked up and saw Duncan had stabbed Penemuel in the back and was hoisting him up so that the fallen angel slid down the sword like he was on a skewer. Penemuel screamed as he flailed his arms and legs.

"How dare you harm my friends! I've lost all patience with you. It's time to finish your long-winded story."

Duncan grabbed the hilt with both hands and swung downward, slamming Penemuel on the ground. The fallen angel hit so hard that his body made an indention in the soggy ground. Duncan pressed his boot down on Penemuel's back and slowly extracted the angelic sword from his quivering body. He leaned down and yanked Penemuel up so that he sat upright on his knees.

"Spoiler alert, your character dies," Duncan announced as he swung his sword. In one fluid movement, Penemuel's head was lopped off, and it tumbled to the ground. His body instantly began to blacken, turning into an ashy, mud pile at Duncan's feet. The rain pounded it until his remains were nothing more than gray slurry.

Devlin helped Rose up to her feet while examining her throat for any injuries. He cupped her chin and tilted her head.

"I'm fine," she insisted. "You don't need to treat me like some porcelain doll. I can take care of myself."

"I know that, but one can never be too careful," Devlin said as he brushed a strand of Rose's hair behind her ear. "You're mortal and the slightest bit of trauma to your body could mean death, especially since there are no more hospitals around."

Rose snorted. "Thanks for pointing that out. If I didn't know better, I'd assume you're looking to see if he damaged your late night snack."

Devlin backed away with a hurt look on his face. He placed a hand over his heart. "Dear, Rose, you wound me with such accusations. If I were sensitive, I'd be crying like a baby vamp that had lost his blood bottle."

Duncan arched an eyebrow. "Baby vamps? Vampires can be born? I thought you could only become a vampire by being bitten by one."

Devlin gave Duncan a wry look and then glanced at Rose. He grinned at her. "As for the baby vamps, I'm willing to make multiple attempts to create one if you are, Rose."

"Pig!"

"As if you haven't thought about it already," the vampire accused her. "Duncan, did you know that earlier she was—"

"DEVLIN!" Rose exclaimed, her face getting red from anger and embarrassment.

"Maybe I should find another place to rest while you two have a go at it back in the cave," Duncan teased. "The least you could do is kiss the guy for fetching you some clothes."

Devlin shuddered. "She kissed me earlier for some fresh fruit which led to other things before you woke up. Hmm, I wonder what her clothes will get me."

"A fat lip and blue balls if you don't shut that mouth of yours, Romeo!" Suddenly, a noise sounded out from behind Duncan, and Rose screamed, "Duncan, watch out! The other angel is behind you!" She instantly created a fireball in her hand and reared back, ready to throw the flame.

Duncan raised his hands in a submissive way as he shielded Purah from the sorceress. He didn't figure the flame would harm the petite fallen angel, it hadn't hurt Penemuel.

"She's okay, Rose," he gently told her. "Purah's a friend."

Devlin raised an eyebrow. "I wouldn't go so far as to say she's okay. More like she's touched in the head, my friend."

"Why would you consider letting her live?" Rose asked. "She's one of the reasons this world is in the shitter."

"Because I know she's okay," Duncan insisted. "Just like I know Devlin isn't a bad guy, despite what he is."

Realization hit Rose, and she let the flame on her hand extinguish. As she did, her lips formed an "O." She knew how he could know they were good beings.

Devlin looked at both of them several times before asking, "Tell me!" he insisted. "How did you know I was a good person? You saw me feeding that night, viciously I might add, and yet you walked on by like I was nothing more than a butterfly on a flower. Care to share the secret that Rose alluded to earlier?"

"WHAT!" Duncan roared at Rose. "You told him about that?"

"No, not exactly but—"

"I confided in you a secret that I have never shared with anyone else in my life, and you go blabbing it to the first person you run across! You said that I could trust you, Rose. I was a fool for doing it though!"

"Duncan," Devlin said sternly, "Rose only said that you had a way of knowing things about people. She didn't betray your trust. She feared you would be angry if she told me, so I didn't press her. Do me a favor," he growled irritably, "leave Rose alone!"

As Duncan clenched his fists, his jaw muscles clenched too. Anger flooded into his mind, engulfing it to the point that he needed to hurt someone. Rose saw violence in his eyes and backed away, causing Devlin to position himself protectively in front of her. Duncan's entire body began to glow with a purple aura.

Devlin's eyes locked on to Duncan's eyes, two alphas asserting their dominance.

"Your fight is with me, Duncan. Leave her out of this! Rose tended to you, kept you safe and this is how you repay that debt?"

Duncan's breath came in quick, heavy spurts as every muscle in his body tensed, readying for a fight. He was about to leap on the vampire when he felt an electrical spark on his forearm. He glanced down to his right and saw the petite, fallen angel hanging on to him, her eyes pleading.

The rains let up some, falling only as a light drizzle now. Purah's sapphire eyes were red, and Duncan knew she had been crying again. He stared at her for a long moment. *What is it about this being that makes me want to shield her from the rest of the world?*

"You need to calm down," Purah murmured to him. Her voice was soft and melodic, creating an emotionally calm cloud for his anger to dissipate in. "If you don't control your emotions, the magic inside you will destroy them...and me also."

Duncan's face paled as her words registered in his mind. He looked at Rose and Devlin and saw the intense fear in their eyes. His friends were afraid...afraid of him! Devlin could have easily teleported Rose to safety. Instead, he chose to stay and help, even though they were both afraid.

He glanced down at his small, fallen angel. "How do I do this? It's getting to be too much to handle." Purah let out a barely audible sigh as she got in front of Duncan, hugging him tightly.

Rose gave her a killing look when she saw Purah holding Duncan so intimately. It irritated her that Duncan seemed to belong in the fallen angel's arms. She could see his anger melting away, being replaced by...what? Love? Rose shuddered.

Feeling Rose's distress, Devlin slipped an arm around her, never taking his eyes off Duncan.

As Duncan's rage melted away, so too did the start of his built up magical energy. Suddenly, he felt lightheaded, and he tensed his muscles in response. Purah tightened her hold on him. "It's okay," she murmured. "What you're feeling is normal when this much energy is being released. Just breathe and let me help you."

Duncan nodded as he concentrated on his breathing. Never in his life had he felt this out of control. Purah seemed to think it was easy releasing this explosive energy, but Duncan didn't agree. Memories filled his mind of frying the ghouls who had attacked him. Even the trees had been scorched. Rose would be dead right now, but she had dived behind a boulder, and his magical energy had passed over her.

Another energy surge shook his whole body, and he shuddered, not knowing how to release it. He felt like a guy trying to disarm a bomb, knowing it could go off at any time!

"I'm taking this energy from you, Duncan," Purah told him firmly. "I want you and your friends to be safe."

"But…but what about you? Will you be okay?" Duncan's voice quavered with concern. He suddenly felt a couple of light kisses on his abdomen.

"I'll be okay, but I have to leave for a while to properly release this energy. I don't want to see you get hurt, Duncan." Purah turned and shot Rose a look that froze her. "While I'm gone, sorceress, you will teach him proper meditation," she demanded. "You will guide him on how to control his ever-growing magic!"

The tone of Purah's voice told Rose she wasn't making a request; she was giving an order. Rose nodded, and a sense of dread filled her when the fallen angel's sapphire eyes flared brightly.

"If you don't do this," Purah warned, "the firestorms will seem like child's play compared to what Duncan will release if you don't help him."

Chapter 19

Purah soared high in the sky carrying the burden she held in her hands. She must get rid of it but not here on Earth. Just a small amount of Duncan's magical energy that she carried could devastate everything in a hundred mile radius, and that was a conservative estimate on her part.

It had been a while since she traveled between dimensions, and Purah couldn't remember feeling this clear in her mind since she'd been injured. Then again, why was she feeling back to normal? Only touching Duncan gave her mind the much needed connections to work properly. Duncan made her whole again.

She glanced down at her hands and saw Duncan's purple energy glowing brightly. It must be his energy that allows this clarity of mind, she thought as she slipped through a thin part of the veil that separated Earth from other dimensions.

It was a dark and desolate dimension, and a being could get lost if she didn't know where she was going. The place she wanted had been used by her fallen brothers and sisters to train for battles over the eons. Even though the directions on how to get there were engrained in her brain, Sorath had always insisted she use an escort.

The head fallen angel never liked her being out of his sight for long and tended to coddle and protect her, which Purah found annoying. She could take care of herself and hated the way Sorath smothered her when she wasn't quite right in the head, which was every single day.

Her memories, fragmented and jumbled as they were, always had one constant among them: Sorath — always with her and always holding her in some way. She shuddered, finding him repulsive. Why do I allow Sorath to attach himself to me like a leach lover?

Purah gasped as memories flooded her mind to the point that she nearly dropped Duncan's energy. "Focus!" She berated herself for the lapse that could have left her in a broken state unable to get back. Get back to where? Anywhere…Just far away from Sorath and the Promised Land.

What about Duncan? Just the whisper of his name in her mind gave her hope. Purah decided not to dwell on the human until she got to the dimension where she would be safe in case her memory decided to leave her again. She didn't know if Duncan felt anything for her, let alone wanted to be around her.

I'm the fallen angel of sorrow and despair. Who in their right mind would want to be around me? Sorath, obviously, but why?

She felt her life was being hit from below with an earthquake and a hurricane from above. Total chaos and no end in sight. As Purah slipped through the familiar entrance in the veil and entered the fallen angels' training dimension, darkness surrounded her, pulling on every nerve of her sanity.

The dimension was a wasteland; barely anything grew here because the sun rarely shined. Mountain ranges jutted out of the sand like something out of a nightmare, their rocky peaks resembling teeth and clasping, bony fingers. In between two rather scary-looking crags sat a small valley, and in its center was a dilapidated coliseum.

The coliseum had cracks and chunks of limestone knocked out of it. Black scorch marks told the story of many past battles as they created a myriad of chaos and destruction. The floor was covered in sand, and in the center of the ring was a stone slab used for the victors to stand on while awaiting their next opponent.

Everything about this dimension bespoke of death, decay, and war which was why the fallen angels chose it for their personal needs as they hid from Earth. There were so few fallen angels left because each fight was to the death and Sorath was always victorious. Only a select few, including Purah, were set aside, never to fight. The hand-selected fallen angels got a front row seat to watch their brothers and sisters die in battles to see who would reign supreme when the time came to create the apocalypse.

Purah landed softly on the sand, barely making a sound. She tucked her wings against her body as she walked towards the stone slab. The energy she held was powerful and starting to become too much for her. She liked that it helped to keep her mind stable, but it came with a painful price: knowledge! Knowledge that she couldn't keep the energy, and knowledge that once she rid herself of it, she would become broken again.

Maybe I can spindle a portion of it in my mind, Purah thought. Was that even possible?

She wasn't familiar with how to do that, but it was worth a try. First things first, though. I've got to release most of Duncan's energy. The energy was violently vibrating her entire body now, and she grimaced as she climbed up to the top of the stone slab.

The slab would make a good conduit since it was buried deep in the ground. Purah lay flat on her back and closed her eyes, trying to coax Duncan's energy out slowly. The moment she relaxed her hold on the energy, it shot out of her like it had come from a cannon. The energy had so much raw power in it that it lifted her off the stone slab a few inches. Purah screamed as she did her best to contain a small portion of the energy for herself.

Just a small dab, Purah thought. She panted heavily as she forced a trickle of Duncan's energy to drip into her brain. The odor of something burning caused her to crinkle up her nose in disgust. She heard rocks crumbling behind her, but she had no margin for error in what she was attempting to do.

If she pushed too much too fast from her body or let too much of the energy into her brain, it could fry all of her synapses and possibly melt her brain completely. All of her muscles tightened as she tried to put up a small, protective wall to seal her brain from receiving too much energy.

A cool breeze blew around her as Purah felt the last of Duncan's energy leave her body. She opened her eyes and for a moment she was blind. Exhaling a large breath, her body relaxed, and her sight returned.

"That was a rush," she said with a smile and sat up. At that moment, it dawned on her that she remembered everything. She laughed and looked around. The coliseum was gone. The stone slab was gone. Even parts of the mountains were gone!

She looked down and saw that a hole had been left in the ground where the stone slab had been. Even her clothing had been burned away during the energy release. That explains the burnt odor, she mused as she took flight. Purah felt more alive than she had in years. She soared high in the dark sky, letting the wind caress every part of her bare skin.

Sorath would not be pleased to see me like this, she thought. Then again, he was back on Earth, and she was here. The tiny bundle of Duncan's energy she had kept for herself made her head tingle, and her mind enjoyed that sensation too. She felt a pang of sadness knowing that the bundle wouldn't last forever because her body's own natural energy would eventually rid itself of it, sending her back into her broken state.

As she flew, Purah was determined to somehow keep the memory of Duncan Morgan fresh in her mind and make it easy to access. Would she remember why he was so special to her when the thought of him crossed her damaged mind?

Purah literally had nothing to write his name on, and it would do no good to scratch his name on her bare skin since it would heal within a day's time. What to do? Purah scanned the grounds and found the remnants of a recent volcanic eruption. She swooped down and grabbed a chunk of obsidian rock and then shot back towards where the coliseum had been.

She dove in the hole left by the stone slab, hunting for a suitable rock that she could carve Duncan's name on. To her surprise, the hole was a crater, and it went deep down in a zigzag fashion, finally opening up to a cavernous area that had many stalactites on its roof. There was even a small spring of water there. Judging from the steam coming off the water's surface, it had to be a hot spring, being warmed naturally by the nearby volcano.

Purah landed on the stony ground of the cavern and lost her footing. She fell hard on her butt and noted that all the rocks were covered with green slime. Algae? Purah didn't understand this dimension at all and wasn't sure she wanted to come back here either.

She used her wings to slightly hover above the rocky ground, making her way to the hot spring. The heat emanating from the spring warmed her, seemingly beckoning to her to slide into the water. That was all the coaxing Purah needed.

She slowly immersed her small body into the spring, bending her knees so the water would cover her up to her neck. Feeling as if she was being smothered in a huge, cradling hug, she laughed out in joy. The spring came up to her waist, so she sat down and dipped her entire body into it. Heavenly, she thought, and she would know that feeling anywhere. Maybe this place wasn't so bad after all. Purah smiled as she lifted her head out of the water. As she looked around at her surroundings, her happiness started to fade.

Someone was here! Purah could sense a great sadness and a despair that was bottomless.

At that moment, she noticed she had trouble focusing. Her mind became cloudy, her thoughts mishmash. "Shit!" Purah scrambled out of the hot springs and found she was sliding on the slippery surface of the rocks. Duncan's energy she had spindled in her mind had come undone and was rapidly leaving her, probably because she had let everything go in the hot springs. Panic seized her mind as she hunted for a rock, anything that she could carve Duncan's name on.

As the energy slowly faded away, desperation covered her. She frantically began to carve his name in multiple areas on her naked body. She grimaced as she carved it into her thighs, her stomach, the back of both of her hands and her forearms. Purah even went so far as to carve his name into several of her wings' tendrils.

"Please," Purah pleaded with herself, "I don't want to forget again! She concentrated on what little of Duncan's energy was left in her head, but it no longer responded. Frustration got the best of her as every attempt to keep the energy failed.

Purah lay down on her side, crying and not caring that the slick algae was leaving a green slime-blanket on most of her body. She balled her hands into fists and slammed both of them repeatedly on the slick, stony cave floor, wailing at the top of her lungs.

"Someone, kill me already," Purah moaned. "I don't want to live like this anymore." She heard the sound of sand falling from the hole where the stone slab had been, but she didn't care. She squeezed her eyes shut.

Several minutes passed as she lay on the stony ground with a blank expression on her tear-soaked face. Finally, she opened her eyes and looked around, noting she was underground. "Where am I?"

Her gaze swept around the cavern and then down at the ground. "What's that?" she asked aloud. She leaned down and snatched a rock off the cave floor. It was green. Putting the rock to her lips, she licked the algae. "Oooh tangy but yummy," she said and continued to lick. A shadow loomed over her, but she was too pre-occupied with the rock to care.

"Purah?" a deep, melodious voice came from above her. "Purah, what are you doing here?"

She looked up and flashed him a huge grin. Wet, green slime dripped down her chin. "Sorath, you're here! Good! Come join me, this stuff is great!"

Sorath crinkled his nose. "Um, no thanks. I believe I'll pass on your invitation."

"Suit yourself, more for me then!" Purah replied as she went back to licking the rock.

"Purah, where are your garments?" he asked. He knew better than to rattle off a series of questions because of her poor memory, but he certainly had plenty of them to ask.

Patience was not something Sorath had been gifted with; however, through the centuries, he had become accustomed to showing patience—when dealing with Purah, at least. No one else deserved his patience because everyone else was held to a higher standard than she. If others couldn't pull their weight, he would kill them.

Purah stopped licking the rock and started examining herself. "I'm not wearing any clothes!" she exclaimed with surprise. "Where are my clothes? Do you have them?"

"No, my sweet Purah, I don't have them," Sorath responded but then gasped at the cuts all over her body. "What happened to you?"

"I don't remember," she said sadly and started to cry.

"Do you remember someone cutting you up?" he demanded.

Purah looked at her wounds. "I think I cut myself. Why would I write...Duncan Morgan?"

Sorath leaned down and gently picked Purah up as if she were a fragile work of art. He examined her wounds closely. At first glance, he could tell they were all self-inflicted, which told him that she was desperate to remember this person's name.

On the ground was a sharp, black stone with blood on it that confirmed she had, in fact, done this to herself. Why? Was this person the one responsible for her current state? Did he assault her sexually?

The mere thought of anyone else's hands on his Purah set his blood to boiling. She was his and no one else could have her! He lifted her so he could sniff her slimy core. He did detect a faint arousal, and it wasn't due to his presence. He also detected an unfamiliar male scent on her, and that infuriated him to no end.

"When I say the name Duncan Morgan, what's the first thing that comes to your mind?" he asked, trying hard to be patient.

She was silent for a long moment. Finally, she said, "Human."That surprised him. Purah was in a dimension that humans were not aware of. He had thought the name might belong to a demon or some other supernatural creature. "I'll have this human found and executed for what he's done to you, my dear. What else comes to mind when I say Duncan Morgan?"

"He killed Penemuel," Purah replied as she ran a finger on her chin and licked the algae.

"Penemuel is dead?" Sorath did his best to hide his joy. "Are you sure of this?"

"Sure of what?"

"Penemuel is dead."

Purah looked shocked. "Penemuel's dead? When did that happen?"

Sorath took a deep breath and calmed his frustration. It was his own fault for being impatient with her, and now he had upset her. Getting answers from her wouldn't be easy. He held her close as he hovered in the air. "Today, Penemuel was killed by Duncan Morgan."

"Yes he was, wasn't he?"

"Why did the mortal fight with Penemuel?"

"He was mad."

"Penemuel was mad at Duncan Morgan?"

"Yes, that's what I just said." Purah glared at him.

"What made Penemuel so mad?"

She thought for a moment and then grinned at Sorath. "He was naked, and I was being cradled in his arms…no wait, he had his clothes on by then…unfortunately."

"A mortal killed one of our kind?" The more Sorath thought about the killing, the angrier he got. He didn't mind that Penemuel was dead. As a matter of fact, he liked that he was dead. But it was the thought that a human would have the nerve to kill a fallen angel that really caused Sorath's rage to get out of control. He couldn't have humans going around and killing his kind. What if it started an uprising among the humans?

Not only had the human called Duncan Morgan killed Penemuel, but he had taken liberties with Purah! How dare he! In his anger, Sorath squeezed Purah tight, to the point of making her cry out in pain, but he didn't notice. How dare this mere mortal touch her! How dare that insignificant bug strut around my Purah naked!

"Let me go, Sorath!" Purah shouted. "You're hurting me!"

Sorath didn't let go. Instead, he took her to the hot springs with the intent of removing the human's filth from her body. Dropping her down hard in the water, Sorath removed his armor and set them on the slimy ground. He entered the pool with her.

Purah stood up. She scrambled toward the bank, trying to get out of the water, but Sorath was already towering over her. He grabbed her and roughly scrubbed all the algae scum from her petite body.

She kicked and screamed at him, but it did no good. Nothing seemed to faze him. Once he felt her body was clean, he grabbed her and dragged her to a nearby wall, pinning her body against it with his own. She was trapped!

With Purah's hands held above her head, Sorath wiggled his hips in between her legs. "I love you, Purah," he said hoarsely as he thrust hard inside her. "No one will ever come between us again. This is for your own good. I will do this for all of eternity until you come to realize that you…are…MINE!"

Chapter 20

"Focus, Duncan. This is something you really need to work on," Rose berated him as they sat across from one another in the cave. It had been nearly two weeks since his powers had come to the surface, and he still had difficulty controlling his inner magic. If what Purah had said was true, and Rose had no cause to doubt her, then Duncan was a walking nuclear bomb waiting to explode. She had witnessed firsthand what his powers had done to the ghouls and how easily he'd dispatched the fallen angel. She shuddered to think what would happen if he completely lost control.

"Damn it, woman!" Duncan snarled, "I'm doing the best I can."

"That's not good enough. You need to work on the basic steps of meditation. That's the only way to control your magic."

"That's easy for you to say; you've been brought up in this sort of thing."

"Quit making excuses and focus on your breathing, asshole! Right now, you're a ticking time bomb!"

"If it makes you feel any better, I'd fly far off into space and explode so none of you would get hurt." He grabbed her katana and slid it towards her. "Might be best to kill me now."

"Quit whining. You've probably been using magic for years and didn't know it. That inner voice comes from somewhere. Only, now that it's requiring a little discipline on your part, you start boohooing."

"I didn't know what that voice was—"

"But you listened to it anyway, didn't you?"

"Yes," Duncan replied begrudgingly.

Devlin appeared out of the shadows. The vampire had been coming by every few days, bringing fresh fruits for Rose and searching for the exact location of the Promised Land that Penemuel had talked about. "May I ask a question?"

Duncan rolled his eyes. "Ask away, Devlin. I'm not going anywhere."

"Don't be rude," Rose admonished. "Go ahead, Devlin."

The vampire produced two bundles of grapes for Rose. Her eyes lit up, and she scrambled off the ground and hurried to claim them. He watched her pop a grape into her mouth, enjoying that her facial expression had gone from excitement to euphoria as she savored the fruit. Duncan cleared his throat impatiently, reminding Devlin to ask his question. "How did you learn to fight…or hunt, for that matter?"

"I had a friend who was into martial arts," Duncan explained. "He taught me the basics. The hunting came from going out into the woods with a grandfatherly figure or with one of my many foster dads that I had growing up. He was a skilled hunter and tracker that wanted to pass on to me that knowledge. He said that one day it might save my life." Duncan nodded his head as he recalled the old man's words. "Oh...how right grandpa was!"

"Hmm," Devlin responded.

Duncan glared at the vampire and growled sarcastically, "Is that all you have to say? If there's more, please share with the rest of the class. No one in here can read minds, you know!"

Devlin chuckled. "That we know of, my friend." He turned to Rose, who was still popping grapes into her mouth. "We might be going about his training all wrong."

"Nonsense," she snapped as she chewed. "He's just being impatient and not wanting to meditate properly."

"No, I think it's you who's being impatient, Rose," he argued. "Remember, he's new to all this. You might have to adjust your teaching accordingly."

Rose glared at Devlin as she shoved several more grapes into her mouth. The vampire went to hold her, but she stepped out of his reach and sat down.

Duncan laughed. "Uh-oh, somebody's in the dog house tonight. Take it from someone who knows; she doesn't like to be told she's wrong."

Devlin shrugged his shoulders and looked at Rose. "Duncan's no closer to controlling his powers than when you first started teaching him. I'd like to try a different approach that will include all three of us."

"Wha..ou..hav..in min..Dvwin?" Rose asked with her mouth full of grapes.

Devlin raised an eyebrow. "Huh?"

She swallowed. "What have you got in mind?"

"This will be risky, but the rewards will be great."

"Get to the point already," Duncan growled impatiently. "Some of us will be old and gray if you keep this cryptic shit up!"

"Duncan, you and I can fight," the vampire explained. "While we fight, you can tell Rose what you're feeling—your emotions. That way, she can guide you as to what you should do if there's an energy build up. You have a hands-on approach to learning, so this method will help you learn her techniques more easily. Does this sound reasonable to the two of you?"

"It sounds insane, that's what it sounds like!" Rose snapped irritably as she stood up. "What makes you think he won't kill you accidentally? Or all of us, for that matter?"

"The training wheels have to come off sometime, Rose. Besides, I've had a little time to observe the situation. Duncan's been focusing, but his concentration doesn't last. He's listening to you, Rose, but patience isn't your strong suit either. Putting two strong-willed, stubborn individuals together makes for a lot of frustration."

Rose was about to open her mouth and rant, but Duncan put a hand on her shoulder, stopping her. "I think this will work, Rose," he stated calmly. "Devlin has a good plan."

Rose shook her head. "I've got a feeling that you two sparring could turn dangerous! What if you lose your temper? You could kill him *and* me."

"Have faith in me, Rose. You're a great teacher, and now it's time to see how much I've learned."

"I have faith in you, Duncan—just not my teaching abilities."

Devlin put a reassuring arm around her and escorted her out of the cave. As Duncan followed them, Rose kept shaking her head. "Throwing all caution to the wind when you're dealing with powerful magic is beyond careless." When they ignored her, she growled, "Typical male bravado! Let's fight and compare our manhood." She rolled her eyes in disgust.

A few clouds hung low in some places, but mostly the sun shined brightly. "Come on, Duncan, it's a nice day, and the acidic rains won't be here for another hour or so," Devlin called over his shoulder.

Duncan grinned. Combat would give him a chance to slap the vampire around. He wondered if he could hurt Devlin in hand to hand combat, especially if he went all out on the vampire. He didn't really plan on going all out; it was just a thought that kept creeping into his mind—a fun thought. Might be good to know for later in case another vampire came along looking for a fight.

"First things first," Devlin announced as he stood a good six feet across from Duncan, "we'll start with hand-to-hand combat. After that, we'll do weapons…but not the angelic sword."

Duncan sniggered. "Scared it might kill you?"

"No, but I suspect it can be used to magnify and channel your magic. If that's the case, then we have it to fall back on if things get a little…" Devlin's voice trailed off as he glanced at Rose. Finally, he added, "out of hand."

"This whole thing is out of hand!" Rose chastised them. "What a brilliant plan: let's grab the nuke, toss it around willy-nilly, and hopefully it doesn't explode in our faces. No, I sure as shit can't see anything bad happening with this dick-sword, clashing match."

Devlin grinned. "Is she always like this?" he asked Duncan and chuckled.

"Pretty much."

"My sweetest Rose, why would I try to slay Duncan with my dick when I could have more fun pleasuring you with it…multiple times?"

Duncan let out a belly laugh that made Rose blush, but it warmed her heart to hear him laughing like that. Ever since he had come to Melona, Duncan had been quiet and serious. True, they both took turns poking fun and irritating each other, but this was the first time Rose had caught a glimpse of what he was like with his guard down. Rose shot Duncan the middle finger, but it only added to his laughter.

"If you two are done playing around," the vampire scolded, "we have some serious business to attend to. Duncan, shut up and get ready for your ass-kicking."

Duncan wiped the tears from his eyes but not his shit-eating grin as he assumed his fighter's stance. He crept closer to Devlin, planning to put the vampire in his place.

Suddenly, a blinding flash of light hit him square in his chest, driving him down to the ground. Despite the searing pain, Duncan opened his eyes and saw that the blinding light was still on top of him. His inner voice urgently warned, *KILL HIM!*

That could only mean the light was coming from someone, but how was that possible? What the hell, Duncan thought as he punched into the light several times. He was rewarded with hitting something solid and metallic and heard a few "oofs" too.

"Pathetic mortal! How dare you think you can challenge the son of God! You will come with me to be judged for the crimes of murdering an angel of the Lord as well as defiling poor defenseless Purah!"

"Sorath!" Duncan growled. As the fallen angel's words settled in his brain, he frowned. True, he had killed Penemuel, but when had he defiled Purah? He used his strength and heaved Sorath off of him.

The fallen angel was thrown up into the air. No longer a blinding light, he quickly assumed the form of Jesus that everyone knew from the portraits that hung in churches.

Duncan scrambled to his feet and shouted defiantly, "Show your true form, Sorath. Save that bullshit savior crap for your dumbass followers!"

"I see I have the correct villain," Sorath called down as he hovered in the air. "You were hard to find. I had to smite multiple worms that went by the name Duncan Morgan. But Purah gave you up."

Duncan felt a pang of anger at the thought of Purah betraying him. How could she willingly do this to me? I trusted her! He glared up at Sorath and shouted, "You going to fight or preach like the late Sully. Might as well add that charge too, asshole!"

Like he had been shot out of a cannon, Sorath raced towards Duncan. Duncan threw a single punch and slammed it into Sorath's face, shattering his nose, but it didn't deter the fallen angel. Sorath swept Duncan off his feet and soared high in the sky with him. And in that moment, they were gone.

"DUNCAN!" Rose screamed.

Chapter 21

Still in the guise of Jesus, Sorath gave Duncan a hard shove, and the man tumbled into one of the dungeon cells. The fallen angel glared at the mortal. No one would have noticed Sorath's demeanor had they seen him because his face falsely glowed with love and understanding, not the hateful stare that he actually wore.

Duncan could feel his gaze, though; it burned into him with malice. As he lay on the floor looking up at his captor, he smirked and mocked, "What, no bed for your honored guest?"

"Count yourself lucky I didn't drop you from the sky on our way here."

"Is that what Jesus would have done? Fly around the world, dropping people like bombs? Huh, I could've sworn that He was all about love and compassion."

"It's not your place to question a god like me." Sorath scowled. "Soon you'll be judged for your crimes against the righteous. Your punishment will be doled out accordingly."

"I'm so glad you took the suspense out of the verdict," Duncan goaded. "My punishment will be what, crucifixion? I'm sure you *nailed* that one back in the day — oh wait, that was the real Jesus. Not some Messiah-wannabe, fallen angel with daddy issues."

Sorath stared at Duncan, silently fuming. Finally, he growled, "Your punishment will be much worse than a crucifixion. That's way too easy for the likes of you." He flashed the man an evil smile. "I intend to make an example of you for my followers to witness. This world will be cleansed soon enough of the filth who got left behind."

From his cell, while laughing, Duncan cried out, "You might want to fix that nose of yours. I wouldn't want you to look so ungodly during my farce of a trial."

Sorath considered the stinging soreness of his nose. "You hit hard for a mere mortal, but that tongue of yours won't make your death come any quicker. Before you die, you'll know the definition of pain."

Duncan let out a belly laugh. "I'm married, so I'm fairly certain that whatever you dish out will pale in comparison to what I've already suffered."

Suddenly, Sorath was back in the man's face, holding him up off the floor by his throat. Duncan kicked at the fallen angel, trying desperately to free himself from the vice-like grip. The lack of oxygen made him light-headed, but it was when Sorath psychically probed his mind that his head felt as if it was going to explode. He gasped as he struggled to suck in air while his lungs instinctively screamed out for it. Sorath's eyes glowed with a harsh crimson red as he probed deeper into the recesses of the man's mind.

Sorath loosed his grip and let Duncan drop hard on the floor. The man had a harsh coughing fit as he inhaled the sweet taste of air again. The fallen angel backed out of the cell with a smile on his face. Duncan glared at the false Jesus and charged at him. Before Duncan could make it to Sorath, though, his body was repelled backwards by an unseen force that knocked him back against the far wall. Sorath laughed as he watched Duncan try to get up on his feet. His eyes glazed over as he staggered along the wall.

"Did you really believe there was nothing to keep you in this cell?" Sorath asked, amused that Duncan still couldn't stand without wobbling and clutching at the wall. "You mortals are all the same, head strong and never thinking. It's so entertaining to see this happen. Why don't you try it again?"

Duncan gave up on the idea of standing and slid down to the floor. He sat leaning against the wall and flipped Sorath the middle finger.

The fallen angel's voice lost any signs of amusement. "Yes, I know of your marriage. I've seen it all in that barbaric brain of yours. Trust me; my punishment will be fitting for one such as you. You'll not enjoy a second of it."

"I'd enjoy it if you would shut up and leave. Your boasting is giving me a headache. Do you get off on pretending to be Jesus? I mean, why this whole charade when obviously you could destroy all of humanity without much of an effort?"

"Everyone has a part to play in life. My part is to be the Messiah your people have prayed for, but you…you are nothing more than a nuisance that needs to be exterminated."

"If humanity is so terrible, then why steal people to keep all to yourself?" Duncan pointed out.

"All gods need worshipers. I took only those who wanted me, who would pray to me and grant me daily tribute."

"You mean they worship Jesus, don't you? The real Jesus. I bet it sucks that they wouldn't worship the real you." He snickered. "If they knew you were deceiving them, they'd probably rip you to pieces."

"Even if they knew my true nature, they would have no choice but to accept me. I own them all."

"If that's true, then why keep up the ruse?" Duncan gave the fallen angel a knowing look. Sorath seemed unable to answer. Instead, he abruptly turned and left.

Duncan felt he had hit a raw nerve with the false Christ, and he was surprised there had been no other rant. Maybe Sorath feels he has no choice and has to remain in this form. Either he fears what his followers would do if his true identity was revealed, or he enjoyed playing a false god.

He knew his time here wasn't going to be pleasant, so why should he make things easy for his captors? He looked around his cell and noted that it was made of solid gold, and there was absolutely nothing in it. No bed to sleep on, no sink to wash his hands in, no…Duncan raised his eyebrows in surprise.

No toilet!

Not even a bucket to go in! Did Sorath's followers not go to the bathroom? Duncan had no problem shitting in the woods or even out in the open, but he was expected to sleep in here!

If I'm to be forced to sleep in my filth, then I'll make it a pain on those who come in here for me. He grinned as he got up and walked over to the cell entrance, where he could hear the invisible energy field humming. He unbuckled his belt, dropped his pants, and kicked them out of his way.

Duncan grunted as he pushed as much stool out as he could and then moved down and did it again. When he was done, he stood up and pissed by the energy field. He grinned as he watched the field corral his urine, not letting it escape. The electrical field sizzled where it touched the urine, sending a shower of sparks flying into the cell. Laughing, he ducked and ran to the opposite wall for safety.

He quickly regretted pissing on the electrical field. Fried piss stank worse than he ever thought it could. As he walked over to grab his pants, Duncan heard the soft sounds of whimpering. Someone was crying. He slung his pants on and fastened his belt while intently listening.

At that moment, a soft voice tugged at his heart and filled him with rage. "I want my mommy! I want to go home!" There were children down here imprisoned like he was, but why?

Careful to not step in his stinky present for the guards, Duncan leaned against the doorway pillar and looked down the hallway. There was a larger holding cell with a wider doorway than his where he saw tiny figures crawling around or lying on the floor.

So many children! What crimes had they committed?

Depressed about his and the children's situation, he walked back to the far wall and sat down. He leaned back against the wall, draping his arms over his bent knees and closed his eyes. There had to be a way to bust out of this cell and rescue the children, he thought, but no answers revealed themselves to him.

He let out a heavy sigh as the burden of helplessness crushed down on his weary shoulders. "That damn angel has to die," Duncan growled. He quickly decided that if he couldn't find a weapon to strike him down with, he'd tear the prick's head off with his bare hands. As he smiled at that thought, exhaustion got the better of him, and he nodded off.

The sound of feet shuffling in the corridor stirred Duncan from his slumber. How long did I sleep? Is it day or night now? It sounded like a group of people, maybe an escort for him. If these guards were here to take him to be judged, then his window of opportunity had arrived.

Duncan scrambled to his feet and stood in a fighter's stance. His muscles tensed as his heart pumped adrenaline throughout his body, preparing him for the impending fight. What's the worse they will do, kill me? Duncan had a feeling that these guards were under strict orders from Sorath to get him to his trial alive, so why not make it rough on the bastards? At that moment, his inner voice spoke. It repeated the same words over and over again.

DEATH...ABUSER! DEATH...ABUSER! DEATH...ABUSER!

As the energy field lowered to let the guards in, Duncan braced for the fight. Suddenly, he stopped and stared. A small group of ghouls trudged up to his cell, their vacant eyes locking on him, and their quivering, slimy lips hungrily munching, wanting to eat him.

A dozen ghouls crowded into the small cell, giving Duncan claustrophobic anxiety on top of his heightened emotional state. Panic gripped him. Thoughts flooded into his mind of being eaten alive. For a second time, he was going to be the main course at a ghoul buffet.

He wanted to use his magic, but he couldn't risk it. The children were nearby, and he had little control over the deadly energy his magic would summon. The ghouls grabbed him and shoved him into the center of the cell where they surrounded him.

As they snapped their jaws at him, he screamed out, "What are you dead fucks waiting for? C'mon! Eat me, already!"

He reared back and let a powerful punch fly into the face of the nearest ghoul. As the dead guy staggered back, the others crowded in on Duncan. He kicked and swung to fend them off, but they grabbed each of his limbs. As he struggled to get free, they ripped away at his clothing, peeling his shirt and pants off like a child shredding a piece of paper.

Their sharp fingernails scratched and scraped Duncan's skin, but that was all they did — no biting or tearing chunks of flesh off. This isn't right, Duncan thought. Chouls don't worry about one's clothing getting in their way when they feed. They eat the clothes too! What the hell is going on?

Once Duncan was naked, the ghouls let him go and backed away from him. As he lay on his shredded clothing, a female voice echoed off the gold cell walls. Duncan felt the hairs on the back of his neck rise as the unseen female squeezed past several ghouls to look at him.

Duncan gasped when he saw the female, and his inner voice cried out again, warning him about her, *DEATH...ABUSER!*

"Good work," she said, scowling at him. "He's now ready for judgment. If he should try anything, feel free to remind him who's in charge now."

Duncan couldn't believe his eyes. He wanted to scream at her, but all he managed was a small, frightened voice, "My wife!"

Chapter 22

Sorath marched up the stairs that led to his private chamber. A turbulent flow of thoughts swirled in his head. As wave after wave of emotions flooded through him, he couldn't decide which problem to concentrate on.

Thoughts that his flock would not accept him if they knew who he really was kept pounding at his heart. More than anything, he needed to be worshipped. He needed to be a god. He should be a god!

He also needed to make an example out of Duncan Morgan. Only, what would Purah do if she happened to see him being punished? Would she remember that they had been intimate? I can't lose her to a mortal!

Should I have her shackled for the duration of his punishment? He had been sending out his elite master warriors to gather and command his ghouls with good results…except for Sully. Duncan will suffer for what he has done to Master Sully. What better way for his followers to mourn than to take their grief out on the one who killed him?

Sorath waved his arm, and the huge double doors were magically flung open. He stomped down the corridor toward his private chamber. The two guards posted outside his door snapped to attention, and one of them opened the door for him.

With his fake façade of love plastered on his face, Sorath stopped and looked at the guards. "We have a prisoner who has done a great deal of blasphemous acts towards our people. One of you gather a group of our ghouls…uh, rather…fallen warriors and escort the prisoner to the central courtyard for judgment. Gather my flock and I'll be down shortly. I need some quiet time before I judge him.

The eyes of both guards sparkled with joy as they bowed and thanked him. One quickly ran to do his bidding. Sorath walked into his chamber. When he heard the door close behind him, he let out a heavy sigh.

Duncan's words weighed heavily on his mind: They worship Jesus and not the real me. If it didn't matter then why keep up this ruse? Why, indeed? he thought as he crossed the room to sit in his wingback chair. Would the people notice if I dropped the charade? Would they even care?

"Damn mortal!" Sorath growled and threw himself down in his favorite chair. He cursed Duncan for playing this damn mind game with him. "Who is he to judge my role in all of this? For centuries, humanity has been praying for a messiah. Now they have one. The people are happy, except the un-chosen ones, like Duncan.

He thought about Duncan. Did he not witness my full power as my brothers and Purah cleansed this world of sin? "Duncan should be grateful that he and his kind are still alive. Instead, they question my decisions!" In his anger, Sorath squeezed the armrests of his chair so hard that they were crushed to a pulp.

He steepled his fingers and closed his eyes, letting his mind roam back to all those centuries ago. He thought about how he put his plan into action. He thought about the real Jesus. He thought about why he had to constantly remain in the guise of Jesus, even though he had utter control over all of his followers.

***

2,000 years ago

Sorath sat silently on a cliff side watching a busy, well-worn road that led into the city of Jerusalem. He concealed his presence from the passing throng of caravans by wrapping his translucent tendril wings around his body. Nothing but sheep and so easily swayed, he thought. It wouldn't take much to control them. Today was a day of much excitement in the region. People had come from all around to either condemn or defend the one who claimed to be the son of God, a man known as Jesus.

Sorath had watched and studied humanity for many centuries, and no matter what the time period, humans always had a constant theme. They were prone to violence and quick to judge before knowing the full truth, and that made them gullible to trickery which made them easily deceived. This, in his mind, made humans the best of his Father's pets to manipulate and gain power. As much as he despised humans, they were the perfect tool to use to spite his Father for casting him and many of his brothers and sisters out of the Heavens.

I refuse to let these hairless apes be more important than me. He spit on the ground as hatred for the humans welled up in his heart. *I do not accept the one known as Jesus to become the savior to my Father's pathetic mortals. Why should this man have the power to grant salvation? What was wrong with it being given to all who pass away in their mortal life?*

Sorath knew this was a contentious way of thinking; it was one of the reasons the War in the Heavens began in the first place. He disliked that the mortals would worship another mortal who had been anointed by their Father to make all this possible.

Blasphemy! Humans in charge of their own salvation would be their own undoing. Sorath decided from the moment he and his brothers and sisters fell that he would ensure that this happened. *These abominations will do the same thing they've always done and that was to create conflict and murders because that was their true nature.*

Sorath sneered as he looked down and saw more people walking by, all their worldly possessions in tow. *It wouldn't take much for these peaceful people to kill one another and take whatever they wanted.* He'd seen this repeat itself too many times to count. *And Father had made them in His own image!*

He hated being in close proximity to these humans, but today was a special day. It was one that he had been waiting for ever since his fall. With each breath Sorath's time was drawing near, and patience wasn't one of his stronger virtues.

A shift in the wind and the soft sound of footsteps walking towards him alerted Sorath that he wasn't alone. A glance over his shoulder let him know who had disturbed his hate-filled musings.

"Your time to rise is almost upon us, brother."

"Indeed it is, Penemuel," Sorath responded coldly. "Why are you here?"

"I'm here to see you in all your glory and – "

"Penemuel, I don't have time for a winded explanation," Sorath growled. "Say your peace and be gone from here!"

Penemuel scowled at Sorath as he replied, "You never were one to mince words. Nor do you have a passion for languages or written words like me, so I shall let that pass. Remember that I too have a vested interest in all of this. I've been writing this story for quite a while now."

Sorath rolled his eyes. "That's all you ever do, but why must you be here to irritate me on this important day?"

"While he still lives, I wanted another chance to see the character that you'll be playing. It will help as I tweak our story. I've been spying on him for a while now and I must say, I hope you can fill his shoes properly."

"What is that supposed to mean?" Sorath glared at the other fallen angel.

"It means when in character, you can't be flying off the handle in a fit of rage when someone says something that you don't like," Penemuel pointed out, not caring if he angered Sorath. "Jesus is a peaceful person who doesn't go around smiting others because they looked at him wrong. I know your temper all too well, brother. It's difficult seeing you as Jesus, so I've been working on a way to resolve this ungodly issue."

"Go on."

"Not yet, I have to find a couple of other things before I tell you more. I don't want to get your hopes up. Rest assured, I'll make this work for all of us."

"Thanks for nothing," Sorath grumbled. "So tell me more about this story you're weaving."

"I thought you didn't care to know."

Sorath sighed in frustration. "I asked, didn't I?"

Penemuel beamed a smile of excitement that made Sorath regret asking him about the story. He knew that Penemuel got zealous about anything he wrote and had seen this reaction in the past. Only now, it was a hundred times worse. Maybe I should flee from here, Sorath thought as he mentally chuckled. Penemuel wouldn't notice that I've gone until next week.

He decided to stick it out because he had, after all, asked, and he was curious on how their grand plan for humanity would work. He knew he had a central part to play. Other than that, though, Sorath hadn't bothered to learn the story because it would take many human lifetimes before the first chapter would be played out.

"My brother, you will be pleased with what I'm about to tell you because this will be, without a doubt, the greatest story ever written! Everything else I've written to this date pales in comparison. Damn, where should I begin?"

"At the beginning!" Sorath shot back sarcastically. Despite his best efforts not to, he felt excitement welling up within him. Penemuel was pulling him into his own world of enthusiasm. On top of that, Sorath also noticed that he was grinning, which was an uncommon facial expression for him. It could mean only one thing: this was a powerful story that Penemuel had written. If it could affect him in this way, he could only imagine the affect it would have on the simple-minded humans. They won't stand a chance.

"In the beginning, God created the Heavens and the Earth."

"Not THAT beginning – the beginning of your story!"

"But that's where it starts. Never mind, I'll give you the shortened version. Since we know that our Father wants the man known as Jesus to be the savior of humanity, I decided to write a story centered around him and have other stories added to it to make a tale that will be talked about and read throughout the ages. It will be known as the Bible!"

"What's so special about this Bible?"

"I've had my influence over all those who are intended to write each book in the Bible. They see what happened, but when they write it down, it will be from my perspective. All who read my work of art will have their own take about what was read, meaning ten people will get ten different messages."

Confused, Sorath asked, "What good is that? Shouldn't they all get the same message?"

Penemuel beamed a toothy grin. "Ah, and that's the beauty of it. There won't be only one religion devoted to this book. Since everyone will get a different message, many will branch off and preach their version of the same gospel. It will make a mass of followers that will blow you away! You will have so many followers that you won't know what to do with them all!"

Suddenly, the fallen angels heard humans shouting in the distance, which told Sorath that the time for Jesus' execution was drawing closer. From his vantage point, Sorath could see it unfolding before him as he used his angelic magic to enhance his vision.

The soldiers were forcing the man to carry his own execution device on his shoulders, a large wooden cross. Blood trickled down his face from the wreath on his head that was made from wickedly sharp thorns. He wore no shoes and had only a woolen loincloth to cover his private parts.

Yes, Sorath thought, humans are an abomination. The fallen angel grimaced as he watched cruel soldiers taking turns lashing Jesus on his back and legs, creating stripes of blood and torn flesh.

They reached a hill known as "the Skull" by the locals. Sorath watched as soldiers drove thick nails into Jesus' wrists and attached them to the cross, causing him to cry out in pain. Crucifixion was a Roman ritual and not a pleasant way to die. It was a method that spoke to the cruelty of Mankind.

Crucifixion used gravity and one's own weight to slowly suffocate people as their arms pulled from the sockets and once the strength in the legs went, the person being crucified would be in a perpetual state of inhalation as the rib cage was forced upward.

After Jesus' cross was hoisted upright, it didn't take long for him to feel the weight of the world literally sitting on his shoulders. This kind of treatment only reinforced Sorath's belief that all Mankind should be wiped off this planet.

Before Jesus died from suffocation, one of the soldiers stabbed him with a spear causing him more misery. Typical human cruelty, cause the victim to suffer before they die. The soldiers pulled Jesus' body off the cross and tossed it in a wooden cart to be carried off to his tomb.

On the third day of Jesus' death, Sorath flew towards the tomb. The entrance was sealed using a huge stone slab and on guard were two soldiers. Sorath smirked as he was able to slip inside the tomb unhindered using his angelic magic to become a being of energy.

Upon materializing, Sorath saw that the tomb was lit up with a small fire and Penemuel was setting up several candles around the body of Jesus. Penemuel had already inscribed angelic sigils and others that Sorath didn't recognize, and for some reason the unfamiliar sigils gave him the creeps.

As Sorath stared at the body of Jesus, he felt a shiver inch down his spine. The sight of Jesus lying on that cold stone made him feel anxious, and he looked away, hoping Penemuel didn't notice.

The only thing Penemuel noticed was that Sorath had finally arrived. Removing the white shroud off Jesus' body, he said, "It's about time you showed up. I was beginning to wonder if you would."

"Lower your voice," Sorath hissed, "there are humans outside."

Penemuel waved off his concern about noise as he replied in a booming voice, "They will hear nothing, brother. I warded this tomb so no sound will be heard. Now it is time to conduct the ritual and take your rightful place as Mankind's savior!"

Sorath let a smile cross his visage. "Yes…so, what do I do?"

"I will recite the incantation and then I shall have you drink his blood which has been tied to the ritual spellwork. But first, you need to add your own blood to the goblet." At Sorath's questioning look, Penemuel sighed as he explained, "When his blood and yours mix together, it ties you to the blood spell. It marks you as the recipient, and it's permanent. It can't be undone. It will allow you to intercept tributes given in Jesus' name which will give you power."

Penemuel handed the fallen angel a small knife and the goblet. Sorath calmly cut his palm and let his blood drip into the goblet while swirling it. Penemuel waved his hand, and all the candles lit up at the same time. He then recited the incantation in the Enochian language.

One by one, each sigil flared brightly, illuminating the tomb with a red light. The tomb hummed with energy, causing dust and rock particles to fall all around them, threatening to collapse the small, hand-hewn cave. Penemuel looked over at Sorath and motioned for him to drink as he cried out, "Drink it all and then you must destroy his body, leave nothing but dust! Do it now!"

Sorath put the goblet up to his lips and chugged it down. The blood tasted bitter and metallic but also had hints of the herbs used by Penemuel. His throat burned as it went down his gullet, making him stagger and causing his eyes to water from the intensity of the spell. He heard Penemuel cry out once more, "Destroy his body now!"

Sorath staggered over to Jesus' body. He was about to place both of his hands on Jesus' chest when suddenly the cave was awash in a blinding light. Penemuel fearfully cried out in surprise.

"What's happening?" Sorath demanded anxiously, blinded by the light.

All Penemuel could say was, "Uh…uh…"

Sorath felt his whole body shaking and vibrating with magic and energy to the point that he believed his head might explode.

Just as suddenly as it had come, the blinding light vanished, leaving only the candles to illuminate the cave. Penemuel gasped as he looked at the stone slab.

Jesus' body was gone!

"What happened?" Sorath demanded again. "What did you do?"

Afraid to tell the fallen angel that the body of Jesus had vanished on its own, he lied. "You were awesome! You caused the body to be destroyed without even touching it!"

"I didn't do that," Sorath argued.

"Yes, you did," Penemuel insisted. He was still shaking, and he gripped the stone slab for courage as well as balance.

In an unsure voice, Sorath asked, "Where did that light come from?"

"Uh…" Penemuel had no idea. "From you," he said, quickly thinking up a believable lie. "After you drank the blood, you had so much power that it burst out of you in the form of the light."

Sorath frowned. "Really?"

Penemuel nodded. "Really!" He watched Sorath grin.

"I feel powerful!" Sorath declared and laughed.

Penemuel breathed out a sigh of relief that the fallen angel had bought into his lie and looked around. Where had Jesus' body gone?

"Now what?" Sorath asked.

"You must be able to disguise yourself as Jesus, so his followers will follow you."

"Okay," Sorath agreed. Concentrating, he calmed his mind and body. In an instant, the magic inside him flowed unhindered, cycling its way everywhere. He looked down and saw that he was now wearing white and crimson red robes instead of his customary crimson armor. His hair darkened and grew longer, and his jaw was now covered in a thick, coarse beard. His skin remained in its unmarred, porcelain color rather than the darker pigment that was customary for this region.

Penemuel smiled as he clapped his hands. "And now you are our Father's savior for humanity! You can shift back into your true form, but you must never do so in front of your followers."

"Why not?"

"Jesus' followers will have faith that you are Jesus. It's that faith that draws them to you. If they see your true form, you risk losing most, if not all, of your powers. In other words, the spell will be broken, and all you will have are broken humans. They will be lost sheep with no purpose and no one to worship or serve."

"I see," Sorath replied and sighed. "Anything else I should know about?"

"Just in case you get any ideas about wanting to kill me, my sword has the power to undo all of your powers," Penemuel warned. He became all cheerful as he added, "Now, for a bit of dramatics. Destroy the tomb's seal and show to the world that you are alive once more…Jesus."

He frowned, thinking about Penemuel's threat of undoing his powers. He would have to take care of that threat — later, not now. He might need Penemuel in the future. But he would definitely take care of that threat!

He walked over to the cave's entrance intending to break the seal by rolling away the huge stone that covered it. He froze. The stone had already been rolled back! He stood, staring stupidly at the entrance as the dawn's light flooded into the cave. Confused, he turned back to Penemuel.

Penemuel looked as shocked as Sorath felt. Suddenly, Penemuel exclaimed, "Wow, you're awesome! You have so much power that the stone rolled away on its own!"

"Really?"

"Really!" Penemuel lied.

***

Sorath snapped out of his memories and back to the present. He was stuck in this Jesus form, and no matter what he did or said, his followers would see him only as Jesus. He could never be himself around them, and it infuriated him.

"This flaw in the spell," Sorath said aloud to himself, "has to be the deliberate work of Penemuel as a way to keep me in line. The spell also kept me from killing Penemuel."

Suddenly, the fallen angel's thoughts went to Duncan Morgan and Purah, and he felt his blood pressure rise. Killing Penemuel was the only good thing that human had done. As he thought about Duncan, he realized that the human had goaded him, nearly causing him to go out and reveal his true nature to his followers! "That would have destroyed everything—all that I had waited for and worked so long for," he growled.

Noise from the center courtyard made him smile. His flock was gathering outside, their zealous hatred for the blasphemer growing by the minute. Their love for Sorath, though, fueled him as they awaited the arrival of the prisoner.

Chapter 23

Rose and Devlin covered a great distance by teleportation, but it was tedious and slow. She had hoped his ability would make their rescue mission go swifter, but it had not. Instead, he had to stop often to rest and feed.

Now they were just a half mile outside a small village. From what Rose could tell as they made their way to it, there were only a few people, and they seemed weary as their heads darted back and forth constantly as if searching for something.

"Have you been here before?" Rose asked.

"Yes, but not for some time," Devlin replied as he took in a deep breath of air. "I don't recall it being this bad though."

"What do you mean?"

"These people are scared. Even this far away, the air reeks of the odor of their fear. My predatory nature is almost salivating."

"Are they afraid of ghouls?" She anxiously looked around them. They were in a valley with patches of small trees here and there. The rolling hills that surrounded them were plush with tall, green grass but still had tell-tale signs of the firestorm. The landscape inside the valley was dotted with impact craters, and much of the ground was scorched and had yet to recover. The mountains in the distance stood as blackened, mute monuments to that horrible day five years ago when the firestorm had rained down on the Earth.

"There might be a few ghouls nearby, but I get the sense that this is something else entirely…" Devlin voice trailed off as they entered the village, causing everyone to stop what they were doing and stare. The people seemed more on edge now.

Rose wondered if it was because Devlin was a vampire. He said he'd been here. Maybe they recognized him. Maybe strangers had been coming through and causing problems. From the traders who had come to Melona, Rose had heard tales about bandits attacking different villages and small settlements.

The moment Rose and Devlin set foot in the village, people scrambled and hid behind various objects. "Go away!" one villager cried out from behind an old whiskey barrel. "We have nothing of value for you!"

Devlin narrowed his eyes at the lady. She wore a tattered, mud-caked dress and looked as though she had been in a fight or maybe a mud wrestling competition. Even though her face was scratched and bruised, Devlin recognized her immediately. "Beth, it's only me...Devlin. You know me. This beautiful jewel beside me is Rose Macready from the village of Melona. We mean no harm. Why are all of you hiding? What's frightened you?"

Beth watched Devlin from behind the barrel, still hesitating to come out into the open. Rose felt bad for the woman and her companions because whatever had happened to them, it had left them not trusting anyone, not even Devlin whom they already knew.

With a scowl on his face, the vampire stomped towards the center of the village. "What the hell happened?" he demanded. "Who's responsible for hurting you? Just say their names, and I'll personally see to it that they never harm you again!"

"We can't say," Beth blurted out, terror slipping into her voice. "He'll have his friends kill us all if we say anything!"

"Devlin, I know that these are your friends," Rose said as she walked up to him, "but we need to go. Duncan needs us, and I'm not sure these people want our help."

Devlin angrily flashed his fangs. "Don't you think I know this? I'm sorry we can't get to Duncan any quicker, but it takes a lot out of me to teleport someone halfway across the world. I need to feed, and whoever hurt these people *will* be my next meal!"

"I've told you before that you can feed on me," Rose growled. "I'm worried about Duncan and you as well."

"Me?" Devlin gasped as if he'd been slapped with a cold fish. "Why worry about me? I'm right here in front of you. I'm not the one who was kidnapped by a fucking angel!"

A sound caught their attention; both Rose and Devlin turned and saw a young girl walking up to them. She couldn't have been more than ten or eleven. Her clothes were badly torn, and her hair was matted with mud and blood. Her face, though, showed more courage than anyone else's in the village.

With pity in his eyes, Devlin pulled out a handkerchief and took Rose's canteen. He unscrewed the lid and upended it to wet the handkerchief. Beckoning for the girl to come closer, he smiled lovingly at her, and she obeyed him without hesitation.

As Rose took her canteen back, she looked the girl over. Her heart broke for her as she saw dried blood caked between the girl's tights, and her small body was covered with cuts and bruises.

Using the wet handkerchief, Devlin wiped away crud from the girl's face as gently as possible. "Who hurt you, my dear? Who hurt my sweet, little Jenny?"

The girl leeched on to Devlin as she sobbed out, "B-bad people!" Tears gushed from her eyes as she tightly hugged the vampire.

More of the villagers came out from their hiding places and walked towards them. All of them were women, and they each looked similar: filthy hair, muddy bodies and shredded clothing.

Sadistic bastards had hurt each of the women. Rose fumed as she stared at them. "Tell us who hurt you," she pleaded. "We want to help put an end to this once and for all, but you need to follow Jenny's example and talk to us."

A curvy, redheaded woman glanced at the others for support before folding her arms across her bare chest. "I'm not sure anyone can stop them. He had all of our men killed."

"Why did you want us to leave, Sarah?" Devlin asked and rocked Jenny in his protective arms as she softly cried.

"He waits for new victims to show up!" Beth blurted out between sobs. "He's nearby, and somehow he knows when 'fresh meat' arrives here."

"Which way does the prick come from?" Rose asked. "We need to set a trap for him."

The women fearfully glanced at one another. Finally, Sarah took a deep breath. "It's hard to explain because it's so strange that you might think we're making it up."

"The fact that you're speaking to a vampire and a sorceress doesn't count as strange?" Devlin grinned as his fangs extended downward and out, glinting in the sunshine as they did.

Sarah smiled sheepishly at Devlin and bit at her bottom lip. Rose felt a twinge of jealousy spike its way to her heart. Were they more than friends? Did Sarah share more than her bed with Devlin? She shook her head and smacked Devlin's arm.

"What was that for?" he whined.

"Nothing, Casanova, just keep those incisor erections under wraps." Rose glanced back at Sarah. "Tell us about who hurt you, so we can help."

"He comes out of thin air, like he's invisible," she explained.

"Suddenly, he's just there!" another woman shrieked and shuddered violently.

"And he brings a decent-sized horde of ghouls with him too!" Beth added. "Todd is his name. You'd think his name would sound scarier, but it's just Todd. When he first appeared here, he asked if any of us wanted to repent of our sins so we could join him in the Promised Land. Naturally, we told him to fuck off but then, out of nowhere, there were ghouls all around us! They k-killed all our men. Todd then commanded the ghouls to bring each one of us to him and…" It was her turn to shudder violently. "If he's a man of God, then his God is sick and twisted for allowing a rapist to run free."

Devlin felt Jenny squeeze him tighter. He grimaced at her distress and held on to her, whispering several times, "It's okay. You're safe with me."

Rose watched the vampire, studying him. Seeing him comfort little Jenny made her heart melt for him. She had her fun lusting for him, teasing him, but Rose knew now that Devlin was the kind of man she would enjoy spending the rest of her life with.

"Todd has returned here several times," Sarah told them. "Each time it's because we have new people in our village. Lately, though, he's chosen to pop in and have his way with us while his ghouls hold us down for him…." She looked away in shame, tears streaming down her dirty face. "I don't think I can take it anymore."

"Why haven't you run away from here?" Devlin asked softly and felt Jenny tense at the question.

"He's watching us!" Beth spat out. "We've tried to leave. He just reappears and surrounds us with his army of ghouls. He told us that we can't ever leave this place. If we try to run away again, he'll have his ghouls cleanse us of our sins like they did with all the men here. We can be spared that fate as long as he can punish us…sexually."

Rose felt sick to her stomach. This Todd was another Sully. Only, Sully wanted to wipe out her village and use it as a trap for unsuspecting traders. Were these men perverted before they got reaped or did that happen after Sorath manipulated them in the Promised Land?

Rose wondered when Todd would show himself. And then she wondered if she and Devlin could fight them off. Suddenly, she had an idea. She decided it would be best to put out a mental call to the animals: "*To any of my animal friends who wish to help, I ask for your aid. There's a terrible man who controls the dead humans that's causing pain and suffering to a group of defenseless women. All who wish to join in this fight please come to me!*" Rose wasn't sure what would show up or if any would come at all, but it never hurts to ask.

"Is there anything else about Todd that seems strange?" Devlin asked.

"After he's done with us, Todd talks to a rock," Beth said. "At least, I think it's a rock, and he always says, 'Back home to the Promised Land.' He and his ghouls vanish then."

Someone in the group shouted frantically, "Oh shit, he's returned!"

Shoving Jenny behind him for protection, Devlin whirled around and stared as a man began to appear. "He's teleporting," the vampire muttered.

Rose wanted to burn Todd to ash but chose not to reveal that she had magic at her command. Instead, she unsheathed her katana.

Todd smirked as he raised an eyebrow, as if unimpressed or bored. The man held what looked to be a small rock or a gold nugget. It glowed as he whispered into it. Just then, about forty ghouls appeared out of nowhere.

Rose glared angrily as Todd leered at her. "Well, well, what do we have here?" he cheerfully asked as he greedily rubbed his hands together. "Not much of a catch, but it will have to do."

He suddenly stood up straight and took on a professional manner. "Newcomers, do you repent of all your filthy sins? If your answer is yes, you will be welcomed in the Promised Land. You will be with Jesus and can bask in His glory. You will be granted everlasting life. If, on the other hand, the answer is no, you will be cleansed of your flesh — so choose wisely."

He turned to his ghoul army. "Gather the villagers and set them aside for later. Anyone who resists me will be cleansed on the spot."

Devlin heard Jenny quietly sobbing as he left her to join Rose. He watched a small group of ghouls circle around the battered women, herding them over to the side. Devlin slid up next to Rose and whispered, "That gold nugget is our key to getting to Duncan. If we can get that, we can open a portal to the Promised Land ourselves."

"Well, heretics, what is your answer?" Todd arrogantly called out.

"Give us a moment. This is a pretty big decision," Rose answered.

"More like a life or death decision," he told her. "You have thirty seconds!"

Rose whispered, "I put a call out to the animals around here for help, but I have no idea if any will come. Do you think we have a chance?"

"I don't have a clue, Rose," Devlin admitted. "I do know this, though; Todd will die today. If we don't make it out of this, I pray he'll be dead, so he won't hurt these women...or Jenny."

Rose nodded as she tightened her grip on the hilt of her katana. They had to get to Todd and take him down or at least get that gold nugget from him. "When Duncan killed Sully back in Melona," she whispered, "he said he had to decapitate Sully because stabbing him in his heart didn't kill him. So Todd's head needs to roll, got it?"

"Got it, my love. Shall I deliver his head to you on a silver platter?" Devlin joked but showed no signs of amusement.

"Times up," Todd announced. "What's your choice?"

Devlin jutted out his chin as he defiantly answered, "We will not bow before a fallen angel who claims to be Jesus. Nor would we want to spend eternity in the company of a pathetic rapist like you."

Todd roared out in anger, "Blasphemers!" He pointed an accusing finger at them. "I should take you before Jesus so He can show you that He is the one true savior. But I won't! You, sir, will be cleansed of your flesh!" His gaze fell on Rose lustfully. "You, my dear, will be cleansed of your sins by me personally!"

Rose snorted as she twirled her katana. "Ha! Go eat a bag full of dicks and choke! If you touch me, I'll cut off that tiny worm you have between your legs!"

Todd snarled as he commanded his ghouls, "Kill the man and bring me the bitch!"

Chapter 24

"I want her made ready for me," Todd ordered, "so rip her nasty clothes off!"

"Real attractive, Todd," Rose taunted as she steadied herself while the ghouls fanned out and surrounded both her and Devlin. "Is this how you pick up all your dates? Why not come and get me yourself or did your phony Jesus make you a pussy?"

"I find it's better this way," Todd explained in a sober voice as if he wanted her to understand, which he really didn't. "You would get winded if you ran from me and so would I. On the other hand, my ghouls don't get winded. They want to help me, so why not have them do the leg work for me? They've become very good at preparing filthy whores for my needs."

Devlin stood by Rose's side, still unarmed and unmoving. He watched in silence as the ghouls crept closer with their teeth snapping greedily, causing that green crud to dribble out of their mouths like salivating dogs.

The rustling of leaves caught Rose's attention, and she looked over in the direction of the sound. Just past the ghouls to her right, she saw a group of animals — all kinds of different species — gathering, waiting for her to give them the go ahead. Above her, in the sky, an assorted array of cries rang out as a cluster of ravens, crows, hawks, and eagles flew in circles, preparing to strike. Rose grinned as she swung her sword with the confidence that Todd and his ghouls were oblivious to the animals.

Devlin opened his coat and unsheathed a short sword. He took a couple of steps toward the nearest ghoul and sliced off its head. Seeing one of their own without its head didn't cause the ghouls to become defensive. They proceed with their attack as if nothing had happened. Did the death of their comrade even register with them? Devlin's hunger was growing inside him, demanding that he should feed.

As more ghouls approached Devlin, he took a fighter's stance and waited to see what their next move would be. When several ghouls got within arm's reach of him, they stopped and stared blankly at him, unsure of what he was. They were programmed to kill and eat people, but the vampire was not human.

He grinned as he moved in towards the closest ghoul's face, baiting it to try and take a bite out him. Todd watched in bewilderment. "What are you waiting for? Kill him, damn you!"

One ghoul pawed the air in front of Devlin as it croaked, "Not alive…can't cleanse…this one."

"That's not possible!" Todd screamed in rage. "If you won't eat him then rip him apart with your hands!"

Devlin slashed first one way and then another with his sword, taking off two ghouls' heads. He then sliced off any hands that were reaching for him. "I've *disarmed* you," Devlin called out to his armless victims with amusement.

At that moment, the ground trembled as a stampede of animals rushed headlong into the fray. Several bulls trampled and gored any ghouls that stood in their path. A massive grizzly bear barreled its way to Rose, swiping its razor-sharp claws through the bodies of the ghouls, causing black ichor to saturate the ground. It stood on its hind legs and roared at the oncoming ghouls that had gotten behind Rose.

Todd groaned in frustration as his ghouls fell faster than he expected. As he put the gold nugget up to his lips, Rose mentally cried out, *"Hear me, my friends! We need someone to snatch that rock from that bastard's hand. Now!"* If one of the animals didn't get that rock fast, a literal army of ghouls would arrive — too many to fight and win.

One of the eagles circling above in the air dive bombed at Todd. It swooped in and snatched the gold nugget so fast that Todd barely knew that it had grabbed it from his hand.

"Hey! Give that back, you damn feathered prick!" Todd screamed as he shook his fist at the eagle. Ghouls appeared from thin air, but some didn't quite make it through the invisible portal and, as a result, there were ghouls that were cut in half or had their heads lopped off inter-dimensionally.

Rose felt that was a small victory, but more ghouls had gotten through before the portal closed. She and Devlin would have to work harder so they wouldn't become a happy meal for the undead.

Crows and ravens landed on top of the ghoul's heads, working to tear out their eyes. Todd glared at the eagle as it landed in a nearby tree with his gold nugget firmly grasped by its foot.

"Bring the bitch to me!" Todd commanded to the new ghouls as he stomped angrily toward the tree where the eagle was perched. "Rip the man apart while you're at it!"

More ghouls encroached on Rose, but with the aid of the grizzly bear at her back, she only had to be concerned with the ghouls in front and the sides of her. She smirked as she swung her katana, knowing that after this wave of ghouls the fight would be over. Then she could wring information out of that pig, Todd...Wait, where was he?

Rose looked around frantically in between her blows. She finally saw him attempting to climb the tree, wanting to get his gold *rock* back.

The ground rumbled once more as the bulls came charging through, knocking down ghouls like they were bowling pins. Devlin took advantage of the carnage and beheaded each of the downed ghouls.

The horde of ghouls is thinning, Rose thought, but if Todd manages to get his hands on that gold nugget, we're going to be so screwed! "You take them out, Devlin; I'm going after Todd!" she yelled as he downed two more ghouls.

He glanced over at Rose and saw her do something he never thought he'd see. Rose had mounted the mighty grizzly and was talking to it as she stroked its massive head. She grabbed a handful of the bear's fur and gritted her teeth. As she twirled her katana over her head, she urged the grizzly forward toward the tree.

Devlin sighed happily, and he beheaded another ghoul. "Oh, how I love that woman."

Devlin decided that it was time to end this charade, so he started teleporting, taking off a ghoul's head with each move. He was swift and deadly, making easy work of the last remnants of Todd's undead army. Using his supernatural speed, though, came at a cost for him. Devlin's hunger was growing stronger with each teleportation, and the need to feed was becoming maddening.

He feared that if he didn't get his hunger under control, he might hurt one of his friends or worse, yet, Rose. He couldn't simply teleport out of here to find the blood he needed because he no longer had the energy to do it. Maybe I could drink from one of these animals, he thought, but then he shook off the idea. No, I need human blood! Devlin could tell his eyes were going red as his hunger washed over him, demanding sustenance.

The massive grizzly bear ran at full speed towards an unsuspecting Todd. As it ran, it swiped its massive paws at any of the nearby ghouls while Rose swung her blade to finish them off. She saw Todd attempting to climb up the tree, but he seemed to be having difficulty finding a good foothold to help hoist him up. As she closed in on Todd, Rose could feel her heart racing and the adrenaline pushing through her body, making her forget that she was nearly exhausted from the battle.

Rose saw that Todd was losing his cool. He grabbed a handful of rocks and started chucking them at the eagle. The big bird squawked and screeched at Todd, but it held on to the branch and the gold nugget too. Rose didn't want the bird to get hurt, so she called out to it mentally, *"Come to me, brave eagle, and hand over the gold nugget."*

Between the rocks whizzing past its head, the eagle took flight toward Rose. Todd turned to track where it flew off to and then saw the grizzly bear barreling down on him. He tried to move out of the way, but the grizzly bear used its massive paw to bat Todd down to the ground.

The eagle landed on the grizzly's back and placed the gold nugget into Rose's waiting hand. She rubbed the eagle on its head and neck, thanking the majestic bird before it took to the sky again. The grizzly hunkered down on the ground to better hold Todd in place. Rose easily dismounted and watched the grizzly toy with Todd the way a cat *plays* with a mouse. The man thrashed his body around, but the bear wasn't letting him go anywhere.

"You filthy beast!" Todd snarled at the grizzly bear. "Take your fucking paws off me! I will have your pelt for this!"

Rose lovingly stroked the grizzly's fur as she walked around to face Todd. She squatted down, enjoying the fact that Todd was pinned and helpless. How ironic, Rose thought, the pious rapist is now the one at another's mercy.

"You wanted me, Todd," she told him, smirking. "Well, here I am. Looks like you're having a pretty bad day."

"You'll be cleansed slowly and painfully once I'm free from this nasty fur ball!" Todd hissed angrily.

"Now that's no way to behave," Rose said as she patted his cheek. "It would be in your best interest not to poke the bear with your insults."

"Don't touch me! I'm immortal and can't die. I fear neither it nor you, harlot!"

"Is that a fact? Who told you that?"

"Jesus, after his angels took me to the Promised Land."

"Is that the same fallen angel who lies to people and says he's Jesus, but isn't?" She chuckled. "I don't think I'd trust the word of a liar."

"Bitch!"

She ignored his insult. "Have you tried dying? Hmm, I wonder if this gorgeous beast here were to—oh I don't know—eat you whole, maybe, would you still be alive? Guess we'd have to check his shit for your pulse." She threw back her head and laughed.

Todd gulped but replied defiantly, "I'm sure I would live. Jesus made me this way and wouldn't make me where a simple beast could take me down."

"And yet it happened, didn't it." Rose tsked several times before grinning broadly.

She looked to her side and saw Devlin standing beside her. He was clenching his hands into fists as blood seeped past his fingers. As she looked up at the vampire, panic seized her. He was in full bloodlust mode; his eyes were completely red with no white showing.

Devlin's gaze bore into Rose's neck, and she instinctively covered her carotid artery with her hand. In this state, he was a dangerous and deadly predator. Without meaning to, Devlin could kill her without much effort, and there was nothing she could do about it.

"You don't know the first thing about being an immortal, Todd," Devlin growled, his voice getting huskier with each word. "But since you can't die, I ought to have no problem bleeding you dry. Why, you would be the perfect drink—never going empty and the refills are free!"

Todd scoffed, "Oh I'm so scared now! The harlot's man-whore is going to bleed me out! Tell me, what exactly will you do with all my blood? Bathe in it or have some sort of satanic ritual that all you heathens enjoy performing?"

In the blink of an eye, Devlin yanked Todd out from under the grizzly bear and held him up off the ground with one hand. The scent from Todd's blood that trickled down his body was intoxicating to Devlin. The vampire swiped a finger in one of the man's wounds and slowly suckled the blood off his finger.

"Your body has the nasty taint of the fallen angel that transformed you. It's bitter, but your blood will have to do."

"Jesus is *not* a fallen angel, you bastard! He's— AARRGGHH!"

Devlin pulled him into a bear hug and sank his fangs into Todd's carotid artery. The man groaned as he squirmed, trying to free his body from Devlin's vice-like grip but nothing worked. He tried kicking, pinching, and clawing at Devlin, but the vampire was unfazed.

Rose got into Todd's face. "You're right. Jesus is not a fallen angel. But then from your actions as a sadistic rapist, I'd say you've never met the *real* Jesus." She glanced down at the gold nugget in her hand and then held it up for Todd to see. "We're grateful for this lovely gift. It will make our trip to the Promised Land quicker and easier."

"Give that…back, bitch!" Todd growled. "No one…goes there…who isn't…saved first!"

"Your pseudo-Jesus took our friend there, and he hasn't been saved. We want him back, and if we have to storm that place and burn it to the ground, we will!"

Even though he was about to pass out from blood loss, Todd still managed a feeble chuckle. "The one called Duncan Morgan will be dead by the time you get there. His body will be beyond recognizable too! Our Lord has judged him for his crimes against our people, and he'll suffer greatly, I can promise you that!"

"Did you know a man named Sully?" Devlin asked as he took his lips from Todd's neck. "Duncan killed him, you know. Wasn't he supposed to be like you, an immortal…undying?"

"Sully can't die!" Todd cried out. "I don't believe this nonsense!"

"Really?" Rose chimed in as she poked Todd in his chest with her finger. "Then why is it when Duncan took his head off did he not revive? I was there, and he was deader than disco. And you're next!"

Todd paled even more at this revelation, and a look of panic washed across his face. All of his smugness and his disdainful, superior words were gone. To Rose, Todd looked more like a scared child than a creepy rapist.

Devlin sank his fangs into Todd's neck again and kept drinking until he felt Todd's body go limp. He slung him over his shoulder and walked back to where all the women were standing, watching him intently. Devlin felt a swell of pride as he dropped Todd on the ground at their feet. "Your immortal captor is down but not dead. If you want to have some therapeutic fun with him, I suggest you tie him down. If not, then cut off his head; either way, he'll die."

The ladies ran to grab whatever weapons they had hidden away. When they returned, each one had a maniacal gleam in her eyes. Beth raised her weather-worn axe and brought it down on Todd's thigh. He screamed, ranting incoherently, but he didn't have the strength to move and could only watch as the woman hacked off one leg and went to work on his other one.

Sarah stepped down on Todd's right wrist and started chopping away at his arm. There was barely any blood left in his body. When Sarah finished with his left arm, she moved over to his right.

Devlin smiled, approving wholeheartedly of the carnage. He gave Rose a side hug, but what threw them all was when Jenny decided to join the fracas.

The little girl walked over with a rusty handsaw in her hand. She stood between the stumps that were Todd's legs and glared at him, snarling. Jenny dropped to her knees and unzipped Todd's tattered, bloody jeans. She grabbed him by his shaft and proceeded to slice it off. He screamed out in pain and horror. But his face paled even more as little Jenny methodically crawled up and sat down on his chest with his severed member in her hand. As he sobbed weakly, she grabbed his mouth and pried it open while screaming over and over, "Eat it, you little harlot!"

Jenny stuffed it into Todd's mouth and manually made him chew it up. From somewhere deep within her soul, her words took on a deep growl as she snarled, "You will swallow what I give you!"

Nausea covered Rose. She was about to empty the contents of her stomach, but Devlin turned and moved her away from the gruesome display of revenge.

The vampire looked back over his shoulder, his anger rising. Todd more than likely said those exact words to Jenny as he forced himself on her. He figured it was only fitting that she do the same to him. I don't need to do any more, Devlin reminded himself. They know how to end it. Let the ladies have their twisted fun with this evil man.

Rose looked at all the animals that had come to help in the fight and gave them all thanks. She felt bad that she didn't have anything to give them in return, but time was running short and she and Devlin needed to get to Duncan.

She pulled the gold nugget out of her pocket and looked up at Devlin. He nodded and motioned for her to proceed. Rose wasn't exactly sure how to use the nugget or if it would work for her at all, but that wasn't going to stop her from trying. Duncan's life was at stake, and he needed them now more than ever. Rose concentrated, focusing on the gold nugget and commanded, "To the Promised Land now!"

There was a static buzz as the air around them became charged with magic. Suddenly, the air in front of them shimmered brightly. Devlin squinted and asked, "Did it work? I don't see anything."

Over the hollering and laughter of the ladies behind them, Rose replied, "Yes, now let's go save our friend!" Arms locked together, they both walked through the shimmering energy and disappeared.

As they appeared on the other side, Rose saw that they were in an expansive room made of solid gold…and filled with ghouls!

When the ghouls saw them, that putrid, green crud immediately started to foam from their mouths. The ghouls extended their arms, reaching out to grasp hold of the newcomers. Devlin swore under his breath as he wanted to put himself between the ghouls and Rose, but there were more ghouls behind them. They were surrounded, and the only way out was either to fight or risk teleporting to another area that could be just as bad or worse.

"I'll do what I can to protect you, Rose. Unfortunately, I've fed, and they can now smell me too."

Chapter 25

The sound of shuffling feet assailed Duncan's ears as he and his undead escorts marched down a barren corridor. The firelight from the orbs on the walls flickered, and the shadows danced, making the ghouls that surrounded him even more unnerving. He was cold and hungry, but it wouldn't do any good to complain since they wanted him to suffer before dying. The flooring under his feet was smooth as ice and just as cold, and it made Duncan wonder how deep down the palace went.

Every so often he would see his wife Pamela glancing back at him. The hate and nasty intent in her eyes told him everything he needed to know. When Sorath had probed his mind earlier, he had seen the painful memories of Duncan's marriage—the fights, the arguing, and Pamela's shrewish behavior. Sorath had decided then to use her as his instrument of torture.

The cold temperature in the corridor made his body shiver, and he knew it had been Pamela's idea to have him stripped of his clothing. He figured she added humiliation and pneumonia to her ever-growing list of cruelties to be done to him. Duncan recalled when they first started dating how sweet and loving she had been, how nothing in the world mattered except the two of them. Shortly after they were married, though, the relationship subtly shifted into mind games and then into mental abuse.

Duncan's mind snapped back to reality as he felt the unmistakable feel of several ghouls touching his naked flesh. He glanced at them; they were foaming at the mouth, wanting to feast on him but couldn't. They looked like starving creatures that had a mouth-watering steak waving in front of them, just out of reach.

"Get your filthy pets to keep their goddamn hands to themselves!" Duncan snapped.

"Why? Are they bothering you, sweetheart?" Pamela mocked. "Are you feeling a little…insecure around my friends? Maybe I should let them get closer to you so you won't feel so inadequate around them." She flashed him a wicked grin, and a moment later the ghouls were shuffling closer to him. Each of the ghouls reached out and touched Duncan, either running a hand up and down his body or gently groping him.

Duncan glared at Pamela as she kept leading the way down the long corridor. What made her so cruel, Duncan wondered as he shoved and smacked hands away from his body.

"Don't hurt my friends' feelings," Pamela called out. "They might take a bite out of you." She shook her head in disgust. "Same old Duncan, nothing but a waste of oxygen. You'll always be a pathetic excuse for a man, and you'll never amount to anything."

"Maybe so, but at least I'm not the one who's slumming with ghouls and a pseudo-Jesus."

"Still mad you didn't get chosen for a higher purpose, babe? Typical of you, Duncan. Always blaming others for you failures. I never understood why you just didn't kill yourself. It would have made my life so much easier. That's right, honey, I loved you that much! Why you never filed for divorce is beyond me."

"Because I made a promise that I would be with you till death do us part, and I always keep my promises, that's why."

She laughed. "You and your old fashioned sense of nobility. Don't you know that doesn't mean shit anymore? All those affairs of mine gave you just cause to leave me, but you didn't go. You know what that makes you, right?"

"A man of my word." Duncan hissed.

"No, that makes you a weak, pathetic, worm and both of us know that worms are spineless. A worm is what I married."

"At least one of us had to make the effort to stay true to those vows. Even after you were taken away from me, I still didn't stray."

Pamela stopped dead in her tracks, halting the escorts. She turned around to face Duncan and had a look of shock on her face. Suddenly, she burst out laughing.

The ghouls surrounding Duncan started to laugh too. Some even pointed their bony fingers at him. He had never heard a ghoul laugh before. Their voices sounded deep, scratchy and hollow. Echoing off the corridor walls, the way they were, the voices were creepy and unsettling, making him shiver violently.

Pamela wiped tears from her eyes. "Wow! What a fucking loser you are! You had what, a five year pass to fuck whoever you wanted and didn't act on it? I'd find that hard to believe but, then again, who would want your sorry ass anyway?"

"I had many opportunities to cheat on you during that time! Ladies were throwing themselves at me, but I never once strayed," Duncan growled against the chorus of undead laughter.

"You didn't stray because there wasn't anyone who wanted you." She laughed. "Just you and rosey palm for the rest of your short life. Me? I've had no problems getting lucky here."

Duncan gasped. "I didn't think you'd be able to do that here in the supposed Holy Land." He shrugged his shoulders and added, "I guess your Jesus is running a palace of ill repute."

Pamela turned around and started walking once more. The ghouls were still far too close to Duncan than he would have liked. He wanted to use his magical energy like he had done when he was being eaten alive, but he didn't want Pamela to be caught in the blast too. She was still his wife. No matter how she treated him, he couldn't kill her like that.

They came upon a long, winding staircase the led upwards, and Duncan could hear the sound of muffled voices coming from somewhere. As they ascended the stairs, he noticed that the temperature was changing. It was getting warmer.

When they got to the top of the stairs, Pamela shoved open a large, wooden door. The bright light of the sun blinded Duncan momentarily, but he kept moving. As he stepped through the doorway, he had to use his hand to shield his eyes. Finally, as his eyes adjusted to the light, he noticed there were thousands of people filling up the courtyard.

He grimaced as he walked out into the hot courtyard. The flooring was made of gold, and it burned Duncan's feet. When people realized he was coming out, a cacophony of noise rose up. The sound of Sorath's raucous, bloodthirsty followers was deafening, and he winced from the pain in his ears. They jeered and hissed at him; some of them spat on him as he walked by them. For the first time in his life, he now knew what it felt like to be public enemy number one.

The escort of ghouls acted as a security detail, shoving and blocking the throngs of people who had one thing on their mind: kill Duncan Morgan.

With maliciousness in her eyes, Pamela looked back at him. "Look, sweetheart, they're your biggest fans! Don't disappoint them like you've disappointed me for so many years!"

Duncan noted that there was a large mound they were walking toward, and it too was created from gold. Movement on top of the walls that surrounded the courtyard caught his attention. Children were on the wall, scrubbing and cleaning it! "Slaves," he muttered. The walls had to be a good two hundred feet tall. If any of the children fell, he was sure they wouldn't be mourned or missed. Probably the ones who died here became fodder for the damn ghouls.

As they walked up to the mound, Duncan saw that the gold had no seams or any creases from where it had been molded. It was as if it was a natural formation, like it grew up from the ground. Maybe that was how Sorath had crafted his palace, summoning the gold from the Earth itself and sculpting it to his liking.

A man ran around like a cheerleader stirring up the crowd of onlookers. He was wearing a uniform, like a guard would, but it was from a different time period. When the man saw Duncan coming up on the golden mound, he shouted to the people, "Finally! The murderous heathen has arrived for his punishment!"

The crowd erupted into a feverish flood of boos and hisses while shaking their fists at Duncan. He felt sick to his stomach. It was like a scene from a movie where the main character is brought before a crowd to be hanged, but Duncan didn't think he would get off that easily.

Pamela walked over and gave the cheerleader a passionate kiss on his lips and then she mockingly glanced at Duncan.

"My descent into madness is complete," Duncan muttered gloomily.

The air in the central courtyard sizzled and buzzed, causing the crowd to do a one-eighty. They now roared with cheers as Sorath seemingly came out of nowhere and magically appeared before them. In his guise of Jesus, Sorath waved and smiled at his followers, enjoying being the center of attention and eating up their praise and worship.

Pamela crooked her finger, beckoning the ghoul escort to bring Duncan to the center of the gold mound. Duncan cringed as the icy cold hands of the ghouls touched his back to push him forward. Duncan edged toward the mound as the phony Jesus gazed upon him.

Sorath gave a dismissive wave. "Thank you for bringing the criminal before us. You may go now."

The ghouls nodded in unison, turned around and shambled off the gold mound leaving Duncan fully exposed to the hateful glares of Sorath's followers. He put his hands behind his back and jutted his chin out at the crowd defiantly.

Sorath turned to Pamela with a loving smile and asked, "Is there a particular reason you had the criminal disrobed?"

"Yes," she answered confidently, "with his clothes on he would feel safe. With them off, your followers will see that he's not a monster to fear. He's only a mere mortal who is timid and weak. Plus, we'll get to see him bleed easier, my lord."

Sorath chuckled. "I like your reasoning, my dear."

Duncan closed his eyes and couldn't believe the words spewing out of his wife's mouth. She was even more sadistic than he remembered.

Pamela moved next to him, looking him up and down before she grabbed Duncan by his hair and screamed, "This evil man needs to bleed for his wickedness against our people!"

The crowd roared to life once more, and Duncan was afraid they would rush at him. If they did, they would tear him apart like a huge pack of jackals on a wounded lamb. Panic set in, and he looked everywhere for an escape route but couldn't find one. Which is just as well, he thought. They would rip me apart if I tried an escape.

The phony Jesus looked over at Duncan and then at Pamela. "Be a dear and fetch the irons; I don't want this one bound in mere ropes."

"With pleasure, my lord!" Pamela exclaimed excitedly and hurried off of the gold mound.

As the crowd parted for her, Duncan saw her open a small hatch that led underground. It was only a few feet from the mound where he stood. She quickly disappeared down through it.

If everyone is up here, he thought, maybe I should be down there. He knew there were more exits out of the underground labyrinth of cells because he had seen arrows pointing toward them. "What the hell," he growled and shot off the mound toward the hatch Pamela had used.

As much as he was sweating, he figured it would be difficult for people to get a good hold on his bare skin. Sorath laughed as he merrily called out to Duncan, "Only the guilty try to run and hide from their judgment, Duncan Morgan! There will be no escape for you today." He motioned to several people. "Fetch him back for me, my children!"

Duncan felt hands all around him, grasping at him as he ran for his life toward the open hatch. When he was within inches of it, someone in the crowd thrust out their leg, and he tumbled over it, falling to the ground with a hard thud. Duncan grunted in pain and stared longingly at the hatchway.

Carrying the irons, Pamela popped her head up through the opening and saw him. She patted his cheek as she purred, "Naughty, naughty, sweet thing. I think I'll punish you myself. Trust me. You won't enjoy it as much as I will, my love."

Duncan felt hands roughly grab his ankles and legs as people pulled him back toward the gold mound. They spit on him. Plenty of them took the opportunity to kick him in the ribs or stomp on his hands and arms as he was dragged by. He barely caught a glimpse of Pamela as she rose up from the hatchway before he got dragged up a small rise.

The hot, golden pavement burned away at his skin, and several people leaned in and pulled Duncan up to his feet. They held him steady while a smug-looking lady punched him several times in the gut. When she was finished, she spit in his face, and everyone laughed.

Duncan was then ushered toward the phony Jesus. He saw that Pamela stood a few feet to Sorath's left and in between the two of them now stood a golden frame. It glimmered in the sunlight, and it answered what Duncan suspected about the palace: Sorath was somehow manipulating the gold that ran deep in the Earth and crafting it to meet his needs.

In the center of the frame was a set of old, rusty iron chains that had a pair of thick manacles bolted to them. The shackles had glowing sigils etched into them.

Sorath smiled as Duncan approached. "Secure the prisoner," he ordered the men. "I can't pass judgment on him if he's not around, now can I?"

They pushed Duncan under the golden frame and held up his arms while Pamela snapped the manacles around his wrists. She caressed Duncan's ass and purred in his ear, "Being shackled suits you. It's something you can't fuck up, but I'm sure you'll find a way. You always do."

"Fuck off, Pamela! At least I haven't been brainwashed by some damn fallen angel like you. Can't you see he's not Jesus? He's—OOF!"

Pamela slugged him in his gut and was about to throw another punch when the phony Jesus spoke up, "That's enough! I must judge him. When he's found guilty, you may lead the punishment on him." He glanced at the man's guards. "Clear the judging mound, everyone!"

While Pamela made her way to a medium-sized wooden box at the base of the gold mound, all of Duncan's captors scattered and melded in with the rest of the crowd. Sorath looked into Duncan's eyes and spoke to him telepathically, *"This is only a formality. You will be punished and put to death for your crimes against me and my people. I know you can use magic. That's why I had your lovely wife place you in these special restraints. They will cut you off from all your magical abilities. No matter what you try, you will fail to escape."*

Duncan angrily lunged at the fallen angel, but he was held fast by the chains. The phony Jesus chuckled as he stepped away to speak with his followers. He held his arms up high and waved his hands so everyone would go silent.

Sorath magnified his voice with his angelic magic as he spoke, "My friends, we are gathered here today because of a terrible tragedy that has occurred — a tragedy that has caused me a great deal of pain and suffering. We have lost a great deal of our fallen warriors as well as a good man by the name of Sully. They all lost their lives doing what they had a passion for in life. They were all cut down by this mortal who stands before you."

The crowd hissed and hurled insults at Duncan, but all he could do was look down at his feet, trying to tune everyone out, especially Sorath. Is it possible to die from a pompous speech? Duncan mused. He recalled having the same thought every few years when politicians would get on the airwaves and promise change, but all they ever did was blow smoke up everyone's asses. Duncan never wanted to take the chance of dying, so he would turn off the television. Now he was stuck here, listening to a smoke-spewing fuck who was his judge, jury, and executioner.

"His name is Duncan Morgan," Sorath continued. "He has not denied that any of these crimes were committed by his hand. In fact, he seems to enjoy boasting about them to me. Now that he is here, he will confess to you and show his true colors. He is the epitome of what the heretics and sinners have become since I had you brought here to be cleansed and made perfect." He turned to the prisoner. Duncan Morgan, do you deny that you have murdered our fallen warriors as well as Sully?"

Duncan remained silent and didn't acknowledge the fallen angel, which only infuriated Sorath. None of his followers could tell he was angry, though, because of the guise he wore. The phony Jesus strolled up to Duncan and yanked his head up by his hair.

"What the fuck is it with you assholes?" Duncan snarled, which shocked most of the crowd, but it didn't seem to faze Jesus. "You're always yanking my fucking hair all the damn time."

"Speak the truth now, Duncan Morgan; it will set you free. Answer the question!"

Duncan snorted. "Speak the truth, you say? What a wonderful concept. Care to go first and demonstrate what it's like to tell the truth? Trust me, folks. He's the biggest liar and hypocrite of us all." Everyone gasped at the blatant, outrageous blasphemy. "Why not show them your true form, *Jesus*?" He said the name with a snide, sarcastic voice.

Several men bolted up on the gold mound with clubs in hand to beat Duncan, but Sorath put a hand up and stopped them. "You're not allowed up here during judgment. Control yourselves until after the trial. You may help punish this guilty man then."

"But lord, we can't stand by while he insults you!" one of the men pleaded. "Can't we soften him so he'll speak the truth easier for you?"

"No!" Sorath bellowed. "Leave now or be the next to stand in his place!"

"Trouble in paradise?" Duncan asked with amusement.

The men cowered back down into the crowd like scared children. Other onlookers went mute and became more subdued, not wanting to anger the Messiah and incur his wrath. Sorath turned around and surveyed his flock, checking to see if everyone was being an obedient sheep. Once he was satisfied they had all been pacified, he locked his gaze on to Duncan. "Speak the truth now, Duncan Morgan; it will set you free."

"In the end, does it really matter what I say? You plan on killing me anyway, so why the big show for your little puppets?"

"It matters not to us, but I believe it would be in your best interest to confess and tell me and my followers about all your sins against us."

"Fine," Duncan rolled his eyes as he huffed. "Yes, I killed many of your Chouls—"

"What are Chouls?" someone in the crowd hollered. Others nodded that they wanted to know also.

"The dead that rose up out of their graves," Duncan explained. "Christian ghouls—or Chouls. Yes, I killed many of your Chouls. I also killed that slimy, scumbag Sully for murdering a lot of innocent men, women, and children who had done nothing to anyone."

"You mean heathens like you, don't you?" someone else called out, and the others agreed.

"I mean good people who went about living in harmony and peace, helping all those who came to our little village. I guess kindness is seen as a weakness to you dumbasses, but we who live beyond these walls struggle to survive every day in the hopes of seeing the next day. Many don't have the luxuries you have here. A lot of people don't have roofs over their heads, and their children are starving because of the evil this fucking fallen angel here brought down on this world."

Someone in the crowd threw a rock at him, but he ducked, and it missed him. "He's Jesus," a man shouted. "He's not a fallen angel. If you can't see that, then you're the dumbass!" They all cheered at the man's words.

Duncan ignored them and went on. "Have any of you been bitten by your undead buddies?" He glared at them, but no one answered. "No? Well, I've been bitten. Just a few weeks ago I was nearly eaten alive, but I managed to slay all the Chouls despite the many bites I sustained!"

Sorath used his angelic eyes to examine Duncan's body from afar and noted that he had no injuries of any kind. Was he lying about the attacks on him? Duncan had to be lying, he decided. No mortal could heal that fast.

Someone in the crowd yelled out, "You look fine; I see no bites anywhere! You are nothing more than a liar and a murderer!"

"I heal quickly, you stupid douchebag!" Duncan looked at Jesus and irritably spat out, "Can we get this over with? I have places to go and Chouls to kill."

The phony Jesus turned away from Duncan with a smile. He raised his arms in the air and cheerfully declared, "You see, this man has confessed all of his wrongdoings. It's time for the world to realize that no sinner is better than us, and they cannot slay any of my flock without retribution." He glanced over at Duncan. "Duncan Morgan, you are found to be guilty of your crimes against me as well as my flock and are hereby sentenced to death. Do you have any requests before we start your cleansing process?"

Better to die a jackass than one of the mindless cowards, like all these people. He wanted nothing more than to be far away from this place, somewhere peaceful and quiet like Melona. I never asked for this life, he thought bitterly, and I sure as hell didn't set out to kill fallen angels either. He sighed heavily. What's done is done.

"Well, I'm waiting," Sorath urged impatiently.

He glanced up at the fallen angel. "Yeah, I've got one request. Reveal your true form or is that too much of a request for you to accomplish?" Duncan spat out, wishing he had some water. He doubted any would be provided to him, so why ask for it?

Jesus mentally spoke to Duncan, "*That's a request that shall never be fulfilled. I hope you enjoy the cleansing; it will last as long as it needs to, Duncan Morgan.*"

Sorath joyfully cried out, "Let the cleansing process begin!" He turned to Pamela. "If you would care to start it off, please."

"With pleasure, my lord!" Pamela purred as she stalked up behind Duncan. She caressed his back as she licked his earlobe and whispered, "Time to pay the piper, my love. Just remember, you brought all of this down on yourself. No one is to blame except you!"

"Shut up and get started, Pamela!" Duncan snarled as he glared at Sorath. "Is everyone here all talk and no action?"

Duncan heard Pamela giggling as she backed away from him. The sound of a heavy whip cracked several times behind him and each time it did, the sound made Duncan involuntarily flinch. Sweat dripped down Duncan's face as she kept cracking the whip behind him, and his anxiety rose with the anticipation of her first strike. It was just like Pamela to torture him with the thought before she did the deed.

Suddenly, he heard the sound of air whizzing behind him. Instantly following, came the searing pain as the heavy whip made contact across Duncan's back.

"Oh, I bet that stung," Pamela mocked as she reared back for another strike. "Here, let me add some more. You know what? I think I'll play tic-tac-toe on your back. Well, the best I can since you'll probably squirm and ruin everything. You always ruin everything!"

CRACK! CRACK! CRACK!

Duncan gritted his teeth to the point that his molars were cracking, and he sensed hot liquid dripping down below his feet. He felt the magic within him building up once again, but with the enchanted shackles locked on his wrists, it didn't come roaring to the forefront like it had weeks ago during his fight with the ghouls. Duncan concentrated and tried to will the magic forward but then another slash on his mutilated back undid it all for him.

Pamela strutted around to where Duncan could see her grinning from ear to ear. "I can't leave your front untouched, now can I, love?" Pamela maniacally cackled as she reared back and swung the whip with a sidearm motion, sending it across Duncan's thighs.

Duncan felt his legs give way. The only thing that kept him upright was his restraints, and even they cut into his flesh under his own weight. Pamela seemed proud of herself so she unleashed several more hits along Duncan's chest and abdomen. He cried out in pain as tears streamed down his face. He snarled, "Fucking bitch! Let's trade places, and I will — AARRGH!"

Another crack of the whip hit Duncan in the mouth at an angle, deeply splitting his lips and causing the area to swell dramatically.

"Sorry, sweetheart. I didn't quite catch that last sentence. Hmm, maybe next time you'll show this whip-mistress some respect."

CRACK! CRACK! CRACK!

The pain was becoming too intense, and Duncan felt as if he was going to black out. Pamela reared back for another lashing, but Sorath stopped her. "That's enough for the moment, my child."

She pouted. "But, my lord, can't I give my husband one more? I know exactly where I want to strike him. It'll be a going away gift from me to him."

Sorath mulled it over for a moment and then said cheerfully, "Of course you can! This is your husband, after all. Give him one that he will always remember."

Pamela beamed with happiness as she called out, "I need him standing upright!" She pointed to a couple of men a few feet from her. "You two," she ordered them, "make it happen now!" The two men rushed up from the crowd and eagerly obeyed her orders.

Despite the scorching heat, shock was setting in, and Duncan's body shivered with a coldness he felt throughout his soul. His split lips quivered from the pain, and he wanted only to pass out. Rough hands grasped his arms and hoisted him up to a standing position.

Pamela motioned to the men. "Spread his legs to look like the Vitruvian Man. He'll stand better that way."

The men kicked at his bloody legs and spread them apart. Duncan knew that Pamela loved art, and the Vitruvian Man was her favorite, for whatever reason. Now he was being used to recreate Leonardo da Vinci's drawing. He just wanted them to hurry up and kill him, but Pamela only stood there eyeing him as her grip on the heavy, blood-soaked whip tightened.

Once he was positioned to resemble the Renaissance masterpiece, one of the men yanked Duncan's head up by his blood-caked hair and made him watch Pamela. She took a couple of steps forward as she wound up the whip for her final strike. "This one is my gift to you, Duncan Morgan, for all the years we've been apart. It must have been difficult on you to be away from me for so long. Since you say there have been no others in your life, let me give you a proper release!"

CRACK!

Duncan's eyes shot open wide as he shrieked as loud as his lungs would permit. The whip had snapped across his groin, leaving a nasty, bloody cut. The pain was too much. His head felt as if it would explode, and his whole being seemed to be on fire. Waves of nausea rolled over him, and he felt his body shutting down.

The crowd cheered and applauded as Pamela took several bows. She walked over and kissed Duncan, biting his split lip as she did. "I love you, Duncan!" Sashaying around and giving the appreciative crowd what they wanted for a few minutes more, she finally left the mound.

Jesus clapped his hands and let his voice boom out. "Well done, Pamela! That was a fitting, parting gift for your soon-to-be late husband. Now that he's been warmed up, it's time for the second phase of his punishment. It's time for a stoning, so grab your rocks and let them fly at this evil fiend!"

Duncan did his best to move away from the small projectiles coming at him, but no matter which way he jerked, the rocks hit him. His body was being pelted from all directions, and he could feel some of his bones cracking from the impacts.

The rocks varied in both size and texture, and each one hurt worse than the last. Suddenly, a solid, smooth rock struck Duncan on the side of his bloodied right temple. After that, his head lolled from side to side, depending on where the rocks hit him. His numb mind slightly registered the rocks as they bounced off his body, and his blurry vision helped him see the bloody pool at his feet. Finally, blessedly, darkness enveloped his world.

Chapter 26

A ghoul extended its gnarled, bony arm and pointed at Rose and Devlin. "Fresh…flesh…" it said with a harsh, grating voice.

"Great!" Rose exclaimed sarcastically. Todd's gold nugget had transported them to a room filled with ghouls, and she quickly unsheathed her katana. There were too many of them to fight and win, and now both she and Devlin were in danger of being eaten alive.

She wasn't sure how Devlin was fairing, but Rose was already feeling wore down from their previous battle with Todd and his ghoul army. With grim determination, Rose cried out as she swung her sword. "Take that!" She sliced heads off and hacked away at any hands that tried to grab her.

Devlin glanced at her, his fangs out and sword at the ready. He would show these ghouls what a vampire could do. He sprang into action by grabbing Rose and using his teleporting skills.

Nothing happened!

Devlin gasped. "What the hell?" He kicked the nearest ghouls away and tried to teleport again. Still, nothing happened.

"I've got a bad feeling about this," he told her. For the first time in his life, he was in a fight he couldn't win. The ghouls may not know how to take me down, he thought, but if they kill Rose, I'll die of a broken heart.

His supernatural abilities were blocked by this place, and he needed to test them to see how badly they had been neutered. He ran at the ghouls while slicing away at their necks and hands. His speed and agility worked fine, and he roared with delight. Maybe he did have a chance to fend off the ghoul onslaught — at least, away from Rose.

"Do you see a way out of here?" she called out as she struck down another ghoul.

"I see a door," Devlin replied grimly. "We'll need to hack our way to it though."

"Can you teleport us to it or are there too many of these dead dicks protecting it?"

"My teleporting has been disabled by this place. I'll do my best to clear a path, though, but I'm afraid the ghouls will swarm you. Can you do any magic?"

"I don't know. Since you can't teleport, I doubt it." Rose grunted as she cut off another ghoul's head and kicked its body down to make several other ghouls trip and stumble. "I don't have the juice to take out the ghouls with my magic. If I did, I'd be doing it right now."

"Try something simple, like a circle shield," he urged. "It won't take much effort. If it doesn't work, then my plan won't work either."

"What plan?"

Devlin suddenly howled in pain as a ghoul bit down on his arm. He glared at it like it was a zit on prom night and sliced through its neck with his sword. The ghoul's head fell to the floor with a thud. He grimaced in pain as he slid next to Rose. "If you can bubble yourself, I can wield your katana and make a bigger dent in them."

"I'm not sure that will work. I can't — "

"The fucking angelic magic may have stopped my teleporting but not my speed!" Devlin growled as he swung his sword in a wide arcing motion, lopping off three heads at once. "You're a sorceress, Rose. You have a direct connection with Mother Earth, herself. Draw on her energies! Hell, look what we're standing on. We can use this gold and make it a conduit for your powers!"

Rose glanced down and saw that the floor was indeed made of gold. She had forgotten all about that after she had started fighting for their lives. How did Devlin know so much about magic and spell casting? Maybe he knew a few witches, she thought. Devlin had been around for centuries so it would make sense that his path would have crossed with a few magic users.

The more she looked at the gold floor, the more she was convinced that she could ground herself into the Earth through it. Gold was an excellent conductor of energy. She closed her eyes and concentrated on the Earth. "I am your child; you are my mother. I need your energy. I know the dead in this room are an abomination to you," she told Mother Earth.

She could hear Devlin fighting the ghouls away from her. "These dead humans should be lying in your bosom for an eternity, but instead they were forced out of their graves by an evil being. Help me kill them once more, so they may return to you, their mother." She could feel the natural energy flowing effortlessly through the gold from Mother Earth into her. The energy healed and caressed her; it reenergized her.

Rose's long, raven hair floated in the air as the room became charged with her magic. With a wicked grin on his face, Devlin glanced over his shoulder at her. "That's it, girl! Now hand me your katana while I deal with these dead assess."

Rose had another plan in mind for her and Devlin. She focused the energy into a large, protective bubble that engulfed both of them. It was a good twenty feet in diameter, and a few of the ghouls got trapped inside the bubble with them. Devlin easily dispatched them.

The ghouls on the outside of the bubble could only touch it. Many of them banged on it while others examined it closely, looking for a weak spot or a way inside. As Devlin calmly moved over to Rose, he extended his hand. "Okay, hand me your sword and let me out of the bubble, so I can take care of this mess."

Irritation covered Rose, and she scowled at Devlin. Her gaze caused the vampire to step back and lower his hand. Her eyes glowed with the magic she was wielding. Devlin groaned as he felt his arousal pique. Rose was beyond beautiful when she was in her element, like this. She was both breathtaking and deadly.

"I want to try something," she said. "It may or may not work, but I'll be damned if I'm letting you fight this battle alone! I'm not a fucking porcelain doll!"

Devlin raised his hands up submissively. "Please don't misjudge my reasoning. I'm superfast. With two swords, I can double their trouble. They won't stand a chance with me, so don't think that I see you as weak, Rose." He paused momentarily and frowned. "I would gladly let them eat me," he said quietly and sincerely, "if it meant you could escape unharmed."

Rose's lips parted in surprise as her anger ebbed. Her heart swelled with happiness, and her whole being was flooded with emotions she had never experienced before. Was this…love? She wasn't sure, but for once she was being seen as an equal in someone else's eyes, and that alone endeared Devlin to her even more.

He flashed a wicked grin at her, causing her heart to race. "What are you waiting for, sweetheart?" he asked in a low, husky voice. "Deal with these dicks so we can find Duncan. I'm curious as to what you've got planned."

Rose blushed slightly as she took in several deep breaths. She closed her eyes and focused on her protective bubble. It lowered slowly, and Rose said as she sat down, "Have a seat and watch the show."

Devlin obeyed. He sat down next to her on the *floor* of the bubble. The loving warmth that he exuded forced her to sidle up against the vampire. She let out a soft sigh, hoping her face wasn't red. Once the protective bubble was about five feet off the gold floor, Rose manipulated it into the shape of a square box.

The ghouls groped and tried to grab on to the edges of the square bubble, hoping to climb up on top of it. Only, the edges now jutted out like razor-sharp knives, and all Devlin could see were decaying fingers falling to the gold floor. Rose gathered more of the Earth's energy to feed into her bubble, and it expanded outward, shoving most of the ghouls back against the walls.

She concentrated, projecting her will into her protective bubble, causing it to have the force of a massive mudslide. Pinned against the golden walls, the ghouls could do nothing but stand and helplessly watch as their bodies were crushed by the bubble. Their heads exploded from the pressure like zits being popped, and Rose retched a little at seeing the black ichor shooting out, splattering against the gold walls and the bubble.

Rose forced the huge bubble to slowly turn all around the room like a carousel of gore. All the ghouls that were pinned in a standing position had their heads ripped off from the movement of the bubble against the walls. "Like scrapping dog shit off one's shoe," Devlin muttered. He cringed at the site but had to give Rose credit for her creative use of the bubble.

"Remind me *not* to piss you off, Rose. I don't think I would enjoy being on the receiving end of your fury."

She let the protective bubble slowly recede back into the Earth as she ungrounded her body. With the bubble now gone, she looked around the room. The color of the walls was now a mix of gold and black slurry. A few ghouls had survived but were in no condition to rise up and cause them any trouble.

Even so, Devlin stood up and held out a waiting hand to aid Rose to her feet. They both walked around the room beheading the survivors. Rose kept glancing at him, watching him from afar and admiring his physique. The man may be old, she thought, but he does have a nice ass.

Devlin was behind her before she realized it. He gently wrapped his strong arms around her chest and softly whispered in her ear, "I could find you by that scent of yours no matter where you hid. No foul odor could cover up something as sweet and intoxicating as your nectar."

Rose shuddered against the vampire and replied in a throaty voice, "I bet you say that to all the girls."

"No…" Devlin hesitated as he took a deep breath and added, "Just to the one I love."

Rose froze, stunned by Devlin's words. How was she supposed to respond? She chewed at her bottom lip as her eyes darted around the room. What am I supposed to say…or do? He said it; does that mean I need to say it too?

Treading uncharted waters, her mind was a bubbling mess of emotions with nowhere to go. The last man she had declared her love for was her father, on his deathbed. Rose had many men in her life, but most of her relationships tended to be superficial, never having any substance to them that went beyond sex.

She wasn't sure if she felt the same about Devlin. What the hell? We're here for Duncan's ass, and tick boy pulls the "L" word on me! She wasn't sure if she should be irritated or flattered by the vampire's admission.

Sadness plagued her heart at the thought of spending the rest of her life with the vampire. The operative word being "her" since Devlin would never age and would definitely outlive her. Would he be heartbroken when I died? Is my being in his life a way to pass the many years without being lonely? Immortality must suck, but why saddle yourself with a person who would only be here one minute and then gone forever?

Devlin turned Rose around to face him. He put his forehead against hers as he cupped her chin in his rough hand. "Don't over think things, beautiful. Just go with your heart; it will guide you to where you need to go."

"My heart is urging me towards…to help Duncan," Rose whispered so softly that she wondered if Devlin had heard her. "I can't be having this conversation. Not here, not now."

"I understand, sweetheart," Devlin assured her. "I'd rather get it out in the open and say how I feel about you in case…"

"In case we don't make it out of here alive?"

"Yes," he murmured as he pressed his lips softly on Rose's forehead. "I hate sounding so gloomy, but it's a reality we need to face. At least we can do that together."

"I like the sound of that." She smiled up at the vampire.

"I'd be honored to fight and die by your side, Rose Macready. I vow to keep you alive as long as I can and— OOf!"

With the hilt of her sword, Rose jabbed Devlin in his ribs. She backed up slightly and cocked an eyebrow at him. "I told you, I can handle myself. Stop trying to shield me from every terrible thing that gets thrown at us. I don't want to have a relationship with someone who sees me as a damsel in distress."

Devlin chuckled. "I know, but you need to give me some leeway here. I'm older than you realize, and old habits die hard."

"Well, prepare for a crash course in The Modern Woman's Etiquette: post-apocalyptic edition," Rose spouted off as she walked towards the door.

He stopped her and pulled her to him.

Rose purred as she leaned against him and pressed her lips to his, planting her hands firmly on his ass. He embraced her, needing to possess her. He groaned as she parted her lips, urging his tongue into her mouth, and Devlin was happy to accept the invitation.

Rose's eyelids fluttered as she grinded against his engorged shaft. Maybe there's more between us than just being friends, she thought in a haze as she felt her core slicken with the want of him. At that moment, she noticed Devlin was tenderly kissing and licking her neck.

"If you're hungry," Rose said between deep breaths, "then take what…you need."

"I hunger for you, Rose," he murmured against her skin, giving her goose bumps. "I want to rip your clothes off, lick every succulent inch of your beautiful body, and then give you a pleasure you never knew your body could experience!"

Rose's whole body shuddered. How can one man's words make me feel so wanted, so desired? Maybe this is what true love is like? Devlin seemed more than capable of following through on his boasting. He had tons of experience—centuries of it—and Rose wanted him to make her body obey all his demands.

She opened her eyes. Realization hit her hard when she remembered where they were. There was a creepy stickiness beneath her feet from the black ichor that had poured out of the decapitated ghouls.

Devlin groaned as she backed away from him. "I don't think this would be the best place for a make out session," she told him.

He adjusted his swollen member and nodded sadly, but he knew she was right. This wasn't the kind of place he wanted for their *first time*. "You have a point, Rose."

"We need to get our asses moving," she said and sheathed her katana. Looking at the wooden door, she felt it was out of place against all the gold and ichor. She yanked on the door handle, and the door creaked open.

Devlin pulled her back a couple of steps and took her place at the door. Peering through the slight opening, he determined that the hallway was empty.

As they walked out into the corridor, Rose crinkled her nose. The place smelled of rotting flesh. A lot of people have died here, she thought.

Devlin kept his sword ready in case someone found them wandering the halls, but he needn't have worried because the place was like an empty tomb. "It's quieter than I expected," he muttered.

"They could all be gathered somewhere torturing Duncan," Rose hissed.

"A place this big could hold thousands of people," the vampire said. "We might have ended up in the one area that is rarely used."

"I doubt it. Everything looks immaculate. There isn't a speck of dust anywhere, and that's saying something since Penemuel said this place was built where the oceans once thrived. Let's split up and search these rooms."

"Are you sure that's wise?" Devlin gave her a look of concern.

"Everything I do is wise," she said and grinned. She walked over to the opposite wall and grasped the door handle of the first room. As Rose opened the door, an avalanche of cleaning towels tumbled down on her.

"Rose!" Devlin bit out a high-pitched whisper. "Are you okay?"

Rose kicked a mass of towels of all sizes off of her and couldn't help but laugh. She looked over her shoulder and gave a thumbs up. "Yep, I found the linen closet. Look, Devlin, I'm on the rag!"

Devlin rolled his eyes as he shook his head. He cautiously opened the door before him. When nothing fell on him, he decided it was a good start. He swung back the door, fully opening it, and stared inside.

He gasped!

Chapter 27

There were scores of children on their hands and knees scrubbing and polishing the floor and walls, all slaving away, the personification of exhaustion. Some of their little fingers were worn down to the bone and bleeding, yet they kept scrubbing and polishing. There were even children on high scaffoldings washing the ceiling, a couple looking terrified they would fall at any moment. Each one in the huge room had on filthy, tattered clothing that either looked too large or too small for the child.

Devlin's anger shot up as he watched these little slave laborers. If I could teleport right now, he thought irritably, I'd set these kids free! Devlin quietly shut the door, not wanting to disturb the children, because he wasn't sure if they could be trusted not to raise an alarm.

As he walked up to the next door, soft voices caught Devlin's attention. He glanced over his shoulder and saw Rose on her knees talking with a small boy who couldn't have been more than eight or nine years old. She was smiling and holding the boy's tiny emaciated hand in her hand. She kept reassuring him she was a good lady.

Devlin opened the door slightly and saw the same scene as he had seen in the previous room. More children were being worked to death, all in the name of vanity. Devlin closed the door quietly and turned around. Rose was walking towards him with the little boy still holding her hand.

The sight of Rose with a child made his heart swell. Whether she knew it or not, children suited her. He could see her aura glow more radiant with love for this child. Outwardly, though, she had a somber expression on her face.

Devlin knelt down on the floor and smiled at the boy. He made an effort to keep his fangs hidden as he asked, "Who is this brave, little boy with you, Rose?"

"Devlin, this is Danny. He found me putting all those cleaning rags away and decided to help me," Rose explained as she squatted next to Danny. "Can you say hi to Devlin?"

The boy's frail body began to shake, and he quickly skidded behind Rose, holding on to her tightly as he peered around her to watch Devlin. Confused, Rose asked, "Danny? What's the matter?"

Devlin let out a heavy, sad sigh. "It's me, Rose. He's terrified of me and what I am."

"Are you sure? Maybe you look like someone who's—"

"No, it's me all right," Devlin insisted. "Through the centuries, children have always behaved like this around me. It's their survival instinct; it kicks in when they sense danger, like when a hungry predator is nearby. You'll have to show him that I'm safe, sweetheart, because he'll never believe anything coming from me."

Rose spun around, taking Danny in her arms to comfort him and give him a sense of security. The boy was filthy and stank. His small body was emaciated, and his jet black hair was long and shaggy, with dried blood matted in it in spots. His brown eyes were sunken in, probably from the lack of nutrition, and he shivered violently.

"It's okay, Danny," Rose said calmly as she stroked the boy's back. "Devlin isn't going to hurt you. He's a good man."

"He's a bad person!" Danny squeaked out through lips that had sores on them. When he spoke, one of the sores cracked open, and a tiny bit of blood oozed out of it. He began to sob. His voice came out scratchy like his throat was parched from thirst. "I just know he is!"

Rose glanced over at the vampire and saw that the little boy's words were affecting him. Devlin looked away as he bit on his bottom lip. Rose thought he might be on the verge of tears. She put her hands on Danny's head and forced him to look at her. "I know what you mean, Danny. When I first saw Devlin, I was scared of him too. I didn't know if he was going to hurt me or not."

"W-what happened?"

"I found out he was a good person, despite that bad feeling coming from him. He can't help that. If you give him a chance, though, I'm sure he'd love to be your friend."

"I can be your friend, Danny," Devlin promised. "Look what I have to share with you." The vampire produced a small canteen of water and a peach. "I may be scary, but I would never hurt you, Danny. I take care of all my friends. Will you be my friend?"

Danny glanced over at the offering, and Devlin could tell the boy was at war with himself, trying to decide if he should take the peach or not. "This peach is as fresh as they come," the vampire said, tempting him. "When you bite down into its soft skin, its succulent juices will gush all in your mouth." He tossed the peach up in the air.

Danny rushed out of Rose's arms and caught the peach in midair. He ran back over to her as he greedily bit into the fruit. The man didn't lie, Danny thought as he felt the juice gush into his mouth. Tears rolled down the little boy's cheeks as he devoured the peach, and both Devlin and Rose smiled.

Devlin slid the water canteen on the floor and said, "There's some good, refreshing water in it if you're thirsty."

Rose picked it up, unscrewed the lid and took a sip before handing it to Danny. He held the canteen like it was made of the finest china and cherished each gulp like it could be his last, which was likely to be true. Rose smiled at the little boy, noting his scarred fingers. "I assume you've been here for a while now. Are your parents here as well?"

"They're somewhere around here, but it's okay that I haven't seen them."

"Why is that?" Devlin asked.

"If your parents come to claim you from the cells, it means you've been chosen for death."

Rose gasped. "What? That's awful!"

"Yeah it is. I've lost two sisters and my brother, so I'm the last on their list. All the people here who have children must show their devotion to Jesus by sacrificing their kids to the ghouls."

"That creep isn't Jesus!" Rose growled. She sighed heavily.

"How many kids are here?" Devlin asked as he clenched his fists, wanting nothing more than to get at Sorath.

"A lot," Danny said as he leaned on Rose's chest for comfort. "I can't count that high. Each week we lose another kid to the ghouls."

Rose wanted to steal this poor boy away from this horrid life. She squeezed Danny tightly, wanting to keep all the ghouls, his parents, and Sorath away from him. She heard a rustling of clothing as Devlin stood. Glancing up at him, she could tell by his face he was thinking the same as her.

"Danny?" Devlin turned away so the boy wouldn't see the red in his eyes. "Do you know where all the people are today? We're looking for our friend who was brought here recently. His name is Duncan Morgan. Have you heard the name?"

The boy's face brightened as he pushed away from Rose and scrambled to his blistered feet. Rose had the urge to grab him and hold him again, but instead she stood up and smiled at him. The boy jumped around, limping a little because of his feet, but acting like a kid who knew all the answers. Danny even surprised Devlin when he took him by the hand and started to lead them down the hallway.

"He's in a cell not far from mine!" Danny explained excitedly as he led them around the corner and up a narrower hallway. "Some of the other kids got to listening and heard lots. Jesus says he's a bad person who needs to be made an example of for killing his people and dead folks — the ghouls! I feel bad for him. He's going to be hurt today — tortured, I think — like right now!"

Concern and worry found a home on Devlin and Rose's faces when they glanced at each other. As they neared a set of wooden double doors, Rose asked, "Are you taking us back to your cell so we can see him?"

Danny froze, staring at them with pity in his cavernous eyes. He shook his head. "I'm afraid for you. If you go down there now, you might get caught. I can lead you there when my work is done in a few hours…when it gets dark." He pointed a shaky hand at the wooden double doors and added, "There's a window in there. Through it, you can see most of this place. You might be able to see Duncan too. I must go now before I'm missed."

Danny started to walk away, but suddenly he lunged at Devlin, hugging him around his waist. Surprised at the boy's move, Devlin hugged the little boy back, but his hands were draped on Danny's neck. As Danny pulled away, he yelped and rubbed his neck.

"Sorry," Devlin said and cringed from hurting the boy. "My nails are sharp. Here, take an extra peach for later."

Danny snatched up the peach and hugged Rose. As the boy ran off down the hallway, they walked towards the wooden double doors. Rose shot Devlin a menacing look as she watched him lick the boy's blood off his fingernail. "Did you really have to do that?"

"Yes, I did. Tasting his blood will help me find him again. And when I do, I'll set all the children free!" Devlin pulled one of the doors open and peered into the room. After making sure the place was empty, he let Rose go through first.

The sound of a whip cracking caught their attention, and they both hurried to a window. The boy had been right. They could see a lot of the golden structure from the window and most of the courtyard.

The courtyard was filled with people. Rose's eyes surveyed the scene wondering what they were looking at. Suddenly, she saw the mound. Then she saw Duncan! She gasped. He was shackled, and if he had not been chained to a pole structure, Rose thought he would be lying on the ground as he looked nearly unconscious.

A woman with a bullwhip in her hand stood in front of Sorath speaking to him. "What's she saying?" Rose asked, and Devlin opened the window so she could hear better.

"Of course you can!" Sorath proclaimed loudly. "This is your husband, after all. Give him one that he will always remember!" The woman jumped for joy and turned back to Duncan.

Rose gasped. "That woman is Duncan's wife! What a fucking bitch! How could she do this to him?"

"With too much pleasure, I'm afraid." Devlin winced and instinctively covered his own groin as he saw the placement of her final blow on Duncan.

They heard the crowd cheer and saw Duncan being pelted by rocks. Rose couldn't stand to watch any longer. She buried her face in Devlin's chest and sobbed.

Holding her tightly, Devlin caressed her head and murmured, "I'm sure this isn't the last of the punishment he'll get from Sorath. Mark my words, Rose. I promise we'll get the kids and Duncan out of here...no matter the cost!"

Chapter 28

With all the swelling in them, Duncan could barely open his eyes. Even though intense pain racked his entire body, he could feel his magical energy flowing throughout him. He cringed and groaned in pain as the grinding of broken bones rubbed together. Is the bone-grinding a way for the magical energy to heal me? He wanted to take in deep breaths, but he could tell multiple ribs had been broken, and they were all grinding away.

The pain was getting to be too much for him, and he screamed out in agony. His body was shivering from cold, and he figured he must be running a high fever. Duncan opened his hands and wiggled his fingers. He immediately realized that was a bad idea as more pain came crashing down on him.

Through his slit eyes, he scanned his surrounds as best he could, but even the slightest movement in his neck shot pain up and down his spine. As far as he could tell, he was back in his cell, and he was still naked." Figures," he growled under his breath.

A heavy pressure landed squarely on his chest, and Duncan suspected that with all the pain and excessive stress on his body that his heart was giving out on him. He mentally laughed. Wouldn't that be a big "fuck you" to Sorath! He would come in here and find me dead from natural causes.

As the pressure swelled beyond Duncan's comprehension, there came a series of small pops that sounded like someone cracking their fingers. With each pop, the pressure ebbed away. As it went, so did the pain in that part of his body.

Duncan mentally thanked the magical energy inside his body because he was sure it was mending him. He wondered, though, if it could release some endorphins to help ease the pain. He heard no response from it, but the sensation that this pain was necessary for healing and growth came to mind.

Okay, either I'm hallucinating or my magic can commune on a more primal level, like sensations. Despite the rest of his pain, a sensation of happiness ran through his mind. After he noticed that the level of pain had dropped, a sensation of sadness came out of nowhere and hit him squarely in his head. Pressure immediately built up in his head, and it momentarily took his breath away. As his ribs mended, Duncan began to breathe pain-free.

The series of small pops now cascaded throughout his head, and it made Duncan think of popcorn kernels popping over an open fire. With each pop, the pressure in his head ebbed, and Duncan felt a wave of relief wash over him. I'm guessing I had quite a few skull fractures, he mused.

This was the sensation he received back: our body has sustained a great deal of damage, and our ribs and skull need repairing; our soft, internal tissue needs mending.

Wait, did I hear it right? Did it say "our body…our ribs"? He frowned. "What exactly are you?" Duncan breathed out.

"I am you, and you are me, and we are one."

Duncan groaned. Just what I needed, more cryptic bullshit, and it's apparently coming from me. He felt pressure building up in his arms and legs, but it was at least somewhat tolerable. From what little he could see, Duncan gazed down at his limbs and couldn't believe his eyes. His arms and legs were literally swelling up like balloons, and his skin was expanding with the swelling — not tearing!

The wounds he sustained from Pamela's lashing only shrunk. They didn't open up or expand. His magical energy was holding the wounds in place, keeping them from doing further damage. Duncan didn't dare move any of his limbs, so he relaxed his swollen eyes and concentrated on meditating. If I can't move, he thought, why not use what Rose struggled to teach me?

Duncan took several deep breaths and used each exhalation as a way to mentally remove the pain from his body, which for some odd reason seemed like the logical step to take. He wondered if he could still hear his magical energy. If so, was that where this idea came from? The sensation of happiness filled his mind which he took as a yes. "How is it that we can communicate now?" he asked.

"As you grew, I grew also. We have always been able to communicate, but you weren't listening until recently."

"Recently? Wait...you're the voice that would warn me about others?"

Happy swirls of energy filled him. *"Yes, but we weren't open then. Once the disaster of this world happened, it was enough of a catalyst for us both. Do you recall the frequent headaches?"*

"Yes, and they were quite painful," Duncan scowled.

"We do apologize for that, but it was a necessary task as we worked to build a bridge between our third eye and enhance our magical channels. Once we were being eaten alive, we were able to focus all of our combined might, and we destroyed our enemies. Our body wasn't accustomed to that much power so soon, so we slept and healed while we grew and became stronger, both physically, mentally, and emotionally."

"Where did you come from? You're not a demon trying to take over my body, are you?"

Anger filled Duncan's mind as it screamed back at him, *"We are way beyond the scum of demons and even the piousness of angels too! We were made by those who loved us and saw that we would be needed here on Earth! We are the product of our parents!"*

"Okay, let's use our inside voice — not so fucking loud! I can hear you just fine. So who are our parents and why haven't they been around for say, all my fucking life? Why did they give up on me?"

"As I say, we have a purpose here on Earth, and our parents had no choice but to put us here."

"More cryptic shit!" he growled. Why can't it just spit out what needs to be said? Doesn't it realize how frustrated it's making me? Duncan recalled growing up, going from one foster home to the next, never knowing if he would have a permanent roof over his head or food in his belly. Why did my parents cast me away like yesterday's trash? Was their situation so dire that a baby was deemed expendable?

Duncan gloomily fumed. "Why do you refuse to tell me anything about them or where I came from?"

A happy swirl of energy rattled through his head. "*You shouldn't fight us; that won't get us anywhere. If we work as one, none can stand in our way. Answers you want, this we know, but so does the broken sadness that is caring for us at this moment in time.*"

Broken sadness? What does that mean? Duncan got a new sensation flowing over his entire body. His skin tingled with energy and stung like bees in certain spots. He opened his eyes and found that he could fully open them now, so he gazed down at his body.

From the nasty lacerations of Pamela's whip to the bruises and abrasions caused by the stones, every wound was meticulously mending back to normal. While this happened, Duncan noticed two things: one, the pain was dropping fast, and he was beginning to feel better; two, for some odd reason, he was cold from the waist down, but from his back and upwards a soft, warm, sensation blanketed him, and it seemed familiar.

Since when did Sorath grow a heart and give him a comfy, warm chair? Duncan tested his neck and felt no pain from moving it, so he chanced a glance to see what he was leaning against. In his mind, he heard the words BROKEN SADNESS spoken as he gazed up at the fallen angel, Purah.

She sat on the floor, her back against the wall, propping him up with her soft, warm body. She looked so beautiful and peaceful as she slept, and a contented smile was on her petite face. Duncan noticed a swirl of happy energy in his mind so he asked, "If you dislike angels so much, then why should you be so happy to see this one? She betrayed us and gave Sorath our location! Doesn't that mean anything to you?"

"If you knew what we've learned from this one, you wouldn't think so ill of her. She is an innocent in all of this."

"I don't see how. She was the one who raised all those fucking ghouls from their graves! She betrayed us to her master and look where that got us!"

"We are where we need to be. Sorath is the fallen angel who has the number 666 upon his essence. He is a deceiver and a liar who will stop at nothing to show up his Creator just for spite. He wants nothing more than the total annihilation of this world. He claimed it was the broken sadness that gave up our location, right? Look at the source before you judge her. You'd be surprised as we were at what she knows."

"She told you these things?" Duncan asked, feeling like he had been left out of an important conversation.

The energy seemed hesitant to speak at first, but then relayed, *"Not so much told us, but we read her mind as she tended to us. Everything became clearer, and there was no deception on her part."*

"So, what did you see?"

The energy abruptly and irritably spat out, *"Ask her yourself if you seek those answers. It's not our place to do everything for us. You have to do this, but keep an open mind and realize that she is our broken sadness."*

The silence in Duncan's mind was deafening as his magical energy spoke no more. Again, he peered up at Purah, wanting to hate her for telling Sorath where to find him. For some reason, though, his temper was toned down.

After the beating I just took, maybe I have nothing left to hate, he mused. He shifted slightly, and his movement woke up Purah. She looked down at him with a smile on her lips, but it was her sapphire eyes that caught and held his attention. They were glowing, and being this close to her, Duncan could see small, white specks in her irises that resembled stars tightening up to form clusters of galaxies.

She was so breathtaking and captivating, Duncan held his breath while he gazed at her. Purah ran her dainty fingers through his thick, strawberry blonde hair and let out a sigh of contentment.

"It's good to see you're finally awake," he told her. "I was worried that we would never get another chance to talk." His nakedness made him uncomfortable around her, so he slipped his hand over his member, which caused her to giggle.

"What's so damn funny?" he growled.

"There's no need to be modest around me, Duncan. It isn't the first time I've seen you in your natural state."

Remembering the waterfall, he agreed. "True, but you're seeing me at my worse…all scarred, battered, and bruised."

"This is true, but I've cleaned the blood from your broken body, and now it looks like it's back to normal. No more scars to mar a perfect body like yours…not even on your manhood parts."

Duncan blushed, which was something he wasn't accustomed to doing. No one ever made his body react like she did. He wasn't normally so self-conscious of his looks, but after the lashes and stoning, all Duncan wanted to do was cover himself up and never show his body to anyone, ever again!

He rubbed his balls and noticed that there was no laceration on them anymore. He perused the rest of his body. The only sign of injury he had was now long, pink streaks of unmarred skin. It was remarkable at how fast the magical energy inside of him was able to mend him.

"See? You have nothing to hide."

"You have a point, but I know I shouldn't be naked in the presence of a beautiful lady. I'm still married, you know…" Duncan wondered about that last part. Am I still married after everything that has happened to me since Pamela was reaped?

Duncan didn't want this burden anymore, but he was a man of his word. Something inside him—OCD, a friend had diagnosed—made him compulsive about keeping his promises.

He noticed a slight shift from Purah and then felt her lips pressed against his scalp. Her soft kiss sent a jolt of electricity throughout his body and despite his best efforts to keep it down, his shaft stiffened in response. Duncan gulped as he sat up, scooted beside her, and leaned cross-legged against the wall next to her.

She reached out and slipped her hand in his. "What's wrong, Duncan? Did that upset you?"

"Purah, I don't know what to think anymore. I'm a married man, but the woman I'm married to is the same person who…" Duncan looked down in shame, "tortured me earlier today. She's a terrible person, always has been, and I guess this place has made her ten times worse."

"The whip-mistress is your wife?" Purah gasped. She thought for a moment before adding, "How else has Pamela wronged you?"

Duncan couldn't look Purah in her sapphire blue eyes, so he gazed down at their clasped hands. "She would be verbally aggressive and say hateful things to me, but people do that to each other, don't they?" He let out an anxiety-filled breath. "She would go to bars and get drunk. I'd be lucky if I found her on our couch the next morning. When she did come home, Pamela would regale me with her wonderful night of alcohol and sex with strangers."

"How long did this go on?"

"Throughout our marriage," Duncan said mournfully. "It started off with mental forms of abuse. She'd tear down my self-worth. She demanded that I work and keep the house clean. Even though she didn't have a job, she didn't have time to cook or clean because that would hinder her fun times at the bar," he said bitterly. "We had many verbal altercations, but I never once laid a finger on her. Of course, that never stopped her from hitting me. For me, divorce was out of the question which seemed to make her more abusive."

Confused, Purah asked, "So why did you stay with her after all that?"

"During our wedding ceremony, we exchanged vows. I said that I would honor and cherish her until death do us part. It may seem silly to you and old-fashioned, but I take my promises seriously. It feels — "

"Sacred?"

Duncan nodded. He hoped she didn't think he was stupid for keeping his vows. All his friends did.

"Did she make the same vow to you?"

"Yes. Most people make those same vows. Why?"

Purah squeezed his hand. "Duncan, I know all this is new to you, so let me explain why you felt so strongly about your wedding promise. When a person with magical abilities makes a vow or an oath to someone, whether it's to another person or to a deity, it's a lifetime commitment. It's not something to be taken lightly because your word is your bond, and the consequences for breaking your word can be severe."

"I think you're wrong about that, Purah. I didn't come into my magical abilities until long after I was married. As a matter of fact, the magic came to me just a few weeks ago and—"

"No, you were born with magical abilities. The magic inside of you is ancient. You have a power greater than anyone else on this planet; that includes both Sorath and me combined."

Duncan thought about it and wondered if the fallen angel was pulling his leg with that last part. How can I be that powerful when I don't know anything about my magical self? He finally looked over at Purah and saw she was smiling at him. He decided this would be a good avenue to explore since she wasn't being as cryptic as the voice in his head, but first he had to ask, "Did you tell Sorath where I was at?"

"No, Duncan, I did not. I would never do that!"

"Sorath claims you told him everything—even how to find me."

Purah's smile faded slightly as she closed her eyes. Duncan figured she was sifting through more broken memories to prove to herself that she didn't divulge his whereabouts.

Why does it matter to me if she did? Duncan berated himself. She's as much a victim in all of this as I am. When did I start to care about her? Purah's beautiful but way out of my league. Don't be stupid and fall for this one.

He did what he could to not think about the fallen angel, but with her this close to him how could he not? His gaze lingered on her pink lips, and he wondered what it would feel like to press his own lips against hers. Could she want a mortal like me? Duncan lowered his gaze from her lips and felt compelled to ogle the rest of her alluring body.

Purah rubbed her hand over her eyes, wiping the tears away. Duncan snapped out of his lustful gazing and pulled her into his arms. He held on to her tightly and let her cry against his bare chest. Stroking the back of her head, he gently asked, "What did you remember…if I may ask?"

"Too much!" Purah exclaimed, her voice partially muffled with a sob. "Not once did I give you up to Sorath, but he knew your name because of my greed for you."

"What do you mean by that?"

"When we were last together, I took your magic inside of me. I took it to another dimension so I could safely dispose of it. I ended up dumping it out, and it burned my clothes off my body. I tried to keep a little bit of it for myself because it was keeping my mind intact, and I was enjoying it. Eventually it slipped out of my grasp, and I feared losing you in the great scrambled mess that is my memory. I carved your name on different parts of my body so I wouldn't forget you." She sighed heavily.

"Sorath found me. Needless to say, he wasn't happy to see what I had done to myself. He became furious and tried washing your stink, as he called it, off of me."

"Maybe that's what he meant when he said I defiled you," Duncan said.

"Huh?"

"Never mind, please continue."

Purah pressed herself against Duncan as she cried even more. "When he couldn't get your 'stink' off of me, he...he threw me against a cave wall and violated me repeatedly." She looked up at Duncan with pleading eyes. "I was stupid for carving your name on my body, but I didn't abuse your trust!"

Suddenly, Purah yanked Duncan's head down and pressed her soft, pink lips against his. He groaned with pleasure as he returned her kiss. In that instant, a surge of energy sparked between the two of them, making them both tremble.

As Duncan pushed away from her, she stood up. He covered his face with his hands, moaning, "I'm no better than Pamela. I'm a cheater too!"

He lowered his hands and glanced up at Purah. She was standing and shaking violently, her eyes closed tightly. Duncan worried that she might be having a seizure, so he stood up and reached for her.

In his mind, he heard his magical voice shout out, *"DON'T TOUCH HER YET!"*

"Damn it, stop shouting! I can hear you just fine! What's wrong with her?"

"She has been granted a vision."

"A vision? You gave her a vision?"

"We didn't grant the vision, but we were a conduit for it."

Duncan rubbed his forehead in confusion. "Okay, if you didn't send it, then who did?"

The magical energy swirled happily in his mind as it stated, *"Our parents!"*

Duncan was stunned by this new revelation. He wanted to go sit in the nearest corner and not deal with reality anymore. What the hell was that supposed to mean? Am I channeling my dead parents' ghosts now?

Purah finally stopped shaking and collapsed. Duncan reached out in time to keep her from falling to the floor and yanked her back into his arms. Her body was hot and sweaty like she had been working out in a gym somewhere. She slowly opened her eyes and, to Duncan's surprise, they were glowing purple.

She shuddered with a euphoric smile. "Now that was one hell of a first kiss, Duncan Morgan!"

"Are you all right?" he asked, concerned for her.

Purah patted him lovingly on his cheek. "Yes," she assured him. "Oh, your parents say hi!"

Duncan smirked at the angel and was ready to ask her about the vision when a female voice roared out from the hallway.

"What the fuck are you doing with my husband, bitch?"

"Giving him what he needs," Purah growled, glaring at Pamela who was holding a small dagger in her hand. "A whore like you could never give him what he needs: Love and respect!"

Duncan had to hold back a snicker as he watched Pamela's cheeks redden with anger. She stormed into the cell with the dagger raised and ready to strike Purah. "You foul, rotten, winged abomination! Unhand my man or so help me I'll cut out that heart of yours!"

Purah stepped in front of Duncan and shrouded him with her wings protectively. When she beckoned Pamela to make the first move on her, Pamela lunged forward at the petite fallen angel. Purah lifted her palm up and commanded, "Freeze, servant of Sorath!" Pamela instantly froze in mid-attack.

Pamela stood as unmoving as a statue. Even her eyes were frozen in place, glazed over as her hatred cemented itself into them. Her breathing became so shallow that, for a moment, Duncan could have sworn Pamela had stopped breathing altogether.

Purah turned to Duncan and said with a mischievous smile, "Don't go anywhere. I'll be right back to attend to you next."

He frowned, wondering if he should be scared or turned on. He crossed his legs and leaned his back against the cold, gold wall.

Purah spread her wings and hovered in front of Pamela, getting eye to eye with her. "Pamela Morgan, you will forget what you just witnessed in this cell. You will not be able to recall being in this cell at all. Do you understand?"

"Yes, mistress," Pamela responded in a monotone voice that Duncan had never heard before.

"Good," Purah said. She placed her petite hand on Pamela's forehead, trying to get a sense of the woman's essence. She gasped. "You're nothing more than a harlot and a deadly snake, aren't you?"

"Yes, mistress."

"You're to go to your chamber and rest. Tomorrow is a big day, and you will need all your strength. You will not recall our conversation or the fact that Duncan is fully healed. Now, strip your clothes off."

Pamela nodded as she peeled off her clothes as fast as she could. When the woman reached for her panties, Purah quickly amended her command. "Keep your underclothes on and then leave us!"

Pamela slipped the dagger into her garter belt and walked out of Duncan's cell without a care in the world.

"Was that really necessary?" he asked.

"Yes it was. I looked into her mind and saw some disturbing things. I felt compelled to make her parade her harlot ass around."

"What did you see?" Duncan asked but not really wanting to hear.

"She's been having a lot of orgies ever since lashing you with her whip. She's celebrating her soon-to-be widow status. Also, Sorath has granted her the opportunity to be your executioner in hand-to-weapon combat."

"Ah, let me guess," he said. "She'll have weapons, and I won't. She knows I won't hurt her." He sighed. "I suppose this will be the last time you'll get to see me alive."

Purah walked up to Duncan and slapped him hard on his face.

"Hey! What was that for?" He rubbed his cheek.

"You're thinking about rolling over and dying tomorrow without a fight!"

"So how do I stop her? Am I supposed to use my supernatural strength and rip her head off? Beheading her is the only way to kill her so how — "

Purah put her right index finger on his mouth to silence him. She gazed up at him like he was the only thing in this world that was precious to her.

Duncan figured if his magical energy could restore her broken memory then he was something she would covet. Was she only using him for her own benefit or was Purah actually falling in love with him? Would an angel fall in love with a mortal? Duncan chuckled mentally. "Not this mortal!"

"Huh?" she asked, confused.

Had he said it aloud? "Nothing."

"I want you to fight Pamela," she said. "It will help you heal in so many ways. If the opportunity arises, kill her! She has broken her vows to you over and over. I know you feel compelled to honor your vow, but according to your parents, Pamela nullified your vow with the way she constantly abused you."

"Are they ghosts or something? My parents, I mean."

"You don't know, do you?" Purah parted her lips in sadness. "I guess that would explain why you know virtually nothing of the magic that resides within you."

"It seems you and my magical energy know more about me than I do. Please tell me about my parents. I was abandoned when I was born. Growing up, I got passed around to different families a lot. If you have time to share, I'd appreciate it."

Purah reached out and hugged Duncan. "I'll tell you all I know. Your mother's name is MoonRose, and your father's name is EnergyBear."

Duncan laughed. "That's their real names? Are you sure of that?"

"Yes," she insisted. "You were put here on Earth to stop Sorath from killing off mankind. Your father is a seer, which means he can see into the future. When he saw that Sorath was going to exterminate the entire human species, he and your mother had no choice but to send you to Earth to put an end to Sorath, once and for all."

Duncan gave Purah a wry look, wondering if she was pulling his leg. "If I was placed here on Earth by my parents, does that mean we are aliens from another planet?"

Purah giggled as she swatted Duncan on his bare ass. "You're not an alien from another planet. Your parents are actually deities in a different dimension, and since you are their child, that makes you a god!"

Duncan's jaw dropped as he paled in disbelief. He was about to rebuke her claim, when his magical energy happily swirled in his mind, chiming in, *"There's the answer you sought. We are one, and we are unstoppable. Sorath will not win as long as we work together. We will bring him to his knees and make him beg us for mercy!"*

Purah giggled. "Your magical energy voice is right. Sorath must die, and only you are capable of this feat."

"You read my mind?" Duncan exclaimed with surprise.

"No, silly!" Purah playfully said as she snuggled against Duncan's body. "I can hear your magical essence talking to you inside your head. It's as much a part of you as you are a part of it."

Now I'm cracking up, Duncan thought. "I'm a fucking god?"

Chapter 29

Devlin and Rose hid in one of the storage closets waiting for nightfall. The vampire held her close to his body for most of the afternoon, and she ended up falling asleep in his arms. He smiled down at her as he watched Rose sleep, her slow, rhythmic breathing becoming hypnotic as her chest rose and dropped like ocean waves.

Rose slept so deeply that Devlin was able to create a pallet from the towels and other linens in the closet, and he lay her down on it so he could sneak out every so often and investigate the place. He never ventured too far from her, though. He knew the only ones that would go in and out of the linen closets were the slave kids; anyone else finding Rose asleep and alone would be catastrophic.

While exploring, Devlin observed a small cluster of people dragging Duncan unshackled towards a door that led downward into the belly of the palace as dusk approached. Either he was going to be tortured more down there or he was being taken back to his cell. Devlin couldn't say for certain, but he was leaning towards the latter.

Walking back toward the linen closet, he wished he could sleep. The more stress he put his body through, the more blood he would need to replenish it. Even though there were ample opportunities to feed in this palace, the pickings so far had been scarce, and Devlin was getting hungrier with each passing minute.

He closed the closet door and watched Rose as she slept, his gaze always managing to go up to her carotid artery. He sighed when he realized that being this close to Rose, the sound of her blood flowing through her body was like a dinner bell ringing. On those few occasions when Rose had willingly offered her neck to him, he had refused it because he didn't want to harm her, but now...

Devlin cuddled next to her, inhaling the sweet pheromones she naturally exuded as well as the scent of her exotic blood that lay just beneath her skin. His breaths became heavy, and his excitement grew as Rose slept next to him, her beauty arousing him.

He pulled her close as he slipped his hand underneath her shirt, his hand gently grazing across the bottom of Rose's soft, ample breasts. "Soft as a cloud and just as heavenly," Devlin murmured under his breath. She let out a quiet moan as he cupped her breast in his hand, caressing her nipple with his palm.

Suddenly, the linen closet door swung open. Devlin had been seen! A big, burly man in a black uniform, with a nametag proclaiming him to be "Gil" rushed inside, snarling at them. "Unclean ones!" He carried an iron mace. "I don't know how you got in here, but you won't be leaving this place alive!"

Startled out of her sleep, Rose sat up. "Huh?"

The man swung the mace in a wide arc, barely missing Rose's head. Using his supernatural speed, Devlin tackled the man. They both went tumbling down on the floor, causing the man to drop the mace. Devlin locked his hands around the man's beefy neck to choke him, but the guy was strong enough to stand up, despite having Devlin draped over his back.

The vampire punched the burly intruder in the ribs, cracking two of them. Despite his injury, the man fought mightily to get Devlin off his back. When he couldn't throw the vampire off of him, he ran backwards into the nearest wall, trying to crush Devlin. "Get off me! Fight me like a man, you fucking coward!"

"Sure thing," Devlin grunted as he got slammed against the wall again, "as soon as I break you in half!" The vampire shoved his arm around the guy's neck and pressed it against his Adams apple.

Rose hoisted the heavy, iron mace up and reared back to swing it. About to lose consciousness from the lack of oxygen, the guy stumbled to the center of the closet. Rose swung the mace like it was a golf club and bashed it against the man's knee. Under both his and Devlin's weight, the burly man crumbled to the ground screaming in pain. He tried to rise up once more, shooting Rose an evil glare as he did, so she swung again and took out his other knee.

"AGGHH! You fucking bitch! I'll kill you for this! I'll—OOF!"

With one more swing of the iron mace, Rose shut the man up as she slammed it down on the back of his head. It made a nasty crunching noise as it connected.

Devlin stretched his back and arms while eying the downed man. "Never let it be said that Rose Macready isn't incapable of protecting herself."

"I couldn't let *you* have all the fun, playing piggyback with Godzilla there."

"I wouldn't necessarily call that fun," he corrected. "It had to be done or he would have split your head open with that mace. Ha! Now he knows what that feels like."

Devlin knelt down next to the unconscious man and added, "Karma's a bitch, isn't it?" He grinned savagely. "Dinner is served, and it's a buffet." As the vampire opened his mouth, his sharp fangs lengthened. He bit down on the man's beefy neck, causing his fangs to make a slight popping sound as they punctured the flesh.

Rose wondered how it would feel if he ever decided to take her blood. Would it hurt? Rose remembered Devlin had not been gentle when he had drunk the blood of Todd, the sadistic rapist. She couldn't blame him for that; the man had hurt Devlin's friends. Taking Todd's blood had been not only an act of feeding but also a form of punishment on the bastard.

Rose couldn't help but watch Devlin as he fed. He was bent over his victim, the way a man bent over his sweetheart as she lay on a blanket at their picnic. Rose heard a soft slurp escape Devlin's lips, reminding her of a wet kiss from an enthusiastic lover. Only, this *kiss* was a kiss of death. She shuddered but couldn't tear herself away from the feeding.

The vampire moaned and Rose wondered if he was turned on by this deadly act. Did it arouse him? That question was quickly answered when Devlin's hips began to gently move back and forth in sensual, rhythmic thrusts. She stifled a gasp as she felt her own hormones release, shooting through her whole body, heating it up.

Devlin moaned again, and despite her best efforts not to, she touched her left breast with her fingers. She felt her core dampen with juices as if she was preparing for a lover of her own. Her breath came in ragged gasps as Devlin's hips increased their thrusts.

He's getting off on this, she thought, and so am I. Her fingers inched their way downward to her aroused core where she gently rubbed at it through her clothing. She fantasized about taking her own victim *lovers* and wondered what it would be like to be a vampire.

Suddenly, Devlin groaned loudly and stopped his thrusts. He raised his head, giving Rose a bleary-eyed stare. His smile was one of satisfaction. He was sated — he'd had his fill. Taking in a deep breath, he focused all of his attention on Rose. He grinned mischievously at her and licked one of his fangs suggestively. When her body heated even more in response to him, the vampire chuckled.

He knew she was aroused; her scent must be tattling on her again. She felt her cheeks heat up and realized she must be blushing. He chuckled again, and she gave him a snooty frown, which made him laugh.

Devlin stood up and backed away from the man. He waved his hand toward the guy. "Hack away, sweetheart. Make sure he doesn't bother us again."

Reaching for her katana, Rose stepped forward. She brought the sword down on the burly man's neck, but the blade didn't go through all the way. It was stuck! She put her foot on the man's shoulder and bent over to jiggle her sword free.

Devlin leaned his back against the wall as he licked the blood from his lips, taking in the view. He smiled, feeling his need growing for her.

With a plop, Rose's sword came free. She huffed as she saw the vampire ogling her. Her heart quickened, just knowing Devlin was hungering for her. And he didn't want her blood!

Again, she hacked at the man's neck, and this time the blade went through unimpeded. She wiped the blood off on the dead man's back and asked, "Enjoy the show, tick boy?"

"I'd be lying if I said I didn't. But, then again, you enjoyed watching me feed, didn't you?"

Rose ignored him as she walked towards the door. She paused so she could peer out into the hallway to see if the coast was clear. Devlin crept up behind her and whispered, "I know it turned you on to see me drinking that prick's blood. Your body betrays you. It instinctively emits the scent of hormones and pheromones when you are turned on. A vampire can smell the slightest of changes in a person's body. Even now, you're excited by the thought of the act. Why is that?" He breathed sensually on her ear.

Rose's heart thudded in her chest, and her breath momentarily caught in her throat as the heat from his mouth cascaded down from her ear to the curve of her neck. Why does he affect me so easily? Wanting to remove herself from his closeness, Rose cautiously stepped out into the hallway with her katana in hand.

Devlin followed her out, his hands clasped behind his back. He easily caught up with her as she crept down the corridor. "Why are you ignoring me, my darling?"

She glanced over at him. A smug, half smile had washed across his sensuous lips. "You need to be ignored."

He chuckled.

"We need to find the stairs that will lead us down into the basement or dungeon or whatever it's called in this place," Rose said as she looked from one wall to the other. "There are so many doors; where do we start?" The doors looked the same to her, like they were all copies stamped out in some weird door factory. How could anyone actually navigate through a place like this?

"Around the corner, there's a set of stairs," Devlin told her. "It will be just past the sixth door on the right."

Rose glanced at the vampire as they rounded the corner. "And you know this...how?"

Devlin smiled as he turned around and confidently replied, "I did some exploring while you slept."

Startled, she stared at him.

"What? I never left you for long." They past the sixth door and came to the stairway. At that moment, they heard a noise behind them. Both whirled around, ready to fight. They gasped in surprise. "Danny," Devlin blurted out, "what are you doing here?"

"I came looking for you," the child explained. "I found your friend. I can show you where he is."

It was then that Rose saw fresh blood on the side of the child's face. "Danny!" Rose exclaimed as she leaned down and hugged the frail boy. She stared at the new wound, trying to determine just how bad it was. "What happened? Are you okay?"

"Yeah," he said sheepishly and hugged Rose back. "Mr. Gil didn't like my work today." Danny pushed away to start down the stairway. "We have to go now while the others sleep."

As Rose sheathed her katana, Devlin growled at the child, "You don't have to worry about Gil anymore. Rose and I took care of him."

The boy started to shake with fear as he thought about the sadistic man. He hoped he wouldn't get in trouble because these two had killed Mr. Gil. Rose saw his reaction and leaned down. "It's okay, Danny," she said in a comforting voice. "We're all getting out of this horrid place." The boy nodded and smiled uncertainly at her. "Lead the way," she urged.

Devlin frowned as he watched the little boy take each step carefully. He would slowly go down one step sideways, stand there momentarily, and then take another step down. On each step, he seemed to pause in order to get his balance.

The vampire wondered if Danny was trying to be quiet as he stepped down sideways or if he had a medical condition that forced him to move down the steps that way. Devlin kept at least four steps between him and Rose so if anyone came at them from behind, there would be room to fight.

The stairway seemed to go on forever. It was lit using small, fiery orbs that clung to the ceiling at different intervals. For most of the way down, the walls were bare. After passing a certain level, though, they were decorated with gold vines and gems of all different colors.

Because of Danny, they were moving at a snail's pace. When Rose was tempted to pass the boy and hurry down the stairs, she forced herself to follow him. He's familiar with this place and the schedule of its inhabitants, she thought. Why complain?

Must be nearing the ground floor by now, Devlin thought as he touched the wall and noted the difference in temperature. Plus, the stairs were noticeably more worn from foot traffic.

Rose started to shiver slightly at the drop in temperature and wished that she had a light jacket on. She thought about how warm she had been upstairs in Devlin's embrace. The thought of his touch always elicited a response from her core, and it was no different now. She glanced back at the vampire, who was smirking as he tapped his nose and wiggled his eyebrows at her.

"Oh grow up, Devlin," Rose whispered irritably.

Devlin let out a soft chuckle. "Hey, I'm not the one who's constantly *happy* when she thinks of me."

"Oh, I forgot; every thought I have must revolve around you. Typical male!"

"Your body doesn't lie even when you lie to yourself, Rose," Devlin said as he polished his nails on his shirt.

"I think I should start calling you a bloodhound. You tend to have that damn nose in my business, when it's none of your business!" she hissed, and the vampire giggled, irritating her even more.

"Shhh!" Danny quietly scolded them. "We're close now. Most people are resting—not everyone though. I don't want them to know we're here. They'd do bad things to us if they caught us."

Rose nodded that he was right. She didn't want anyone alerted, especially the ghouls.

They made it to a small landing with a door that had more of the decorative gold vines on it, which was in far contrast to the ones on the upper levels.

Thinking of the ghouls, Rose whispered over her shoulder to Devlin, "Were there any other rooms that had ghouls hidden away upstairs?"

"Only one," he answered. "It looked like a training room of some kind. Maybe that's what the big man was doing up there. He might have been training the ghouls and saw me."

"The dead folks you saw probably ratted you out to Gil the Giant. He was working to be an elite warrior and ghoul master. He had to control the dead folks by talking to them or using his brain."

"Like telepathy?" Rose asked in surprise.

Danny frowned and whispered, "I don't know what that is. Some of the people here can talk without moving their lips and others hear them inside their heads. Dead folks can do the same. It's creepy and scary." The little boy involuntarily shivered, just thinking about it.

When they approached a landing that had a door, Devlin passed Rose and the boy on the stairs, getting in front of them. He pulled the door open just enough to peek out. A long, open corridor lay before them. "This has to lead to the main courtyard," the vampire said.

The floor was decorated with four oversized runner rugs that formed a crucifix, and where the rugs intersected was a half sphere made from gold, its top smooth and flat. A place of worship came into Devlin's mind as he pushed the door open farther and walked through.

With a panicked look on his face, Danny stepped around Devlin. His little, emaciated body shook with fear, and Devlin found himself admiring the kid. Danny was scared to death. He knew what would happen to him if they were caught. Yet, he was willing to lead them to their friend. "The door on the far left," Danny whispered, his tiny voice quavering with fear, "leads down to the dungeon where your friend is being kept. Hurry! Follow me!"

An uneasy feeling settled over Rose like some dark shroud had descended down and was covering her. The sense of dread and foreboding that the shroud was causing assailed her mind, and she nervously glanced over at Devlin. He too looked anxious. Did he have his own shroud? He was definitely on guard, ready for a fight. Looking for comfort, Rose placed her hand on the hilt of her katana, but she found no reassurance.

Maybe this bad feeling is because we're now out in the open, Rose thought and nervously looked around.

Devlin kept his hand on the hilt of his sword, expecting someone to walk out of the many doors and sound the alarm. He sadly shook his head as he watched the little boy inching along, still walking like he did when he went down the stairs. The vampire realized this was new because when they first met Danny, he had walked like a normal boy should.

"Danny, what's wrong with your leg?" Devlin whispered.

Rose gasped as she noticed his movements. "Yes, when did you hurt yourself?"

Danny froze in his tracks and hung his head, letting his little, bony shoulders slump. He sniffled as he uttered, "I didn't hurt myself. I was punished today."

"Who did this to you, Danny?" Rose asked angrily as she grabbed the boy's arm and turned him to look him in the eyes. He kept his head down and his eyes averted from her gaze. Suddenly, the fiery orbs along the walls brightened so much that Rose, Devlin, and Danny had to shield their eyes.

When the lighting in the corridor dimmed to a tolerable brightness, Rose and Devlin saw that they were surrounded by a huge throng of people, each carrying a weapon. Another bright light shined as it descended down and landed on the half sphere.

"Ah, thank you, little one, for delivering these assassins who killed our fallen warriors and Gil," Sorath spoke merrily. "I see that Duncan has loyal friends willing to die in a futile rescue attempt."

"Danny?" Rose blurted out. "I thought you—"

"Were helping you two out?" Sorath interrupted. "My child, he was helping you until we persuaded him to help us. If he would draw you two out of your hiding place, I wouldn't toss him in the barracks to sleep with the fallen warriors."

"By *persuaded*," Devlin growled, "you mean that you beat him and broke his little body?" He angrily unsheathed his sword and made a beeline for the fallen angel who was pretending to be Jesus. With her katana drawn, Rose also charged the pretender.

Sorath laughed and lifted his hands. Magic shot out and both Devlin and Rose were stopped in midstride. He flicked his fingers and disarmed them of their weapons.

"Pathetic humans! You cannot beat me," Sorath said with a smile on his lips. Behind his benevolent smile, though, Devlin and Rose could sense Sorath's evil. Why couldn't his followers do that? "You thought you could come in here and murder me? I'm a god, and no mortal can slay a god, especially one as powerful as I am."

"Wow! He's got an ego the size of Texas! I'm so impressed," Rose shouted sarcastically. "I guess you have to keep reminding yourself that you're a god and not just the pitiful fallen angel with daddy issues that you really are!"

Sorath cast a killing gaze on Rose, trying to break her will. He wanted her to bow down before him so his followers could see it, but she somehow was able to defy him, which infuriated him even more.

Devlin watched the exchange of warring wills between the two. He concentrated hard and, suddenly, he had some control over his own body.

He figured he wasn't going to survive a fight with the horde, so he threw back his head and laughed. He dropped to his knees and mockingly bowed before Sorath, cackling and shouting out, "We're not worthy! We're not worthy! All must bow before the mighty asshole!" He heard Rose laugh.

Sorath pointed at the intruders and commanded his followers, "Bind them in shackles and take them to the arena! We'll see how long they mock me!"

Rose looked down at Danny. The boy was sobbing. He glanced up at her, shame covering his little face. "It's okay, Danny," she assured him. "You didn't do anything wrong. Everything will be okay…so enough crying." She smiled lovingly at him.

Several well-armed men yanked Devlin to his feet. The men aimed their swords at his neck and heart, and a woman placed iron shackles on his wrists.

When the woman approached Rose, she sneered as she backhanded the sorceress across her cheek. Other men rushed between them to keep Rose from attacking the woman. Rose thrashed and kicked at the woman, but one of the men holding her slammed his fist into her gut, causing her to double over in pain.

"Leave her alone!" Devlin snarled and got backhanded too, but he didn't flinch. He knew attacking the men would be useless. There were just too many of them. These guys weren't mindless ghouls. They were logical-thinking men who were completely loyal to the one they believed to be Jesus.

The woman yanked Rose's arms up and clapped the shackles around her wrists. For good measure, she slapped Rose in the face when she was finished, before walking away.

The phony Jesus laughed and mocked them while they were being escorted away. "Maybe next time you'll obey me, harlot. Though in a few hours, I guess that will be a moot point as you will both die along with your friend, Duncan Morgan! But don't you fret; I have a special punishment in store for the two of you."

Chapter 30

Duncan was startled awake by something that had been thrown on him. He jerked up to a sitting position and saw several men standing at the entrance to his cell, their weapons drawn. A small group of ghouls stood behind the men acting as their backup. Duncan glanced down and saw that they had tossed a dingy, white shirt and tattered, black pants on him.

"Nothing but the best for me, huh?" Duncan smirked as he examined the clothing and saw that they were at least the right size. How would they know that? Then it dawned on him: Pamela!

"Shut up and get dressed, murderer," the tall, redheaded man spat out. "The time has come for you to atone for your crimes against us."

He slipped on the dingy shirt and crinkled his nose from the different pungent odors that wafted up out of the fabric. It smelled of decay, blood and rot, so he figured the shirt had been stripped off a dead man's body. Was the former owner lying around somewhere or had these belonged to a ghoul?

As Duncan stood up, slinging on the black pants, the men entered his cell for him. A combination of disgust and malice had settled in their eyes, and a couple even looked like they were about to have some fun with him. He shrugged. He didn't care. Death was the worst they could do to him, and he would probably be wishing for that soon enough.

They have to get me safely to my execution, Duncan thought, and he chuckled as he shook his head. He tugged on his boots as the redheaded man asked, "What's so damn funny?"

"Nothing," Duncan smirked. "Just wondering if you brought enough people. I'm a really dangerous fellow, you know?"

"Silence!" the redheaded man shouted as he grabbed Duncan and shoved him back against the wall. He placed his forearm on his throat and growled, "If we had a choice in this matter, we would gut you like a fish and slowly feed you to the fallen warriors while you watched!"

"I've already been eaten once so that threat doesn't scare me," Duncan snarled out defiantly.

The redheaded man bared his teeth at Duncan like a mad dog. He raised his right hand to strike him. Suddenly, the man's mouth dropped open. He roughly grasped Duncan's chin and turned his head from side to side, examining him.

"What in the devil happened to your wounds? How is this possible?" He looked over his shoulder to the other men. "Carlos? George? You saw his body, right? Didn't he have bruises and lash marks?"

The men all grumbled amongst themselves before one of them stepped up and took hold of Duncan's shirt. "One way to know for sure, Dave." The man yanked up Duncan's shirt so all of them could see his chest. They gasped in unison as they stared at perfect and untouched skin. There was not a hint of bruising or lacerations from the punishment he had received from the whip-mistress less than twenty-four hours ago.

"He's clean! Nothing! It's like he was never punished!" the befuddled man exclaimed as he touched Duncan's abdomen.

"Seriously," Duncan smirked, "if you're going to paw at me, at least buy me a drink or two. OOF!"

Glaring menacingly at him, Dave gut-punched him. Duncan coughed as he tried to catch his breath, but Dave leaned in and barked, "Who did this to you? Who healed your sorry ass?"

"Sorath did this to me," Duncan said, chuckling. "Maybe you should go talk with him about this travesty."

Dave blinked in confusion as he tried to wrap his mind around the name. "There's no one here by that name!"

"If you say so, but he tends to go by the name of Jesus around here. His real name is Sorath, though."

"You're so full of shit, you damn heathen!" Carlos hissed.

"Jesus has many names—Lord, Savior, Divine One," Dave growled. "I know them all. Not one of them is Sorath! Do you think we're stupid enough to fall for your trickery?"

Duncan laughed. "Well…yeah!"

George roared in anger and reared back his sword, about to plunge it into Duncan's chest. Carlos and Dave both grappled with the man to wrestle away his weapon.

"Let me go!" George yelled out. He focused his anger on Duncan. "Guys! He doesn't deserve to stand there smiling and breathing!"

"You're so right, George," Dave growled as he struggled to restrain the man. "Unfortunately, though, it's not our place to kill him. Just take pride in the fact that we get to deliver him to his execution and watch him die!"

George struggled to get free of his friends' hold. Finally, he relaxed, but he kept a baleful watch on Duncan.

"Good choice, George," Dave said in a soothing voice. He too wanted to kill the heathen, but he knew his place and stayed in it. A man lived longer around here doing that. "Jesus wouldn't be pleased if we ruined the example he wants to make of this piece of shit."

"Yes, George," Duncan said cheerfully and pushed himself away from the wall. "I'd hate to see you fall from Sorath's good graces. So let's get this over with; take me to the party."

The men roughly shoved him towards the cell entrance. He glanced back at them as they stepped behind him with their weapons at his back. Although he didn't know why, Duncan felt as though he could sense Purah and that she was still in the cell with him. He stopped and turned around, smiling, feeling her strong presence.

One of the men swung him around again. "Get going!"

Still smiling, Duncan obeyed.

The ghouls stepped aside, creating a funnel for him, herding him towards the center where they surrounded him. The men in the cell hurried to the front of the throng and proceeded to walk towards the main door of the dungeon.

As the dungeon door closed, the sound it made echoed off the gold walls. Purah opened her wings from around her body and spread them out wide. It was difficult for her to observe Sorath's men being so cruel to Duncan, but she dared not interfere with them.

She knew Duncan could take the punishment, but that didn't mean she was going to feel callous about it either. Purah made sure to siphon off more of Duncan's magical energy for herself so that it would keep her mind sharp. Her heart had soared when Duncan turned around and gazed at her, even though she was hidden behind her wings. He knows I'm here with him, Purah thought, and it makes him happy.

She wanted to watch over Duncan, keep him safe and alive. She vowed that the first chance she could get, she would steal him away from his executioners. But where could they go? Sorath would be furious, and he would find them no matter where they went. After Duncan's energy had cleared her mind, she had discovered that she and Sorath shared a bond. Maybe that was how he found her in the training dimension.

She walked behind the throng of men and ghouls as they herded Duncan down the hallway. She cringed at the pain and sadness that emanated from the dungeon. The misery from all the captive children held down here fed her natural empathy, and she soaked up their pain. As she walked by the children's cells, her heart hurt from all their broken spirits.

The curse on her was a terrible price to pay, but Purah was convinced she had done the right thing by defying the Creator. She had received brain trauma in the battle, and now with the help of Duncan's energy she was able to think logically again and remember.

She had been cast down to Earth as a punishment, but now there was a light at the end of the tunnel, and that tunnel ran through her broken memories. Duncan Morgan was that light. Just a while ago, she had watched over him as he slept. She had communed with his magical energy, and it was doing something to her she hadn't expected. It was permanently healing her mind. For the first time since The Fall, Purah had hope that her torment and confusion would one day be just a bad memory altogether.

How can I keep Duncan safe and get Sorath off our backs? She stopped and silently leaned against the wall near one of the cells? Penemuel's blood magic had made Sorath so powerful — too powerful! Who can I turn to for help against him?

The other fallen angels had been killed off long ago during the competitions. They had fought to see who would stand with Sorath and become his right hand — his lieutenant.

Purah closed her eyes and concentrated on all the names and images of her fallen brothers and sisters. Every image turned into a dead end road. Suddenly, an answer burst into her mind as if it was a flash as bright as the sun. She gasped as she opened her eyes. The answer was clear to her. Now all she needed was more energy to make the long journey.

She walked to the center of the dungeon and let her voice carry to all the children. "Hear me, little ones! You haven't made the palace perfect and spotless for Jesus lately. You have been lax in your assigned chores!"

A chorus of whining and pleading ensued, and she could almost feel each child's eyes as they welled up with tears. Purah soaked up their despair and sadness. As the energy built up amongst the slave children, she realized that it was not coming fast enough.

She hated doing it, but it was the only way to save them all. "Jesus is greatly disappointed in all of you," she added. "You know what that means: no food or water until all of your terrible work is fixed!"

The air in the dungeon filled up with the sounds of moans and crying. When the children realized that no food or water was coming, it caused a massive wave of depression in the little slaves.

Their horrid, pathetic energy hit Purah hard. She dropped to her knees with a smile as the children charged her up. It may have been a cruel lie to tell them, but it didn't matter to Purah. She had to look and feel strong when she got to her destination because her brother could easily smite her on sight without a second thought.

Fighting broke out in the cells as children accused each other of screwing up and more sad energy followed. Once Purah got her fill of the energy, she sealed it off so none of it could leave her body. She unfurled her tendril wings and flew out of the door at a blinding speed, leaving the palace. As she soared towards the sky, she looked for a thin spot in the dimensional veil. Suddenly, she found it and shot through it.

Duncan was escorted out to the central courtyard. It was filled to capacity with onlookers and hecklers, but Duncan noticed this courtyard was a different one. This new place did not have the gold mound where he had been lashed and stoned yesterday. It also did not have the golden frame that he had been shackled to.

"Where the hell are they taking me?" he muttered aloud as he looked around.

"Patience, it will all be revealed soon enough," Duncan's magical inner voice spoke to him.

"Patience is one thing I don't have at the moment," he growled. "I want to get this over with!"

"If what our broken sadness told us is true, will we be letting our wife kill us without a fight?"

"What choice do I have?" Duncan grumbled. "I'm still her husband, and she knows I won't hurt her."

"That grants us the advantage we need," the voice hissed. *"If we can work together as one, she will be the one to die today and not us."*

"Easy for you to say. Why are you so gung ho on killing her when we could simply escape?"

A sense of anger consumed Duncan's mind, and he knew it came from the Other. *"We know how Pamela has treated us ever since we met her! We've been together since we were born, and we've strived to keep us both safe. You refused to heed the warnings when it came to her. When we met her, your hormones ruled your head. Stupidly, you married her, and we had to sit by and idly watch as she destroyed our manhood in so many ways. Yet, you were too stupid to get away from her. Running away isn't an option today. Since there's no escape, we WILL fight her!"*

"And if I refuse?" Duncan asked with suspicion.

"Then we will take command and dispatch her. We refuse to let us die in vain because of an oath that she broke long ago. Our parents are watching us, and they know this is our time to shine. If we fight, we can bring peace and safety back into this world!"

"If they are watching, why don't they step in and stop this from happening? Since they are gods, they could easily destroy Sorath and his army."

"They can't interfere because they have rules against it, especially when it comes to a realm that isn't theirs."

Duncan laughed. "Politics?"

"They would have to petition other deities that watch over Earth before they could make a move. Since they foresaw our current plight, they long ago petitioned for us. We were granted the right to live among the mortals here. Our purpose in this world is to protect it from those who would see it burn."

"How is it that you know all this?"

"I asked our parents, and they answered."

Duncan shook his head as he chuckled. "You make it sound so simple. It must be since you're magical and connected to them somehow. I guess calling them up on a cell phone is out of the question. I don't seem to have other-worldly coverage."

His magical energy gave off a sense of amusement. *"To talk to any deity, one must speak their name and possibly give an offering of something they prefer. Once one works with that deity enough, one can ask that they commune with you in person or through one's mind. Since MoonRose and EnergyBear are our birth parents, they will always answer our call and will come to see us in person if need be."*

Duncan considered that and wondered what it would be like to actually see and talk to them. He wasn't sure that he wanted to see them at all after they had dropped him off in this world, to be all alone, never knowing if he would have a roof over his head, a bed to sleep in, or have food and water to survive. What kind of parents would do that?

"Why should I care if I ever see them?" Duncan grumbled. "They wanted me to be a hero here without any guidance or knowledge. Bang up job so far, Mom and Dad!"

"Don't be so hard on them or us!" the magical energy berated. *"It was hard on them both to let us come to Earth and live here without them. They want us to end this terrible evil that is destroying the Earth, but they also want us to come home and be a proper family too."*

"Great!" he growled sarcastically. "Go home to mommy and daddy and forget all this shit ever happened! Ha! I'd rather be dead and rotting somewhere. I'd—"

"Don't worry, heathen, you'll be dead soon enough!" George hissed from behind Duncan.

"I think he's cracking up," Carlos said, laughing. "He's been talking to himself a lot. His body may be healed, but his mind is gone."

The crowd parted, revealing a set of stairs that led down into a large arena that had to be a good twenty foot deep. As Duncan descended down the stairs with his ghoul escort, he noticed the ground was covered with sand, instead of the gold the other arena had. Towards the center of the arena, he saw Rose and Devlin.

"How the hell did they get here?" he muttered in surprise. They were both staked to the ground, chained down securely, but at least they were alive. And as far as Duncan could tell, they were unharmed.

Duncan was roughly shoved off the bottom step. He stumbled but managed to right himself before he could fall. He felt the sand shifting under his boots and looked down at it. It was squishy soft but thick and would make running difficult, but that was exactly what he did. He bolted away from his escorts and ran toward the center of the arena where his friends were chained. "Rose! Devlin! Are you two okay?"

"Just peachy, Duncan!" Rose sarcastically replied. "I've been making sand angels all night with Devlin. Care to join us? How's your day been?"

"Rose is all right, thankfully," Devlin said. "She's been—"

Suddenly, his eyes grew wide. "Duncan, look out!"

Chapter 31

Duncan was slammed to the ground by an unseen force that left him shaking his head, trying to clear it. He scrambled to his feet and looked around. The crowd roared with delight as if an invisible gladiator had scored on him. He sighed heavily, brushed the sand off his face, and reached out to see if he could feel his opponent.

Just as he suspected, the air crackled, and his hand tingled when it got close to the energy. It was a barrier, similar to the one that kept him a prisoner in his cell. Withdrawing his hand, he realized that a little more voltage added to the barrier could kill him.

The loud screaming and heckling turned into a chorus of loving cheers as Pamela and Sorath approached the stairs. The phony Jesus had his arms out, welcoming the cheers from his followers. He stopped walking, soaking in the love of the crowd and smiling, but Pamela continued her trek towards her husband.

With a maniacal grin on her lips, Pamela stomped up to Duncan. She twirled her broadsword with an expertise that made Duncan realize that she had been practicing. He wondered who she had practiced on. He watched her as she turned and basked in the crowd's love for her. She was a star!

Duncan glanced over at Rose and Devlin. "One way or another," he called out, "I will free you two." He turned, trying to figure out how to survive this and not hurt Pamela in the process. Every idea he came up with, though, ended badly for both of them.

"We are one, Duncan, and we have a plan," his inner voice told him.*"It will require staying alive long enough for it to succeed."*

"Care to share or is that too much to ask?"

"Evade her attacks and wear her down. Cause her to be guided by her anger. Cause her to make a mistake. We will win this if we can evade her while we attempt something."

"So that's the whole plan?" Duncan snorted with disgust. "Dodge her attacks and hope for the best while you go off and do something else? This day just keeps getting better and better."

"Trust in us and all will go well."

"Why do I get the feeling you're not telling me everything?"

"We are one, and we both know this."

The reluctance of his inner voice to share his plans made Duncan wonder if it meant killing Pamela. He noticed that the magical energy was slowly building up in his body. His heart raced and sweat beaded up on his forehead and upper lip. Worried more about why his inner voice refused to share his plans, Duncan ignored Pamela and paced in a circle like a caged lion ready to pounce.

Sorath's voice boomed, echoing off the walls of the arena, as he called out cheerfully, "Welcome, my followers! Today you'll witness what we do to all those who kill our friends and oppose us." He pointed at his prisoner. "Duncan Morgan murdered Sully, many fallen warriors, and my dear friend, the angel Penemuel. Our halls may be lively and full, but these heinous acts of barbarism make our home feel empty to me."

The crowd grumbled in agreement, so Sorath pointed his finger at Rose and Devlin, adding, "The ones who are restrained were caught sneaking around in our home. They murdered Gil and many of our fallen warriors. They are as evil as Duncan Morgan!"

The crowd jeered loudly, many calling for the prisoners' deaths. Sorath had to raise his hands to quiet them. Again, he pointed at Rose and Devlin. "I've done my best to keep all of you safe from the cruelties of this world, but seeing those two in the Promised Land only reinforces what I've been saying all along. After today, we will march forth into the world and cleanse it of all the remaining heathens. Only after this is done, will we be able to live in peace for the rest of our eternal lives!" He continued on and on about heathens and their deaths.

Whipped into a frenzied state, the crowd roared with cheers once more. The phony Jesus cast his gaze down on Duncan. "Pamela," he called out. She ran to him, ready to do his bidding. "It's time to execute your husband. Are you up to this task or should I get another in your stead?"

"No, that won't be necessary, my Lord," Pamela replied excitedly and stomped closer to Duncan. "It will be my pleasure to honor you by killing him."

"Very well," Sorath cried out jubilantly, "let the executions begin!" The crowd erupted in a loud cheer.

Duncan glanced back at Rose and Devlin, wishing like hell he could bring down Sorath's energy barrier and free his friends. They would have a fighting chance then. He debated with himself on using his new abilities to try and jump over the energy barrier, but he wasn't sure if it was a wall or a dome.

Still ignoring Pamela, he bent down and snatched up a small rock. Hurling it over where he thought the energy barrier would end, he carefully watched it. The rock hit the barrier and slid against it, bouncing several times. To Duncan's surprise, the rock suddenly stopped, suspended in midair.

"Okay," he said aloud, "jumping is out of the question." He turned his attention towards Pamela.

Watching him, still with that maniacal grin on her lips, she now caressed her broadsword lovingly, like it was a prized possession. The ghouls shambled away so Pamela could have plenty of room as she hacked her husband to death. They positioned themselves back at the stairs so they could block Duncan's only escape route.

As she moved close to him, Pamela pressed her lips against the side of her broadsword. After she had kissed the blade, she announced in an evil-sounding voice, "This is the kiss of death, and I'm going to seal your fate with it, sweetheart."

Duncan put his hands up in surrender, pleading, "Pamela, don't do this! Is this really what the true Jesus would have you do? Murder your husband? He's not Jesus; he's a fallen angel."

She ignored his pleas. "An eye for an eye, Duncan," she sneered. "That's what this is all about, and I'm ever so happy to mete out this punishment for your crimes. Any last words before I gut you like a fish?"

"Yes, please release my friends," he begged. "I won't put up a fight if you would grant me this one request."

Pamela stopped dead in her tracks and hesitantly glanced back at her phony Jesus. Duncan could sense them communicating with each other telepathically.

"How did your body heal so quickly?" she asked as she looked back at Duncan. "Hmm, I guess it really doesn't matter, does it?" Realizing she was the star of this show, she raised her voice so the crowd could hear her. In a dramatic voice, she called out, "Your request has been heard, and our Lord Jesus has been moved by your sacrificial act. Therefore, your friends will be set free from their bonds."

The spectators were stunned into silence. They had wanted to see all three of the heathens die, but they didn't want to boo at their lord's generous decision. So they merely sat, watching the drama unfold.

The ground suddenly vibrated beneath Devlin and Rose. "What's going on?" Rose worriedly asked the vampire. Before he could answer, their shackles sprang open. Not wanting to risk them snapping shut again, Devlin scrambled up off the ground and stumbled clumsily over to Rose. He helped her to her feet, and they both struggled to keep standing.

As the vibrations got more intense, the spectators nervously looked around, trying to hang on to anything that might help them keep their balance.

Duncan dropped to one knee and watched as the spikes along with the shackles were being pulled down into the sand. Both Rose and Devlin stumbled to get away from the area, fearing the place would become a large pit of quicksand.

Pamela stabbed her broadsword into the sand to help stabilize her footing. Duncan could feel the magical energy inside him growing, increasing with strength as it readied him for a fight. Unlike the energy he had felt when he fought against the ghouls or Penemuel, this energy felt more stable and under his control.

Rose and Devlin noticed the walls surrounding the arena were shimmering as everything vibrated all around them. Where the sands met the walls, three rectangular tunnels rose up like submarines breaching the water's surface. As the sand and dust cleared, Rose saw dark figures moving around within the tunnels.

Devlin's predatory eyes glared at the nearest tunnel. He gasped and bit out, "Fuck!"

"What is it?" Rose asked, but she already knew the answer.

"Those tunnels are filled with ghouls, and they're marching this way!"

Duncan spun around as he stood up, furiously looking towards the phony Jesus. Pamela was laughing manically as she leaned on her broadsword, watching the ghouls head their way. Duncan felt his magical energy boiling out of control, and he roared, "You fucking promised to let them go, you son of a bitch!"

"Jesus kept his promise by releasing them," Pamela announced loudly, making sure the crowd—her audience—heard her. "They aren't restrained anymore. That's all he promised." She watched as the ghouls slugged through the thick sand. "It's dinner time," she hollered at the ghouls. "Eat up. Don't play with you food now!"

Happy that the ground had stopped shaking and that they were going to see all three prisoners' killed, the spectators laughed at Pamela's little joke. "As for letting them go," Pamela told Duncan, pulling her broadsword from the sand and pointing it at him, "Jesus felt it would be best to have them cleansed first. Hopefully, you'll get to witness it…if you survive that long." She shook her head. "No," she said and grinned, "you won't get to see it!" She let out a war cry, thrusting her sword at Duncan as she did.

He sidestepped her, tripping over his own feet as the sand gave way underneath him. He quickly rolled away as Pamela slashed and stabbed at him. She glared at him, stalking closer, and he sprang back up to his feet, panting heavily.

Duncan put his arms up in a fighter's stance as he stepped backwards. Pamela's sword sliced toward the top of his head. He ducked and batted the blade away with his forearm, maneuvering past her. He kicked Pamela on her hip, sending her to the ground. The crowd roared out its displeasure.

"Whip-mistress? Sure. Sword-mistress? Not so much, huh?" Duncan smirked.

Pamela snarled as she grabbed a handful of sand and flung it at Duncan. The sand hit him in the face. He staggered backwards as he attempted to rub it from his eyes. Squinting, his world had become a blur with a dark figure moving closer to him.

Pamela chuckled as she mocked, "I bet you didn't see that coming. What's the matter? No witty remarks or comebacks? You should drop down to your knees and let me take off your head. Let's end this pathetic game now."

Duncan heard a swishing sound and then felt searing pain in his left forearm. He groaned as he grabbed his arm and quickly backed away. Magical energy filled his body to the point that all his muscles were vibrating with a massive power that he had never felt before. For the first time in his life, Duncan felt alive—really alive! Inside his throbbing head, he heard his inner voice say with pride, *"We are one now, and we shall prevail!"*

Duncan backed into a corner where the energy barrier and the wall met. Still unable to see straight, he wasn't too confident as to which way he should go. Pamela twirled her broadsword in front of her, knowing it would keep Duncan disoriented. She slashed it at him, making sure he could hear the swishing noise. "Stuck like a rotten child in a corner," she cackled out. "It's been fun playing with you, my dear, but this game must come to an end. Question is, should I make this quick or draw it out slowly?"

"Knowing you, it will be the latter of the two!" Duncan mumbled bitterly.

"Oh how right you are, sweetheart!" Pamela purred as she slowly circled him. She took a few fake swipes of her broadsword at him, causing him to jump, and she laughed when he did. Suddenly, she swung her sword for real. It arced down, hitting him on the bend of his leg.

Duncan roared in pain and dropped down to his knee as his leg gave way. He saw a shining object swing in front of him and then more pain hit him as Pamela slashed him across his chest. Sorath's throng of followers screamed excitedly with each swing of her blade.

So this is how it ends? Duncan thought. Carved up into a million humiliating pieces before a bloodthirsty crowd of mindless sheep?

He was ready to shout at Pamela to finish it, but his inner voice piped up, "NO! We'll not die so easily! If you won't fight, then we'll have to do it for us!"

"It's over," Duncan spat out and grimaced in pain. "We're done!"

"Why must you give up on us when victory is within our grasp? Every cut she makes, we've been healing. Our leg is good enough to walk on once more!"

"What the hell do you want from me?" Duncan shouted.

Pamela viciously scraped her blade across his forehead and grinned mischievously.

"Lift our arm and we can end this! Get ready to move. Pamela is preparing for the killing blow!"

Chapter 32

"Can you use your magic, Rose?" the vampire asked frantically.

Rose held the palms of her hands out and focused on them, trying to create a fireball. When nothing happened, she grunted in frustration.

"Can you ground yourself and create another protective bubble?"

"I don't know," she whined. "It's hard to concentrate with all those ghouls pushing down on us. I'm scared; we've got no weapons!"

"You work on grounding yourself, and I'll keep an eye on our *dead friends.*"

"I'll do what I can, but I'm making no promises." She sat down on the ground to make a better connection to the Earth.

Devlin put a hand on her shoulder, and she looked up at the vampire. He cringed slightly when he saw that doom had settled in her eyes. He forced a smile at her, and Rose could see the concern on his face. Her heart swelled as she looked into his eyes and felt the love he had for her. She suspected that he could see the same in her eyes as well.

"I love you, Rose," he said softly. "I'll do everything in my power to keep you safe from harm." Devlin glanced back at the encroaching horde of ghouls and sadly added, "but no guarantees…unfortunately."

He turned to move away, but Rose grasped his hand and squeezed it. He looked back at her with a pent up breath and wished like hell that he could use his teleportation right now. He wanted to take her back to his place. There, she would be safe from this nightmare. She was so beautiful, smart, and strong willed that Devlin had fallen for her the first day he had seen her back in Melona. Since then, his feelings had only grown more as he got to know her.

"I understand completely, Devlin," she said and smiled sadly. "Before it's too late, though, I want to tell you that I love you too, darling. I never thought I would find someone that I could truly feel like this about. I don't want you to die, and I'll do everything in my power to protect you!"

"But no guarantees?" Devlin smiled and kept glancing back at the slowly approaching ghouls.

"None, whatsoever, but fuck it!" she spat out defiantly. "I'm going to do my damndest!"

Devlin leaned down and pressed his lips firmly against her soft ones. She eagerly returned his kiss, but then Devlin pushed away from her. He gave Rose a curt nod as he flashed his fangs at her before turning his full attention to the ghouls. He let his claws extend fully as he anxiously awaited the walking dead to make their first move. He wanted to rush headlong at them, but he refused to leave Rose unaided and exposed. Her safety alone was what kept the vampire from attacking.

Rose turned her back on Devlin to block out all distractions. She took several deep breaths to help calm and center herself. Needing to send her emotional energy into Mother Earth to ground herself, she concentrated on the job at hand. Taking the form of spiritual roots, her energy easily slipped out of her body, which was encouraging.

She worked at guiding the roots down through the sand for several feet before they ran into the gold flooring of the palace. Gold is a great conductor, she thought. Rose smiled as she attempted to use its properties to strengthen her magical connection to the Earth.

Suddenly, she felt something wrap around her roots and rip them from her body! She screamed in excruciating pain as her body was grabbed and pulled face first onto the ground.

With her heart thudding in her chest, she tried to wrap her mind around the fact she was in so much pain. "Son of a bitch, what just happened?"

Now, the magical energy felt as though her grounding roots had been slingshotted back into her body where they were reverberating violently. She groaned as she reached behind her and tentatively rubbed her tailbone, cringing as she did. She could still feel where the main root had been, and it hurt like hell.

Devlin saw Rose lying in the sand and shouted in a panic, "Rose! What's wrong?"

"Nothing!" she grunted out. Groaning in pain again, she tried to catch her breath. She pushed herself upright. At that moment, she heard laughter and the mocking voice of Sorath inside her head!

"Ahh, my little harlot! Magic is not allowed in the arena. Your magic has been officially cut off, and you have to survive using your physical attributes against my fallen warriors. I'm sure they will make easy work of a powerless sorceress, like you. Rest assured, your flesh shall be slowly torn from your sin-filled body." He laughed so loudly inside her head, she grimaced.

Rose glanced over her shoulder and saw Devlin pacing back and forth, his claws extended and his eyes almost completely red. He looked vicious and deadly, but there was no way he could take out all those ghouls by himself. She watched the undead slowly slogging through the thick sand toward her and Devlin.

She stood up; her legs felt shaky from what Sorath had done to her, but she was determined to stand with the vampire. I may be cut off from my magic, Rose thought stoically, but that doesn't mean I won't go down without a fight!

The ghouls had swelled to a staggering number and now several small groups shambled towards them from behind. Devlin sensed Rose approaching. "Make your protective bubble now, Rose!"

"I can't. Sorath has me cut off from everything, even Mother Earth, herself."

"What will you do?" Devlin narrowed his red eyes.

"What else is there for me to do? I have no choice. If I have to fight on his terms, so be it. But if I'm going to die today, I'm going down swinging!"

"I want you behind me at all times! I can protect you —
"

"Hello!" She snorted half-heartedly. "It doesn't matter where you strategically place me, Devlin. We're outnumbered a good hundred to one! Do you really think we're getting out of this alive? You might get out, but I won't!"

"Damn it, Rose, don't think like that! Give me a chance to—"

"No, Devlin! As much as I love the fact that you're willing to protect me when I'm practically helpless, I'm as good as dead, and you know it too. If I'm to die, I want to be by your side when it happens. I want to be on my feet fighting like hell, not cowering in a corner for Sorath's amusement."

***

Pamela leaned down and roughly grabbed Duncan's chin. She pressed her lips against his and then purred, "What I want from you is your death, Sweetheart. I thought that was pretty obvious but, then again, you were never very bright. That being said, though, I think I will split your head open…just to prove my point. I'm really very sorry that you're blind and can't witness your friends being ripped to shreds right now. It's quite the sight."

Duncan could barely hear Rose and Devlin over the crowd's deafening roar. Rose was screaming frantically, like she was in great pain. Devlin sounded worse, almost monstrous. Despite the sand, Duncan forced open his eyes. Without warning, the color of purple flashed brightly in them. The sand was gone! His eyes were clear!

Pamela stared at him in surprise. When she saw the change that had come over him, a wave of terror washed over her. She frantically pushed away from him and lifted her broadsword high above her head.

Duncan felt the irresistible urge to thrust out his arm as if he were reaching for something that wasn't there. His inner voice boomed with magical energy inside his head as it screamed, "*COME TO ME NOW!*"

Pamela let out a squeal of joy when she saw his arm up. He looked as if he was pleading for mercy. As she brought her broadsword down at him, Duncan saw a flash of purple streak towards his hand and felt his fingers tighten around something hard.

Again, his inner voice shouted out an order. "*Move right and swing our arms to the left!*" Duncan seemed to go into slow motion mode, like he had no control over his own movements.

Instinctively, he shifted to his right and swung his outstretched arm to his left as the voice had commanded. At that same moment, he realized that he was now holding a familiar looking sword. It was glowing with purple flames!

He heard horror in Pamela's screams, and he stupidly looked at her, not knowing why she was screaming. Then he saw them.

Pamela's forearms, hands still attached, lay on the sand, blood gushing out of them like raging rivers! He gasped in horror. The sword had sliced through her arms so swiftly that he hadn't felt any resistance from either her muscles or her bones.

Pamela's screams quickly turned sickening as she stared at her arm stumps. She wailed in shock as her eyes jumped from her spurting stumps to the amputated limbs on the sand. Her right hand still tightly held on to her broadsword.

As shock descended over her, she felt a great, black emotional shroud engulf her, preparing her body for an eternal stay. Pamela stared up at Duncan, tears streaming down her face. "You weren't supposed to hurt me! You promised that you would never hurt me!" She stared at him in despair. At that moment, her mind suddenly focused on him. "You…you're healing!"

"Yes I am, aren't I?" Duncan said coldly as the cut on his forehead mended without a trace of a wound. "Now it's time I end our relationship and our marriage on my terms…" Duncan chocked up as he added tearfully, "I loved you so much in the beginning, Pamela! I would have done anything for you!"

"I hate you, you fucking worm of a man!" Suddenly an idea hit her. "Heal me too!" she pleaded and thrust out her spurting stumps.

He shook his head.

As she saw the purple-flaming sword coming at her, Pamela started to scream. The sound that tried to escape her lips, though, was interrupted by the blade as it sliced through her neck, lopping off her head.

The crowd fell eerily silent as Pamela's lifeless body dropped down to the ground. Duncan heard Rose scream. He whirled around, turning his attention to the energy barrier. Duncan felt his magical energy course through his body, and he was able to channel it into the angelic sword.

Rearing back, he violently stabbed the sword into the energy barrier. Instantly, it exploded. The blast knocked down hundreds of spectators above the arena and caused the ghouls to pause and look his way.

He picked up Pamela's broadsword and twirled both it and his angelic sword, howling out an angry growl. The look in his eyes was so fierce and deadly that death itself must have flinched and backed away as he ran headlong towards his friends and those who were about to hurt them.

**

Rose cringed as she heard Duncan's howl, but she didn't dare look away from her vampire. Devlin was so tightly wound that he might explode if she touched him. He jerked his head to the left as more ghouls reached out for him. In a flash, he was ripping off the heads of the nearest attackers.

His supernatural speed took Rose by surprise as he made easy work of the first group of ghouls. She watched him, grabbing and gouging, hitting and kicking, and he momentarily gave her hope. She grinned as he stomped back to her, waiting for the next group to arrive.

When Devlin rejoined Rose, he looked like a nocturnal predator, his lips curled back in a snarl and his fangs extended. His hands were now drenched in black ichor, and he resumed his pacing.

"I can do this! I can protect you, Rose!" Devlin snarled but never looked her way. He seemed to be concentrating on his powers.

"I believe you," Rose replied softly, but she still wasn't quite sold on the idea. Devlin may have his speed and killer instincts, but there were still too many ghouls and only two of them. Rose bit her bottom lip as her anxiety increased when more ghouls shambled past the ones Devlin had killed.

The vampire roared as he moved once more to kill the oncoming threat. He slashed throats with the claws of one hand and ripped heads off with his other hand. Another group of ghouls pushed forward towards Rose, their mouths already chopping and covered in that sickly, green crud.

At that moment, more ghouls swarmed Devlin. They pawed at him, trying to get a firm grip on any part of the vampire's body. He weaved and ducked, sliding out of their grasp. When he couldn't get to their heads, he sliced off their extended hands, just for good measure. That might not stop them from biting him, but they couldn't grab him.

Rose automatically flung her hands forward to throw several fireballs, but nothing happened. She cursed Sorath for repressing her magic. *What's the point of being a sorceress if I can't burn some assholes alive?* She wanted to run in and help Devlin, but there was nothing she could do. Devlin roared in pain as one of the ghouls managed to take a bite out of his back.

Rose couldn't stop herself from bolting towards her vampire. To hear him in pain like that tore at her heart and made her want to pull him back from the fight. She needed to protect him. Suddenly, she yelled, "Hey!" as a ghoul grabbed her by her hair and dragged her away from Devlin.

Rose lost her footing and fell to the ground, but that didn't deter the ghoul that had a handful of her hair from pulling her back into the waiting throng. She desperately dug her heels into the sand to slow the ghoul's movement, but all she got for her trouble was more pain in her scalp.

Frantically, she hit at the ghoul. Maybe I can break its arm, she thought in a panic. The ghoul let out a haunting laugh that could only be made by the dead, and its' words made Rose's skin crawl.

"Cleanse you…we…hunger for…your flesh. We will…eat you…slowly, unclean one…"

The ghoul turned and reached down, grabbing Rose roughly under her arm. It yanked her up momentarily and then tossed her on the ground, face first. Rose spat out a mouth full of sand. It was then she noticed feet all around her.

A lot of feet!

Panicking, she squirmed and tried to crawl away but was assailed by hands from every direction. They flipped Rose over onto her back and held her down by her arms and legs.

"Make her…cleansing last. Jesus commands…this…"

The ghouls surrounding her all dropped to their knees. That close, Rose could actually see their cravings for her flesh in their ghostly eyes. Their mouths quivered hungrily for her. Rose wanted to scream for help, but in her terror-stricken state, she let out a high-pitched squeal. Even that didn't last. The ghouls pulled her sweater up to her chin, and the green crud from their mouths dripped along her abdomen.

Suddenly, the first of the ghouls leaned down and sunk its diseased-ridden teeth into Rose's soft flesh.

She screamed in horrendous pain as more of her flesh and muscles were gnashed and pulled away in chunks. One of the ghouls held her head up by her hair but didn't make a move to bite her. Realization hit her: they wanted her to watch them as they ate her alive!

More bites rained down on her. The ghouls lifted her legs up in the air and took bites from her calves! Rose screamed as loud as she could, but she wasn't sure anyone could hear her. There was a good chance Devlin was already dead.

Horrendous pain overwhelmed her, and she felt her mind clouding. She knew shock was setting in on her. It was just a matter of time before death would give her blessed relief. She prayed for it to come quickly.

From somewhere nearby, Rose heard a terrible growl and a primal scream that would have caused her to freeze in her tracks.

Devlin!

He was either being ripped apart or the one doing the ripping. Maybe he will get these things off me, she thought as her body started to shake. Even though she was lying on hot sand, she felt a terrible coldness engulf her—an eternal coldness that only the dead could understand.

The ghoul holding her head up leaned down and rasped, "Not done...with you...yet, heathen." And then it sunk its teeth down in the bend of her neck. Rose panted heavily as more tears streamed down her cheeks.

An explosion of energy boomed all around, and the ghouls paused for a moment. Several of them stood up and looked toward the source of the sound. Others, though, continued biting down on Rose's limbs. Devlin frantically attacked every ghoul he could reach, but with each one he downed, another one jumped in to take its place. Rose consumed his mind. Each time he heard her screams of pain, it cut deep into his heart with a precision that only a surgeon could match.

"Devlin!"

The vampire shredded two more ghouls as he got closer to Rose, but it still felt like she was a million miles away. He kicked, punched and ripped off more heads, but he didn't seem to be making a dent in their numbers. As he killed one, five more took its place.

He prayed Rose would be alive by the time he got to her, but he knew in his heart that was a pipedream.

"Devlin!"

"Rose!" He couldn't see her, but she was still alive!

"Devlin!" The vampire frowned. That wasn't Rose's voice. He cast a killing look in the direction of the voice. Duncan was running at full speed towards him. The man was carrying his angelic sword in one hand and a bloody broadsword in the other.

Duncan heaved the broadsword, sending it twirling end over end, and it landed in the sand two feet from Devlin. The vampire snatched up the broadsword and let out a furious roar as he sliced his way towards the ghouls that had his Rose surrounded.

"I'M COMING, ROSE!" he howled frantically.

The ghouls that were holding her down and gnawing on her limbs stopped suddenly, as if they had all received a command that only they could hear. They stood up and quickly formed a line with one goal in mind: stop the crazed vampire that was approaching them!

Each one had blood covering their mouths, a sign that they all took part in hurting Rose. Devlin glared as he swung the broadsword, cleaving heads off. He used his supernatural speed to sprint around the ghouls. As the last of the ghouls dropped to the ground dead, Devlin stabbed the broadsword into the sand and carefully pulled Rose up into his arms.

"Oh g-gods!" Rose stammered as she shook uncontrollably from the deadly cold of shock. "The p-pain…it h-hurts so b-bad!" Her lips quivered as if she was freezing.

"It's okay, Rose," he said gently. "I'm here now, and I won't let them hurt you." Devlin stroked her hair lovingly.

"K-kill me!" Rose pleaded. "I-I can't...take it!"

Devlin held back the tears as he inspected her body. The ghouls took their sweet time at picking where to bite. They hadn't torn her to pieces quickly, like they normally did, which told him they wanted her to suffer.

He wanted to pick up the broadsword once more and behead every single one of the ghouls that kept piling into the arena, but he couldn't bear to leave Rose in her vulnerable state. As he stared down at her bloody body, he didn't have the strength to hold back his emotions. He cried while shaking his head, "I failed you, Rose. I couldn't protect you, darling, and now you're paying for my failure." He began to sob.

"No, I t-told you it was g-going to..." Rose babbled incoherently as her eyes rolled back in her head. "Just end m-my...misery," she begged. "Kill...me...now!"

Chapter 33

Duncan ran up and stood next to his friends. When he saw how bad Rose was, he growled, "Get her and your ass behind me! You take care of her by the vampire way, and I'll deal with these pricks once and for all."

Devlin gasped. "You want me to turn her? Right here? Right now?"

"If you want her to survive, you've got no choice. Do it for her sake, Devlin. I'm not losing either one of you today! I know you love Rose, and that's fine by me."

Panic filled Devlin as he looked down at her. "She's too far gone; it may not work. This isn't a guaranteed transformation like in those damn movies. She may die!"

"She's going to die if you don't try. What does she have to lose?" Duncan snarled as he grabbed Devlin by his arm. "Either way, Rose will no longer be in pain. If she dies by your hand, Rose will be grateful for that!"

"I...love y-you..." Rose croaked out to Devlin.

Duncan placed a hand on her forehead. When he touched her, she appeared to calm down, and her body stopped shaking. He glanced at the vampire and said coldly, "Do it before my magic wears off. I'm going to clean house, so get behind me!"

Tugging her sweater back down so he wouldn't have to see her wounds, Devlin sighed heavily and quickly glanced around. She was so close to death, he was surprised he didn't see a grim reaper nearby. He gently scooped Rose up into his arms, holding her body close to his. He got behind Duncan.

Rose reached her hand up for Devlin's face but only made it to his chest. She smeared the black ichor around, getting it all over her hands. The vampire cringed as he looked down at her. "We'll clean you up soon, darling."

"Your eyes...are so red," she said weakly. "Can you...paint my...nails that...color?"

Hearing her ramblings made tears run down his cheeks once more. The dying were often out of their heads just before the end, and he again glanced around for a grim reaper. Not seeing one, he told her, "Of course we can, my darling. Any shade of red you want." Devlin sat down with his back to Duncan while cradling Rose on his lap. Her head lolled against his chest.

He didn't know how to tell her, so he just blurted it out, "Duncan wants me to make you a vampire. He says that's the only way to save your life. Are you okay with that?"

"Will I...suck your...blood?" Rose asked and gave him a weak smile.

He leaned down and kissed her neck. He could smell her blood as it coursed through her body, and it seemed to call to his hunger like a dinner bell. He shivered violently, and Rose looked up at him.

"Are you okay with becoming a vampire?"

She closed her eyes.

Devlin bit down on his own wrist, causing the blood to ooze out. He held his wrist to Rose's lips. "Drink up, my little vixen."

Rose managed to open her mouth a little, and the vampire's blood trickled down her throat. She was so weak that Devlin was surprised she was still alive. He quickly gave thanks to the vampire goddess Lilith and looked around for grim reapers again. He gasped!

Hundreds of grim reapers stood on the walls surrounding the palace. Their black robes fluttered in the hot winds, and their scythes glinted in the bright sunshine. They all stood like statues, watching, and seemed to be waiting for something to happen. Devlin wondered which one was for Rose. Which one was for him?

He looked down at Rose and smiled. Her death pallor looked different. Was that a hint of blush in her cheeks? She looked a little better, he decided. Glancing up at the reapers, he hoped he wasn't healing her just so a reaper would take her in a fight.

He leaned in towards her neck again and whispered by her ear, "My turn to bite you, sweetheart. Keep drinking until you can't drink anymore."

Rose murmured something unintelligible but kept on drinking the blood from his wrist. Devlin brushed Rose's hair aside and slowly licked her neck along her carotid artery. He felt Rose shiver as she tilted her head more to the side for him.

He ached to pierce her soft skin, and he opened his mouth, causing his fangs to extend downward even more. With a small pop, Devlin's fangs entered Rose's neck and went straight into her carotid artery. He felt the blood gush into his mouth in spurts.

Euphoria struck Devlin as he lapped up Rose's blood. Her blood was the sweetest he had ever tasted, and it took all his willpower to hold back his hunger's demand to drain her dry. His eyes rolled back in his head, and he noticed that his member was now fully erect. It throbbed painfully, demanding to be let out of his tight pants.

Devlin tried to ignore his swollen member and let out a silent prayer to any gods or goddesses to help Rose survive the transformation. He didn't want to lose her; he couldn't see himself without her. To live an eternity without her by his side...

He would rather die!

Duncan stoically stood before the massive horde of ghouls as they shambled towards him and his friends. He gripped the hilt of the angelic sword tightly, causing the blade to glow with a purple flame. He could sense that the ghouls were communicating with each other and could feel the uncertainty in their collective, dead minds somehow.

"They are uncertain of what we are and fear us, Duncan," his inner voice explained. *"They have witnessed a mere fraction of our power and are now hesitant. Shall we show them more?"*

At any other time, he would have felt shocked by his inner voice's ability to hear the ghouls' thoughts. Now, though, his world had dramatically changed to the point that nothing surprised him anymore. "You can read their minds," Duncan muttered quietly.

"I can feel the energy that binds them and keeps them alive. It is similar to ours, but ours is natural where theirs was created through summoning. Enough of our energy can break the bonds that keep them living. We proved that weeks ago outside Melona, but you don't remember that."

Duncan shuddered with the recollection of being eaten alive by the ghouls near his village. It was a memory that he would have preferred to stay buried. Seeing Rose with all those bite marks on her body didn't help either. They made the memory of his attack flood back into his mind. He wanted to use the same kind of energy blast that saved him, but he was unsure if he could do it, let alone control it.

"Is it possible to recreate that blast of energy?"

The inner voice chuckled. *"Indeed it is. Now that we're one, we can use our blade as a conduit for the blast. Together, our focus can control where it goes. Hold the weapon with both hands and concentrate on the ghouls. Imagine them burning to ash. Our power will manifest itself as we do this. When we are ready, we'll release it on them!"*

Sorath, still in the guise of Jesus, stood at the edge of the arena, just behind the ghouls. He had been able to stop the woman from using her Earth magic, but Duncan had managed to use his like there were no enchantments or sigils warding him off. Sorath had been as shocked as the spectators when Duncan had armed himself and beheaded his wife, and the sword he had wielded was Penemuel's angelic blade!

Impossible! No mortal can wield one of our sacred weapons, he thought. Maybe it's not an angelic weapon.

Sorath decided he would need to get closer to see if it truly was Penemuel's sword. For now, though, he wanted to witness his fallen warriors killing the man. I can inspect the sword better when I pry it from his cold, fleshless hands, Sorath mused as he steepled his fingers together and smiled.

Movement caught Sorath's eye, and he looked up. He gasped as he saw hundreds of grim reapers on the walls surrounding the palace. He stared anxiously. He hadn't called them; he didn't need them. Why were they here? What was about to happen? Were the reapers here for Duncan and his friends?

No, there were far too many of them!

He shuddered as truth overwhelmed him. Looking around for help, he realized with a sickening feeling in his gut that he was alone. He had made sure to kill all his friends over the eons, and now when he needed them, they were gone!

Chapter 34

Duncan grasped the hilt of the angelic sword with both hands and took several deep breaths. With his steely gaze focused on the massive horde of ghouls, he felt his inner, magical energy building up. He imagined that he dumped a huge vat of gasoline over the ghouls and, right before his eyes, he saw each one of them coated with a purple haze.

His inner, magical voice gave off a sense of pride as it responded, "Good, you're growing stronger." That meant the purple haze was real and that he had done it.

Duncan roared as he thrust his sword forward and released a blast of purple flames that swept through all the ghouls. They moaned and shrieked as they tried to put out the flames, but nothing they did could extinguish the fire.

One by one, the ghouls disintegrated, leaving behind clouds of blackened ash covering the sand where they had stood. Duncan made sure to send the purple flames through the tunnels and wipe out any ghouls that were still lurking within them.

Breathing heavily, he lowered his sword and let a smile of satisfaction cross his lips. Sorath's followers went completely silent as shock washed over them. They had never witnessed such raw power in their lives. A man finally spoke up and asked, "What is he? Is he a man or a god?"

A woman pleaded with the phony Jesus, "How can he do these things?"

Another lady asked, "Are you not our one and only God?"

Still, a man demanded loudly, "How is it that you can't kill Duncan Morgan?"

The questions sounded more like accusations, and Sorath's anger grew with each one. Doubts were seeping into his followers' minds, and he could fell their respect toward him weakening. His godly image had taken a hit when Duncan had killed Pamela, but after the massacre of his fallen warriors, the people were now considering whether Duncan was the all powerful one.

It took everything Sorath had to not double over in pain. A god's power comes from the people's beliefs in him, and he could feel a massive loss of power. His head throbbed from the loss, and he frantically looked around at his followers. Most stared at Duncan in awe. He knew that when a god's last believer stopped believing, the god always died.

Unable to listen to his people anymore, Sorath gave Duncan a malicious gaze and flew towards him like a ball shot out of a cannon. He slammed into Duncan's midsection and grabbed the man. With Duncan in his arms, the fallen angel flew upwards with him, trying to gain altitude as he did.

As they flew upward, Duncan could now see through Sorath's guise which meant his power was weakening fast. He reached out and grabbed Sorath's tendril wings and started ripping them from his body as they soared into the air. Sorath howled in pain, and they came crashing back down on the sand below, with Sorath landing on top of Duncan.

He had only pulled part of Sorath's wings out, but it was enough to keep him from taking Duncan up in the sky and letting him drop to his death.

As he punched Duncan in his face repeatedly, Sorath snarled, "This is your fault! If you hadn't meddled in my affairs, none of this would be happening now! You have no idea of how terrible my wrath will be!"

Duncan was finally able to block Sorath's punches. He rolled his hips, trying to shake the fallen angel off of him, but it did no good. He threw punches of his own into Sorath's ribs causing his hand to sting as it made contact with the fallen angel's body armor. Duncan's blow was just enough to knock Sorath off him.

He scrambled to his feet, assuming a fighter's stance, as he waited for Sorath to make his move. When the fallen angel rose up and glared at Duncan, he noticed the man held something in his hand. Duncan was shaking it so Sorath would be sure to notice it.

"Are these yours, Jesus-wannabe?" Duncan mocked as he threw Sorath's tendril wings at him. "Looks like you've been grounded by a human. I'm sure that's gotta sting that over-inflated ego of yours!"

"My ego will be soothed by your death!" Sorath reached over his shoulder and unsheathed his crimson sword. "I'm done playing nice. I gave you the chance to repent yours sins and have your body cleansed, but you spat in my face at every turn. I'm going to enjoy ripping your heart out and placing your head on a spike at the entrance to my palace. I want everyone to see what happens when someone defies me!"

Duncan yawned as he extended his arm and called his angelic sword to him. "If you planned to kill me with your preaching, then you have succeeded. You've bored me to death." He twirled his sword. "Your move, Mr. Wannabe-Messiah."

Sorath narrowed his gaze as he inspected Duncan's purple, flaming sword and felt a cold chill run up his spine. "No! That's Penemuel's sword! How is it that you can wield his weapon, you abomination?"

"What? This?" Duncan said cheerfully as he twirled the angelic sword. "Penemuel was kind enough to donate his sword to me, so I repaid him by using it to kill him. I'm thinking about expanding my collection. Yours would make a nice addition." He laughed. "Care to donate now or should I just take it from you?"

"Never!" Sorath roared as his anger got the best of him. He slashed and stabbed at Duncan with blinding speed, but none of his blows got past the man's defenses, which only added to the fallen angel's anger and frustration.

Duncan could hear his inner voice urging him, "Stab Sorath and pierce his armor!" He wanted nothing more than to take off the fallen angel's head, but his inner voice was insistent that he stab him first. Who was he to argue with it? After all, it was the one keeping him alive. Duncan completely understood that if he didn't have his inner voice aiding him, Sorath would have already sliced him into a thousand little pieces.

Duncan pressed his attack on Sorath, and with each clash of their blades, sparks flew. The flames on his sword flared bright purple, and Sorath was blinded momentarily. Duncan used all his strength and kicked Sorath's knee. The fallen angel cried out in pain as he collapsed down on the ground but managed to parry away Duncan's following blows.

Sorath reached down and grabbed a handful of sand and flung it at Duncan's face. Duncan frantically rubbed the sand from his eyes and staggered backwards.

Sorath glowed slightly and stood up. Sneering at Duncan, he put all his weight on his crippled leg and grimaced from pain when he did. He hobbled towards the man, steadying his body for a killing blow as he commanded his leg to heal itself.

"You fought well for a mortal, but now you must face my final judgment." The fallen angel glanced around at the totally silent spectators. They were enthralled at what they were witnessing and seemed unable to move. Sorath raised his hands and announced loudly, "And the verdict is death!" He waited for the expected cheering, but it didn't come. Still, his followers sat transfixed, waiting for the finish of this drama to be played out.

Duncan got just enough sand out of his eyes to see Sorath with his sword raised above his head. The fallen angel stopped glowing, and a malicious grin spread across his perfect visage as he brought his sword down on Duncan.

With his magical energy, Duncan threw a hook punch so hard and fast that his fist connected with Sorath's blade and knocked it out of his hands. The sword flew across the arena and ended up buried halfway into the wall.

The crowd gasped in unison and then went quiet again, waiting expectantly.

Sorath could only stare at his own sword as it vibrated. The fallen angel snapped out of his daze and tried to go after it, but Duncan snatched him by his remaining tendril wings and pulled him back to him.

"This is for all the hell you put this world, my friends, and myself though!" Duncan hissed as he pressed the tip of his sword against Sorath's back.

"My armor is enchanted, you fool!" Sorath said and laughed. "Even though you have an angelic weapon, it will not pierce my armor!"

"Really? Well then let's put those enchantments to the test, shall we?" Duncan replied as he focused his magical energy into the angelic sword and thrust it into Sorath's back.

The blade slid through the armor as though it were made of water, giving little resistance. Sorath howled in agony as Duncan hoisted him up in the air, letting his body slide down to the hilt of his sword.

Impaled, the fallen angel looked down at his chest in disbelief. Never in his existence had his armor failed to protect him. He could feel the blade's magical sigils start to dissolve into a liquid. Toxic ink that had been used to inscribe the sigils now soaked into his body like his skin was a sponge. As the magical poison spread throughout him, his body felt like molten lava was being injected straight into his veins. Sorath's perfect skin was now blistering and turning black wherever his veins happened to be.

The fallen angel cringed as he felt the weakness in his power. He was losing more of his followers. Their belief in him as a god was waning fast and sure. At that moment, a small burst of energy popped, and Sorath's guise as Jesus was gone!

Again, the crowd gasped in unison.

Suddenly, the sand shifted and flowed through a large pipe as the gold floor took its place. The floor rose to the level of the first row in the arena, causing Duncan to be closer to the people.

Sorath's followers all stared at the fallen angel in disbelief, their mouths gaping open. Duncan kept a close eye on them, just in case any of them got the notion to try and help Sorath, but they all looked lost. Eyes vacant and void of all malice, the only emotion Duncan could see in them was sadness — the sadness that comes from utter betrayal, something Duncan knew only too well.

"This is the one you worshipped all these years!" Duncan shouted as he shook Sorath like a flag for all to see. "His name is Sorath, and he has tricked every one of you into doing terrible things. He's not Jesus! He is no Messiah, just a pathetic excuse of a fallen angel!"

Duncan gripped the hilt of his sword with both hands and slammed Sorath down on the golden floor, pulling the sword from his back as he did. Sorath doubled over in a fetal position as the toxic ink burned inside him. He gasped as the total loss of power was vacuumed out of his body. "I am a god with no believers!"

Duncan poised himself as he prepared to decapitate the fallen angel. At that moment, the sound of someone slowly clapping caught his attention. He turned his head in the general direction of the sound and saw Purah standing meekly next to a being made of pure light.

Duncan squinted as the light dimmed, and he saw the figure of a man that had perfect, unmarred skin and was dressed in black leather from head to toe.

The guy's hair was long and flowing, even though he was standing still and there was no breeze! The source of his light was in his tendril wings which made it clear to Duncan that he was facing yet another angel.

The unknown angel strolled towards him with a smile that made Duncan both weary and cautious. "Well done, Duncan Morgan," he said in a melodious voice. "You have won the day! Purah was kind enough to tell me all about you and the troubles happening down here on Earth. I see, though, you have everything well in hand."

Duncan narrowed his eyes and demanded, "Who the hell are you?"

The unknown angel chuckled. "Funny choice of words, Duncan. I've gone by many names throughout time. I've been known as the morning star and the Son of Dawn, but you may call me Lucifer."

All humor left his voice as he added, "And I've come to collect what is rightfully mine!"

Chapter 35

A hellish chill shot down Duncan's spine as he stared at Lucifer. "Collect?" He glared at the fallen angel suspiciously as his hand tightly gripped the hilt of his angelic sword, anticipating an attack. "What are you looking to collect…exactly?"

Lucifer noted Duncan's expression and stance had changed slightly, so he lifted his hands up as he shrugged his shoulders innocently. "Only what I'm entitled to take." A slight smile crossed his lips. "Let me rephrase that: only *whom* I'm entitled to take."

Duncan stiffened, ready for the attack. "If it's a bloody fight you want, Lucifer, then by all means let's go!"

Lucifer coyly smiled as he made a tsk tsk sound with his forked, serpent's tongue.

"If I were here for you, we wouldn't be standing here having a civilized chat. You mistake my motives, and that is only natural, considering what you've been through. You know of me; you don't know me. Let's make the best of this chance encounter and sit a spell, shall we?"

A swift shift of wind behind Duncan caught his attention. When he turned to look behind him, he saw that an ornately carved, wooden chair had been placed there. He glanced back at Lucifer who was now sitting down in his own chair, only his was made of marble and encrusted with many colorful gemstones. A round, granite table now separated Duncan from Lucifer.

Duncan heard a noise coming from under the table, and he leaned down to have a look. The table's two massive legs had Sorath pinned securely to the gold floor, where he still writhed in pain.

Lucifer shrugged his shoulders slightly and softly chuckled. He motioned for Duncan to sit. The man could tell that he wasn't dealing with an arrogant fallen angel like Sorath or Penemuel. He got the sense that Lucifer was smart, cunning, and powerful—yet, he wanted to talk, not fight.

Duncan sat down and stared at Lucifer. "What the devil do you want to talk about?"

Lucifer let out a soft laugh as he looked over his shoulder. "You're right about this one, Purah. He's quite the bold one, and I do find him amusing."

Purah walked up and stood by Lucifer's side, never looking him in the eyes.

"Tell me, darling," he said, "why do you want to be with him?"

"Duncan's a good person," she answered in a pleading voice. "He can heal my fractured mind and make me whole again."

"So you plan on using this alien god for your own personal gain, is that correct?" Lucifer asked flatly.

"What does Purah wanting to be around me have to do with anything?" Duncan demanded irritably.

Lucifer's eyes flared a bright white. "Everything and nothing, but I have to ask her these questions. She came to me at great risk to herself, pleading for my aide to keep Sorath away from her. I want to know what her plans are, and I *do* expect answers!"

"I see," Duncan said and frowned. He looked at Purah. "Why didn't you call for his help before now?"

With tears welling up in her eyes, Purah gazed at Duncan. "How could I when Sorath had me on such a tight leash all these centuries. I didn't know if Lucifer lived or not. Sorath was paranoid. So sure another fallen angel would try to take his throne here on Earth, he became hell-bent on destroying all his competition."

She sighed heavily. "Now add in the fact that I couldn't remember things for more than a minute or two. I'd never have made the journey to Lucifer's realm, let alone have the strength to stand before him, if it weren't for you, Duncan."

Lucifer placed his hand on the small of Purah's back and gently caressed her. Duncan jealously glared as he clinched his fists, which Lucifer noticed and chuckled.

Duncan wondered if this bastard was testing him. He wanted to flip the granite table and throttle Lucifer until his head popped off his shoulders. He hadn't realized just how possessive of Purah he had become until now, and seeing her so near Lucifer, reacting to his touch the way she was, made him cringe.

"I see that you both favor each other," Lucifer said in a bored tone. "I asked our sweet Purah how she would feel if I decided to take you from here and keep you in my realm for all eternity. In all the centuries that I've known her, I'd never seen her so willing to fight to keep a mortal safe. Then, again, you aren't just a mortal, are you, Duncan?"

Duncan grinded his molars. "What did you force her to do to keep me safe?"

"Me?" Lucifer spat out, trying for an innocent tone. "I didn't make her do anything against her will." He smiled at her. "She was more than willing to do whatever I asked of her, weren't you, Purah?"

Purah shrugged her shoulders but couldn't look Duncan in his eyes. "I didn't want to lose you, Duncan. If that meant going through with any kind of humiliation or degradation that Lucifer desired, then so be it. You are all that matters."

Duncan shot to his feet as he growled, "If you hurt her in any way, I swear that I'll—"

"Sit down, Duncan!" Lucifer ordered and took his hand from Purah's. "This whole heroic, male-bravado thing is getting old fast. Like I said, I want to chat, not fight."

As Duncan sat back down, still casting a killing look at Lucifer, the fallen angel continued, "That's better. What Purah is saying is absolutely true. When my brothers or sisters come to me for anything, I always insist that they do something to prove it's worthy of my time."

He stopped momentarily and smiled at Purah. "Since the time of The Fall, I've taken it upon myself to watch over my brothers and sister." He frowned. "Since it was my actions that lead to our expulsion from Heaven in the first place, I feel responsible for them. I've known of Purah's...condition, and I've felt guilty that she's had to needlessly suffer. When she came to me, I noticed that she had changed. I asked how it happened that her memory had been restored. She told me a grand story about you, your lineage, and the kindness that you gave her when others wouldn't."

Duncan relaxed slightly but kept his hand ready to grasp his angelic sword. He had heard many stories about Lucifer, mainly that he was a deceiver and that he created hate and chaos in order to take one's soul to Hell for eternal damnation. Yet, Lucifer now seemed more like Purah's protective relative. Duncan got the feeling that he was being judged. Lucifer wanted to see for himself that he was truly worthy to be with Purah.

"The picture she painted of you was one of perfection and greatness," Lucifer said matter-of-factly. "Hmm, I did expect you to be taller though."

"And I expected you to have horns and a pitch fork!" Duncan snorted.

"Ah, and be red skinned with a pointy tail and goat legs?" He laughed. "Some fool saw a satyr and decided that must be the image of a fallen angel. I must confess, though, that the pointy tail and red cape was my idea. I had a little fun with a few drunken priests back in the day and since then it has stuck. Humans are too slow to understand and too quick to judge which is why I can't stand my Father's creations." He sighed, remembering. "Though there have been a few humans who I enjoyed during my time down here. I had done a certain rock n' roll band a solid as long as they wrote a song in honor of me."

Duncan grinned. "Let me guess, the Rolling Stones?"

"Bingo!" Lucifer threw back his head and laughed. "I told them that it would cost them their souls since all they wanted to do was drugs and binge drinking during their career. Tell you the truth, I liked Keith Richards best of all. He was awesome at playing guitar, so I made it where he would survive longer than any of the others by taking the life forces from other humans who didn't deserve it, like that Justin character, and gave them to him so he could play for a long time!"

"Pretty sweet deal," Duncan agreed, "but did they know about that small *soul* detail?"

"Of course not," Lucifer said, chuckling. "What can I say? I'm a fan, and they did write a nice song for me. Though the band is now long dead, Keith still lives on in his own world, still playing for those around him." Lucifer sighed as his gaze went distant for a moment. Suddenly, he blinked as he looked at Duncan with a slight gasp. "You look famished, Duncan. Where are my manners?"

Lucifer waved his hand over the table, and a feast magically appeared before Duncan. There was a tray that had an assortment of cheeses and fruits, like grapes, apples, and oranges.

In front of Duncan was a golden chalice filled with red wine and a plate with slices of ham, beef, and several chicken legs. The centerpiece of food had a bountiful amount of assorted meats and fish to choose from, and their aromas were as intoxicating as Duncan knew the wine would be.

Duncan picked up an apple with a raised eyebrow. "An apple? Really?"

Lucifer shrugged his shoulders slightly. "What can I say? I'm a sucker for the old classics. I know you might be worried that I've done something to all of this, but I haven't. I would tell you to trust me but I haven't earned trust from anyone for several millennia. I know you struggle with trust too. I—"

The table bucked and shook, spilling wine all over it. Lucifer fumed as he snatched up a huge turkey leg. Holding up a finger, he said, "One moment please." He ducked under the table where Sorath was imprisoned.

"You have no right to hold me like this! You—OOM!"

Lucifer shoved the huge turkey leg into Sorath's mouth, mid-rant. He got in his face and growled irritably as he patted Sorath on his cheek. "Be quiet! I'm trying to have a conversation, and you're being a spoiled, little brat down here."

Sorath's face paled more than normal as he looked upon Lucifer's visage. His whole body began to quiver in fear of his brother.

"It's very rude to talk with your mouth full. Be a good boy. Don't make me come back down here again and have to tell you twice, understood?" With a curt nod from Sorath, Lucifer smiled, patted his head, and went back to his chair. Lucifer pursed his lips and said, "Sorry about that, Duncan. Sorath tends to behave like an entitled brat." He waved a hand over the table and all the wine that had spilled disappeared, and Duncan's chalice was full once more. "And he's a messy brute too. Now, where were we?"

"Talking of trust," Purah answered before Duncan could. Lucifer nodded as he steepled his fingers under his chin. He watched Duncan for a moment before saying, "You've been hurt a lot in your life, haven't you?"

Duncan snorted as he picked up his chalice. "Who hasn't?"

"Fair enough, but I've been reading your life story ever since we sat down, and I'm amazed that you kept going on when there were many times you should've just given up. You've been burned in the past by those you cared about, and it has kept you at arm's length from those you love. Tell me, will you treat dear sweet Purah like that?"

Duncan shook his head. "No, I don't think I could do that to her." Suddenly, his eyes grew wide. "Hey! You've been reading my mind? Wow, and you wonder why no one trusts you!"

"It's better than asking questions and getting lies in return. If you had the skill to read minds, which you do at a rudimentary level, you would do it too."

"What makes you think I have that skill?"

"It's the voice in your head that's kept you alive. It's warned you about treacherous people. It's your inner voice, as you call it, but really it's an aspect of your god nature. Do you know how long it's been since I've encountered a real god?"

When Duncan shook his head, Lucifer went on, "I've only encountered one other. For all the good he did in this world, mortals had him crucified. My wayward brothers and sisters hatched out a plan to make his story theirs, just to spite our Father."

Duncan picked up a piece of chicken and greedily stuffed it into his mouth. Lucifer smiled as he looked on and then he said, "Jesus of Nazareth was a god…a demigod, actually. His mother was human, you know?" He got a faraway look in his eyes as his mind went back two thousand years. "I had a lot of interactions with him—mostly trying to make him look like a hypocrite." He sighed. "He was so strong willed and passionate that I grew to respect him greatly. The day he died, I wept."

"Now, that's surprising!" Duncan said and stuffed his mouth again.

"I knew my brothers and sisters were there desecrating his mortal image for their own gain. I grew furious and wanted to strike them all down!"

"So why didn't you?" Duncan asked in between bites. "You knew where they were going to be. Why didn't you take them out?"

"Because I promised Penemuel that I wouldn't interfere. He gave me a copy of his manuscript and told me to read it and learn it well because one day I would have to put Sorath down myself.

"Naturally, I went to where Jesus was buried, but I couldn't enter the tomb due to the many wards and sigils Penemuel had placed on it. Even though I couldn't go inside, I could still eavesdrop. I listened to their plans. According to the Bible, Jesus was to return, and we were to have an epic battle where he would win and cast me and all my followers into some sort of fiery pit to burn for eternity. Naturally, I didn't understand how that could be possible since Jesus wasn't on Earth anymore. Hearing the meat of their plans, though, gave it all away, and so I stayed away from Sorath."

"So you feared that Sorath would be able to best you in the guise of Jesus?"

"Indeed, yes, but you must understand that he is a powerful angel…nowhere near my strength, of course. By using the guise of Jesus, people worshipped him. That worship creates power. With the spell they cast and using the Bible as a reference, Sorath garnered more power than any angel that had ever existed. He essentially became a minor god, so there was no way I could best him in battle like you did, Duncan."

"I don't get it. If he was as powerful as a minor god, then how could I have stood a chance against him in the first place?"

A half smile creased Lucifer's lips. "Because you have something he doesn't: lineage. You're the product of two gods." He chuckled.

"To compare your power to Sorath's phony Jesus would be like comparing an apple to a freight train. The differences are greater than you know. It's one thing to use dark magic to make oneself as powerful as a god, but there's nothing stronger than being either a real god or the seed of a god.

"When Purah told me about you and your lineage, I was intrigued and wanted to see you for myself. We got here, but I couldn't get inside the palace. Sorath's magical enchantments and sigils kept me away. Once you stabbed him, you broke his spells. Penemuel's sword was the key to undoing it all."

"So did Penemuel know about this? I know he thought I was nothing more than a mortal, but did he foresee something like today coming?" Duncan asked and sipped his wine.

"Hardly, but he knew better than to trust Sorath with all that power. Not wanting Sorath to go unchecked, he made his own sword into the key to undoing the spells they had cast together. He wasn't much of a fighter, but he was smart enough to know that Sorath would one day kill him."

"So how am I able to wield Penemuel's sword?"

"You're the seed of gods. That automatically makes you stronger and more powerful than our kind. When I say I won't harm you, I mean it. I know that even without much effort, you could easily wipe the floor with me."

As Duncan took in all this new information, he looked around the palace and at all of its inhabitants, wondering what would become of all them. Grim reapers still stood on the walls, waiting patiently.

Suddenly, his thoughts went to Rose and Devlin. Were they okay? Did Rose survive the transformation, or did she perish from the shock of her wounds?

Duncan leapt up from his chair. "My friends!"

Chapter 36

"The vampires?" Lucifer asked.

"Yes," Duncan bellowed frantically. "Rose is dying! I've been so wrapped up in all of this that I forgot about them!" He turned to leave. "How could I have forgotten them?"

"They're both alive, Duncan," Purah declared, trying to ease his mind.

Duncan frowned. "Wait…did you say vampires, as in *two* vampires and not just one?"

Lucifer nodded and smiled. "There are two."

Duncan looked at Purah. "You're sure they're both alive?"

"Yes," she insisted. "I saw them just a while ago."

"Sit," Lucifer said in a tone that sounded more like an order. "I have one more question of you."

Duncan sighed and sat back down. He wanted to go to Rose and see for himself that she was truly okay, but Purah said she was fine, and he believed anything the little fallen angel told him. She would never lie to him. He glanced over at Lucifer. "What's your question?"

"How do you feel about Purah?" the fallen angel asked. He leaned forward in his chair as if he were studying the man.

Purah looked up at Duncan. In her eyes, he saw great sadness as she gave him a melancholy smile. He could tell she was worried that he didn't feel the same way about her as she did about him. When he smiled lovingly at her, all the sadness left her eyes, and she smiled brightly at him in return.

As he stared at Purah, he thought, how can I not love her? And since I decapitated Pamela, I'm a widower now. No one else stands between us. Purah's the only one I want to spend the rest of my life with. How could I not?

Lucifer watched Duncan intently and occasionally glanced over at Purah. He stood up from his chair and whispered something into Purah's ear that made her blush. She turned and hugged Lucifer before walking over to Duncan.

Confused, Duncan told Lucifer, "Wait, I haven't answered your last question."

"Yes you did. You don't need words. Your heart spoke loud enough for you. You two were meant to be together, and I give my seal of approval on this union. Stand up, please."

Duncan's cheeks flushed slightly as he stood up. Another swift shift of wind behind Duncan caught his attention again, and he saw that his chair was gone. He looked back and saw Lucifer was standing. The table and Lucifer's chair had disappeared as well. All the food was now in bags, and the bags were on the floor beside Lucifer.

Sorath had been bound with shackles on his feet and wrists. His restraints shimmered with energy and became almost translucent. Lucifer made a motion with his hand, and Sorath shot up to a standing position, the turkey leg still crammed into his mouth.

Duncan snickered which was rewarded with a baleful gaze from Sorath. Purah sidled up next to Duncan and put her arm around his waist, leaning into his solid body. Sorath growled incoherent curses as he watched Purah, his prized possession, being held in the embrace of a mere mortal.

Lucifer looked Sorath up and down and then announced, "What was once yours is now mine. That includes all of your followers as well as you, do you understand me?"

Sorath glanced down several times at the turkey leg, wanting to answer, so Lucifer yanked it from his mouth.

"This is an outrage! You have no business being here, brother! You chose to hide in your own realm because you knew you could never best me in combat! What gives you any right to take my people or me for that matter?"

"Poor, dim Sorath." Lucifer tsked his tongue. "All brawn and no brains. I'm only going by the marvelous script you had Penemuel wrote two millennia ago. Did you take the time to read the Bible?"

Sorath stood, silently glaring at Duncan, so Lucifer snatched him by his chin and hissed as he got in his face, "Well I did! You do realize that there's a section that states there's only one true God and that your people are supposed to worship only Him, don't you? When you decided to play the role of Jesus, you became a false god and since these sheep worshipped you as such, they committed a sin to which I have the honor of collecting them because that's my role in all of this. If people don't repent of their sins, they come directly to me!"

"I don't believe you!" Sorath snarled loudly, despite Lucifer's firm grip on his chin. "The only reason you're here is because I'm powerless, and you want to take my place!"

Lucifer chuckled as he let go of Sorath's chin and patted him on his cheek. He turned around and walked over towards Duncan and Purah. "No, Sorath, I'm here because Purah came to me, pleading for me to save her man. She wanted you out of the picture so the two of them could live happily ever after. Naturally, I said that I couldn't do anything for her, but when she told me of Duncan Morgan and how he had been healing her fractured mind, and how you'd been sexually mistreating her..." He paused to caress Purah's cheek. Suddenly, he angrily whirled around, his eyes blazing white. "I figured I should watch the outcome of today's wonderful, heavyweight fight."

"I knew it! You're the reason that heathen was able to wield Penemuel's sword! You managed a spell to do it or had him sell his soul for the power to defeat me! How dare you use a mortal as your weapon to bring me down, you snake!"

"Alas, if that were the case then why am I here? None of my magic could penetrate your golden whore house. You were bested by no mere mortal, Sorath. The being standing with Purah is the seed of gods from another dimension. Since you never actually fought one until today, you would not have known that you were destined to fall—and fall you did! That's how he could wield one of our weapons. Both his parents are deities that placed him on Earth to take you down. I met them earlier, and they confirmed this to me."

"What the hell?" Duncan exclaimed. "Does everyone around here get to meet my birth parents but me?"

Purah looked up at Duncan and patted him on his chest. "Don't worry, my darling, I promise you will get to meet them soon enough. They want to see you, but they didn't want to distract you from your task here."

Sorath glared at Duncan, wanting to rip his heart from his chest as he spat out, "You should've killed me when you had the chance! From now until the day you die, keep an eye over your shoulder because one day I will be there to kill you!"

Lucifer walked over to Sorath, put his arm around him, and looked into his brother's eyes. "If you think keeping me out of here was easy, then imagine how it will be trying to escape my realm—a realm, over which I have full control. You can walk freely in it, but that will be after I'm through torturing you for all the wrongs you've done here!"

Sorath paled and gulped audibly. "You can't be seriously considering taking me down there! By what right have you to claim me?"

"Since your ignorance of the Bible is obvious, I shall tell you. In the book of Revelations, you and I are to fight it out—*Jesus!* According to the book, you win and cast me into a lake of fire for an eternity. That doesn't sound right to me. But in light of what has transpired here today, I'd say that battle has already been fought and won. To make things right, I'm casting Duncan in the role of Jesus since he is the seed of gods and you, Sorath, get to play the part of the devil." He pointed to himself. "Me!" Grinning, he added, "Since you corrupted so many lives and created so much war and death on Earth, my domain shall be your lake of fire. You will be tormented forever. How's that for a twist on an old classic?"

Looking towards the crowd of lost souls, Lucifer walked away from the stunned fallen angel. With several gestures of his hands, a large, fiery chasm opened up in the ground. The hole widened out so close to Sorath that he was forced to run from it or he would have fallen inside.

Lucifer's voice boomed out as he commanded, "Here me, all those who followed the man known as Jesus! You were all led astray by the false Christ. In your faith, you know it is a sin to worship false idols and gods so, therefore, I command you to go forth into the lake of fire and accept the fate that awaits you! As you were bound to the false Jesus, you are now bound to me. Go now and enjoy the torment that awaits each and every one of you!"

The people wailed as they fought the compulsion to go into the chasm, but they had no choice. No matter how hard they tried to keep their feet still, they walked toward the fiery abyss. One by one, they fell into the pit. As they fell into the chasm of torment, grim reapers flew down from the wall, recording each soul as it left its dying, physical body.

Purah shook, and her eyes fluttered with the influx of fear and despair coming from the crowd. Duncan held on to her tightly and looked at Lucifer with concern for her.

The fallen angel shrugged his shoulders. "It's her curse, and it's feeding her right now. Once the people have all entered the lake of fire, she'll be fine."

"What of Sorath's followers who aren't here?" Duncan asked, wanting to take Purah far from this horrid place.

"A similar hole will appear, and they will have no choice but to obey my command." He started to say something else but stopped suddenly. "Oh, I almost forgot. Purah, be a dear and release the dead from your summoning. Their souls are mine as well, and I don't want them to go to waste."

Purah stepped away from Duncan and rose up into the air. She hovered there with her hands outstretched. Her sapphire eyes blazed brightly as she muttered a chant that Duncan couldn't understand. He felt the power, though, behind each word. Before long, a dark, misty trail poured into the chasm from all directions.

Duncan stared in fascination. The dark mist was actually the souls of the ghouls, and he knew that the world would now be a safer place without them lurking in the shadows.

Lucifer proudly smiled as he turned around and forced Sorath to walk back towards the chasm.

"No, brother! Don't do this!" Sorath pleaded. He squirmed as he tried to dig his heels into the gold floor to slow his momentum. "I've not wronged you!"

"You soiled the name of my good friend Jesus with your little spellwork. You've raped our sweet Purah throughout the centuries, and I can't overlook that. Trust me when I say that magic of any kind always comes with a price, and now you shall reap what you've sown!"

Sorath felt something hard smacking him on his chest. He looked down and saw it was a bar of soap attached to a twine necklace. As he neared the edge of the chasm, Lucifer grabbed the collar of Sorath's crimson armor and tore it from his body like it was made of paper.

Sorath howled in pain, feeling as if he had just had his limbs removed. He dropped to his knees clutching his abdomen as he watched his angelic armor disintegrate into a metallic dust before his eyes.

Lucifer leaned down and whispered into his ear, "Now that you've been properly dressed for your eternal Hell, know that every time you lose this soap-on-a-rope, you will get what you gave poor Purah in her broken state of mind." He laughed.

"I've cursed the soap so that it will fall to the ground from time to time. You must bend over to retrieve it, and you *will* try and retrieve it—don't think that you won't try. The soap has been so cursed that you will have no choice but to bend over and retrieve it. As soon as you bend over, you will be raped on the spot by the ugliest and meanest fucker in Hell!"

Lucifer put his hand on Sorath's back and, one by one, his tendril wings turned to dust. Sorath wailed in pain from the loss of his wings.

Lucifer grabbed Sorath by the scruff of his neck and jerked him to his feet. He placed his foot on Sorath's back and gave a hard kick, sending the fallen angel tumbling into the fiery chasm. Lucifer watched his nemesis for a moment as the fallen angel fell helplessly toward his doom.

Finally, Lucifer turned around with his eyes blazing hot white and said to Duncan, "Treat her well, Duncan Morgan. I'm rather fond of her and don't want to see her harmed. If you hurt her, I shall return. With Sorath's sheep in my domain, I grow stronger and may decide to make a go at what he couldn't accomplish."

"I will love her like no one ever has, and you have my oath that she'll be treated with respect. Her mind will be whole once more. As for your threat, know that *if* you decide to be as stupid as Sorath and try to take control of Earth, I will be here to stop you. You'll be put in a place where that lake of fire will look good to you! It's my birthright to protect Earth, and I'll do so at any cost!"

Lucifer smirked as he spread his blinding white wings. He gave Duncan a two-finger salute as he took to the air and disappeared. Sorath's followers were still dropping into the chasm as Duncan looked past it and saw Devlin cradling Rose in his arms.

"Come on," Duncan told Purah.

As they waded through the mindless crowd, Duncan squeezed Purah's hand. "I gave my oath to love, respect, and care for you, Purah. I love you and you know I'm dead serious about my oaths."

Purah's cheeks flushed slightly as they maneuvered towards Devlin and Rose, squeezing through the herd of people being forced into the chasm.

Devlin was sitting on the ground, rocking Rose in his protective arms. Duncan and Purah hurried up to them. The vampire seemed oblivious to his surroundings at first, but then he muttered, "She will live; she has too!"

Duncan examined Rose and saw that her wounds were bright red with infection, but they were improving. He was about to put a hand on her forehead to feel her temperature, but Devlin hissed at him, showing his fangs in defense like some guard dog, ready to attack.

Duncan heard his inner voice urging him, *We can heal her!* He felt the magical energy swell up inside of him, wanting to heal her. "Devlin, it's Duncan," he said softly. "Let me check to see if she's all right."

"She's fine! I've got her; I'll care for her!" Devlin snarled.

"Do you want her wounds to heal or not, jackass?" Duncan snarled back, catching both Devlin and Purah off-guard. Duncan wondered why the vampire thought he could heal her. Where did that notion come from?

"I've *turned* her," Devlin whined, "but…but I'm not sure she'll survive the trauma to her body."

Duncan's eyes glowed purple which made the vampire shiver. Devlin stared at his friend with a little disgust and a lot of fear.

"Our magic can and will heal her body if you'll give us a chance," Duncan promised him.

Devlin still wasn't certain. Finally, his shoulders slumped forward, and he lowered Rose onto the ground as gently as he could.

Duncan sat down and slid Rose into his lap and held her, keeping a cautious eye on Devlin as he did. The vampire was too protective of her. Duncan was afraid that if he made Rose cringe in pain, Devlin might lunge at him.

Duncan heard his magical inner voice say in a calm manner, *"We have the gift of healing from our father, and we too can heal. Rose's body will mend like ours does. Once that happens, her vampire blood will take over, and she will live!"*

"I've never healed anyone," Duncan muttered. "What do I do? How do I heal her?"

"We are healing her as we speak. It's simple enough, especially when it's someone we care about. Love heals all wounds and mends all scars."

Devlin stood up, planning to pace, but as he glanced down at Rose, he saw her entire body glowing purple. The bites were mending quickly. He became excited as the first of Rose's bite wounds healed completely, leaving fresh, pink skin in its place. The vampire felt a hand on his shoulder, and he looked over to see Purah.

She smiled at him. "No need to fret, vampire. They're taking good care of your woman. You can relax."

Confused, Devlin asked, "They? What do you mean by *'they'*? Aren't you helping Duncan with this healing?"

"This is beyond my skills. Duncan is the seed of deities. His father is a powerful healer, and Duncan has inherited that talent." She saw more confusion on Devlin's face. "Duncan is a god too, and that's all I will say on the matter. Ask him, if you want more clarity, but revel in the fact that he's saving the love of your life."

A soft murmur caught Devlin's attention, and he looked down. Rose was waking up. She tried to sit up, but Duncan held her securely in her place. Her head lolled to the side as she muttered, "Did we win?"

"Yes, sweetheart, we won," the vampire cooed at her as he squatted down beside her. "Now you are healing quickly with Duncan's help."

"Oh goodie!" Rose giggled weakly. A thought suddenly entered her mind, and before she passed out, she uttered frantically, "Are the children safe?"

Duncan didn't know how to answer her. He glanced over at Devlin and then up at Purah. The petite fallen angel shrugged her shoulders as she turned around. "I'll go fetch the little ones." She took a few steps and then suddenly stopped. "I don't know how we're going to get them out of here," she said over her shoulder.

"What do you mean?" Devlin asked.

"It's going to require a huge transport vehicle," she explained. "Outside these walls are more environmental dangers than I can count."

Devlin slipped his hand into his pocket and produced Todd's gold nugget. "I'm sure you know how to operate this thing, but will it still work now that Sorath is gone?"

Purah walked back and took the nugget from him. She focused on it for a few seconds. "You're right. Sorath's magic powered this. He's gone, and along with him went his magic." She started to hand the nugget back to Devlin but suddenly stopped when she heard a man cry out in fear as he neared the chasm. "The sadness from these people might be strong enough to make it work with *my* magic."

Duncan smiled. "Then by all means, get that sexy ass moving! The sooner we are away from this place, the better I'll feel. Gather the children, and let's *all* go home!"

Epilogue

Rose awoke in her luxurious, king sized bed and stretched her arms over her head with a growling yawn. Devlin was already up and gone. The little shit, she thought, didn't bother to wake me before he left. "Guess I'll have to kick his ass for that." She smiled.

A few days ago, Devlin had admitted that he had *turned* her—made her a vampire. He explained that he and Duncan had been afraid she would die from the ghouls' bites which were instantly becoming infectious. Rose had taken the news of becoming a vampire much better than Devlin had expected. He had thought she would be furious at him for not giving her a choice in the matter. After all that she had been through, he figured having or not having a choice would be important to her. But it wasn't.

She was sad that she couldn't remember her *turning*. Had Devlin enjoyed biting into her artery? Had it been erotic for him? She sighed, knowing that she'd probably never remember the act, but she had been too close to death.

She swung her hips to the edge of the bed and nearly knocked over the IV pole. Devlin had been feeding her with blood through the IV for the last week because he hadn't wanted her to be overwhelmed all at once by the urge to feed. For Rose, though, this was getting old fast.

Running her tongue over her sharp fangs, she purposefully nicked it slightly so she could get the taste of blood in her mouth. Her eyes rolled back in her head as the small amount of blood covered her taste buds. The sensation was heavenly!

She yanked the IV from her arm and shrugged on her robe. Shoving her feet into slippers that had little, red roses on them, she smiled. He spoils me too much but then again, who am I to complain? She walked over to the French doors that led out onto a small balcony. Opening one of the doors, she stepped outside to enjoy the view from her new home. No matter how many times she did this, Rose couldn't get over the fact that she was now living in a mansion. Even an old mansion like this one impressed her.

The estate was large, and an eight-foot tall wall surrounded it on three sides. Only the front of the land beside the road wasn't walled off. The grass was kept mowed down by a small herd of goats that wondered aimlessly about the grounds. There was a large fountain in the center of the courtyard that had been converted into a drinking well for the goats and other animals, and it doubled as a bath for the birds as well. The old mansion also had solar panels in different sections of it, put there by a previous owner, so there was more than enough electricity. But what Rose loved best about the house were the hot showers.

The property was surrounded by a large forest that teemed with all sorts of wildlife, but there was another reason why she liked the forest so well: it kept the house hidden from prying eyes. And after what she'd been through, Rose valued her privacy. Yet, she was a gregarious woman by nature, and she knew instinctively that too much privacy could be a bad thing, at least for her.

She sighed, remembering Melona. Now that the ghouls were gone, she hoped people would move into the huts and give the old place new life.

"They'd have to clean it up first," she said aloud and shuddered, remembering the dead bodies—parting gifts from the ghouls.

She shook her head, trying to ward off the depression that was trying to settle over her. She sighed with loneliness as she thought of all the friends she'd lost at Melona. Life would never be the same for her. There would always be a hole in her heart left by her friends and Melona itself. Again, she sighed.

Wondering what she would wear today, she glanced down at her clothes. She had on silk pajama bottoms and a pink T-shirt with black lettering that read: *Rose is undead, this much is true; If she hadn't just fed, the next meal would be you!*

She smiled. "Devlin, you're one seriously insane vampire."

Devlin had put the lettering on her shirt in his screen printing room. When she had first seen his hobby room, she had laughed. "Hey, this is great!" she had exclaimed. "You can bring in extra income. We'll be able to afford to fix up this old place."

She had said it as a joke, but now her words didn't seem so farfetched to her anymore. As she thought about that "extra income," she stared out at the forest. "What are you hiding?" she whispered to the trees. Her head filled with fantasies. "You're hiding acres and acres of beautiful, level land — like pasture land, maybe — with a creek running through it." She smiled at that. "A place to build a new village!"

Rose was a natural business woman. She was smart, honest, likable, and she could charm anything out of any man. "New Melona!" She liked the sound of that. A new village would mean new friends, barter riches, and most importantly, something to do with her time! She needed something to keep her busy; she wasn't the kind of woman to sit around doing nothing.

"There had better be a good place for a village out past you," she warned the trees. "If there's not, you're going to be in serious trouble!"

She laughed and shrugged off her pajama bottoms and t-shirt. Looking around the room, she wondered what she would do today. She walked over to her closet and chose a long, black skirt and a white, off-the-shoulder, gypsy blouse.

Leaving her bedroom, she headed down the long hallway for the stairs. As she got to the head of the stairs, she stopped, feeling a little lightheaded. She had promised Devlin she would stay in bed until he returned, although both of them knew she was lying as she said it. When the vertigo faded, she started down the stairs.

She wished Devlin was here today. The house seems so empty, she thought as she headed toward the patio. She wanted to sit outside in the shade under the back portico and enjoy a little bird watching in her backyard. She hoped she might see the wolf pack she had heard howling last night. I'd like to get acquainted with you guys, she called out mentally to the pack, but she got no response from them. She frowned. She was different now—a vampire. Would that matter to this new pack of wolves?

She sat down on an old chaise lounge that Devlin had found while prowling for blood and lay back. Devlin was away finding suitable foster homes for the last of the children. She had wanted to go with him, but they both knew she was too weak from the vampire transformation.

Devlin was using the gold nugget to teleport Sorath's slave children back to the various countries in the world. Rose had insisted that French children be taken back to France, Spanish children back to Spain, and so on.

"There are no more countries," Devlin had whined, wanting to place them all nearby.

"It's only right!" Rose had been adamant about it, and Devlin had complied by taking the children to their different homelands.

But as loneliness threatened to overwhelm her, she again wished he was here with her. Duncan and Purah were both gone too. A few days ago, after escorting American children to nearby villages, they had left to see Duncan's parents in a different dimension.

She felt, rather than heard, the pack of wolves as they crossed the meadow at the back of the estate. Rising up, she started to go after them.

"Rose!"

She gasped out in fear as her heart landed in her throat. She jumped, whirling around, mentally preparing for a fight. Devlin was standing in front of her with a definite frown on his face.

"You promised me you would stay in bed!" he growled.

She put her hand over her heart in a useless attempt to slow its thudding. "I thought I'd get up so you could scare me to death!" she said sarcastically.

Devlin shook his head in disgust. "When are you going to start minding me?"

"Never!" she hissed with a haughty voice, in a tone that dared him to argue with her.

Despite himself, he smiled a little and leaned in towards her, pressing his lips firmly against hers. She moaned from the kiss as hormones flooded her body.

Without warning, Devlin slipped something into her hand and closed her fingers around it. Rose begrudgingly broke away from his smoldering kiss to see what it was.

"I thought you would enjoy using these," he said and grinned. "I got some from Germany, Scotland, and even a few from China. I know you'll love the ones from Mexico."

Rose looked down at the large, brown bag in her hand.

"Open it," he urged excitedly. He seemed like a kid wanting his mother to open a present he had made for her.

She opened the bag and peered into it. She saw thousands of seeds. They filled the large sack nearly to the top. None of them were packaged separately and labeled by type. They were all lumped in together!

"What are they?" she asked, with a sickening feeling in her gut.

"Seeds, silly," he said, laughing. "You've seen seeds before. Everyone in Melona said you were the best gardener around." A thought suddenly shot into his head. "You're okay, aren't you? The *turning* didn't hurt your brain, did it?" He stared at her as if she might be a halfwit or something.

"No," she growled as she looked at the mess inside the bag, "but I think it hurt *your* brain!" She glanced up at him. "Do you know what kind of seeds they are?"

"Of course I do," he assured her. "There are apple seeds, orange, grape, corn, tomato, lettuce and a bunch of other things…all kinds. Duncan said you loved peppers, so I found some in Mexico. I thought you'd enjoy having a garden again. I'm sure Duncan and Purah, as well as other guests, will love the food you grow."

She pulled a single seed out of the sack. "No, what I mean is, can you tell one seed from another? Can you tell which seeds are apple seeds and which are lettuce?" She held the seed out to him. "What kind of seed is this?"

He frowned and then shrugged. "What difference does it make? Put it in the ground and see what grows." He smiled happily at her. "Problem solved!"

It took all her willpower not to knock him upside his head. "Guess who's going to help me sort them," she growled.

"Why are you going to sort them?"

"Because I'd like the tomatoes growing in one row and the apple trees growing in another one." She sighed heavily. "We just won't know which row is growing what until everything starts to sprout."

Suddenly despondent, Devlin hung his head. "I was sure you'd love them," he muttered.

Her heart melted. He was that little boy in front of his mother again. Only his mother was rejecting his present.

She tiptoed up and kissed him deeply. "I do love them," she assured him softly. "I can't wait to start planting them." She narrowed her eyes at him. "But you're still going to help me sort them."

Devlin grinned. "It will be our special project." He hugged her. "I know the last couple of weeks have been difficult on you, so I figured you would enjoy getting back to working with nature." He waved his hand towards their property. "Pick an area for your garden rows; it's all yours. I'll do my best to deter the goats from devouring our crops."

She glanced down at the sack of seeds and wondered just how well he would do with the goats. "We'll fence the garden. The goats can't eat what they can't get to."

When he agreed, Rose dragged Devlin down onto her chaise lounge and kissed him passionately. "I love you so much," she cooed at him.

He smiled and caressed her cheek with the back of his fingers. "Not near as much as I love you."

She started to argue with him, but she heard a noise inside the house. "Who's here?" she asked.

"No one," he said and frowned. Afraid there might be a random ghoul still around, he instantly shot up to his feet. "Stay here!" he ordered.

Rose got to her feet too. "If there's going to be a fight, maybe I can help," she said, thinking of some evil human who might have spotted the big mansion. She followed Devlin into the house.

"Duncan! Purah!" Devlin exclaimed as he saw the two lovers walking through the house.

Rose grinned as she watched them. Duncan stopped and let Purah move forward towards Rose. The petite fallen angel looked different in a way that Rose couldn't explain. There was a shimmer in front her, and she walked funny.

Purah was scooting her feet along the marble flooring, but she didn't appear to be hurt, as far as Rose could tell. Purah's lips curled up slightly as the shimmering in front of her glowed a sapphire blue. Then Rose saw through the shimmer. The glow was coming from Purah's wings.

The fallen angel's wings were curved around her shoulders, covering the front part of her body up to her breasts. Purah suddenly outstretched her wings, letting them naturally return to her back where they belonged. What she had been hiding was now exposed. "Do you know this little guy?"

"Danny!" Rose squealed. She put the seed sack on a small table and held out her arms. The little boy rushed over to her, grinning from ear to ear. She hugged him tightly as tears streamed down her cheeks. Devlin hurried to them, happily wrapping his long arms around Rose and the boy.

Duncan smiled as he walked up to Purah and slid his arm around her waist. "This young man said he wanted to visit another dimension with us and then go home. When we asked him where home was, he said wherever Rose and Devlin were."

Rose gasped. "Oh, Danny!"

"Welcome home, Danny," Devlin said and watched the boy grin up at him.

"Is there anything for a kid to do around this place?" Duncan asked. Walking to the glass patio doors, he looked outside. A huge oak tree stood not far from the patio in the backyard. "I guess I could make him a tire swing," he muttered.

Rose laughed. "While you make the swing, Danny can join me and Devlin in our *special* project." She glanced over at the seed sack. "Now that I think about it, you and Purah can help sort the seeds too."

***

That night, after everyone was asleep, Rose lay in bed beside Devlin. It had been a perfect day. Danny was now asleep in the room next to theirs. He had spent most of the afternoon finding things, like rocks and pinecones, to decorate his new bedroom.

Duncan and Purah were in one of the mansion's many guest rooms. They could hardly be called guests anymore, though, because Rose and Devlin had asked the two lovers to move into the house permanently with them, and they had agreed.

As she snuggled against Devlin, she heard the wolf pack howl. They were near the property's back fence! Rose quietly slipped out of bed, threw on her robe, and stuffed her feet into her house shoes. She padded silently down the hallway to the backstairs that led into the kitchen.

By the time she got all the way to the back gate, she was beginning to regret going outside. Her breath came in labored pants from all the physical exertion and she leaned heavily on the gate as she opened it. "I thought vampires were supposed to be strong," she mumbled irritably.

Suddenly, she heard growling. Her strength may not have come in yet, but her new vampire eyes worked just fine. She saw six wolves standing nearby. They were ripping the meat off of a large deer they had taken down. The alpha male looked over at her and yipped, giving the others a signal to look up. Now they all stared at her…and started to growl viciously.

She thought about taking a step back, slamming the big, wooden gate shut, and running back to the house. Hopefully, the wolves wouldn't know they could go around the tall wall and into the front of the estate. That part of the land wasn't fenced off the way the other three sides were.

At that moment, the big alpha male stalked toward her, growling and snarling, causing the others to leave their dead prey and follow their pack leader...to her!

As her heart thudded in her chest, and every part of her mind called out for her to run, she took a deep breath and summoned all of her powers. I'm a sorceress, she reminded herself, shaking violently with fear. I can do this. I've done it before!

"*Stop!*" she ordered in a strong, demanding, psychic voice. She knew the wolves couldn't understand her words, but they could psychically feel the meanings of them. "*I want to be your friend – one of your pack.*"

No response.

The wolves kept coming! The big alpha male suddenly stopped, but it seemed to Rose that he was about to lunge at her.

She dropped to her knees, getting her head close to the ground. She tried again. "*I want to be part of your pack?*"

The alpha snarled viciously at her, but she heard — or, rather, felt — his words go through her whole being, mostly down her spine. His communication was something to the effect of, "*Who the hell wants you to join? We don't need you!*"

She could sense he was about ready to give the command to attack. In seconds, she would be as ripped apart as that big buck over there. She cringed, regretting her decision to leave her warm bed and Devlin. Who would take care of little Danny?

She had no choice now. What was done was done. She immediately rolled over on her back. For a wolf to expose its underbelly to another wolf was an act of submission. It was a way for the wolf to say to the alpha or any other wolf, for that matter, "Hey, I know you're the boss, and it's okay by me. I'll do whatever you want me to do."

The big alpha stopped and stared at the woman. It had never seen this reaction by a human. The woman had spoken to it, and it had understood her!

"My name is Rose, and I want to join your pack," she told the alpha psychically.

"This human is strange!" the alpha growled, and the others agreed by growling back.

"Maybe it's a human trap," another wolf cautioned. Rose heard the words inside her head, but her ears heard them only as two yips.

"Let's get out of here!" still, a third wolf warned. More yips.

The big alpha must have agreed because it turned and loped across the pasture, its pack following closely behind.

"I live in that house," Rose called out psychically to the alpha as she scrambled to her feet. *"You'll be back, and I'll still want to join your pack!"*

She watched as the wolves broke into a run, quickly disappearing into the woods. She smiled. "Well, at least they didn't attack me."

"You're lucky," a voice behind her split the night air.

She whirled around. "Devlin! How long have you been standing there?"

"Long enough to know that you're crazy," he hissed irritably.

She walked up to him and wrapped her arms around his waist. "Crazy about you," she purred at him.

"No," he argued, "just crazy!"

She laughed as she let him carry her back to their mansion. "What's for breakfast in the morning?" she asked.

"Blood," he said simply.

"What about lunch?"

"Blood."

"And dinner tomorrow night?"

"Blood."

"Devlin, darling, you have no imagination!"

The End

www.ingramcontent.com/pod-product-compliance
Lightning Source LLC
Chambersburg PA
CBHW071341020726
47502CB00001B/197